MW00813843

IN ASHES
BORN

Cover art by J. Daniel Sawyer
Background nebula graphics from Hubblesite.org

ISBN-10: 1-940575-08-7
ISBN-13: 978-1-940575-08-7

First Printing: May, 2016

For more information or to leave a comment about this book,
please visit us on the web at:
www.solarclipper.com

Publishers Note:

To my grandfather, Ralph M. Lowell.

He taught me to fish and the value of work.
He was a gentle soul
who always smelled of fresh cut wood and tobacco.
May he rest in peace.

The Golden Age of the Solar Clipper

Quarter Share
Half Share
Full Share
Double Share
Captains Share
Owners Share

In Ashes Born
To Fire Called*
By Darkness Forged *

South Coast
Cape Grace*

Tanyth Fairport Adventures

Ravenwood
Zypherias Call
The Hermit Of Lammas Wood

* Forthcoming

IN ASHES BORN

NATHAN LOWELL

Durandus

Chapter One
Port Newmar: 2374, May 25

A lot had changed on the campus since I'd left it in '58. Sixteen stanyers in the life of a public institution would do that. From the observation deck, I could pick out the hulking edifice that was Hutchins Gym. The buildings still hugged the ground, most a single story. Where the old admin building used to be, a new glass and steel office tower stood shoulders above the tree line. I snorted as I realized that it couldn't be more than five floors, but it towered above the rest.

"Captain Wang, sar?"

I turned to find a cadet waiting at attention. "Yes?"

"Commandant's compliments, sar. I'm to show you to the Visiting Officers Quarters and see that you're settled comfortably, sar."

"At ease, cadet."

He snapped to a perfectly rigid parade rest.

I sighed and read his name badge. "Mr. Udan? Is that Ou-dan or You-dan?"

"Oo-don," he said with the emphasis on the second syllable.

"I'm glad I asked. Thank you, Mr. Udan. Please stand easy."

His posture relaxed fractionally, but he didn't look anything like comfortable. The two stripes on his sleeve marked him as a second-year student.

"Looking forward to a summer cruise, Mr. Udan?"

"Sar?" He looked genuinely perplexed.

"You're second year. Isn't the academy on summer break?"

"Oh, yes, sar. The cadet has not qualified for a summer cruise, sar."

"I see. Well, in that case, lay on, MacDuff."

"And damned be him who first cries 'Hold! Enough!' sar."

His answer forced a laugh out of me.

He came back to attention and held a flat palm toward the ladder off the observation deck. "Your quarters are this way, sar."

With a final scan of the campus from the terminal overlook, I nodded to him and led the way down the ladder, both grav-trunks trundling along behind. Out on the tarmac, I heard shuttle engines warming up with their characteristic whistling whine, a sound I hadn't heard since I left. It sounded like home.

The terminal lay nearly deserted. The outgoing traffic had cleared out as had the half dozen mechanics I'd shared the ride down with. They'd left me to my own devices in the back of the shuttle while they carefully kept eyes forward and voices down. After letting me debark, they'd arrowed straight for the terminal exit.

"Would the captain prefer to walk or ride, sar?"

"Walk, I think, Mr. Udan, and if it wouldn't strain your training protocol too much, the captain would prefer to be called by his name."

Red crept up the back of the boy's neck. "Of course, sar."

"Good," I said. "VOQ still over by Admin?"

"Yes, sar."

"Walk with me, Mr. Udan. You can regale me with tales of student life." I set off at a stroll toward the exits and smiled to myself when Mr. Udan fell into step.

"Tales of student life, sar? I'm sure the capta—uh—I'm sure I don't know what you might find amusing about student life, sar."

"Commandant Giggone still holds the flag here?"

"Yes, sar."

"I'd have thought he'd have retired by now."

"He, sar?" Udan gave me a sharp side-eyed glance.

"Commandant Giggone. Robert Giggone?"

"Oh! No, sar. Commandant Alys Giggone."

I laughed again. "Small universe."

"So I'm told, sar." Udan stepped forward to trigger the automatic doors that opened onto the plascrete plaza fronting the terminal building.

"How long has she been here?"

"I believe this is her fifth term as commandant, sar. She was here when I got here, but some of last term's graduates knew her father."

We strolled down the tree-shaded path toward a cluster of smallish bungalows sheltered in the stunted trees.

"She was my first captain," I said. "She put me in for the academy herself."

I saw Udan giving me a skeptical look out of the corner of my eye. I grinned at him. "Don't look so surprised. She recommended a lot of students. I was number thirty-four. I have no idea how many she ended up with."

He stopped in front of one of the bungalows. "This is your cottage, sar."

I looked at the comfy little building, all brick and wood. White roses bloomed on a trellis highlighted by the late afternoon sun. "I used to trim these roses when I was a cadet, Mr. Udan."

He cocked his head and looked at me, surprise painted on his face with a broad brush.

"It's true. I had problems with the physical training so I was assigned a rather unorthodox teacher."

"And he had you pruning roses, sar?"

"*She* had me pruning roses, trimming trees, raking leaves, and planting flowers. Among other things."

His brow furrowed as if he couldn't make sense of what I'd told him.

"What self-defense discipline have you worked with, Mr. Udan?"

"G'wai G'wah, sar. Some tae kwon do."

"When I was here the PT instructor said I had the killer instincts of a lawn chair. He brought me out here to meet my new teacher." I smiled at him. "I'm hoping she's still here. I could use some refresher work."

"How long ago were you here, sar?"

"Class of '58."

He shook his head. "I don't know any instructors who've been here that long, sar."

"Is the old dojo still there? The one with the big windows behind Hutchins?"

He blinked. "Well, there's a building over there, yeah. Big windows and almost overgrown with ivy and vines, sar."

I smiled. "And have you ever noticed a gardener working the grounds? Older woman? About this tall?" I held up a hand to show what I meant. "White hair. Wears a floppy canvas hat? Her name is Margaret Newmar."

"I don't know that name, sar, but there's a little old lady who tends a lot of the gardens. I see her around sometimes."

"That's her."

"She was a martial arts instructor, sar?"

"I still am, Mr. Udan." The voice came clear and piping on the late afternoon air.

We turned to find *Sifu* Newmar strolling toward us along the path, her ever-present gardening gloves in one hand and a pair of trimmers in the other.

I locked my hands together and bowed, student to master.

She smiled and handed her gloves and trimmers to Udan before returning the bow, teacher to student. "I'm pleased to see you, Captain."

"I'm pleased to be here, *Sifu*."

Her left eyebrow twitched ever so slightly and her lips curved up on the right. "You always were polite." She shook her head. "But you still can't lie worth a damn."

I had to laugh. "I've been practicing."

"You'll never be a good liar. You have other admirable qualities."

Mr. Udan's eyes looked like they might bug out of his head.

She held out her hands to him for her gear. "Mr. Udan, you have duties, I believe."

He stopped in mid-salute on realizing she wasn't in uniform and just nodded. "Yes, sar. Ma'am. That is. Yes." To me he said, "If there's anything you need, Captain? There's a card on the desk inside." He came to attention and saluted me, holding it.

I returned the salute. "My compliments to the commandant, Mr. Udan. Thank you for your assistance."

He nodded once and strode off toward the admin building.

"He's a good lad," Margaret said. "He just doesn't pay attention to the details."

"You know him?"

"I know of him. He's one of Alys's problem children."

I looked after the retreating cadet. "That why he's not on summer cruise?"

Her lips twitched but she just winked and shook her head. She looked to the rose bushes beside the door. "What do you think of those iceberg climbers?"

"I think you've been saving them for me." I looked at her. "How'd you know I'd be here?"

She lifted one shoulder and let it fall. "We may be in the ivory tower, but I still follow the news. After what you've been through? I'm half surprised you haven't shown up sooner."

"And Chief Stevens told you I'd be coming?"

She pursed her lips and gave me a half smile. "Maggie Stevens is a sweetheart. She'll be here later in the summer, I think."

"You don't think she'll stay with DST?"

She looked at me. "No. She got what she went for. She'll be back to work on the new edition of the book by the end of July. Wouldn't surprise me if Alys convinces her to stay on and teach in the fall."

I gave a little laugh. "And what about me? What do you see

me doing?"

She handed me the trimmers. "For starters? Those climbers need some attention. Why don't you give them some."

I looked down at my dress uniform. "I should probably change."

"Practical thought," she said. "I'll be on the floor at 0600, if you'd care to join me. Maggie says you need some help with the Four Corners."

"I may not have been as diligent as I might have been over the stanyers."

She sniffed. "It'll come back." She ambled back the way she'd come. "Bring the clippers back tomorrow," she said over her shoulder. "Might be more work for you."

I laughed and pulled my trunks into the cottage, locking them down and rummaging through to find a shipsuit I could wear to garden in.

Funny. I'd forgotten the smell that clipped roses have. Sure the flower itself smells like a rose, but the stems—fresh with sap, green-smelling. There's a musky fug to it that I'd completely forgotten until I clipped the first stray runner from the bush. That scent took me back nearly twenty stanyers.

Back before I'd graduated.

Back before I'd found Greta.

Back before I'd found my father.

Back before I'd lost it all.

I kept sniffing because my nose kept running in time with my eyes as if they competed in some contest of runniness. Each time I did, the sharp scent of snipped rose stem reminded me to watch where I clipped, where I put my fingers.

The mess call bugle sounded but I kept pruning. Being a captain meant I could eat when I wanted. If nothing else, it meant I could go into town to find something to eat. Besides, only a meter or so of climbing rose remained. I could finish by the time they piped the colors at sunset.

Chapter Two
Port Newmar: 2374, May 26

I'd forgotten reveille. The academy wasn't actually a military academy per se, but they followed many military customs as molds into which they poured cadets. The administration had installed speakers across the campus and programmed the appropriate recordings. I'd heard the evening mess call and evening colors, but I'd forgotten the welcoming of dawn. It all came back to me with the brassy notes echoing across the campus.

To be fair, the call came from a distant speaker and probably wouldn't have awakened a sounder sleeper. I might have ignored it had my day been free of encumbrance. As soon as I heard the first few notes, I crawled out of the rather comfortable bed and did the needful before climbing into workout clothes. Reveille sounded at 0530 and *Sifu* Newmar would be on the floor in her studio at 0600. If I wanted to be on time, I'd need to arrive well before that. Breakfast would have to wait until after our session. I grabbed the clippers and headed across campus.

The morning air carried a familiar tang, the sky above almost translucent as the primary kissed the eastern horizon. Proximity to the water kept the air temps from swinging too wildly, but a faint morning haze turned my march across campus into a stroll through a green fairyland. In the distance I heard an engine turn over and then catch with a low rumble. In a few moments, a large tractor trundled out onto the parade ground, huge squishy tires barely caressing the grass as it drew a mower along behind. The green scent carried clearly, wafting on a stray breeze.

I arrived to find the studio empty. The local primary had risen high enough to cast ample light on the floor so I bowed to the studio and took my position. The old warmups and stretches came back to me. At least some of them. It felt good to be in that space again, to be moving my body and feeling the muscles work. I focused on my balance, on being suspended from the top of my head and keeping a balanced center through my core. I often thought of it as my own planetary axis, aligned with gravity and free of any axial tilt.

The warmth of the primary's radiation stroked my face. It promised heat later in the day, but the freshness of morning clung to my nose, the air soft on my skin. I could still hear the low thrum of the tractor mowing the parade ground ever so faintly over the rushing of my own blood in my ears.

"Good morning, Captain Wang." *Sifu* Newmar stepped into the studio with her usual quiet grace. "I saw that you finished the roses. Did you remember to bring the clippers?"

I stopped and bowed, student to master. "I did, *Sifu*."

"Are you through pruning?" she asked. Her seamed face turned toward the light as if she were a flower addressing the day.

I took a moment to consider. She asked no questions lightly, and she knew I'd finished the roses. "I'm not sure, *Sifu*," I said.

"You arrived here the first time with thirty kilos."

I nodded. "With friends to support me and the idea that I'd have a career waiting for me when I left."

She turned back to me and gifted me with a small smile that reached from her lips all the way up to her eyes. "Shall we begin?" Without waiting for me, she took the opening position and led me into a Jung Long Form.

At the end of the first hour, she called a halt. Sweat drenched my workout clothes, and I felt as wrung out as a recycled scrubber filter. "Tea?" she asked, gliding off the floor as if the previous hour had been nothing at all. For her, I'm sure it had been.

"Thank you, *Sifu*."

"Do some of the cooldowns while I heat the water," she said, stopping me from following her into the cooler, dimmer confines of the studio.

"Of course, *Sifu*." I took the position and began an exercise she called Pumping Chi. It consisted mainly of slowly crouching and pressing down with outstretched hands, then reversing to stand up with palms upward.

"Beautiful Lady's Hands, Ishmael. Beautiful Lady's Hands."

I felt my lips curl into a smile and relaxed my hands. She always knew, even when she couldn't see me. I let myself forget everything. I became quiet in my head and let the repeated movements carry me. I focused on my hands pressing down even while relaxed. I felt the lift of my thighs when I pulled up. My breath moved in synchronization with my movements—inhaling on the rise, exhaling on the fall. My body became a bellows, pushing out and pulling in.

"Tea's ready, Ishmael."

I finished standing and let my arms drop to my sides, feeling the burn in my muscles and enjoying the feeling. I let my eyes close and took two more full breaths, letting them all the way out before taking the next. I listened to the sound of my blood pulsing languidly in my ears, waves on an inner sea. I turned to see her watching me from the shadows.

"Come. Sit."

I followed her back into the cool recesses where she kept a cozy nook. She used a cast iron kettle and a porcelain teapot. Her cups—each unique—found homes in an old wooden sorting tray. I noticed one empty slot in what I'd remembered as a full rack. "You're missing a cup?"

Her fingers went to the empty slot in gentle caress. "It fell." She pulled two cups from their slots, seemingly at random but I'd seen her pour tea too many times to be fooled. Turning to me she said, "Nothing lasts forever. Even teacups." The smile tugged the corners of her lips. "You can keep them safe on the shelf, but that's not what teacups are for."

I sank onto the cushioned chair opposite her and folded my hands on the buttery smooth wooden surface.

She placed the solidly formed, simple clay cup without a handle in front of me and kept the flowered porcelain for herself. It looked like it should have had a saucer under it. It reminded me of something from long, long ago with its cheery flowers, soaring birds, and generously flared rim.

I remembered watching her perform this same ritual when I was a cadet. She seldom picked the same cup twice for herself and the cups for her guests always appeared to have some symbolism. I considered the white shape in front of me as she tilted the teapot over it. The rich, dark tea steamed as it flowed into the simple bowl. She lifted the spout and then lowered it to fill her own cup without spilling a drop. I knew part of it was the teapot, a classic from someplace far away. Part of it was her practiced skill in using it. She placed it on a hot stone slab and leaned forward to let the warm steam from her cup waft across her face.

I tested the surface of my cup with fingertips before committing myself to gripping it. The smooth glaze retained sufficient coolness as the cup's mass slowly absorbed the heat. I took a careful sip and managed to avoid burning my tongue.

"You're out of practice," she said.

"With tea?"

She gave a slight nod toward the practice floor.

"I let my discipline slide."

"You've risen very fast, Ishmael."

I stared into the simple cup of tea, admiring the smooth lines of the clay and satin finish of the glaze. "I flew too high." The words came to my lips unbidden but once uttered I knew them too well.

When *Sifu* Newmar didn't answer, I looked across the table. She was smiling at me.

"What?" I asked.

She lifted the brightly colored cup to her lips and took a slurping sip from its gold-touched rim. Without taking her eyes from mine, she placed it back down on the table. "What would you have done differently?" The smile never left her lips. "Knowing what you've learned? Would you take a different path?"

I sighed and shook my head, looking down into my cup again. Small bits of leaf and sediment hung suspended in the tea like dust motes in a sun beam. I stared at them, hoping they might offer some insight. "I let myself become too rigid."

"Say more."

I glanced over at her. "What I learned on the *Lois McKendrick*, I took with me."

"Commandant Giggone will be gratified to learn that."

"I took it too far. I ignored the evidence of my own eyes and clung to dogma instead of adapting to new understanding."

"Sort of like tai chi, eh?" One corner of her lips curved up and she hid the crooked grin behind her teacup.

I felt my lips responding with a smile of my own. "I'm out of practice."

She nodded and replaced her cup on the table. "You've some pruning to do and perhaps some new seeds to sow. You'll have a few weeks to practice, I think."

"I was planning on a few months."

"Plans are not actions." Her eyebrows lifted and her smile broadened. "We've rested long enough. Drink up. I have time for a couple more sets before I need to visit a leggy lilac bush across campus." She stood and crossed to the sideboard to rinse out her cup.

I lifted my cup and drained it to the dregs. "What would you like me to prune? More roses?" She grinned at me over one shoulder and offered a shrug. "I'd like you to cut down your baggage. Can you weed out enough to get down to one grav-trunk?"

Her answer surprised a laugh out of me, but it also made me pause. "It's everything I own."

Her eyebrows expressed much more than words might have. She turned to the floor and bowed before stepping into the sunlight.

Chapter Three
Port Newmar: 2374, May 26

An onshore breeze brought the iodine pinch of saltwater from the bay. The system primary had cleared the tree line but hadn't yet warmed the air. The coolness of it soothed my skin and made the sweat on the back of my shirt feel chilly.

I had nearly made it back to my cottage when Cadet Udan found me on the path.

He saluted sharply but didn't hold it. Completely understandable since I was out of uniform. "Sar, Commandant's compliments and would you join her for lunch mess at the Officers Club at 1200 hours?"

"I'd be pleased to, Mr. Udan."

"Thank you, sar. I'll let her know."

"Carry on, Mr. Udan."

As he marched away in proper cadet form, I marveled that I had ever been that young. I wondered what happened to that boy, then snorted and resumed my stroll toward the shower. It hadn't even been twenty stanyers since I'd been a cadet. It seemed like much longer.

As I strolled, the images from the *Chernyakova* came back to me. I hadn't thought of that for a long time, but it had only been—what? I couldn't remember. When I counted back on my fingers, I realized it had only been three stanyers since we'd jumped into Breakall and found the ship adrift. Less than that, really. Closer to two and a half. A year on the *Agamemnon* and a year on the *Iris*. Only a few months since I left my last ship to the tender care of Christine Maloney.

As far as I knew, the *Chernyakova* still waited for auction in Breakall. The first two auctions had failed. I wondered what would happen with the next one. Docking fees added up over time.

The roses around the door looked fully recovered from my ministrations. The white double blooms seemed to shine in their own light against the rich green foliage. The pile of clippings had disappeared from beside the path.

I stripped off the soggy workout clothes and dropped them into the refresher and rummaged in my grav-trunks for clean shorts and my dress uniform. I could have gotten away with a set of utilities, but lunch at the O Club meant I'd be on display. I owed it to Alys Giggone to put on a good face.

As I sorted through the trunks, *Sifu* Newmar's words came back to me. I'd left Neris with less than twenty kilos of worldly possessions. I'd arrived on Port Newmar with thirty. Looking at the two trunks, I knew they tipped in at nearly two hundred. With that thought, I grabbed my shower gear and headed for the bathroom.

I was pretty sure *Sifu* Newmar had not been talking about just the physical baggage. Seeing the physical manifestation got me wondering how I'd measure the psychic baggage. With roses, you could learn where to clip. A branch out of place here. A stem gone wrong there. Clipping that to open the center and this to foster bushiness. Physical baggage can be measured in mass or volume or both.

How did one measure psychological baggage? Where—and what—would one clip?

Alys Giggone hadn't changed much. I hadn't seen her since I left the *Lois McKendrick* but the image in my mind matched the smile that greeted me when I stepped into the O Club at 1145. "Captain Wang!" She waved me over to the bar. Her pristine undress whites showed off her tan and sported a commandant's fleet arrow on the collar.

I dropped my hat on a hook by the door and crossed the uncrowded bar. I could feel myself grinning back at her. Heads turned to watch me. Faces showed curiosity more than anything. It looked like a slow lunchtime. I suspected most of the permanent party had their own quarters and transients didn't spend lunch hours there. Perhaps I was just unfashionably early.

"Commandant, thank you for the invitation."

She snorted and held a hand for me to shake. "You're allowed to call me Alys. At least at the bar. What'll you have?"

I shook her hand. "Coffee any good here?"

"Better be." She turned to the bartender. "Mike, coffee for the captain, if you please?"

"Of course, sar." He found a heavy china mug embossed with the academy logo in gold and filled it from a thermal carafe behind the bar. He slipped it onto the polished wood in front of me. "Cream? Sugar?"

I shook my head and reached for the handle. After a tentative sip I nodded my thanks. "She's right. This is good."

He beamed and took his polishing cloth down the bar.

I perched my rump on the tall stool and settled in beside her. "I'll admit, it's a bit surreal."

She snorted again. "You'll get used to it. You didn't socialize with the other captains out there in Diurnia?"

"None of them were my first skipper."

She gave a short chuckle at that. "No doubt." She took a pull from her glass. "So, last time I saw you, you were worried about how to pay for the academy. Got your loans paid off yet?" Her lips curved up in a half smile.

I laughed. "Yeah. I didn't have to take out that much, and I had that paid back before I made second mate."

"Told ya," she said with a bump of her elbow. "Now look at you. Captain and everything after only, what? Sixteen stanyers?"

"Something like that. I came up fast but I had a lot of help pushing me up the ladder." I toasted her with my mug.

She smiled and nodded. "I heard about Maloney. Geoff was a good man. My father always thought highly of him."

"Didn't you?"

She shrugged. "Didn't know him that well. Father knew him because they had committee business together. Seems like I'd barely taken over here when we got the word that he'd passed on."

"Well, he gave me my start, even if it was as bait."

She looked at me with one eyebrow arched in query. "Who? My father or Maloney?"

"Both, actually." I shrugged. "Your father recommended me when Maloney showed up at the academy after graduation looking for a green third mate."

"And you took it?"

"I didn't have a large number of choices. A lot of the class had shipped out by the time Maloney made me an offer. I was afraid I'd be here doing another year just because I didn't have a berth." I took a sip of the coffee.

"You said bait?"

I nodded. "Long story." I chewed on the inside of my lip as I remembered it. "It was pretty bad. I think that was the first time I was ever punched by a senior officer. By anybody for that matter."

"Punched?" The look of amazement stretched her eyes wide and left her jaw hanging.

"On the bridge. First mate caught me by surprise with a punch to the gut."

"Oh, Ishmael. Your first berth out of the academy and you got a bully first mate?"

I shrugged. "I had no idea. My only saving grace was that I knew I had no idea. It's a miracle that I wasn't booted for insubordination."

"You? Insubordinate? Is that why he hit you?"

I shook my head and opened my mouth to tell her, but Mike returned.

"Commandant? Captain? Your table is ready."

A steward in a spotless white uniform showed us to a table in the corner. I hadn't seen a table dressed that well since Jimmy Chin's Plum Blossom on Welliver. From the immaculate white table cloth to the precise placement of embossed silver and a single yellow rose, the staff had created a work of art.

"Anything wrong, Captain?" the steward asked as I stood there gazing.

I glanced at his name tag. "Not at all, Mr. Armstrong. Your work?" I waved a hand at the table.

He smiled and I realized he was much older than the typical cadet. "I've been doing it for some time now, Captain. Practice makes perfect."

I nodded agreement and slipped into my place across from the commandant.

"We'll have the special, Rubin," she said. "Another coffee for Captain Wang and if you could bring me another iced tea?"

He smiled and nodded. "Of course, Commandant." He disappeared through a swinging door that wafted some delicious aromas as he passed.

She looked at me and raised an eyebrow. "Punched?"

"I interfered with the first mate's watch section. He punched me for it."

"That's conduct unbecoming in most circles." She rested her elbows on the table, her fingers steepled in front of her face.

"The captain approved of his tactics."

She sighed. "I'm surprised Geoff put up with that."

"He didn't, but he didn't have the lawyers to back him up."

"Ugh. I understand the reasoning but when something's obviously wrong, finding the legal justification can be a real pain."

"Literally, in this case."

"For you?" she asked.

"For the women they assaulted and left in medical."

Her expression went dark and her brow furrowed. "That's unconscionable."

Mr. Armstrong returned with the drinks and small cups of soup, interrupting her train of thought.

"Old news. Blacklisted and never got another job as far as I know."

She shook her head and addressed her soup. "My spies tell me you met Frederica deGrut."

"She gave me my stars," I said. "She was on the *Tinker* as cargo master. Took command when Maloney cashiered Burnside and Rossett."

"I read that in the bulletin." She looked up from her soup. "That she'd taken command. Not how it came about."

I turned to my own soup. Something about it tasted familiar. It carried a spicy flavor and a richness to the mouth that I'd never found after leaving the *Lois*. "This reminds me of Cookie's soup."

She grinned at me across the table. "I'm not surprised."

"What? He's here?"

She gave me a half shrug and a smile. "Rank hath some privileges. He was getting ready to retire, but I convinced him to join the permanent party staff here. He'll be out to say hello as soon as they get the luncheon served."

I looked around and realized that the place had filled up while we chatted. The few faces that had turned in my direction when I entered had become a sea of discreet glances. "Are these all permanent party?"

She shook her head, glancing around. "Several are summer faculty. Some are graduate students. We've a fair number here for a seminar on economic modeling that starts in a couple of days." She cast me a knowing look at that last bit.

"What, you mean like the stuff Pip did?"

"Very much like the stuff Pip did." Merriment seemed to set her eyes dancing.

I sat back. "No."

She nodded. "Third Annual Symposium on Economic Modeling."

"No."

"Yes. He's due to dock at the orbital sometime late tomorrow."

I had the strangest feeling. "We're talking about Pip, right?"

"Cargo First Phillip Carstairs, these days," she said.

"Pip? Here?"

"Keynote speaker."

"Pip."

She gave me a small laugh. "Yes, Pip. The one-time red-headed terror of the spaceways. Your ex-bunkie and cause of half my gray hairs."

I glanced up by reflex and she tutted.

"Sorry," I said, running a hand across my mostly naked scalp. "Mine started turning and abandoned ship. Seems I inherited it from my father."

Her eyes narrowed. "Your father. Wasn't there something about him?"

"Yeah." I took the last spoonful of soup and pressed the cup back from the edge of the table. "I didn't know where he was when you were trying to get me into the academy."

"I remember. It wasn't a problem in the long run. Probably helped you." She finished with her soup. Mr. Armstrong swooped in to remove the empties.

"Your plates will be right up, sars," he said and disappeared again.

"Did you ever find him?" she asked.

"I did. He owns a restaurant on Diurnia Orbital. Does very well for himself as the chief cook and bottle washer."

"Is that why you went to Diurnia?"

I shook my head. "Maloney made the only offer. It was just coincidence. I stayed with DST until I started Icarus. I only discovered my father was on station a few months ago."

"Wait. What?"

Armstrong came out with a tray and settled two plates of Cookie's spicy beefalo in front of us. I took several moments to inhale the aroma that took me back to a time I thought I'd remembered. The scent of dusky spice wafting across the table made me realize that my memory contained only a hollow shell. The smells of too many ships and too many half-decent meals had dulled the edge. I closed my eyes and inhaled, nearly overcome by the aroma. I almost cried. When I opened my eyes, Cookie's dark face and gleaming smile met mine.

"So, Captain Wang," he said. "You've come a long way from the mess deck."

I rose and, propriety be damned, gave the man a hug. "Not so far as you might think," I said. I stepped back and became aware of the amused glances around us. "Thank you," I said. "You—" I shook my head unable to form words for a moment.

"Thank you, young Ishmael," he said. "You've made me proud."

"You've made *us* proud," the commandant said.

"Sit. Eat." Cookie pressed me back into my chair. "You two have much to catch up on and I have a kitchen to run. You'll be on-planet for a while?"

I nodded.

"Excellent. We'll have a chance to catch up ourselves when duty is not so pressing." He glanced down at the commandant with a nod and a smile before ducking through the kitchen door.

I took my seat again and shook my head. "You're just full of surprises, Commandant."

"Alys," she said. "You're not in my command and I'm not one to stand on ceremony."

"Alys," I repeated and shook my head again. "It feels strange. You've always been the captain to me."

"I remember my first captain, too," she said. "He retired before I took the *Lois*. Hiram Longstreet. Starched martinet of the old school. Thank gods I knew real captains before I met him. We never met again after I came to the academy." Her lips twisted in a wry grin.

"Having met Rossett, I'm glad I met real captains first, too."

She laughed. "Speaking of real captains, what actually happened between you and Cassie?"

"Cassie?" I momentarily blanked on the name. "Captain Harrison?"

"You remember. The captain who gave you a recommendation on the basis of having met you on the brow watch one night?" She took a forkful of beefalo and grinned at me.

"What did Captain Harrison have to say?" I asked.

"Something about a mirror."

"I just offered her a different perspective on reflection," I said. "How is she?"

"Excellent. Running a very profitable triangle trade in Ciroda these days with her new husband and first mate. Her elder daughter will be a cadet in the next class."

"You mean kids who weren't born when I came here are now old enough to be cadets?"

She snickered. "Kids who weren't born when I made captain are now captains. Just wait. Your turn is coming."

We ate without talking for a bit. The beefalo tasted better than I remembered. Cookie had had nearly two decades to perfect what I thought had been perfect at the time. Perhaps it was just my memory.

"How come you took over here?" I asked.

"I've been sending my father cadets for stanyers. Seemed only right I should sit on the other side of the desk for a bit."

"Don't you miss being captain?"

She grinned at me. "Do you?"

I poked at the beefalo with my fork a few times and thought

about it. "Yes. No. Maybe," I said after too long a pause. "I'm a bit burned out, I think."

She shrugged and scraped the last of her meal off the plate. "Happens. That's why we have the facilities here."

I nodded and pushed my plate back, too full to finish. "I remember seeing the officers come and go. *Sifu* Newmar had rather a large following."

"She still does. I think more people come back to visit her than for any other reason."

"I never thought I'd be one of them."

"You've had a rough couple of stanyers."

"Yeah." I scanned the other patrons and tried not to think about it.

"Have you talked to anybody?"

I looked back at her. "Talked?"

"Psychiatrist? Psychologist? Counselor?"

I shook my head. "That's why I came back here."

"I can give you a referral."

"I've got a standing date with *Sifu* Newmar."

Alys smiled. "I know Margaret better than you. She's probably already given you three impossible things to do."

"Three?" I knew of two but couldn't imagine the third.

"One, she wants you to master your form."

"Agreed."

"Impossible because it's a form of practice. Of meditation."

"I expect I could reach mastery in a few more decades."

"Yes, but impossible because you'd need to take a teacher with you to practice and you've got a career to consider."

I had to agree. "She also wants me to prune."

"Prune what?"

"Baggage, apparently. I already pruned the roses at my cottage."

"Your physical baggage?" She raised an eyebrow. "I didn't see that one coming."

"I've got two trunks of stuff. It's everything that came off my last ship."

"All your worldly possessions."

"All my physical ones, anyway."

Mr. Armstrong showed up to take the empty dishes. "Refills? Dessert?"

I looked at Alys. "You probably have duties to attend to."

She looked at the chrono on the wall above the bar and shook her head. "Curriculum committee meeting in a stan. Nothing until then." She turned to Mr. Armstrong. "If Cookie has some of that vanilla mousse? I'd take some and a refill on the iced tea."

He looked to me. "Captain?"

"Just coffee. That meal was enough to last me for a week."

He grinned. "Coming right up, sars."

Alys brought her gaze back to me. "So. Any idea how long you'll be here?"

"How long can I stay?"

She shrugged. "The academy doesn't just exist for the molding of fresh new officers. Some really smart person recognized that command carries its own unique burdens, so they made arrangements for our students to come back whenever they need to. When they can."

"That's why it's mostly senior grades?"

She gave a shrug. "We get some others, but yeah. Captains have more say over what they do than third mates."

"How long can I stay?"

"Long as you pay for the cottage," she said with a twinkle in her eye. "But I'll warn you that if you're still here come fall, you'll find yourself in front of a classroom filled with shiny new cadets all looking for words of wisdom from the famous Captain Ishmael Wang."

I snorted. "After the settlement from DST, I think I can afford to live here for a few centuries." I toyed with my coffee mug for a moment. "Famous?"

"You will be by the time I get done building you up."

"Whew."

"No, seriously. You're not famous-famous, but people who follow the field know your name. You might not be the youngest captain on record, but you might well be the youngest owner. Certainly the youngest land-rat to make it to owner." She smirked a little as she leaned back to let Rubin deliver her vanilla mousse. "People notice that."

Rubin topped up my coffee and disappeared again.

Her words didn't make me feel much better about things.

"So, what do you want to do, Ishmael?" she asked around a delicate spoonful of creamy fluff.

I took a deep breath and shook my head a little. "Practice my form. See if there's anything I can get rid of in my baggage. Beyond that? I don't know."

She nodded and took another bite of her dessert.

"I should probably talk to somebody."

"I knew you were smart. I'll send you a contact when I get back to my office. He's expecting you."

I nodded and took another sip of coffee. "What would you have me teach?"

She shook her head. "As I remember you were brilliant at systems and comms. Maybe astrogation. You could be the remedial math tutor. Doesn't matter. You won't be here that long."

"I won't?"

She shook her head again. "Pip's coming."

I laughed at that. Really laughed for the first time since leaving the *Iris.* The other patrons looked in our direction with smiles, reminding me that we weren't alone. I laughed anyway.

Chapter Four
Port Newmar: 2374, May 28

When Pip got off the shuttle, I recognized him immediately. His hair had gone white, his girth had expanded a bit, and he sported a trimmed goatee, but I recognized his grin as soon as he turned it on me.

"By Athena's nether beard! Ishmael? The one man in the Western Annex I need to find and you're waiting for me?" He grabbed me in a bear hug and pounded my back.

I hugged and pounded him back.

"When Alys told me you were coming, I almost lost it," I said.

"You've caught up with her then?" He snagged his carry-on bag and nodded toward the terminal entrance. "Come on. I need to get settled in, and we need to talk."

"Oh, yeah. We had lunch at the O Club a couple of days ago."

"You've seen Cookie, then."

I nodded. "Old home week here, isn't it?"

He bulled through the doors and trundled toward the cottages. "Well, Bev is off somewhere with her hubby. They're doing a nice fast-packet trade out of St. Cloud last I heard. Forget what they called it. *Epiphany*? *Eridani*? *Ephemeral.* That was it."

"I thought she was going off to work the family ship."

He shrugged. "Opportunities are everywhere, but berths are always in demand. Maybe she outgrew them."

"Heard from Bril?"

He shook his head.

"I've not heard from anybody since I left here," I said. "How do you stay in the loop?"

He waved a hand as if swatting at a fly. "I've been in and out of Port Newmar a dozen times or more since we left. Gossip always comes home to roost."

"Any scuttlebutt on Mr. Maxwell? Mr. von Ickles?"

"Captain Maxwell retired and works for the CPJCT now. He's the orbital manager up there." He pointed up.

"No."

"Yep."

"What are the odds?"

"Well, he's married to Alys Giggone. I'd say the odds were pretty good he wouldn't be too far away."

"What?"

"You didn't know?" he asked, stopping to look at me as if I were some kind of odd flower beside the path. "Seriously?"

"I didn't know she was even married, let alone to him."

"Second hub for her, I think. She's got a kid or two stashed out in Dunsany Roads somewhere if I remember."

"Do you have files on everybody?"

"Oh, no." He shook his head and resumed his march toward campus. "Only the important people."

"Von Ickles?" I asked.

"Captain von Ickles commands one of the new Manchester Eighty-Eights for Federated Freight. He's on the *Lois's* old route over in Dunsany."

"He stayed?"

"They treated him well. Moved him up as he made grade. Why wouldn't he?" He turned into the path that led to the cottage across from mine. "They pay a nice seniority bonus, you know?"

"What happened to the *Lois*?"

"They retired her from active service about a decade back. Not sure where her hull is now. Probably melted down and recast."

That thought made me sad but everything has a life span. Especially ships subjected to the rigors of the Deep Dark.

"Where'd they put you?" he asked.

I jerked a thumb at the cottage across the way.

"Handy." He nodded toward his own. "Come in. They should have stocked my fridge for me. We can catch up."

"Stocked your fridge?"

"Yeah. I come here often enough that I leave a standing order for supplies."

I shook my head. "I don't get out enough."

"You got stars," he said, nodding at my collar. He looked me in the eye. "Scars, too, I'd guess."

That might have been the first time I'd ever seen Pip serious.

"You got an earring," I said. "Makes you look like a pirate."

He grinned and flicked the small silver hoop in his left ear with a fingertip. "Lost a bet. Best bet I ever lost." He turned to the cottage, resettling the strap of his bag. "Come on. Let's get out of this harmful radiation and under cover."

"Harmful radiation?"

He pointed at the system's primary hanging over the treetops to the south west. "You have any idea how much damage that thing can do?"

I chuckled and followed him inside. The day had become warm but the clouds forming just offshore promised an evening light show when they came inland.

Pip stashed his bag in the bedroom, tossed his coat over the back of a chair, and went face first into the small refrigeration unit in his kitchenette. He emerged with a pair of bottles and a beaming smile.

"I keep thinking I should stock up on this stuff." He held out a bottle to me. "You know you can only get this on Port Newmar?"

I took the bottle with the familiar label—a square-rigged sailing ship with a bone in her teeth appeared to be sailing across the night sky. "What? Clipper Ship Lager?"

He nodded and flipped the cap off. After a long pull from the bottle, he grinned and smacked his lips. "We lived on this stuff, but they don't distribute off-planet."

I took a sip from mine and remembered only too well how much of it I'd consumed as a cadet. "Really? I thought we drank this because it was cheap."

He threw himself onto one end of the sofa and pointed me into the chair across from him. "That, too, but you have to admit. It's local. Consistent product. Reasonable flavor. Not too big a kick. Not too heavy. Not too watery." He took another pull. "It has a lot to recommend it."

I dropped into the chair and took a long drag from my bottle. "It's the nostalgia factor."

He shrugged. "Nothing wrong with remembering the past."

I didn't say anything to that. I hid my face behind my bottle as I took another drink.

"It's good to see you, too," he said.

I grinned at him. "I'm still a little off balance. I can't believe you're here. And giving a keynote address?"

"Why not? I started this conference. It's grown from a half dozen modeling geeks from the academy. Third annual and we're expecting to get a couple dozen people from the various shipping lines along with some data mongers from around the Western Annex. Saltzman's sending somebody this year. We'll have a couple from Federated."

"This is the same stuff you were doing back on the *Lois*, right?"

He nodded. "Humble beginnings on the mess deck with your mother's old computer. Yup. It's a lot bigger now."

"You learned more math?"

He laughed, a low chuckle in his chest. "Yeah. Well, that, too."

"Do you have to prep or anything for the keynote?" I asked after a few moments.

He shook his head. "It's nothing to write home about. Mostly thanking them for coming. I've got a little song and dance about the latest work on applying structural equations to profitability on extended multi-cargo runs. It's a lot more than we used to do by guess and good instincts in the old days. Single-cargo ships have an interesting problem. They can't diversify risks across multiple cargoes. It's one of the reasons Eighty-Eights are climbing so fast in the ranks of ships."

"I was on a Barbell. It worked pretty well for bulk hauling."

"I know." He looked at me over the top of his bottle. "That's what I wanted to talk to you about."

"About bulk hauling?"

He shook his head and leaned forward, anchoring his elbows on his knees. "About Barbells."

"Not much to tell. Unwin-built. Single-can design. Rated at two hundred metric kilotons. Lock the can in place and off you go. Without a can they're two bricks on a soda straw."

Pip nibbled on the inside of his lower lip as he looked at me. "You were on the *William Tinker* for a lot of stanyers. Started there when you graduated and stayed there until you made captain."

I raised my eyebrows. "You have a file on me?"

He grinned. "I said. Only the important people."

"What else do you know?"

He pursed his lips and squinted at me like he was reading something in his head. "Married, divorced. Made captain a couple stanyers ago. Moved to the *Agamemnon*, a fifteen-metric-kiloton tractor, also with DST. Flew her for about a stanyer before Maloney died, and then started your own company. Sold that a few months ago to the new CEO of Diurnia, one Christine Maloney who just happened to be your cook on the *Iris*." He saluted me with his nearly empty bottle. "Did I miss anything?"

I thought of the sapphire eyes and the bubbling laugh. I shook my head. "Those are the high points."

"There were some low points, too," he said.

I nodded. "A few. We all have them, don't we?"

He nodded and drained his beer. "Too true."

"So enough about me. What have you been up to? Cargo first?"

He shrugged. "Not much to tell. One of the cousins is the skipper for the *Prodigal Son.* We've managed to stay solvent and I've worked up through the ranks. Cargo first is all we can justify in that small a ship. I took the exam and hold the rating, but there was never any reason to claim the rank. It's not like I'm going to get paid more or passed over. Besides, I'm getting the owner's share less a franchise fee to the old man. Shares have been better than I ever imagined. Which is why this modeling symposium started. People took notice of how well we were doing."

"Your father had nothing to do with that, did he?" I asked.

He smirked. "He fought it at first. Made it clear that I had to keep the profit coming and cover the costs of my own ship. He held the note, but I paid the bills with interest."

"How long did it take you to pay it off?"

"Well, it was a twenty-stanyer note."

I smiled. "So, you paid it off in ten?"

He grinned. "You know me so well."

I raised my bottle in a toast to him. "Congrats. That got his attention, did it?"

"It did. Of course, he kept up on our trading the whole time. We're part of the family fleet after all and he's still the chairman of the board." He went to the fridge and pulled out another beer. "You want one?"

I shook my head. "One's my limit for the afternoon."

"Lightweight." He came back and sat down again.

"Married?" I asked.

He shook his head. "Never found the right person. Really wasn't time to get involved."

"So you brought the *Son* here?"

"Sure. We picked up a hot priority over in Dunsany and made a tidy profit on the run."

"Just cooling your heels for a few days?"

"Roland is doing some maintenance on the engines and upgrading the sail generators."

"Roland?"

"Captain Roland Marx. Second cousin on my mother's side. He's the captain of record and has the engineering certification for that power plant."

"But can he cook?"

Pip shook his head and laughed. "Gods, no. He keeps us moving. I keep us fed and keep the profits rolling in."

"Just the two of you?"

"For now. He's planning on trading me out soon for a better-looking model."

"He's leaving? What'll you do for a captain?"

"Well, yes, and no. He's actually planning on staying with the *Son.* I'm planning on leaving."

"You're leaving your own ship?" I could feel my jaw stretching open.

"Buying a new one, I hope."

"You must be doing well."

He looked down at his hands. "Yeah. Well. That's what I wanted to talk with you about."

"So you weren't kidding about looking for me?"

"I knew where to find you. I expected to be flying to Diurnia to do it when the conference is over." He didn't look up, just kept worrying the corner of the label on his bottle with a thumbnail.

"So? What did you want to talk about?"

He glanced up at me for a moment and then looked down again. "What can you tell me about the *Chernyakova*?"

Chapter Five
Port Newmar: 2374, May 28

My beer was nearly empty but I drained it anyway. The memories of bloated bodies and of living in the smell of corrupted flesh soured the brew, but it was something to do with my hands while I processed the question.

Pip cleared his throat. "That bad, huh?"

I put the empty bottle on the coffee table and leaned back in my chair. "Yeah. Actually, a bit worse than you might imagine." I wiped a hand across my mouth but it did nothing for the vile taste there. "What do you want to know?"

"Condition of the vessel?"

I shrugged. "It's been a couple of stanyers. Last I saw of it, it was a mess."

"Mess, how?"

"No spares. Systems missing components. Broken panels in the backbone. Stores completely inadequate."

"Structural problems?"

"Not that I noticed."

"You commanded the salvage crew."

"Yeah." I kept my eyes open and focused on his face because closing them meant seeing things I never wanted to see again.

"They'll hold the next auction in about a month."

"Third time's the charm," I said.

"You stand to make a lot when it closes."

"Yeah. That's what they tell me. It's how I was able to finagle the financing to start Icarus."

"I figured. Musta thrown a few wrenches in the works when it never closed."

I shrugged. "I had worse problems."

He gave me a long stare. His earring gleamed in the afternoon light streaming in the window behind him. "Wanna talk about them?"

I shook my head. "Alys is setting me up with a therapist and I've got *Sifu* Newmar to keep me grounded."

"She's a treasure, that woman."

"Which one?"

He laughed and took a slug from his beer. "Both, I guess."

"Why do you want to know about the *Chernyakova*?"

"I'm going to bid on it."

"Why?" I asked.

"The Barbell class is a unique vessel. Secure cargo. Massive capacity. Absolutely reliable ship. Relatively small crew compared to ships like the Eighty-Eights."

"And you want one to test your model."

He grinned at me and the twinkle in his eye took me back two decades. "You aren't as dumb as you used to be."

"Why *Chernyakova*?"

"Ship itself isn't that old. The space frame is rated for a half century and it's barely scratched ten stanyers. Generators, fusactors, and engines should all be sound." He eyed me. "Unless you saw something?"

"Maintenance logs weren't exactly trust-inducing."

He sat back and cradled his beer on his chest, frowning at the ceiling. "So, we may need some overhaul."

"The last two auctions have failed."

"Yeah. I know." His grin grew more predatory than friendly. "They've also changed the terms. They dropped the reserve and minimum bid is down to fifty mill."

"What was it before?"

"Reserve was a hundred and fifty with a one percent penalty. Sealed bids."

"So bid two hundred mill and realize the ship was a dog?"

"Pay the two mill to get out from under it," Pip said. "Is it a dog?"

I took a deep breath and blew it out, trying to sort out my emotional response to the ship from the actual facts. "It'll need some work. I wouldn't trust the Burleson drives in a pinch. They'd need to be recalibrated. The inside probably needs to be completely refurbed. That stench got into everything. I had to burn the uniforms I wore over there."

"Seriously?"

I chuckled. "No, but I thought about it. I smelled that ship for weeks after."

"It's also an open auction," Pip said.

"Not sealed bid?"

He shook his head. "Registered credit balance deposit in escrow before you can bid. They want that ship gone."

"So if you bid it and win?"

"They already have your credits. Losers get theirs back."

"How the heck can you finance something like that?"

"Deep pockets." He shrugged. "Or a good banker who'll float the loan in advance."

"How deep are your pockets?" I asked.

"Not as deep as yours." He shrugged again. "Deep enough and I've an appointment with my bank tomorrow. I've enough of a credit line to cover what I intend to bid."

"What do you intend to bid?" I asked.

"My limit is a hundred and ten. With what you've said, I think I need to chop that back to ninety to leave some cash for refurbishment."

"The ship's been docked for a couple of stanyers now."

He nodded. "I have reserve funds for maintenance and updates, but it's not enough to replace a Burleson unit."

"You'll need crew."

He nodded. "Yeah. I'll need a captain, engineering, and steward. I've already taken the cargo master exam so I'm certified as chief. I've got some relatives we can tap for mates, and I'm planning on hiring from the pool when I need them. Probably from Diurnia."

"Where you going to get the work done?"

"Unwin has a maintenance yard in Dree. I was planning on jumping over, but you say the ship's not spaceworthy?"

I thought about it. "We sailed her into Breakall. They were on their way out of the system when they gassed themselves. One jump?" I shrugged. "If it can pass a decent engineering inspection, it'd probably be all right."

Pip's lips twitched back and forth as if he were chewing on that information. "All right. I'll take that under advisement. Unwin must have some jump-capable tugs available or on retainer."

"Moran runs the tugs around the stations in the whole quadrant. Maybe they have some."

"Might not need one, but I'll factor that into the mix," Pip said with a nod.

"What's a new Barbell cost?" I asked.

"I found a used one over in Ciroda for half a bill. New ones are almost twice that."

I whistled. "I shouldn't be surprised, but the level of the reserves, I'd have thought less."

"How much was your Higbee?"

"I got it for scrap price. Thirty-five mill."

"One fifty is the scrap value of the *Chernyakova.* Even the knackers didn't want it for that."

"Any idea why?"

"Superstition?"

"How much bad luck can you get when you melt down the hull?"

He shrugged. "Who knows. I suspect the scrap dealers weren't paying attention. Other than its history, there's nothing to indicate that the ship needs much more than a crew and stores to get underway."

"You know the closing bids on the last two auctions?"

"Scuttlebutt is that they were both somewhere north of two fifty."

"And they both folded rather than take it on."

"Yep," he said.

"Didn't they get an inspection before making a bid?"

"I've got the prospectus here if you want to see it." He fished in his pocket and pulled out his tablet. He flipped a couple of pages and then slid the device over to me.

The pictures looked right. I flipped through the photos. Inside shots showed some cosmetic damage to the bulkheads including the broken one that I remembered in the spine. They'd apparently cleaned out all the trash and junk. Berthing areas showed bare racks without mattresses. Galley was completely empty except for the built-in steam kettles and ovens. Images of the bridge showed all the consoles in place but the stains on the deck looked familiar enough that I thought my stomach might rebel.

"Looks too familiar," I said, swallowing against the bile.

I flipped past the images and read the actual description. "They haven't sold the cargo?" I asked.

"As far as I can tell, they never unloaded it. It's still in there. It'd be part of the salvage claim, at any rate."

I flipped through the document. "Isn't there a manifest?"

"Near the back. It's supposedly a can full of hydraulic fluid from Martha's Haven bound for Diurnia."

"At least it's not kitty litter."

"What?"

I shook my head. "Never mind. Long story. You think the fluid's any good?"

"It's probably frozen. I wonder how they unload it."

I shrugged. "Not my problem. They must have some kind of can warmer that lets them pump it out. Two hundred metric kilotons of hydraulic fluid isn't something you chip out with a hammer and chisel."

I stopped at the engineering reports. "According to this, the generators, fusactor, and Burleson drives are within specification."

"Yeah, well, that's why I wanted to talk with you about it."

I shook my head. "We didn't have any problems sailing her in from where we found her, but I wouldn't get underway until we replaced the missing alarm circuits."

"Missing alarm circuits?"

I settled back into my chair. "How much do you know about this?" I slipped the tablet back across the table.

"Only what I've gotten from the public documents and a bit of scuttlebutt from here and there."

"Crew died of carbon monoxide poisoning. A rag fire in one of the after engine compartments."

"How's that even possible?"

"They'd taken the alarm module out of the system. The sensors detected the gas, but the alarms didn't go off."

"Wouldn't the gas have smothered its own fire?"

"Not before enough gas got into the environmental system. It took three days to burn up and then burn out."

"Ouch."

I nodded. "Once the level got critical, the crew pretty much all dropped within a few ticks of each other."

Pip closed his eyes and shook his head. "And you found them?"

"Yeah."

Pip blew out his breath. "Well. That's nasty."

"Yeah."

"So, I suppose you're not interested in being captain?"

I blinked at him. "Captain? Of the *Chernyakova*?"

"Assuming I win the auction."

The realization struck me like a rock to the head. "That's why you wanted to find me."

He gave me a sheepish smile and a small shrug. "You aren't going to stay ashore forever. I thought you might feel up to a new challenge."

"Are you mad?"

"I've always been a little mad. You know that."

I sat there for several ticks. All the memories of that ship washed through my head. The sights and smells of death. The horror of what had happened rose in my chest. "You don't know what you're asking," I said. I barely heard my own words over the rushing in my ears.

Pip nodded. "You're right. I don't. I can't imagine what that must have been like."

I took a couple of deep breaths and tried to unclench my hands from the arms of the chair.

Pip leaned forward again, his elbows on his knees. He reached forward and placed his beer bottle on the table between us. He seemed to be studying the table top as if for some flaw. "What I can imagine is that you'd never let anything like that happen again. For a lot of people it's a bad luck ship. A death trap. You were there and saw it. You know what caused it and you know how to fix it. You saw it yourself. First hand. It's just a ship. A ship with a tragic past, but one that you might be able to turn around. One that you might be able to make into something noble again."

He looked over at me. His eyes dared me, but the rest of his face stayed flatly neutral.

I stared at him and recognized the fear that lay beneath my memories. He hadn't called me afraid in so many words but he knew just which buttons to push to get me to see it. The thought of setting foot on that ship again made my skin crawl. I had to wipe my palms on the thighs of my uniform.

Yet there was something in his suggestion. Something that appealed to my insecurity in a horrible, scary way. My bank account held enough credits that I never had to work another day in my life. I could do anything I wanted. Find a rock and live out my days on it. Get a yacht and sail around. I could retreat from the universe and stop worrying about power dynamics and personnel management and trade routes.

I might live long enough to forget those sapphire eyes.

I didn't want to do that. Any of it.

Part of me wanted to go somewhere that I couldn't get anybody else killed, but the life of a dilettante held no appeal. I knew that—whatever else had happened—my future lay in the Deep Dark. People died in space all the time. Probably every day, and most of them because somebody cut a corner or made a mistake without sufficient backup. The *Chernyakova* was a monument to that shortsightedness.

I looked over at Pip.

"You could sell vacuum to an orbital, couldn't you."

He grinned. "You'll do it? Be captain?"

"I need to think about it."

"What's to think about?"

"Whether or not I'm fit to command."

He threw up his hands and flopped back in his seat. "I never met anybody more fit," he said. "Even now, with your head up your backside and acting more like Hamlet's father than Hamlet, you're more fit to command than half the captains in the fleet."

I should have said something like "What do you mean?" or "Head up my backside?" but what came out was "Since when did you read Shakespeare?"

Pip scuffed his feet on the floor and refused to meet my eyes. "I had some time on my hands and stumbled on some old books. Sue me."

"Guy's been dead for centuries."

He glared at me. "Your point?"

I laughed, my entire train of thought so completely derailed I completely forgot whatever I had meant to say. I just kept chuckling. Nobody had quoted Shakespeare to me since my mother died, and now it had happened twice in the last week. The wonder of it struck me funny. That one of them came from Pip made it even funnier. After the horror and seriousness of the conversation we'd been having, you could have put a whoopee cushion under one of us and it wouldn't have been as funny to me.

Eventually Pip started laughing, too.

It took some time for us to rein in the giggles. I'm not sure why. It wasn't that funny.

"Lemme think about it," I said after we'd gotten to the chuckle-and-sniff stage.

"All right. Ponder," he said. "I still don't know what you're going to ponder. You can't stay ashore any more than I can, fat bank account or not. You'll need a new berth eventually, and at least with me you won't be bored."

He almost got me laughing again but I stifled it.

Somebody knocked on the cottage door before I could answer.

Pip stood and crossed to open it.

A woman wearing a spacer crop haircut and a set of utility khakis stood there, hand ready to knock again. "Phillip!" she said.

"Katharine! My gods and garters, woman. It's so good to see you!" He gathered her up and they hugged. He stepped back and held her at arm's length. "When did you get in?"

"Yesterday. I've just been lazing around the campus, but heard you'd come in on the afternoon shuttle."

Pip ushered her into the cottage, and I stood to meet her.

"Cargo First Katharine Munroe, meet Captain Ishmael Wang." He waved a hand in my direction. "He was just leaving."

Her eyes goggled a bit as she stared for a moment too long before blinking and looking aside. "Sorry, Captain. I didn't mean to stare." She glanced at me and then at Pip. "You're the Ishmael Wang from Diurnia?"

I shrugged. "Yeah. I guess. I came in from Diurnia."

"I'm honored to meet you, Captain." She tamped down whatever fangirl impulse had seized her and held out her hand.

I shook her hand and offered a smile. "Call me Ishmael," I said.

"Are you here for the conference?" she asked. "I didn't see your name on the attendee list."

"No. I'm just here for the food."

She blinked and glanced at Pip who snorted.

"At any rate, I've got some thinking to do and I'm not very sociable when I think," I said. I headed for the door.

Pip said, "You can attend if you want. I know who to bribe to get you a badge."

I stopped at the door frame and shook my head. "Thanks, but all I know about economic modeling is buy low, sell high."

Ms. Monroe snorted. "You'll fit right in with some of these dinosaurs." Her eyes went wide and she all but slapped a hand across her mouth.

Pip laughed at that. "She's right, but do what you need to. We can talk later."

"I can't believe I said that out loud," she muttered.

I chuckled and pulled the door closed behind me. I stood on the stoop for a moment and let my eyes adjust to the late afternoon light. Pip had given me a lot to think about. I needed to find some space to foster that thinking.

Behind the door I heard Katharine Monroe say, "You know Ishmael Wang and you didn't tell me?"

Pip's laughter followed me down the path.

Chapter Six
Port Newmar: 2374, May 29

I wouldn't have thought the simple, almost gentle movements of tai chi could have taken such a toll on my body. The third day with *Sifu* Newmar reminded me that I'd neglected my practice far too long. I felt it when I bowed to the empty floor, right along the back of my thighs. I felt it in my calves as I started the warmups, pushing and pulling an imaginary ball. I felt it in the back of my neck and across my shoulders every time I did anything with my arms.

I was so focused on the burn that I didn't notice her enter until she spoke. "Have you trimmed down your baggage yet, Ishmael?"

Her voice didn't startle me. It was too soft for that. I was too deep into the movements to let it jump me. "Not yet, *Sifu*."

"Hm."

I stopped my warmup and looked at her. She had her head cocked to the left and her eyes squinted at me.

"Well, you're making good progress anyway," she said. "Let's do Yang Short Form today. Your Snake Creeps Down needs work." With a bow to the floor, she took her place and dominated my attention for the next stan.

Eventually she said, "Enough. Tea." She waved a hand in a rolling gesture. "Cooldown for you."

I grinned and took a stance, letting the soft morning air wash away the heat in my muscles as I flexed slowly and evenly. I had to focus on my forearms to relax my hands. I let myself feel the moisture in the air, smell the green of summer and the faint salt from the ocean. Shipboard air never feels like real air. It never smells quite right; it isn't alive and moving. While it never stays still, it never touches your skin the way real atmosphere can.

I heard the whistle of the teapot and slowed my cooldown even more.

The sweat stuck the back of my tunic to my skin. A small trickle of moisture traced down the side of my face, cooling as it evaporated.

"Tea is ready."

I finished my cycle and released the pose, holding the chi for a few moments before releasing a breath and turning to the kitchen. The flowery scent of a jasmine blend reached me when I paused to bow to the floor.

"You really are doing much better, Ishmael."

"Thank you. I've missed this."

"Your muscles are sore." It wasn't a question.

"Yes. Thighs and calves mostly. Some across my neck."

"You're carrying a lot of tension in your shoulders." She crossed to the cup rack and paused, one hand raised to select the day's cups. She lifted a shallow tea bowl from one slot and an antique porcelain cup with a gold rim and a brightly painted scene of birds and willow branches from another. She placed the bowl in front of me and poured a portion of the jasmine into it.

"How do you know which cup to choose?" I asked.

Her smile was so delicate it barely showed as she poured tea into the nearly translucent porcelain. "I don't. A cup is a cup. It holds tea." She placed the pot on the warming stone and looked into my eyes as she lifted her cup. "Why? Do you see significance in my choices?"

"You never pick the same cups twice in a row."

"No two days are exactly alike. I celebrate them each for what they are."

"You always pick a cup that seems appropriate for your students, even though I'm not sure what that means." I touched the rim of the tea bowl in front of me with one finger and decided to wait for a few moments before trying to lift it.

"Can you explain a bit more?"

"The first morning, you gave me the simple clay cup. No handle. No adornment. You kept the brightly colored one with a wide mouth."

"What do you divine from these selections?"

I shook my head. "I don't. I feel like there's a pattern, a commentary or message or something. I just can't put a finger on it." I shrugged. "That's why I asked."

She sipped her tea and nodded.

"Do you see a comment about value? Yesterday, you used the small Yixing clay cup while I used the much larger Chientan porcelain. Today, I've given you a clay bowl while I drink from an antique Wedgewood."

I shook my head and chewed my lip for a moment before speaking. "That's not your style, *Sifu.* I've never heard or seen you make any judgments. The lowest cadet to the highest captain. The commonest of weeds to the brightest of blossoms. You seem to approach each the same way, appreciating each for what it is."

"My goodness. You've become quite the philosopher." Her eyes fairly danced with the merriment held behind her lips.

I laughed for her. "I sound pretentious."

She shook her head. "You speak your mind. I'm flattered that you think me so filled with hidden depths that even simple acts like choosing a teacup are freighted with meaning." She pursed her lips as if trying not to laugh and hid her mouth behind the bone china.

My tea had cooled enough to lift the bowl, and I used both hands to keep it steady. The flowery tea served as foil for the smell of wood and polish and sweat. Even the faint tang of the hot iron tea kettle blended with it. The sip washed across my tongue and filled my mouth with summer.

"Thank you, *Sifu.*"

"For what?"

"For the tea. For being here."

"We all need an island of calm in the sea of life."

I smiled. "Even you?"

"Even me. The plants are my island. The practice takes me into myself but the gardening reminds me that there's a world outside."

"I would never have considered them in that light."

"Too much like work?" she asked, the smile playing around her lips again.

I laughed and shrugged. "Yes. I'm spoiled by my air-conditioned comfort and clean surroundings. The bugs and dirt seem foreign."

"Dirt is life. The bugs help more than they harm."

"Then why do you spray them?"

"I don't do that very much. Only when the balance is disturbed. My goal is to restore balance, not kill bugs."

I looked at the tea bowl on the table in front of me, balanced artfully on a base that seemed too small but proved to be remarkably stable in practice. I glanced at her cup with the flaring rim and the too-narrow base. My gaze swept the rack of teacups, picking out the shapes and colors there, finding the ones I'd used and those she'd taken for herself.

"I think I'm not done pruning yet, *Sifu.*"

"Maybe not, but something has shifted your balance. I noticed it when I entered."

"How do you know what to prune?" I asked.

"Sometimes you don't. Sometimes you just see what's not working and start trimming. A bit at a time and eventually you find the balance is restored."

"What if you don't see what's not working?"

She paused to tip her teacup up and drain it. "You should visit the lilac plantings on the east side of Building H. You might find inspiration there." She moved to the sideboard, rinsed out the Wedgwood, and set it in the drainer. "We've time for another few sets before I need to meet the groundskeepers."

I followed her lead and was soon sweating on the floor again.

She released me after morning colors and I found myself walking the circuitous route over to Building H. It housed the astrophysics classrooms in a rambling two-story building with a small observatory on the roof. Everyone had to spend a semester dealing with optics and angles, with stellar sequences and orbits. Some complained that it served no purpose when we could literally fly out and see the objects in question. It fascinated me, and I often marveled that our progenitors back on Earth had managed to learn so much simply by using such rudimentary tools. While our detailed understanding had changed over the centuries, the basic theories still governed our understanding of the universe around us.

When I got there, I had to check the position of the system primary to make sure I was on the east side. As I approached the building, I saw no lilacs. The planting beds beside the building looked empty. I remembered pruning those lilacs when I'd been a cadet. Every spring after they blossomed, we had to prune back about a third of the stems and watch for those that had gotten too large.

I had to walk right up to the beds to find the answer. I crouched down and ran my hand across the stumps sawed off flush with the ground. A bit of nearly dry sap stuck to my fingers. The entire stand had been taken back to root. I stood and surveyed the width of the building. Here and there I spotted the beginnings of new growth. A sprig of green here. A tiny stem with a few leaves there.

I wiped the sap off my fingers on the side of my pants and headed back to my cottage. Clearly, I had a lot more pruning to do and a decision to make about Pip's offer.

Chapter Seven
Port Newmar: 2374, May 30

The therapist that Alys Giggone recommended turned out to be a thirty-something beanpole with a flattop haircut, slightly bulgy eyes, and an infectious grin.

"Malloy Gains," he said when I made it to his office for my first appointment. "Mal to my patients."

I shook his offered hand and grinned back at him. I couldn't help it. "You know that means 'bad,' right?"

If possible, the grin got even wider. "Why do you think they call me that?" He pointed to a comfy-looking chair. "Have a seat. Tell me why you're here."

I settled into the chair and felt it hug me. It was a bit disconcerting. "I'm not sure why I'm here. It's just—given the last few months—it seemed like a good idea."

He pulled another chair over and sat down where he could look at me. For several heartbeats that was all he did. "So, death, dismemberments, serious illnesses. Money?"

"Yeah, pretty much. Not so much dismemberments."

His bulgy eyes blinked slowly and I had the sense that he had to refocus on me. "For most of my patients, that's a joke." He paused. "Not so much the money." He settled himself into his chair and clasped his hands around one knee. "Tell me a story."

"What kind of story? You want to know how my mother died?"

He blinked that slow blink again. "Do you want to tell me that story?"

I shrugged. "I can. It was a long time ago, but I thought therapists wanted to know about your mother."

His grin came back. "Not all of us. How did she die?"

"Flitter crash back on Neris. Two decades ago."

"Senseless, no warning. Left you on your own?"

"Yeah. Company planet. They were going to deport me unless I got a job. Just a few weeks after I turned eighteen."

"What did you do?"

"That's when I met Alys Giggone."

"So, now I know how you got to the academy and made captain at such a young age." He pursed his lips and looked up at the ceiling. "What do you want to get from these sessions, Ishmael?"

"I don't know. For a long time I've been focused on moving up the career ladder, making enough credits to be comfortable, and now I have." I shook my head. "Over the last couple of stanyers, I made captain, bought a ship, started my own company, and then sold it. Money isn't a problem. I'm probably considered wealthy at this point."

"More than a million?" he asked.

"More than a hundred million." I shrugged.

"Yeah. You're wealthy. If that's a problem, I'll take it from you." He winked at me. "And I think my hourly rate just went up."

"It's certainly life changing levels, but it's barely enough for a down payment on another ship." I thought of the *Chernyakova.*

"What was that?" he asked, sitting up and waving a finger in my direction. "What were you thinking about then?"

"A ship. A salvage claim I have on a ship over in Breakall. I commanded the salvage team that recovered it."

His grin remained but his brow furrowed. "Tell me about that."

"Crew gassed themselves on a rag fire. We found the ship on a ballistic course on its way out of Breakall. I took a skeleton crew over and stabilized the ship, and waited for the TIC forensics team to examine the remains."

"You said that pretty smoothly. You've told this story before."

"Just the other day, actually."

He nodded. "It must have been horrific."

"We found the crew where they'd dropped. Most of them in their bunks. Some at duty stations."

"How could such a thing happen?"

I felt my jaw clench. "They removed the alarm-system board from their engineering section. Environmental instruments picked up the rise in carbon monoxide, but the alarm couldn't sound because the board wasn't there."

"That makes you angry," he said.

"No, it frustrates me."

His grin came back full force, and he just raised his eyebrows.

"Yes. It makes me angry."

"Why?"

"It was so senseless. They were operating on a shoestring, sure, but to take out the alarm? Gods, how much could it have cost to replace it?"

"Senseless. Another senseless loss," he said.

I took a deep breath and the image of Greta's body lying on the decking, her blood staining the back of her shipsuit, filled my mind. "Lots of senseless death."

He settled in again, putting his feet flat on the floor and folding his hands in his lap. "And now we come to the real problem. Who was she?"

His comment caught me sideways. "My engineer. My lover." My eyes stung and I had to swallow a couple of times. "My friend."

"Senseless death."

"She got between an assassin and his target. It was an accident."

He did that slow blink thing again. "That hardly seems like an accident."

"She was in the wrong place at the wrong time. She took a knife that was meant for somebody else."

"And you think it was an accident?"

"I think I caused it." I couldn't seem to catch my breath. "If she hadn't been with us, she'd still be alive."

"Well, if she'd never been born, she'd never have died, either." He gave a little chuckle. "The loss part. Sure. This was a woman you loved."

I nodded but couldn't find breath to speak. "She pushed me away at first. I was being an ass."

"How so?"

"I had this really rigid stance about relationships among the crew."

He nodded. "That's not unusual in commercial environments. The power differential can feel insurmountable."

"She was amazing. She had the sharpest sapphire blue eyes. Brilliant engineer. Learned at her father's knee." I looked up at him. "She was my conscience. Once I nearly made a fatal decision. If it had gone well, we'd have made a few credits. If it had gone wrong, we'd have all been smeared across the surface of an airless planet."

He nodded. "Then what?"

"The longer we were together, the harder it was for me to see her there, just out of reach. She was everything I ever imagined. Brilliant, clever, gorgeous. A truly gifted engineer and a great shipmate."

"Sounds like she'd have made a good mate-mate."

"Except she was crew."

"So you let this idea that because she was crew she was untouchable get between your head and heart."

I looked down at my hands. The white knuckles surprised me; I unclenched the fists. "Yeah. When I became too much of an ass about it, she took me to the cabin and told me that it was impossible, that we'd never have a relationship. That I wasn't going to be anything more to her than a captain."

"Ouch."

"Yeah. It made it better. A little."

"How so?"

"Well, it wasn't just my ethical considerations that stopped things from progressing. She didn't care for me that way."

"Unrequited love was easier to deal with than holding the key to happiness and not being able to use it?"

I looked at him, but his grin stayed in place. "Something like that."

"That changed. What happened?"

"I started my own company and left the ship. She followed me a few months later. We hashed it out when we didn't have the captain-crew barrier between us."

"And then you hired her anyway?"

"Well, more like we formed a partnership. I couldn't fly without an engineer, and she couldn't engineer without a captain." I rubbed a hand across my eyes, trying to dispel the images.

"So you blame yourself because she's dead?"

"If I hadn't started the company. If I'd been smarter about it. If I hadn't hired her on." I felt my breath shuddering in and out and had to stop for a moment. "She'd still be alive."

"All right, let's talk about this captain-crew barrier for a bit. Tell me about that."

"Easy. I don't screw with crew. Never have. Well, except her."

"That's charming. Where did you hear that?"

He surprised a short laugh out of me. "It started with Alys Giggone."

His eyebrows shot up. "You had the hots for Alys?"

I laughed again. "She was my first captain. The *Lois McKendrick* was my first ship. They had a nonfraternization policy aboard."

"No intimate relationships among the crew members."

"Yeah."

"Was it enforced?"

"How do you mean?"

"Did you ever see anyone engaging in fraternization? Did they get punished? Was it part of the standing orders?"

"I never observed it. It was just part of the culture of the ship." I paused thinking of Bev and Bril. "We lost at least one crewman because he wanted more latitude."

"He liked the idea of bunk bunnies?"

I coughed in surprise.

"I've heard the term before," he said.

"Yeah. And he was roundly derided for his predilection."

"You were what? Eighteen? Nineteen?"

I nodded.

"And you were good with this rule?"

"It made things a bit difficult for me, but I understood the rationale."

"And you didn't want to be seen in the same light as that other guy."

I shrugged. "My mother raised me alone. I learned a lot from watching her suffer."

"So, do you wonder why we headshrinkers like to talk about mothers?"

He caught me off guard with that one, too. "No, I guess it makes sense."

"Were you ever on a ship where this nonfraternization rule wasn't in place?"

"My first posting out of the academy was a den of depravity called the *William Tinker*."

"Den of depravity. That's a bad thing?"

"It was. I'm not being overly judgmental with that. The captain abused the crew sexually and allowed his first mate to do the same. That went all the way to torture, assault, and hospitalizations. At least one crewman died under suspicious circumstances."

He twitched and the grin left his eyes, but remained fixed on his lips. "What did you do?"

"That was my welcome to the fleet as an officer." I sighed. "I did what I could. Worked with the crew that would work with me. I was the only male officer who didn't abuse them."

"Why didn't Geoff Maloney do anything?"

I shot him a glance.

"Yeah. I've seen your public jacket. Alys sent it over," he said.

"Back then none of the contracts allowed for appeal outside of the chain of command. What the captain did in space stayed on the ship until and unless the captain brought in the authorities. With the contracts he had, Mr. Maloney's lawyers felt he had no grounds for dismissal and cautioned him against risking the company in court."

"Yet, you broke it open."

I shook my head. "No, I was just the catalyst. I didn't actually do anything. That was the chief engineer and the cargo master. The first mate had his bully boys attack me one night. It didn't work out well for the mate, and the captain made a mistake. That allowed the company to step in, remove him from command, and replace him with a captain who could bring in the authorities to put an end to it."

"And you stayed there until you made captain."

"I did."

"I see." He glanced at the chrono. "Well, our time is up for today but that sounds like a good place to pick up next time. How long will you be on-planet?"

"I was planning on a few weeks, but it may only be a few days."

"All right. We'll have to move fast. I'm going to give you some homework."

"Homework?"

His grin lit up his entire face again. "Yeah. The family we're born in has values and mores that color what we believe for our entire lives. Usually those values provide a firm foundation for growth. If they didn't, the family of origin wouldn't exist."

"All right."

"Sometimes, those values get—oh—misapplied, we'll say. As each subsequent generation passes on the values, those values can evolve. Even be outgrown."

"I'm with you." I understood what he was saying but I wasn't sure I liked where he was going.

"So, between now and our next session, I want you to ponder your families of origin and what values they passed on to you."

"Families?"

"Your mother is your initial family of origin and you're carrying a lot of her influence with you. Then Alys Giggone took over as a kind of surrogate mother, and the values you learned in her family are even stronger."

The perspective twisted around in my head and then locked down. "Yes. I can see that. All right. When is our next session?"

He nodded and stood. "Tomorrow. 1100 hours."

"All right." I stood and headed for the door. "What do I owe you?"

"Commandant Giggone has the tab. You're good."

I looked at him in confusion. "What?"

His grin went all the way to the twinkle in his eye. "She has a budget for captains who need help. I'm on retainer."

"Nice deal. Do you get many?"

He sighed and nodded. "Unfortunately, yes. Command messes up people who aren't sociopaths to begin with. Empathy starts chewing on the good ones. Ego blinds the bad ones. A well-adjusted sociopath makes the most effective captain, but few people want to serve with one."

"Job security for you?"

"There is that consideration." He held out a hand. "Tomorrow, Captain."

I shook the hand and left his office. He'd given me a lot to think about.

Chapter Eight
Port Newmar: 2374, June 3

I didn't see Pip during the conference except to wave to in passing at the O Club or on the path to our respective cottages. He drew a crowd every evening, and I often heard the discussions—and laughter—well into the early morning hours. They didn't keep me awake. Just something I would be aware of when waking in the night or hear as I dropped off to sleep.

My sessions with Mal Gains continued to be interesting even if I didn't find them terribly fruitful. He introduced me to more family-of-origin stuff. He placed great store in the idea that I'd been raised in a culture of academe with its values of knowledge, truth-seeking, and reputation but then shifted to the culture of spacer with values like dependability, competence, and upward mobility.

Having achieved the upward-most mobility by becoming an owner, I suppose it was not too surprising that I felt at a loss as to what to do next. There was no new step up to take. My guilt over Greta didn't help. I still had trouble with my anger. He assured me they existed; the white-knuckle sessions when we talked about my divorce and the *Chernyakova* supported his assertions.

The question that left me staring at the ceiling at night was "What do I want to do now?"

I found so many different facets of that question to examine in detail.

The first challenge was trying to tease out what I wanted from what I felt like I should do. I had worked under an external obligation for so long, the idea that I might have some say in what I might want—and the privileged position that allowed me to actually consider it—left me floundering.

Gains had asked, "If you could do anything you want, what

would you do?"

Once I ruled out the physically impossible things—like going back in time to save Greta—and the things that I felt unqualified for—like starting another shipping company—I was left with a large empty space. I'd achieved everything I'd set out to do. Everything I'd imagined I might do. I was at a loss as to what I might do next.

I continued my sessions with *Sifu* Newmar, of course, and felt my body responding even after so short a time. I had to force myself to remember I'd only been on-planet ten days. Even with the growing heat of summer, I found my workouts with her became less strenuous. I'm not sure if it was because my form was improving or because my muscles were regaining tone. I suspected some of each.

She continued to give me simple cups with narrow bases while taking brightly painted porcelain or bone china cups for herself. I kept trying to find some meaning in those choices. Random choice would have suggested that I might get a cup with a handle occasionally. Instead I consistently got the simplest forms that made the function of tea-drinking possible.

I kept circling back to Pip's offer to be captain of the *Chernyakova*. I'd been operating under the notion that I needed a job for so long that the idea I didn't have one—and really didn't need one—provided a constant tension. On the one hand, I had enough credits to stay in the cottage on Port Newmar for the rest of my life and live comfortably. I could even move to an orbital and live there in the finest hotel and not scratch my credit balance for a century.

It took Cookie's wife to point me to a path I hadn't noticed.

The conference was due to wrap up on the fourth. I suspected Pip would be anxious to head to Breakall for the auction. Cookie had the evening off and invited me to dinner at his home. He lived off-campus in a comfortable single-story house well away from the space port but with a charming view of the bay from the back porch.

His wife, Eloise, welcomed me with open arms. "Rafe has told me so much about you. I'm so glad we've finally met." Being hugged by her was like going home.

She ushered me through the house and out onto the back deck where I found a collection of comfortable-looking lounge chairs and Cookie tending a compact grill. She pressed a cool glass of some citrus drink into my hand and winked before disappearing back into the house.

"So, Ishmael. What do you think of my view?" He waved his tongs at the ocean.

"I never took you for a waterman, Cookie."

He smiled and flipped over the chicken breasts before answering. "Myself? I prefer the desert. The soft light. The shifting sands.

Even the shimmering of the sun in the distance."

"So you have an ocean view instead?"

He grinned and made a circling gesture with the tongs. "You know of many deserts on Newmar?"

I laughed. "No. I suppose not."

Eloise returned with a huge bowl of green salad in one hand and a cloth-covered basket in the other. As Cookie's gaze followed her, his smile seemed to soften.

He caught me watching him. "The only sight I really need to see, eh?"

Eloise looked at him. "What silliness are you spouting now, old man?" The laughter in her voice reminded me of someone much younger.

"Nothing at all. Merely contemplating our wonderful view with my old friend."

She placed the bowl and basket on the table and turned her face to bask in the cool breeze coming in from the sea. "It's truly amazing. I never imagined we'd live where water lay so plentifully on the land." She smiled broadly at me, and her eyes crinkled at the corners. "And now we do."

Cookie said, "This chicken is ready for you. Are you ready for it?"

"It smells wonderful, Cookie." I rose and took the indicated seat at the small table while the two of them executed what must have been a much practiced dance of last-minute preparation.

The meal proved to be as good as I could have imagined. The spices and textures took foods that I felt I knew and pushed them into places I never knew existed. The sweet burn of the marinade on the chicken melded with the crisp crunch of the greens and the homely flavor of biscuits, one I'd nearly forgotten over the stanyers. We washed it down with a chilled citrus drink that balanced sugary sweetness against a puckery sourness. Cookie pulled out a hot granapple cobbler for dessert and topped it with a scoop of ice cream.

"You married a good cook, Eloise," I said as they cleared off the dishes and returned with a coffee carafe and small cups. "I feel like I put on two kilograms just at that one meal."

She gazed at Cookie and pursed her lips. "He is an excellent cook, but I didn't marry a good cook."

Cookie grinned back. "You've taught me well, dear one. I just took your lessons to heart."

She turned her smile on me. "I married a good *man*," she said. "The rest flowed from there."

"You taught him to cook?" I asked.

"Oh, heavens, no," she said. "He's been a cook as long as I've known him. He has a way with the spice rack, you know?"

The way her face lit up and the look on Cookie's made me think there might be more to that statement than met the eye. Her hair might be graying and her skin no longer smooth, but Eloise's fire still burned hot.

"So, tell me, Ishmael," Cookie said. "What will you do now?"

Eloise reached over to cover his hand with one of hers and looked to me, her eyes sparkling in the evening light.

I groaned. "That's the question everyone asks, and one I have no answers to."

"What would you like to do?" he asked. "Surely there's some path you've not taken yet."

His knowing look told me he remembered his own advice to me in the mess deck of the *Lois.* To choose a path before I found myself on one that I hadn't chosen. "You once told me that I should consider that I'm on the path I'm supposed to be on."

He nodded. "I'm surprised you remember."

Eloise patted his hand. "You often have more influence than you think, old man."

I toyed with my coffee mug and pondered. "I feel like I'm at the end of my path. I don't need to walk it anymore."

Cookie nodded and turned his hand around so he could hold his wife's hand in return. "There's only one end to the path, Ishmael. You're not there yet."

"If you were, you wouldn't be eating chicken with us," Eloise said, an amused smile on her lips.

"I've gone through the list of things I might do. I've spent the last week pondering." I shook my head. "Longer. I only came back to Port Newmar because I didn't know where else to go. What else to do. Now that I'm here? I still don't know."

Cookie nodded but Eloise spoke. "Perhaps it's because you needed to be here. Something totally unexpected may come along. Something that couldn't happen anywhere else."

I chuckled.

"Something tickles you?" Cookie asked.

"Yeah. I can't tell you all the unexpected things that have happened. Finding Alys Giggone as the commandant of the school. Learning that she married Benjamin Maxwell and that he's now in charge of the orbital up there. Finding you here." I shook my head. "Running into Pip again. The only thing I expected—well, hoped for—was that Margaret Newmar would still be here and teaching tai chi."

"You see?" Cookie said. "The universe is filled with challenges and opportunities. You could stay here and teach."

"Funny you should mention that. Alys Giggone said that if I'm still on-planet come fall, she'll have me teaching."

Eloise shook her head. "You don't want that?"

I took a deep breath and considered for a moment before releasing it slowly. "Of all the paths I might follow, that's the one that I probably know the best. I grew up on a campus. My mother taught ancient literature. I know that life. Know it well."

Eloise nodded, her deep brown eyes nearly black in the fading light of day. "Not your path."

I shrugged. "Perhaps it might be."

She shook her head. "No. If a familiar path called you, your feet would already be on it."

Cookie's white smile flashed. "See why I married her?"

"You married me because you love me. The rest is just fringe benefit, old man."

He shrugged. "That, too."

Eloise looked back to me. "In the ten days you've been here, have no other paths presented themselves?"

A chill ran an icy finger down the back of my neck. "Well, only one that I can think of."

"Pip," Cookie said.

I glanced at him. He shrugged.

"That man has made more plans than I've made biscuits," he said.

I laughed.

Cookie leaned toward me. "Consider that most of them succeed."

"The operative word there being 'most,' " I said.

"What is his plan?" Eloise asked.

"To bid on a ship at auction and use it to test his economic models."

"He wants you to be captain?" Cookie asked.

I nodded.

"Did you tell him no?" Eloise asked.

I shook my head. "I told him I need to think about it."

"Why didn't you say yes?"

"I have history with the ship. Lots of very bad memories."

"What's the real reason?" Cookie asked.

I looked at him. "Real reason?"

"There must be something else. A ship is a ship. You and Pip worked well together on the co-op. Both of you have learned many lessons. You cannot doubt Pip."

I shook my head. "I don't."

"Will the ship do what he believes it will?"

"Probably. The performance only needs to support his model or prove it wrong."

"Can he do it alone?"

"Without me as captain?"

Cookie nodded.

"Probably. I'm not the only captain in the Western Annex."

"Then why do you doubt yourself?" Eloise asked.

I had to think about that and peered into my coffee mug as if the answer might appear floating on the dark surface. The horror of the *Chernyakova* still made my palms sweat, but the objective facts of the matter remained. I really did know what was wrong with the ship. I knew how to make it right. I knew how to fly it and how to make it profitable. From a pure investment perspective, it might be the best opportunity in the whole Western Annex.

I looked up from my mug and into their patient faces. "I don't. It was the wrong deal," I said. "I just didn't recognize it."

Chapter Nine
Port Newmar: 2374, June 4

By the time I got back from Cookie's, I didn't feel like braving the post-conference party still underway in Pip's cottage. It sounded like a good time from where I stood at my front door, but noise discipline held and the level chopped down at 2200. The noise didn't disappear, but it fell enough that I was only distantly aware of it. It didn't really matter. I wasn't ready for sleep and I had a lot to do.

I started with my grav-trunks.

What did I really need out of that massive pile of collected clothing? While I'd done a rough sort back on the *Iris* as I packed to leave, I set myself the task of paring down to a single trunk.

I pulled the trunks out of their storage slots and parked them in the living room of the cottage. A handy dining table served as a sorting and folding surface, and the sofa and chairs worked nicely as places to stack stuff I wanted to sort.

Two stans later, I had a mess. I couldn't seem to make any progress at all. Every time I thought I had a handle on it, I wound up thinking, "Well, I might want this sometime."

In a relatively short time, clothing festooned the living and dining rooms. Some civvies. Mostly shipsuits and uniforms. All of them still fit. Probably. I'd purchased all the civvies during my shopping trips with Stacy Arellone back on Diurnia.

I looked around at the chaos and realized that I had only one physical thing from my childhood on Neris—a picture of my father as a young man sitting at a restaurant table. I'd scattered my mother's ashes in the sea here on Port Newmar while I was a cadet. I hadn't even kept the urn. Her portable computer was long gone. I had some digital images and the one printed photograph. I picked up the dog-eared image and looked at the smiling face of the man who had been such a mystery for most of my life. I'd stared at the back of his head for stanyers not knowing I sat only meters from him as he worked the grill in his own restaurant.

I'm not sure I'd have recognized him even if he'd turned around and stared right at me.

I surveyed the mess again, holding the photo and wondering where I should put it. Almost two hundred kilograms of stuff and the only thing I found I couldn't replace was a photo? Not even a current photo. I had new digital images of my father and me together on the orbital at Diurnia. Something about holding the one thing that had survived, the one link to my childhood on Neris, seemed important in a way I couldn't explain.

A cloth-wrapped bundle on the coffee table caught my eye.

The photo wasn't the only thing I couldn't replace. My whelkies. Christine Maloney had offered a lot of credits for the collection. I couldn't part with them for credits. I couldn't leave them behind. I really needed to find their owners. Or keep them safe until they found new owners for themselves. I couldn't believe I'd overlooked them when pulling all the stuff out of my trunks. I picked the bundle up and tucked it under my arm.

I must have made quite a picture standing there in the middle of the night. The lights in my cottage blazing. Me barefoot, wearing a tatty but comfy old shipsuit with a *William Tinker* patch on the shoulder, staring around at what looked like ground zero in a clothing explosion. The realization of what it might look like if somebody was to call made me laugh. Not just little giggles but real laughter. With nobody around to see, nobody to bother, I didn't hold it back but let it roll. After a few moments I couldn't have stopped if I wanted.

That's when somebody knocked on the door and I heard Pip's voice. "Ish? You all right in there?"

I stumbled through the clothes, almost tripped on a pair of ship boots, and slipped the latch on the door, laughing all the way.

Pip's eyes got round when he saw me and the mess I'd made. I laughed harder as he rubbernecked through the door, taking in the whole effect.

As my laughter wound down, I was able to gasp. "Come in. Come in."

He took a step over the threshold. "Love what you've done with the place."

"Thanks. I'm just doing a little pruning." I leaned out to look across the path. "Party over?"

He nodded, still scanning the room, eyeing a pair of jeans that had gotten thrown over a lamp. "Conference done for another stanyer. We'll do it again next year. Probably."

"Good. Good. We need to talk."

He nodded. "Yeah, we do, but perhaps we should do it when you're sober and it's not the middle of the night."

"I'm perfectly sober." I didn't help myself with another little giggle.

He raised one eyebrow at me. "All right. How about when I'm sober and it's not the middle of the night?"

I glanced at the chrono. It read 0135. "Where does the time go?"

He shrugged and grinned at me. "Time flies when you're havin' fun. You gonna hit the floor tomorrow at 0600?"

I used an elbow to clear off a corner of the table and put the package of whelkies and the photo down. "Planning on it."

"All right. I'll get some sleep and sober up a little. Knock on my door when you get back and we'll go find some breakfast."

"Sounds good."

He picked his way back across the mine field of discarded clothing toward the door. At the threshold he turned to me with a grin. "This mean you're gonna be my captain?"

"Yes. No." I shook my head. "Maybe."

"I'm not that drunk, Ishmael. You sure you're not?"

"Positive. I'm not going to be your captain. You can't win that bid with what you're planning to spend. The breakers will take it for scrap value now that they know they can get it cheap. Ninety million won't cut it."

His grin faded and his brows came together above his nose. "Then what do we need to talk about?"

"I'm not going to be your captain. I'm going to be your partner."

"What?" He shook his head. "I must be drunker than I thought. Partner?"

"We'll hash it out tomorrow but you can't win that auction with your level of resources."

"And you can?"

I shook my head. "Not by myself. If we pool our funds, we can outbid the breakers and still have enough left over to refurbish the ship and get her crewed up and ready for space."

His grin came back. "Just like old times!"

"Go sleep. I need to try to get a nap in before Margaret Newmar wrings me out again in a few stans."

He nodded and only stumbled a little bit getting out the door and closing it behind him. A few moments later I heard his cottage door close in the silence of the early, early morning. I made one last survey of the room and blew out a deep breath before slapping the light switches and shuffling off to my bed.

I had no idea what I'd do with the mess out front, but the mess inside me felt a little less hopeless for the first time in a long, long time. I zipped out of the shipsuit and crawled between the sheets, letting the garment fall to the floor as forgotten as a snake's shed skin. I'd no sooner closed my eyes when the brassy tones of reveille pulled me back from dreamland.

I didn't groan when I crawled out and stepped into the shower. It wouldn't have done any good, and I really wasn't the kind to groan when there was nobody around to appreciate it.

I felt almost human when I stumbled into the living room to find a pair of shorts and a fresh ship-tee. I felt a little exposed padding naked and damp through the cottage, but managed to find enough clothing to wear for my workout among the piles of "what do I do with this?"

I slipped out of the cottage and struck out for the studio. The fogginess inside my head burned off as I crossed campus. The fresh morning air, cool and damp, pulled the last of the sleep from my muscles. When I got to the studio, I was ready to go and started my warmups immediately. I had to struggle to push the coming discussions with Pip out of the way and focus on the movements and my balance, but within a few ticks I found my pace and relaxed into the discipline.

"Good morning, Ishmael."

"Good morning, *Sifu*."

"Rough night?" she asked.

I ended my warmup cycle and turned toward her. She stood at the edge of the floor, her head turned slightly to one side in a birdlike gaze.

"Short night. I didn't get to sleep until nearly 0200."

"Ah," she said and nodded. "What were you doing up so late? Or should I not ask?"

I smiled. "Pruning."

She beamed. "That's what it is. I knew you looked different this morning. I should have realized."

"Different?" I almost laughed. "How can you tell?"

She shook her head, that same quirky smile on her lips. "Something about your stance. It's looser, more balanced maybe. Your posture has changed. You'll find the chi flows better today, I think."

Her answer surprised me. "Really?" I looked down at my hands and arms. "I haven't noticed it with my warmups yet."

"It's either that or the fact that you're wearing one blue and one green sock," she said.

I looked down to find my feet clad in different colored socks inside my tai chi slippers. "Yes, I might not have actually finished pruning last night before I was interrupted."

She nodded, her lips pursed. "That would make sense. Mr. Carstairs called, no doubt."

"Actually, he did." I shrugged. "He came to find out if I was all right. I'm not a night owl as a rule, but I started late in the evening and just got carried away."

She nodded again. "I can see how that would happen. Well, we should get to it." She bowed to the floor and we began the morning's lesson.

For some reason I kept messing up Four Corners. We'd worked on it for days and I had thought I'd gotten the movements down. That morning, dealing with the complexity of the forward and backward movements and the shifts to each of the four directions seemed beyond my ability to grasp. After I missed it twice in a row, she called a halt.

"Tea," she said. "Your socks have you thinking about your feet and not focusing on your balance."

I looked down, dubious that such a minor thing could be causing my problem, but it seemed as likely as anything. I had no better explanation so simply started my cooldown.

"Not today. You're not overheated. Come sit while I brew."

Surprised, I took my place at the table and watched her graceful, practiced movements filling the kettle, measuring the tea, and setting it to steep when the water boiled. "You know the water boils at one hundred and two degrees here?" she asked.

"Really?" I shook my head. "I thought it always boiled at one hundred Celsius at sea level."

She shook her head. "Earth standard measure that's been adopted as a standard. Same as the standard hour." She lifted the kettle off the burner and rested it on the warming stone.

"I knew about the hour. Sixty standard minutes each of sixty standard seconds, each measured by so many vibrations of a subatomic particle in some kind of matrix that I knew once to pass the test but have never had to deal with again."

She smiled. "Newmar's atmosphere is just enough denser that it raises the boiling point two degrees. It's one of those things that we take as it's presented and don't think about. The difference is small, barely noticeable unless you measure." She poured the water over the tea, one of her blacks with a strong herbal component. "That's why I let the water cool, just slightly, on the stone before pouring."

"That helps the infusion process by keeping the temperature low enough to infuse the water without sublimating the volatiles?"

She smiled at me. "You paid attention in chemistry class."

"I like good coffee. Water temperature matters there, too."

While the tea steeped, she glided to the cup rack. "Which cup would you choose for yourself today, Ishmael?"

"The simple white one you gave me the first day."

She pulled it out of the rack. "This one?"

"Yes, please."

She selected another one for herself, a plain china mug that I might have found on the mess deck on almost any freighter in the fleet. Flat on the bottom and nearly cylindrical in shape.

She placed them on the table and poured the tea.

"How did you remember which cup?" she asked.

"I don't know. I always look to see what cup you pick for your students and visitors. You never seem to pick the same cup twice, which always made me think you remembered which cup they'd had before."

"You found that remarkable even though you remembered well enough to believe that I knowingly picked a different cup each time."

"I guess I never thought of it that way."

"You're an excellent observer, Ishmael. You pay attention to details."

"Thank you, *Sifu*."

"Yet sometimes you overlook the most obvious. That doesn't always work in your favor."

I looked down at my cup. I thought of Greta and how I'd been blinded by my own biases, my own dogma. "True."

She sipped her tea and placed the cup back on the wood with a hollow thump.

I glanced up and saw her regarding me with as serious an expression as I've ever seen on her face. She almost always had a smile or a near smile.

"What would have happened if you had not met Alys Giggone?" she asked.

"I'd have been deported, probably."

"Then what?"

I shook my head. "I have no idea. I never thought about it."

"Yet at the time, the notion that you might be cast adrift in a sea of unknown with no skills, no credits, and no support terrified you enough to launch yourself into the Deep Dark."

"Yes."

"In all that time, have you never considered what must happen to the people who are not fortunate enough to find their Alys

Giggone in the nick of time?"

The question caught me by the nose and tweaked it. "I—no. I was so focused on what was in front of me, I never thought about anything else."

Her smile came back, just teasing the left corner of her lips. "Just as you were so focused this morning that you didn't notice you wore two different colored socks."

I grinned. "Apparently."

"Or a pair of workout pants with the seat ripped out."

I felt the heat flash across my skin. "What? Really?" I stuck a hand back to feel for confirmation that I'd been working with her all morning with my boxers hanging out the back.

Her smile blossomed across her lips but it didn't reach her eyes. "No," she said. "But you weren't sure for a moment. Your reality shifted just enough for you to question what you thought you knew."

I nodded, more concerned with her eyes than her lips.

"Your time here is nearly done. As you sail back out into the Deep Dark, consider that question. What happens to the people who fall through the cracks? The person you might have been had you not found Alys Giggone in time."

I nodded. "Thank you, *Sifu*. I will."

"While you ponder that, look around. Really look. Look beyond what you think you know. Look beyond what you've been told. Look beyond the hundred degrees and find the reality where it lives."

I knew she was trying to tell me something, but couldn't quite wrap my head around it, not even enough to ask her for clarification.

She tipped her mug up and drained the tea from it. "I've got business this morning, so we'll have to end our session here for today."

I nodded and lifted my cup to finish my tea as well.

"Stay. Take your time. Turn out the lights when you leave." She stood and rinsed her cup, leaving it in the drain as always.

I watched her cross the studio and stop at the door.

She turned once more. "While you are considering, consider this. How does an assassin get paid?" With a final wave, she slipped out the door, closing it behind her with a quiet snick.

I sat there for a very long time, considering.

When I finally drank my tea, it was cold.

Chapter Ten
Port Newmar: 2374, June 5

I had to knock twice before a rumpled Pip answered the door, blinking at the morning light. "Morning already?"

"Up and at 'em," I said.

He backed away from the doorway and I followed him into the cottage. The living room was surprisingly neat, given the party I'd heard. Pip shuffled into the kitchen and I followed. He pulled two mugs from the cupboard, slopped some coffee from a thermal carafe into each, and handed me one.

I took a sip and sat at the table, hunched over the mug cradled in my hands.

He sat across from me and raked a hand through his hair. "You look like hell," he said. "I'm the one who's hung over."

"Long morning," I said, shaking myself to try to release the spell that Margaret Newmar had cast. "We need to talk."

He nodded. "Yeah. If I remember, you said that last night. Partners?"

I shrugged. "Seems the right answer."

He yawned, winced, and took a pull from his mug. "What're you thinking? Joint partnership?"

"Incorporation. Limited Liability as a minimum, but filing for incorporation isn't that hard and leaves us some options for financing in the future."

Pip blinked and offered a half smile. "My goodness, how quickly they grow up!"

"We'll need a lawyer and some board members," I said.

"And an engineer."

"And a ship," I said. "But if we lose the bid on the *Chernyakova* we can lease one short-term."

Pip raised his eyebrows as if stretching out his face and blinked a few more times. "You *have* thought about this."

"Yeah. A bit."

"Why don't you look happy?"

I shook my head. "Margaret Newmar asked a few questions this morning that I hadn't thought about. I'm not pleased with myself that I've never thought about them."

He leaned forward, bracing his elbows on the table. "Such as?"

"What if I hadn't found Alys Giggone back on Neris? What would have happened to me?"

He snorted and lifted his mug to his mouth, speaking into it. "Knowing you? You'd have been a land baron by the time you turned thirty." He took a sip and set the cup down. "Why's that so important now?"

"I don't know. Something's out of whack and I've just never questioned it before." I chewed my lip rather than say anything else.

"They're not your problem."

"Who's not?" I asked.

He sighed. "The people who fall through the cracks. The ones who don't find an Alys Giggone. This is your conversation. Try to keep up."

"Yes, but where are they?" I asked.

"You ever visit planet-side?"

I shook my head. "Neris and Port Newmar."

"Company town and college town. Not exactly typical, but how much time did you spend actually in town when you were here?"

"I wandered around a bit."

"I'm not talking about drinking at the Flying Mermaid." He rubbed a hand over his face. "You ever visit South Side?"

I shrugged. "Not that I remember."

"You'd remember."

"Wait, wasn't that the part of town they warned cadets about?"

"Yeah. They promised captain's masts for cadets caught there. You ever wonder why?"

I shook my head, feeling very dumb.

"Most cadets caught there have trouble finishing their training. That's a big investment to flush away for a night on the wild side." He took a slurp from his mug. "How desperate were you back on Neris?"

"I don't even remember. Pretty desperate. I signed up for a job I knew nothing about on a ship that would take me away from the only life I'd ever known."

He nodded. "And you had a full belly, warm clothes, and a safe place to sleep."

I felt a cold draft slide down my back.

Pip spun his mug between his fingers and looked across the table from under bushy, snow-white brows. "You were in Diurnia. You ever run across a place called Odin's Outpost?"

"Yes. In deep space equidistant from Dree, Breakall, Welliver, and Jett."

"Ever visit it?"

"No. Just flew by. It was close to the shortest course from Dree to Jett and Breakall to Welliver. We pulled a double jump into the dark and then back out to port."

"What do you know about it?"

"Not much. It's seen as a kind of destination for those who are looking to get out from under CPJCT control. Scanners showed a lot of traffic in and out when we flew by. We never stopped for a beer. Lots of stories. Supposedly started by a one-eyed guy when his ship lost its Burleson drive on a routine jump through the region. I had a second mate who was convinced it was actually a pirate hangout called 'High Tortuga.'"

Pip grinned at that. "Really?"

"He saw pirates everywhere. Anytime anything happened on the ship, it was pirates."

"You flew with him long?"

I shrugged. "Stanyer. He could thread a needle like nobody's business."

"He sewed?"

"Astrogation."

"Oh, yeah." Pip shrugged. "Hung over. Did I mention that?"

"Couple of times. You want breakfast?"

He swallowed a couple of times. "I'll settle for a handful of analgesics for now, thanks." He got up and went into the bathroom. I heard him rummaging around for a moment followed by the sound of a pill bottle popping open. He returned with his chin held up and took a slurp of coffee. "There."

"What about it?"

"Huh?"

"Odin's Outpost?" I asked. "This is your conversation. Try to keep up."

He offered me another sideways grin. "Hung over. Did I—?"

"You mentioned it."

He shrugged and topped off his mug before holding up the carafe with a question on his face. I pushed my mug over, and he topped it off, too.

"You ever wonder why Odin's Outpost exists?"

"Not really. Emergency resupply. High rollers who like a little danger to spice up going broke."

He slouched into his chair and buried his face in his mug for a moment. "Yeah. That, but as a business model?"

"Seems to be working for them."

Pip sighed. "It's a gateway."

"Gateway to what?"

"The Dark Side."

"You're making this up."

He shook his head, somewhat gingerly. "No. We jumped the *Bad Penny* through the Deep Dark on our way here from St. Cloud, remember?"

"Sure. I've done it myself flying around Diurnia. What of it?"

"Well, what if—and I'm just talking hypothetically here—what if there were stations not sanctioned by the CPJCT?"

I took a belt of the coffee. "Hypothetically."

He gave a little sideways nod of his head. "Hypothetically."

"So, no trade regulations. No orbitals," I said.

"No regulations. Period."

"No law?" I asked.

He shrugged.

"We joked about how Odin disposed of the bodies, but I guess I never considered that was something real."

"You never run out of freezer space out there," he said with a nod toward the ceiling.

I took another sip of coffee and something Geoff Maloney's bodyguard had told me once came unbidden from the back of my mind. "Some other hidey hole," I muttered.

"What?"

"Nothing. Something a little bird told me once. How many of these gateways are there?"

He shrugged. "I've found one in Ciroda. There's at least one in Diurnia. Two in Dunsany. There's rumored to be one here in Venitz. They're not exactly regulated so they don't appear on any official charts."

"Not even as a HazNav?"

"HazNavs only appear on regulated routes."

I pondered that as I sipped my coffee. "How do you find this Dark Side if it's not on the charts?"

"It's not on official charts. If you know a guy who knows a guy, you can get them."

I snorted. "You know a guy who knows a guy?"

He smiled. "Of course."

"That's all beside the point," I said. "We have a company to form. A ship to buy."

Pip sat up straight. "Indeed we do." He held his mug up and I clinked mine to it across the table. "To better deals in the afternoon," he said.

"Better deals!" I took a gulp and looked at the chrono. "Speaking of which, it's almost lunchtime. I need a shower, and then we need to make some notes to take to the lawyer."

Pip lifted an arm and gave himself a sniff. "Yeah. Good plan. You're a captain. Call the O Club and catering service for 1230. That'll give me a chance to sober up, get cleaned up, and see where Roland is with the repairs. We need to be in Breakall in time for the auction in a few weeks."

"Can we make it?" I asked, suddenly aware of just how long the voyage could take.

He grinned.

"All right, then," I said and left to do the needful.

I crossed back to my cottage, the fug of low tide pinching my nose. I looked up at the clouds building in from offshore. Looked like a storm brewed to the east. It would make the evening hours a bit noisy if history was any predictor.

When I opened my door, I remembered why I was wearing two mismatched socks. I scrounged around for a clean set of khakis and pondered what to do about the mess. I eyed the chrono. It flipped over to 1137. A stan before lunch.

"Priorities, Ishmael. Call. Shower. Mess."

A card on the desk had the information I needed to place the order for lunch. The steward assured me it would be delivered at 1230. Being a captain had its advantages after all.

That amusing thought accompanied me into the shower. It took next to no time to strip down, sluice off the worst of it, and slip into my undress uniform. I had to scrounge around for a set of stars and realized I had a collection of them that needed to be put on the dining room table with my photo and the whelkies. I smiled at myself in the mirror as I pinned on the scarred stars that had belonged to Fredi's grandfather. I always got a little boost when I put them on. If only they could talk.

I found a pair of matching socks and slipped on a pair of comfy shipboots before surveying the wreckage.

"Priorities," I muttered and began a triage. 'Must keep' was the small collection on the dining room table. I checked to see that both trunks were empty and mentally labeled the one to starboard 'Toss It' and the other 'Could Live Without.'

I started on the table because we'd need that to eat and plot. Any shipsuit that wasn't new and pristine went into the 'Toss It' bin. I tossed most of them. Civvies went into the 'Could Live Without' since I'd gotten all of them on Diurnia, but were all a stanyer old. Most of the socks, ship-tees, and boxers went into that trunk as well. Those with worn elastic, sweat stains, or other problems went into the 'Toss It' bin. The painting clothes from the *Iris*, I understood, but I wondered where I'd gotten into so much blue paint while in my shorts. My two good dress blues and one good dress white uniforms went into the 'Must Keep' pile along with two sets of intact undress khakis.

By the time the steward arrived with luncheon, I'd cleared the table and the couch of litter. The 'Toss It' trunk was full to overflowing, the 'Can Live Without' had its own share, and still stuff festooned the chairs in the living room. The pile on the table had grown, but I suspected it weighed less than the twenty kilos I'd imagined as a goal.

I accepted the hamper from the steward at the door and thumbed the receipt.

"I can set it up for you, if you like, Captain."

I eyed his name tag. "Not necessary, Mr. Brewster, but I appreciate the offer."

"Thank you, Captain. Just leave the hamper on your doorstep when you're done. We'll send somebody over to pick it up later this afternoon, if that's satisfactory?"

"Excellent, Mr. Brewster. Thank you for your consideration."

He nodded and scampered back up the path toward the O Club just as Pip came out of his cottage and crossed to meet me. "Lunch, I hope?"

"Soup and sandwiches. That all right?"

He nodded and followed me into the cottage. "You've had the maid in since I was here last."

"Just a little light straightening and a round of toss out," I said, placing the basket on the end of the table.

"Looks like mostly toss out."

I took the pile of must-haves and moved them to the cleared couch to make room for lunch. Pip popped the lid on the hamper and burst out laughing.

"What?"

He looked over at me. "Just soup and sandwiches?"

"That's what I ordered."

He shook his head and unloaded the dishes. "Cookie thought we needed more than soup and sandwiches." He slid a note across the table to me. It read:

'If you're going to take over the Western Annex, you two will need more than soup and sandwiches. Enjoy!'

I tried to see past Pip's arm and the lid. "What'd he send over?"
"Oh, there's soup. Chicken curry, if my nose isn't mistaken. A pile of biscuits. At least one beefalo dish that I can't place but smells yummy." He peered into the bottom of the hamper. "And a whole granapple cobbler, if I'm any judge. And I am."
We spread out the food, grabbed implements of mass ingestion, and began plotting.

Chapter Eleven
Port Newmar: 2374, June 6

Morning found me crossing campus in thick fog. A cold weather system had blown in on the overnight storm and the warm air over the land gave up its moisture in the form of fog and heavy dew. I knew the path by heart, or thought I did. I still jumped when the side of Hutchins Gym loomed at me with a shift in the wind.

Pip and I had been up late hashing out plans, and we'd consumed our weekly ration of Clipper Ship in the process. On top of the short night I'd had before, it was all I could do to drag my sorry carcass across campus.

I arrived soggy, groggy, and lost in the morass of what-if's that *Sifu* Newmar had left me with the day before. The lights were on, gleaming behind the large windows, and I found her in the kitchen.

"Good morning, Ishmael," she said. "Are you ready to begin?"

"I am, *Sifu*."

"What do you need work on?"

"I'm still too weak for Snake Creeps Down. It leaves me struggling for Rooster Stands after it."

She nodded. "That you recognize it says a lot. Very well. Let us work on Yang Short again today."

She strode out onto the floor, pausing only to bow before stepping to the front of the room. The dimness of the fog outside reflected her form in the glass of the window as a backlit silhouette. Her black uniform cast a stark contrast to my informal workout clothes.

She stood for a moment and we took our breaths at the same time. As I let it out, the world shrank to my balance, my form. We danced together in perfect synchrony, my gray sweats a shadow behind her black reflection. At the end of the first set she stopped and eyed me me up and down.

"You've finished pruning?"

The slow, even beating of my heart marked the moments as I thought. "Not yet, *Sifu*, but I think I have made some progress."

"Are you down to one trunk?"

"I believe I'm down to twenty kilos."

Her eyebrows shot up at that. "And yet you think you have more to go?"

"Some baggage is harder to trim than others."

Her face relaxed and the smile that bloomed felt like the sun burning through the clouds. "That you recognize that," she said, "says even more." She turned back to the window and took the beginning stance—arms down, feet shoulder width apart, weight centered on her core. "Dance with me," she said, and we began.

She led the dance in a form I didn't recognize. The movements came smoothly, one after another but in no pattern I recognized. After the first few, I stopped trying to figure it out or anticipate the movement. I simply followed, focusing on my breathing and maintaining my balance. We swooped into Snake Creeps Down and flowed into Rooster Stands on One Leg, but moved to Grasp Sparrow's Tail and then Wave Hands As Clouds. With each movement she flowed as water flows over stones, with no apparent pattern but as inevitable as gravity. We danced for nearly a stan without pause before she drew up to the closing, her arms rising and then falling to lie as she had begun—arms down, feet shoulder width apart, weight centered on her core.

We stood like that for several moments. The waves in my inner sea, washing the shore in a slow even rhythm. My breath, the wind across the waves.

She moved then, just slightly, turning her head to speak over her shoulder. "Thank you, Ishmael."

"Thank you, *Sifu*."

"Shall we have tea?" she asked.

"That would be very nice."

"Then we shall."

I joined her in the kitchen, taking my place behind the table as she heated the water and poured it over a measured portion of tea. She offered me a smile as she chose a cup I'd never seen before. As usual with her choices for me, it was a simple cup formed without a handle, a dimple pressed into the bottom as if it had been hand-molded from clay and pressed upwards with some artisan's thumb. When she placed it on the table, it looked as if it belonged there. As if it had been formed there.

She drizzled a bit of the steaming tea into it and then into her own. She'd chosen another simple cup without handle and apparently without glaze. It was the first time I remembered her using one without a handle since I'd arrived.

She placed the teapot on the warming stone and took her cup in the tips of the fingers of both hands, lifting it as if in salute before taking a sip, her breath pulling air in with the steaming tea to cool it as she drank. It made a slurping sound that my mother might have found rude but which I recognized as part of the tradition.

I followed her lead and we sat there, unspeaking, for several heartbeats. My cup felt heavy in my hand, but balanced.

"Do you still think I have a message in my cups, Ishmael?" she asked, her voice so low that it barely rose above the sound of the morning breeze.

I looked at her collection, still missing one cup. I looked at the cups she'd chosen for each of us. I thought about what message she might have and what message I might see.

I smiled. "I think your messages are less about what you say with them than what they tell you about your students."

Her face relaxed into a pleased smile. "Now, you begin to understand," she said. "I'll be away for the next week. I suspect you'll be gone by the time I get back, but you may use the studio as long as you remain on-planet."

I nodded my thanks. "If our plans work out, Mr. Carstairs and I will be leaving in a couple of days."

"You'll be traveling much lighter than when you arrived, Captain."

"I will."

"Good." She tipped up her cup and drank down the tea. "When you're ready, come back to see me and perhaps we can dance again."

She rose and flowed away, all of her movements—from rinsing the cup to stacking it in the drainer to gliding out the door—as smooth as water. I felt like an ox next to a panther by comparison.

I sipped my tea, listening to the quiet. The light levels grew steadily as the system primary heated the atmosphere and the fog sublimated again. I heard the sounds of small birds chirping in the bushes behind the building. The tea she'd prepared had a strong tannin component that almost bit the tongue, but a sweet, almost fruity, aftertaste at the back of the tongue cleared it away. As the light level grew so did my awareness of time and place. I almost felt like I was waking from a dream, as if I'd come fully awake and realized I was still in my bed.

I shook my head and gulped the rest of my tea, took care of the empty cup, emptied the tea kettle and pot, disposed of the used leaves, and left everything draining. At least she wouldn't come back to a pot full of mold. A glance at a small chrono tucked in beside the cooktop showed I had just time to get cleaned up before meeting Pip.

I walked back to the cottage and spent a few ticks throwing more clothing into the 'Toss It' bin and contemplating the remaining uniforms. On the one hand, all I needed for shipboard work was a workable collection of shipsuits. Even dress uniforms would stay hung in closets for the most part. I cast a slightly jaundiced eye at the civvies, but I still hadn't found a decent tailor. Until I did, those would have to do.

The chrono ticked over to 1050. I expected Pip at 1100 so I jumped in the shower. Shipboard living was good practice for the "hurry up shower." I was out, dressed, and mostly dry before Pip knocked on the door at 1105.

"Second thoughts?" he asked when I slipped the latch to let him in.

"About the partnership?" I shook my head.

He blinked a couple of times. "About what?"

"I don't need all these uniforms, do I?" I pointed at the collection of undress and utility khakis still strewn over the furniture in the living room.

He coughed out a single laugh. "If that's your biggest problem, we're golden."

"Where'd you get your bag?" I asked.

"My bag?"

"The one you flew down with."

"Oh, standard luggage module. Chandlery, where else?"

I shrugged. "I don't get out much."

"Probably find something similar at the academy store. Maybe even one with the academy logo on it. Rah! Rah!" He waved his fists as if he held pom poms, with a mischievous grin on his face and his eyebrows halfway to his hairline.

"Where are we on the checklist?"

"I talked to Roland. Ship'll be ready to make ship noises by tomorrow. He figures if we leave within a couple of days, we'll be there in plenty of time."

"How much is plenty of time?"

"A week before the auction."

I gave a low whistle. "The *Son* has some legs in there, huh?"

"That's what we specialize in. Long legs. High value. Low mass."

"No wonder you made money flying in from Dunsany."

"Son, we make money on every flight."

"What are you flying back to Breakall?"

He shrugged. "Dunno yet. I'll grab something on the way out the door."

"I'm impressed."

"Don't be. It's all tricks of the trade. I put the word out with one of the brokers upstairs when I arrived. We'll have several to choose from by the time we file an outbound flight plan."

"You'll pay a broker?"

"Fees are cheap money with the kind of cargo we carry."

"All right, then. Ship? Check. Lawyer?"

"We're having lunch with Alys at the O Club at 1200. She'll know."

"Hear back from your father?"

He frowned at that. "No, but I only messaged him yesterday. If he's out in the back of Dunsany Roads somewhere, it may take a bit to catch up to him."

"We still need to iron out the contingency clauses."

"Like dissolution, death of a partner, and all that?"

"Yeah. How do we break deadlocks on votes."

"We also need at least one more member of the board," Pip said.

I pondered that for a couple of ticks. "I'd really like to open that up to the engineering officer, but I don't expect we'll hire one until we already have the ship. And we need to be incorporated before that happens."

"I'm not too keen on having more members of the crew as board members. What if we need to fire one?"

I remembered Gramps Bailey and nodded. "Good point."

"Any flashes of insight for the name?" he asked.

"Nothing I want to put on letterhead. I've spent most of the time since we broke last night either asleep or trying to make sense of Margaret Newmar."

"Is she being enigmatic again?"

"You have no idea."

"Well, let it percolate. I haven't anything more original than Carstairs and Wang, Inc."

"C&W?"

"Yeah. Probably. Why?"

"I've heard worse, but there has to be better," I said.

"Agreed."

"Shall we mosey on over to the O Club and grab a Clipper Ship before lunch?"

"Don't you still have some in your fridge?" I asked.

"Of course, but I'm hoping to save that for the trip over to Breakall."

"I'll buy you a case, if you want," I said.

"A case won't cut it. How much mass in a pallet of the stuff?"

I laughed. "Don't ask me. You're the cargo master."

He shrugged. "Just cargo first, at the moment, thanks."

"Hmm."

"What, hmm?"

"How's that for a name?"

"Hmm? Kind of vague, isn't it?"

"I was thinking more of 'Cargo First,' "

He gave me a long-suffering look. "We can do better. Come on. I hear a beer calling my name."

We trundled up the path toward the O Club, taking turns offering bad names to each other.

"Secure Can."

"Can D. Man."

"Barbell of Doom."

"What if we decide to expand the fleet?" I asked.

"Barbells of Doom?"

I shook my head. "Cargo Crew."

He looked at me as if actually considering it. "I like that but I think there's already a CC out there."

"Hamlet's Ghost?"

"It's my turn. You had Cargo Crew."

"Sorry. Sheesh. You're going to be this touchy when we're partners?"

He cast me another pained look. "Worse. Hush. Let me think."

I waved a hand rather than speak and spoil his concentration.

"Beer Runners."

I looked at him. "Seriously. That's the best you got after all that buildup?"

"All right, Mr. Captain. What've you got?"

"Black," I said.

"Black?"

"Black, Inc."

"That's really bad."

"What? You want Red?"

"Red, Inc.?" he asked.

I nodded.

He took a deep breath and blew it out through his nose. "This is going to be a long day."

I held the door for him at the O Club and he sailed through. "We'll think of something," I said.

He grinned at me in passing. "We always do."

Chapter Twelve
Port Newmar: 2374, June 6

Alys Giggone leaned over her salad and swept her gaze back and forth between Pip and me. I couldn't read the expression on her face, but I thought it might be either indigestion or amusement. "Let me get this straight," she said, her voice lowered to the point where I needed to lean in to hear her over the ambient noise of a lively lunch hour. "You two are going into business together?"

Pip nodded. "Yes, sar."

She shook her head. "Don't sar me, Carstairs. At least not at lunch."

"Yes, ma'am?"

"Skip it," she said.

"Yes, we're going into business together. If we can find a lawyer to make it legal," he said.

She waved a hand. "Lawyers are easy. I know several. Tell me about this partnership."

Pip looked to me and shrugged.

"You know about the *Chernyakova*? It's in my jacket."

"You commanded the salvage detail. Yes."

"It's had some problems and still hasn't sold. The auctions kept failing. There's a new one in a month."

"And you two terrors are going to bid on it?"

I nodded.

"And use it to start a fleet," she said.

Pip shrugged. "I don't know about a fleet. It's a ship. Bulk hauler. I want to test my model against a single-cargo vessel. We've had some good confirmation on diversified cargo ships, but the data on single-cans is less robust."

"You're going to buy a ship and go into business as an experiment?"

We both shrugged. "Why else?" I asked.

She sat back in her chair and took a forkful of salad. She kept looking back and forth between us as she chewed. "Profit?" she suggested.

"Ideally," Pip said. "It'll be hard to keep the experiment going without it."

She ran a finger under her nose as if stifling a sneeze. "I see."

"I could retire and live comfortably for the rest of my life," I said. "I've no real need to make more."

"You will if you sink it all into that ship," she said.

I gave a half shrug to concede the point. "I'm pretty sure we can make a profit. At least enough to get our money back. Worst case, we liquidate the assets. We'll probably get the ship for a bit over scrap value. If we put a few credits into it, bring it back up to spec, we'd be able to double or triple that investment without carrying a can."

"I can see that," she said. She took a sip of her iced tea. "So what do you need from me?"

"Recommendation for a lawyer who can get us incorporated in time to participate in the auction in Breakall next month," Pip said.

She pulled her tablet out of its holster and flipped through a few screens. She clicked a couple of functions and both of our tablets bipped. "There are three. Two are here in Port Newmar. The third is upstairs. I've done business with all of them."

Pip looked at his screen and nodded. "Perfect. Thanks."

Alys took a few more bites of her salad and pushed the plate back from the edge of the table. Mr. Armstrong showed up at her elbow and pulled it out of the way. She continued to eye us silently while he arranged our entrees before fading into the background again.

"Who's going to be on the board?" she asked.

"Us," I said. "We'll need one more."

"Three more would be better," she said.

"Why?" Pip asked.

"Less chance of a two-against-one bloc developing," she said. "Who'll be chairman?"

Pip pointed to me. "Also CEO."

I felt my eyebrows rise. "Did we discuss that?"

He shook his head. "Captain runs the ship. You're always going to have the veto."

Alys said, "Not necessarily. Consider keeping those functions separate."

"Which?" I asked.

"All three. Chairman, CEO, and captain. The function of the board is to oversee the strategic and operational direction of the company and to monitor the company's performance."

"The extra set of eyes," Pip said.

"Exactly. It'll be hard to be objective if the chairman is also the captain."

Having filled all three roles at Icarus, I could see the wisdom.

Pip looked to me across the table. "Who?"

"How?" I asked.

"How is easy. We get together once a stanyer and have a party," Alys said.

"We?" Pip asked.

She grinned. "You don't think I'm going to let you two have all the fun, do you?"

Pip frowned. "I'm not sure this is such a good idea."

Alys's grin evaporated and her lips pursed. "Why?"

"We're going to be on the ship. When we're the board, getting approval is easy. With a board spread around the Western Annex?"

She shook her head. "Private company. You only really need to satisfy the stock holders. One of the roles of the board is to make sure the stockholders are happy."

"Meaning we earn enough credits to justify the investment," Pip said.

"You two are the savviest traders I've ever seen. It's not a question of whether or not you can keep the shareholders happy."

Pip and I traded a glance that reminded me of so many other times when Alys Giggone had left us wondering what was happening.

"What is the question then?" Pip asked.

She leaned in. "How do I become one?"

"What? A shareholder?"

Her grin changed to a full on smile. "I always knew you were clever."

My fork scraped plate before I even realized I was eating. I found myself shaking my head, trying to clear it and catch up.

Mr. Armstrong cleared the empty and filled my cup without asking.

Alys leaned back and tapped the table with one index finger. "Basics. How many shares were you planning on?"

"Twenty-three," Pip said.

"Interesting number. Why?"

"I'm representing Carstairs, Ltd. They committed a hundred and ten million to the venture. We planned on having it just be an extension of our operation."

Alys shook her head. “Little ships, big profits.”

“Oh, you know my father?” Pip said, his lips curled up in an almost sardonic grin.

“I know your Aunt P,” she said.

“Good enough.”

“I’ll toss in another hundred and twenty,” I said. “That’ll give us two hundred thirty mill in capitalization. Leaves me with a majority voting block and captain of the vessel.”

“Ten million credits per share,” Alys said without so much as blinking.

I laughed.

“What’s so funny?” Pip asked.

“We’re throwing numbers around that would take my breath away if I thought about them too long.”

Pip shrugged. “They’re just numbers.”

“So you two already have nearly a quarter billion credits? Just between the two of you?”

“Well, my family,” Pip said. “And him.”

“For a land-rat, you clean up nice,” she said with a wink in my direction.

“I had a good teacher,” I said.

“How much do you think the ship will cost?”

Pip said, “Two failed auctions had high sealed bids north of two hundred mill.”

“Failed how?”

“High bidder defaulted and paid the penalty to get out from under the debt.”

“Twice?” she asked, eyes wide.

Pip nodded.

Alys looked at me. “How bad is it?”

“Looks good on paper. In person? Not so much.”

“Structurally sound?” she asked.

“It seemed like it to me. We sailed it in from about nine AU. Once we got it stabilized, we had no problems with the sails, keel, or kicker. Fusactors stayed stable. We didn’t notice anything like cracked ribs or the like. We didn’t really look.”

“You just wanted to get it docked and get off it,” she said.

“Pretty much.”

“Certified engineering inspection found no major flaws in the structure or major fixtures,” Pip said.

“That’s what you meant by looking good on paper?”

“Exactly.”

“Why’d they forfeit? Barbells are expensive ships. Those were good prices.”

Pip looked at me with an eyebrow raised. "You were there."

I sighed. "I've had nightmares about that ship since I went aboard. The photos in the prospectus show a cleaned-up ship. Somebody must have cleared out the trash and thrown away the stained mattresses." I looked to Alys's plate. "Are you done eating? If not, we might want to hold off on this discussion."

She cleared her throat and shook her head. "I've heard enough."

"I figure we'll need to do some major refitting to make her habitable," I said. "She's probably spaceworthy, based on the engineering report, but living aboard would be challenging until it's refitted."

"Scrap value?"

"Around one forty."

"Your bid?"

"We'll start at ninety and hope none of the breakers are represented," Pip said.

"Start?" Alys pounced on that word. "It's not best sealed bid?"

"Last two were. Hundred fifty mill reserve. Best sealed. One percent default hidden in the fine print."

"They're taking it to open auction?"

"They want that ship gone. Third time's the charm."

"Why didn't they go to the next highest bidder?"

Pip shrugged. "Don't know. Maybe they tried. Maybe there wasn't another bidder."

Alys shook her head. "This business would be so much easier if there weren't people involved."

We both laughed.

She looked at us, her brow furrowed in contemplation. "So you two galoots are going to jump over to Breakall, bid on this death ship, and expect to walk away with it for a fraction of its worth?"

Pip shrugged. "That's the plan."

"Your father know about this plan?" she asked.

"I've sent him a message. I can't commit the family credit without his approval. I should hear by tomorrow. Next day at the latest. We need to get the paperwork in the mill, even if we don't sign and finalize until we hear from him. The more work we can get done before we hear, the faster we can get the thing nailed down after."

"What if he turns it down?"

Pip looked at me.

"Then we go to Plan B. I'll kick in fifty mill, he'll kick in five. We'll lease a ship, maybe one of the Damien Fifteen tractors, and keep going."

"Not a single-cargo ship, but limited diversification is better than nothing," Pip said.

She pursed her lips and nodded. "I'm impressed you've got a Plan B."

"There's a lot depending on stuff we have little control over," I said. "Plan B is much more modest, has lower levels of risk and lower upside potential, but it's also much more contained."

"All right," Alys said. "In either case, you'll want a board. I still want a piece of this action, if you'll let me invest."

"Seriously?" Pip asked. "We could crash and burn here."

She shook her head. "I'd be willing to bet on either one of you alone. Together? I don't want you leaving the planet until I can get in on this."

Pip laughed.

"Seriously. Between the two of you, one will always see an opportunity the other won't. You did it on the *Lois*, and I didn't see any indication that either of you slowed down much when you got out on your own."

Pip looked to me.

I shrugged. "Let us talk it over. I've got no objection on the face of it, but we'd have to come up with a new capitalization scheme."

Pip leaned forward. "How much were you planning on investing?"

"Plan A, I can't match money bags over there." She smiled at me. "Ben and I could each kick in ten. That would give us each one share and keep your splits largely untouched."

"Captain Maxwell?" I asked.

"He's the only Ben I'm willing to speak for at the moment," she said. "We could both be on the board and you'd only need one more. If I can rustle up one more investor, each of us buys in with one share and you two will still have the voting stock between you."

"Would he be interested?"

"He'd divorce me if I let you two get away without him."

"Plan B?" I asked.

"Same deal. One share per board member. Smaller investment for a smaller goal."

"Can you find somebody else who'd kick in ten million credits?"

She laughed. "The question is which of them do I like well enough to bring aboard."

Pip looked at me. "Captain's shares must be nice."

I nodded. "They are."

She snorted. "I was a captain for a long time. Even little bits add up over time."

Pip gave her a grin. "And when invested properly can yield big dividends, eh?"

She gave a kind of sideways nod and a knowing smile. "I'll admit you two are not my first venture into the wilds of industry. That's as far as I'll go."

Mr. Armstrong came to clear the plates and offer desserts.

I shook my head. "We've got work to do."

Pip looked like he might be thinking about it but shook his head after a moment. "He's right."

"I guess that's it then, Rubin. Thank you, and put this on my personal tab, if you would?"

"Of course, sar."

"Personal tab?" I asked, more out of surprise than anything.

"As commandant I have a budget for entertaining visiting dignitaries. It includes meals here."

Pip smiled. "And this was personal business."

"Precisely, Mr. Carstairs. The governing board frowns on sticking the academy with the bill for personal business." She stood and tugged the hem of her tunic to straighten it. "I'll let you gentlemen get on with your day. Please keep me in the loop and I'll forward the name of any other interested parties as soon as I have them finalized."

We rose with her.

Pip cleared his throat. "You know even if we get this ship, we're probably going to do some unusual things with it?"

She laughed loud enough to draw the attention of diners on the other side of the room. "I'd be disappointed if you didn't." With a nod to each of us, she sailed out of the O Club leaving Pip and me standing by the table.

"That was ..." I ran out of steam.

"Different?" Pip suggested.

"At least."

"Unexpected?" he asked.

"Definitely."

"Strange?"

I nodded. "Yes. Almost as strange as the question *Sifu* Newmar asked me the other day."

"Purple?" he asked.

"Now you're just trying to see if I'm paying attention."

We headed for the door, threading our way through a room full of smiling faces, most of whom seemed to know Pip well enough to nod to.

Outside, I said, "You've a lot of fans."

He shrugged. "I'm not sure about the fan part, but a few people know me. Most of them were here for the conference. There's an astrophysics seminar next week, so they're probably staying around."

"We still don't have a name," I said.

"You're not going to start with the punny names again, are you?" he asked as we sauntered down the path to the cottages.

"I can't promise, but you go first."

"Secured Hauling," he said after a moment of biting his lip.

"Cans to Go."

He gave me a look. "Seriously?"

"Don't judge. We're brainstorming."

He rolled his eyes. "Two Guys and a Ship."

"There's more than two of us."

"Don't judge," he said, with a smirk.

"Deep Space Transport."

"Deep Dark Transportation."

"Bulk Freight," I said.

He thought for a few more moments. "I got nothing."

I sighed. "Me either."

"Brick on a Stick," he said.

"Interstellar Transport Services."

He looked at me. "ITS?"

"Is there one?"

"We'd have to check the registry, but we could do worse. It's kinda generic."

"True, but it's your turn."

"Speedy Delivery."

I groaned.

"No judging," he said.

"Yoyodyne."

"Wait, I've heard of that, haven't I?" Pip asked.

"You read much twentieth-century English lit?"

"No. Do you?"

"Not lately. That's where it's from."

"Huh."

At the cottages, we split up. Pip went to make an appointment with one of the local lawyers and check in with his captain. I went to try to finish pruning.

I knew Pip would succeed in his tasks.

I wasn't so sure about me.

Chapter Thirteen
Port Newmar: 2374, June 7

Being in the studio alone felt odd. Not quite wrong, but without the life that *Sifu* Newmar brought. I hit the floor at 0600 and ran through a few iterations of Wu Long alternating with a variation on Yang Short that emphasized leg strength. I still had trouble with lifting myself to Rooster Stands on One Leg after Snake Creeps Down. I either cheated it on the Down or trembled when pushing myself back up on one leg.

After three or four passes, my muscles said "No more."

I was doing something wrong, or I really needed to spend some time toning up the femoral muscles. Massaging them with the heels of my hands, I suspected it might be some of each.

My tablet bipped and I pulled up a message from Pip.

"Lawyer appointment. 1000 in town."

I acknowledged and shut down the studio. I didn't know if anybody else would use it, but I left it in good order, just in case.

It didn't take long for me to get back to my cottage, get cleaned up, slip into some civvies, and meet Pip.

"Any word from your father?" I asked.

He shook his head. "Not yet. Message may not have found him yet, or he's taking it up with the family council."

We caught the 0915 shuttle from campus to town and skidded into the lawyer's lobby with five ticks to spare.

"Glad we didn't miss that one," Pip said out of the corner of his mouth as we pushed through the office doors.

The lawyer, one Krista D. Ball, Esq., ran a posh operation. The receptionist showed us to a small conference room just off the lobby. "Ms. Ball will be with you in a moment, gentlemen. Can I offer you refreshment? Water? Coffee? Soft drink?"

"Nothing for me, thanks." I was always leery of drinking free coffee.

"I'm good," Pip said.

She slipped out of the room and we took chairs on opposite sides of the head of the table.

At the stroke of 1000, Ms. Ball sailed in trailed by an assistant wearing a conservative business suit that looked like it had been tailored for him. Long habit had both of us on our feet before the door hushed closed behind her. "Gentlemen," she said. "It's always a pleasure to work with officers."

Pip and I looked at each other's civvies and then back at Ms. Ball.

"Alys doesn't send many crewmen my way." She smiled. "She speaks highly of you but I can't help wondering what she found funny. Please. Sit." When we sat and left her the seat at the head of the table, she paused. She took it but only after I watched her weigh the other possibilities. Her assistant took a seat away from the table, near the door. "How can I help you?"

"We're going into business together and would like to incorporate," Pip said.

"Easily done," she said with a small frown. "It's generally a simple transaction. Why do you believe you need my services?"

Pip took a deep breath. "Well, maybe we don't, but neither of us is up on admiralty trade law, and the CPJCT can be finicky when it comes to who owns what and what they do with it."

I saw her lips twitch as if suppressing a smile. "Indeed," she said. "Perhaps you can give me a better understanding of what you're planning?"

I waved at Pip. "You're better at this."

"We're forming a corporation to test the viability of an economic model of trade when applied to non-diversified cargo carriers."

Ms. Ball's eyebrows shot up and then lowered in a frown of concentration. "So, you're going to do what in terms of business activity? Buy a bulk freighter and experiment?"

In all the time I'd known him, I couldn't remember Pip ever being speechless. His mouth just opened and closed a couple of times before he closed it, took a deep breath, and nodded. "Actually. Yes."

"Very well, then," she said. "You haven't purchased the vessel yet, have you?"

"No. It's going up for auction in a few weeks. We want to be incorporated so we buy the vessel in the corporation's name."

She made a little "mmm" sound and nodded. "Good plan. Not required but probably cleaner that way. How's your capitalization?

I assume you're planning to keep this a private corporation?"

"Private. Yes. We've pooled our resources. I'm representing Carstairs, Ltd.'s share and will sit on the board as their representative."

"Carstairs, Ltd.?"

"Family company. We run a fast packet fleet based in Dunsany Roads but serving most of the Western Annex."

"You have documentation certifying you're the authorized agent of record for this transaction?"

"Yes and no," Pip said.

She raised one perfect eyebrow. "Please elaborate."

"I came here to speak at the economic modeling symposium at the academy. My father granted authorization to bid on the vessel leaving Dunsany. When I came here, the plan was for me to purchase the ship for the family."

"Not form your own, independent, company," she said.

"Correct."

She turned to me. "You must be Captain Wang."

"I am."

"What part do you play in our little drama?" From anyone else it might have sounded snotty.

"Mr. Carstairs planned to hire me to be the captain of his ship."

"You're rated for operating this vessel?"

"I am."

"How did this change from being a simple contract for hire to a partnership?"

"I refused his offer and offered a partnership instead."

"May I ask why?"

"His capitalization wasn't enough to obtain the ship and put it in spaceworthy condition. His estimates of cost were too low, and he relied on the engineering reports in the prospectus to ascertain the vessel's readiness."

She looked to Pip. "How much were you authorized for?"

"A hundred and ten million credits."

"What kind of ship is it?"

"Unwin Barbell design. Two hundred metric kilotons."

She swiveled her head toward the assistant. "Alexander?"

"New from the yard, over a billion depending on fittings. There are three used in Venitz. The lowest is four hundred million, but needs new fusactors. Scrap price around one hundred fifty mill depending on salvageable fittings."

"Thank you, Alexander." She looked to Pip again. "What made you think you'd be able to get the vessel for so little?"

"The auction has failed twice and the terms have changed from sealed best bid to open auction. The reserve has also been lowered."

Ms. Ball hadn't been terribly animated to begin with, but she seemed to freeze in place at Pip's words. She stared at him for several heartbeats and then looked at me. "You're going for the *Chernyakova*."

"You know of it?" I asked.

"It's been the talk of legal circles around the Annex for months."

"Does that make a difference?" Pip asked.

She sat up in her chair a bit and gave her head a little shake. "No. It's just one of those odd coincidences." She tilted her head and said, "Alexander?"

"Open point on Captain Wang's involvement."

"Thank you." She turned to me. "You said Mr. Carstairs relied on the engineering reports for his estimates."

"Yes."

"You have special knowledge of the vessel?"

"I do. I commanded the salvage crew that flew the ship to Breakall."

Her eyes grew slightly wider at that. "Your captain filed the salvage claim for Diurnia Salvage and Transport?"

"She did."

"So you were aboard when ...?"

"Yes."

She cleared her throat before speaking again. "Your contribution to the partnership?"

"I hold a master's license with appropriate certifications for that vessel and a hundred and twenty million credits to augment the capitalization fund."

Her head twitched just slightly. "And who provided those credits?"

"I don't understand," I said. "They're mine."

She gave me a small smile. "Mr. Carstairs represents his family's interest with his contribution. You're telling me, you—personally—have a hundred and twenty million?" Her eyebrows told a tale of skepticism that amused me greatly.

"I have more than that, but I'm only committing a hundred and twenty."

She stared at me, her careful mask slipping as her brain tried to process. Her head turned, ever so slowly but her eyes never left mine. "Alexander?"

"Captain Ishmael Horatio Wang. Class of '58. Employed by Diurnia Salvage and Transport until December, 2372, when he left to form his own company, Icarus. Earlier this year he sold the company and all its assets to Diurnia Salvage and Transport for an undisclosed amount. His estimated net worth is in excess of a hundred and fifty million credits."

Pip looked at me across the polished table. "You've been holding out on me."

I shrugged. "I like to have a bit in reserve."

Ms. Ball's lips curved into an O as if she might be going to say something, but she closed her mouth without speaking. She stared at me for several long moments and then looked to Pip, who simply shrugged and grinned. Her head nodded, just a little bit up and down. She took a deep breath and then blew it out. "Well," she said. "Now I know what Alys found so funny." She took another deep breath. "All right, gentlemen. I apologize. Commandant Giggone sandbagged me with you two. I'll owe her for that. I'm not used to people coming in here with even half a plan, let alone some idea of adequate financing."

We both shrugged.

"We're kinda new to this, too," Pip said. "He's done it once on his own but this is our first partnership and to my mind, it seems more complicated than signing a form and moving on."

"Yes, I think you're right. Between your family's interests and Captain Wang's involvement, this should get pretty gnarly." She paused then and looked to me. "Wait. You commanded the salvage team?"

"Yes."

"Then you'll get a portion of the proceeds?"

"My share is ten percent."

"Net or gross?"

"Gross, I think, but it's all tied up with DST's legal team."

Pip stared at me. "So, whatever we bid? You'll get ten percent of it back?"

I grinned. "I like to have a little bit in reserve."

"You sneaky son of a beachcomber."

"I try."

"Gentlemen?" Ms. Ball said. She folded her hands together on the table in front of her. "How can I help?"

"We need a partnership agreement so we can incorporate to push this crazy project forward. We're going to buy that ship—or rent one if we can't win it—and start hauling freight."

"Very good," she said. "Have you given any thought to shares? Share values? Terms for things like board of directors? Who'll be CEO, chairman?"

Pip nodded. "Yes. I can send you our notes, if you like?"

She looked at Pip. "Of course. You have notes." She said it with a kind of lilt in her voice that sounded suspiciously like it contained the unspoken words "How cute." She cocked her head. "Alexander?"

"If you could beam those to me, Mr. Carstairs?" He held up a small tablet. "Secure link. Pin 1066."

"Battle of Hastings," I said without thinking.

He blinked at me.

"My mother was an ancient lit professor back on Neris. I learned a lot of extraneous history."

"Sent," Pip said.

Alexander looked down at his device and started flipping pages. He kept flipping long enough that Ms. Ball turned her head again. "Alexander?"

"Ma'am, we'll need a day to go through this and see if there are any conflicts or internal inconsistencies."

She spun in her chair to watch him flipping pages. "What?"

Alexander's cheeks puffed up as he flipped and flipped and flipped. "I've got terms, conditions, clauses for dissolution, expansion, bankruptcy, buyout, death of principal partner. Oh, a nondisclosure agreement?"

Pip shrugged. "Seemed prudent."

"Do you expect us to sign it?" Ms. Ball asked.

"Oh, no," Pip said. "That's for members of the board and anybody else with inside information on the operational details of our company. We expect you to respect attorney-client privilege."

Alexander made a sound that reminded me of a laugh but wasn't quite there.

"So, Ms. Ball?" I asked. "Would you be able to help us? We'll offer a retainer for your services as corporate counsel."

"It's in here," Alexander offered without being asked.

"I don't know, Captain Wang. We can certainly help you with your immediate needs but being on retainer is—"

"Ma'am?" Alexander said.

She turned to look at him, red climbing up the back of her neck. "Yes?"

He nodded, very deliberately.

"Thank you, Captain. Yes, I think we can do business," she said, twirling her chair back to face us.

Pip grinned. "Now you know why Alys was laughing," he said.

She grinned back at him. "Alexander? Have Rosalind clear my calendar for today. Grab a couple of those bright faces in the back and let's see if we can get something done."

"Yes, ma'am. I'll have Rosalind clear your calendar for the rest of the week and bring in Robert and Virginia to help sort through this."

She turned to look at him.

He held up his tablet and shrugged, a "trust me" look on his face.

Ms. Ball chuckled and slapped the table once lightly. "Yes, Mr. Carstairs. Now I know." She addressed Alexander. "Don't just sit there. We've work to do."

He grinned and scooted out the door.

Ms. Ball turned back to us. "There's the matter of clear title to the funds, Mr. Carstairs. What were the terms of your agency?"

"Durable power of attorney for all purposes related to the auction and acquisition of the *Chernyakova*. Letter of credit in the amount of one hundred ten million credits for deposit in escrow at the bank of record on Breakall."

"Are you a lawyer, Mr. Carstairs?" she asked.

"Cargo master."

"Of course." She pondered. "That might be a problem. While the power of attorney gives you access to the funds, it's earmarked for a specific purpose."

"I've messaged my father for instructions and amended documentation."

"When do you expect a response?"

"Any time now. He should have had the message yesterday or the day before."

"What if he doesn't approve?"

"We have a Plan B," he said.

"Of course," she said. "Was that in the notes you sent to Alexander?"

"Of course," he said.

Chapter Fourteen
Port Newmar: 2374, June 7

Ms. Ball and her team proved to be quite effective in handling our needs, offering several suggestions on clauses we'd missed and ways to streamline some of the things we'd taken notes on. It helped that Pip and I had seen our share of contracts over the stanyers. Much of the incorporation stuff looked familiar from when I'd formed Icarus, and Pip had seen a lot of partnership agreements because Carstairs Ltd. had arrangements with several other small haulers around the Western Annex.

Our original idea had been for me to form a partnership with Carstairs Ltd. and use the partnership as the basis for forming the corporation. Ms. Ball convinced us that it was unnecessarily complex because incorporating—and allocating ownership shares based on financial contribution—was actually a more robust scheme. It provided the protections we needed while affording us some flexibility if one or the other of the parties wouldn't or couldn't continue.

It took the rest of the day to satisfy them that they had the details they needed, but we counted it time well-spent.

At the end of the day, we still lacked two things—word from Pip's father and a name.

We left Ball and Associates to draw up the paperwork for both plans, minus the name which we'd plug in as soon as we had it.

"We'll need another day to finish adding all the boilerplate and common clauses," Ms. Ball said. "I'd recommend incorporating in New Farnouk but you'd have to take the papers there to do it and maintain an office there."

"Why?" I asked.

"Taxes, mostly. New Farnouk is the tax haven of the Western Annex. Part of the charter that formed the CPJCT originally and created the Annex."

"It's only five points different and subjects corporate records to a higher level of scrutiny, though, right?" Pip asked.

She nodded. "Five percent can be a lot of credits, and the scrutiny is largely automated unless they decide to call for a physical audit."

Pip scowled and looked to me with a small shake of his head.

"It's pretty common," Ms. Ball said. "I know several reputable service companies that provide the requisite office address and records storage."

"We could also file in any Confederation port," Pip said. "Like here."

Her eyes widened slightly at this. "Yes," she said. "Or Diurnia, since that's the seat of record for the quadrant."

Pip shrugged and pushed back from the table. "Let us think about it and get back to you when we have a name and word from my father."

"Of course," she said and gave a little shrug.

We stepped out of the cool offices into the oven of late afternoon. The buildings and sidewalks captured the system primary's heat and held it. The only relief came from a light, onshore breeze. I felt the sweat trickling down my back under my shirt almost immediately as we shuffled our way toward the shuttle stop.

"What's the problem with New Farnouk?" I asked.

Pip frowned again and shook his head. "CPJCT oversight is invasive and constant. When you file there, you report company performance monthly—not quarterly—and they monitor all your financial and operational data. If something's out of whack, the physical audit involves flying all your assets to New Farnouk for an inventory audit."

I winced. "I'd hate think of how long it would take to fly a Barbell from Dree to New Farnouk. Even through the Deep Dark that would take weeks."

"Months, more like."

"How do the big carriers like Federated do it? Can you imagine having to fly every Federated ship to New Farnouk?" I asked.

He made a gesture with his thumb and forefingers. "That five percent you save in taxes? You don't get to keep it."

"Then why do they bother?"

He grimaced. "I'm not really sure. Father registered Carstairs in Dunsany Roads. It's not exactly the same thing as a full corporation, but a lot of the same rules apply when it comes to oversight and reporting. Private corps don't have to make the information public, but we still have to tell the Joint Committee." He glanced at me. "Didn't you have to do this with Icarus?"

"Some. I left most of it to the financial service company that set us up."

His eyebrows went up at that. "The same one that screwed you over for the share price?"

"Yeah. Among other things." I closed my eyes for a moment and tried not to see the images playing in my head.

Pip sighed.

"Not my problem anymore," I said. "Christine Maloney's got a whole fleet of accountants and lawyers to keep her in compliance."

He clapped me on the shoulder and we kept trudging. "Should we eat in town? We're already here."

I ran a finger around the inside of my collar and unfastened another button on my shirt. "Only if it's someplace cool."

"It's all the thermal mass. Paving, buildings. It gathers the heat and the breezes just move the heat around in these plascrete canyons."

We took the cross street that led to the harbor proper and the wind came more directly off the water instead of being funneled through the buildings and picking up heat. The temperature felt like it dropped ten degrees just walking two blocks. Maybe I was just getting used to it.

Pip nudged me and nodded to a restaurant on pilings stuck out over the water. A trellis shaded the back deck and the breeze fluttered the greenery. "Suppose they serve Clipper Ship?" he asked.

The sign above the front door displayed a bird of prey with white and black plumage and a fish in its talons. "Osprey's Nest." I shrugged. "Local beer. Local restaurant. We can ask. You ever eat here?"

He grinned. "Yesterday."

I backhanded his shoulder and he led the way in.

The maître d' smiled at Pip. "You're back."

"Could we sit on the deck?" he asked.

She glanced at me. "Two of you this afternoon?"

"No, just one of me. It's usually sufficient, but this guy—whom I have never seen before but has been following me all day—will join me."

She smiled at me. "Does he always talk like that?"

I shook my head. "That's what people usually ask about me."

"All right, then." She grabbed a couple of menus from the rack and led us on a circuitous route through the dining room to an air door leading to the deck. Inside, the place felt cozy; the way the sweat on my back chilled down, I'd have bet the AC was cranking. Along the walls, and even on some of the inside pillars, paintings hung in attractive frames. Some had small stickers beside them. Most had some kind of accent lighting that showed them off against the dark wood of the walls.

The deck outside didn't need any decoration. The trellis held up a green canopy of some type of vine bearing thousands of tiny white flowers. It cast the entire deck in a cool, green light. A breeze teased the leaves into a regular shimmer while the vista of water, boats, and docks down the harbor drew the eye out and away.

She stopped at a four-top, stripped away the extra place settings, and dropped the menus in the middle of the table. "Here you go, gentlemen. Daryll will be right along to take your orders."

We hung our jackets on the backs of our chairs and settled in. I felt the tension leaking out of me as I watched a sailboat tacking across the mouth of the harbor.

"White Sail," I said.

Pip scowled at me.

"What?"

"Seriously? White sale?" he asked.

I shook my head and pointed at the boat. "Not White Sale. White Sail."

He still shook his head. "Didn't you ask that the other day?"

"We've tried so many, I've forgotten."

Daryll showed up. Pip ordered two Clippers and Daryll left.

"Didn't you want anything?" Pip asked.

Pip always made me laugh. A characteristic I thought I'd need if the deal actually went through.

"I'll get coffee when he comes back," I said.

"I'm telling you. You should take advantage of the beer while you can."

"Beer Barge, Inc."

His mouth twisted into a grimace so funny, he could have been sucking on a lemon. "We're not changing the name of the ship. Just the company," he said after a moment.

"Soyuz Inc.?" I asked. "It means 'union' in Russian."

Daryll came back with the beers and Pip gave me one. "Two more of these and an order of the calamari?"

"Comin' right up."

"Maybe," Pip said, "but you've had three and I'm still trying to enjoy my beer. Hush, now. Lemme think." He took a swig of beer and rolled it around in his mouth before swallowing. "Flea Market Traders," he said after a few moments.

"Deep Dark Delivery," I said.

He made a face. "Possibilities, but it's still my turn."

Daryll came back with a plastic basket filled with deep-fried breaded squid and another pair of beers. "You guys know what ya want yet?"

"We're thinkin'," Pip said. "Give us a couple minutes." He reached for a menu and flipped it open while Daryll wandered back inside. "I had a burger here yesterday. Pretty good, but I bet the fish is better."

I grabbed a chunk of the calamari and waved it at Pip. "You know they fly this in from Blanchard, don't you?"

"Yeah? It's just the next system over." He took another bite. "How do you know?"

"No squid here. They were never introduced. The nearest place is Blanchard."

He shrugged. "You're suggesting they ship the fish in, too?"

"It's possible."

"I'm still having the whitefish sandwich," he said.

I looked at the menu and shrugged.

Daryll popped up again. "What can we get started for you?"

Pip ordered his sandwich and I took a chance on the fish and chips. The menu claimed it was a local whitefish—probably mouta—beer-battered and deep-fried. I figured it should hold me to breakfast.

I lifted my beer and poured some of it down my throat. I had to give Pip credit. Ice cold beer on a hot day, looking out over the water? It hit the spot after being locked up with the legal team all day.

The bottle made a thunk noise when I put it back on the table. I chuckled.

Pip looked at me out of the corners of his eyes. "What's so funny?"

I turned my head the way Ms. Ball had and said "Alexander?"

He laughed, too, and the people at the next table looked at us with "Were you talking to us?" all but printed on their faces.

"What do you suppose she pays him?" Pip asked.

"No idea. Probably enough. That was some serious skill there."

He shrugged. "Less than you might think."

"Really? He had my file—at least the public parts—nailed down."

"When we go back, look in his right ear," Pip said.

I started to take another slug of my beer, but stopped. "His what?"

Pip pointed to his own right ear. "He's wired for sound. My guess is that mics in the ceiling transmitted our conversation to the bright faces in the back room that Ball was talking about. They did the research on the fly and fed the puppet in the corner."

"She pulled his string and they fed him the answer to the most obvious question."

Pip nodded. "Just a guess, but even if it wasn't the answer she wanted, it was close enough to fool us."

"He perked up enough with our notes."

"He did. Which makes me wonder what his relationship with the charming Ms. Ball might be. He recognized the legalese and all the clauses we threw into that thing."

"And the retainer offer."

"That, too," he said and toasted me with his bottle. "That was brilliant."

"That was nothing. I lost more than that in the first week of working with William Simpson."

"Great fish and little godlings. How much are you worth anyway?" He turned his head and pulled back a bit to look me straight in the eye. "None of this wishy-washy stuff."

His look made me self-conscious. "I'm not sure with any degree of accuracy. Something between a hundred forty and a hundred sixty million. Depending on how the accounting rules treat my salvage claim. I don't count it as income until I see the credits in my account. Some of the CPJCT rules on accounting show it on my balance sheet as an outstanding receivable with an estimated value of twenty million based on the last two auctions."

"Ah, accountants," Pip said and clinked the neck of his bottle to mine. "We'd be broke without them."

"It didn't seem that hard in the academy. Debits on the left. Credits on the right."

"Yeah. That's accounting for officers. A good accountant is worth his weight in gold because he can take one set of numbers and make them say three different—completely legitimate—things depending on what you need them to say."

I looked at him hard and he shrugged.

"All right. I'm exaggerating, but only a little."

"Do we need to hire one?"

He shrugged again and took a short pull from his bottle. "Probably wouldn't hurt. We don't want to pay Ball and Associates to run our books for us. The board would probably feel better if we had one."

"Where do we find an accountant?"

Pip shook his head. "Beats me. Anybody worth having is probably too busy to take us on."

"We used a payroll service that Simpson lined up. They handled most of the receivables and sorting credits from our income to the various bills. Bastard was probably skimming that account, too."

"That's the second time you've mentioned him. That name's familiar but I can't place it."

"He was the financier who set up the Icarus paperwork."

He frowned. "No, it was something else. Something recent."

"He was arrested by the TIC for assault, murder, embezzlement, and a few other things I've probably forgotten."

Pip's eyebrows rose slowly. "And he was your money man?"

"He came highly recommended by DST."

"Seriously? He had them hoodwinked, too?"

"Oh, yeah. One of his subsidiaries through a holding company run by a shell ran a bodyguard service so well thought of that all the high-level corporate officers—and a lot of the lower ones—used it."

Pip's eyes narrowed. "This can't end well."

"One of the things the guards were supposed to do was protect their clients from unwanted coverage in the newsies."

"That's an impossible task. Anybody with a face hanging out in public is fair game to those people."

"Made even doubly so because the guards regularly proved how much their services were needed by taking pictures of their clients on the sly and selling them to the press."

Pip looked at me, beer bottle raised halfway to his gaping mouth. "My garters and braces, that's brilliant!"

"Also just slightly illegal under the terms of their agency contracts."

He shook his head. "I bet it wasn't."

"What?"

Pip took a sip and leaned over the table toward me. "Look, this guy was a high-end money guy. I bet he wiped his butt with three-hundred-page contracts every day. He was either a lawyer besides or had two hotshots on staff. There's no way he's going to set this up and then make it so he's hung by his own damn contract." He shook his head. "If he was half the crook you say? He was way smarter than that."

I laughed. "Damn, I missed you."

Daryll brought our food and another round of beers. I looked at Pip who just shrugged.

Daryll smiled and asked, "Is there anything else?"

"Yes," I said. "Would you bring me a coffee? Black."

"Of course."

"Thank you."

He bustled off and we dug into our meals. I had to admit the view wasn't bad. Pip must have seen my expression.

"What? You think we came here for the food?"

"You said you ate here yesterday and it wasn't bad."

He shrugged and took another bite of his fish sandwich. "It's not bad. And the beer is cold. And the view?" He waved a hand at the light gleaming off the water of the harbor and the picturesque view of boats and docks. "You gotta admit. Not exactly the view we get from the cottages."

I sighed. "I'll grant you all that."

"All right then. Quit bitchin' and relax. We still need a name."

He was right. The food wasn't bad. The chips were hot and not overly greasy. The batter on the fish was a bit heavy and the fish itself was a little soft, but it wasn't bad.

Daryll came back with my coffee and, predictably, it wasn't bad.

I sat back and listened to the wavelets lapping the pilings under us. The breezes made the leaves and flowers on the trellis dance in time with the glinting waves in the bay. I watched the boats in the harbor and forgot about it. This wasn't something I'd see in the Deep Dark. There were no warm zephyrs in the cold vacuum between the stars.

Pip was right. We weren't there for the food.

Chapter Fifteen
Port Newmar: 2374, June 7

Daryll brought me another coffee and kept taking away Pip's empties. I'd had two with him. I'd lost track of how many he'd had since. I was fairly certain he felt at least as relaxed as I did. The system primary had slipped nearly to the tree line in the west. Daryll kept asking if we wanted dessert.

"We'll just finish this round and go," Pip told him.

I might have felt guilty except the tables on either side of us were free.

"Yanno?" Pip said. "We're going at this wrong."

"You couldn't have thought of that before we retained counsel?"

He shook his head. "Not that. The name."

"Oh, yeah. Stella d'Oro."

"I get a gold star?"

"No. As a name."

"It's my turn."

"But you're not offering any."

"I'm trying to tell you. Hush."

"All right," I said. "You know you're about half in the bag, though, right?"

"Yes, but you're not. Are you going to listen?"

I waved a hand for him to continue.

"We've been picking random names. No rhyme. No reason. They sound good, or funny, or they're just random words that pop into our heads."

"True. Your suggestion?"

"Who do we want to be?"

"You mean a name? I thought that's what we were trying to figure out."

He squinted against the glare. "Are you sure you're not drunk?"

I lifted my coffee cup in toast. "Unless Daryll has slipped a little something extra in here, I'm pretty sure."

Pip ran a finger across the tip of his nose. "Is your nose numb?"

I touched it. "No."

"Must be mine."

"Your point?" I asked.

"Oh, brand-wise. Who are we? What do we represent?"

"We haul big cargo." I shrugged. "What else is there?"

"That's kinda thin, brand-wise."

"I thought so, too. That's why I didn't bring it up."

"We're doing research. Kinda."

"So? Cargo Lab?"

He blinked at his beer. "That's not bad."

"Yes, it is. It was a joke."

"No, it wasn't. That's not bad."

I blew out a breath. "I hope you can walk. I don't fancy dragging your drunken butt to the shuttle stop."

"All right." He upended the bottle and drained it. It slapped down on the table with a hollow thunk. "You ready?"

"We should pay first."

Pip raised a hand. "Daryll? Our tab, my good man."

Daryll was there before Pip could lower his arm. "Here you go, sir. We hope you found everything satisfactory."

Pip keyed in a tip and I looked over to make sure it had the right number of zeros on it before I let him thumb it.

"What're you doing?" he asked.

"Just checking." I released his arm. "Carry on."

He glared at me and thumbed the tab.

Daryll smiled and nodded before standing well back while Pip levered himself up from the chair.

I'll give the man credit. He stood, found his jacket, and slipped it on before walking in the wrong direction.

"Ah, the exit is this way, sir?" Daryll said, herding Pip toward the door.

"Restroom?" Pip said. "I should probably go before we leave."

"Just through here." Daryll led us out of the brilliant late afternoon sun and into the darkness inside. Not many people had shown up for the dinner hour. I realized that it was well past the dinner hour when we walked past a Clipper Ship Lager logo on a chronometer done up like a ship's wheel.

About halfway back, Daryll pointed Pip to the appropriate door and stood back, apparently ready to resume herding duties if needed.

Pip nodded and disappeared into the head.

Daryll looked at me with an odd expression until I realized what he wasn't saying.

"Oh, I'll just make sure he doesn't fall in," I said and joined Pip in the head.

After doing the needful and washing up, I held the door for Pip and followed him out.

We hadn't gone more than three steps when he stopped so suddenly, I nearly ran into him.

"You lost?" I asked.

"No," he said. "I think I'm found."

"If you start singing 'Amazing Grace' in here, they're going to kick us out."

"Stop being so damn sober for a tick and look." He pointed to one of the paintings on the wall.

The accent light illuminated a smallish piece with a tag beside it. A simple black metal frame held a collection of stylized flames. At first glance they looked random but the longer I looked the more of the pattern I saw until I found they created the image of a bird made completely of these delicate flames. It was beautiful.

Pip leaned over to peer at the tag. "Firebird. Fifty credits. E.J."

Daryll appeared from the dimness of the dining room. "Gentlemen? Is everything all right?"

"This painting. It's for sale?" Pip asked.

"Yes, sir. You can take it with you, if you like. Just pay at the desk on the way out."

I thought he'd placed special emphasis on the words "on the way out," but I really couldn't blame him.

Pip nodded. "Yes. I'll take it. The artist? A local?"

Daryll shrugged. "I suspect so. Most of them are. They'll be able to tell you at the desk. On the way out."

Pip stared at Daryll for one long moment. "I'm not going to hurl on your shoes, lad. And I'm on my way out. Relax."

Daryll actually gulped. He also had the sense to simply nod.

Pip lifted the painting off the hook and peeled the tag off the wall. It left an outline on the surface where it had been hung. "Been here a while, eh. Good," he said. He turned to Daryll. "So where's this desk on the way out?"

"Right this way, sir." He led us back to the maître d's desk and muttered something in her ear.

"Ah, you'd like to purchase the painting?" she asked.

"I would," Pip said. "Anything you can tell me about the artist?" He offered the tag.

She took it and pulled a tablet from a cubby under the desk. She flipped through a few screens and smiled. "Yes, Erik James. Local artist. He has several other pieces here if you'd like to see them?"

Pip shook his head. "Just this one. Where can I find Erik James?"

"His contact information should be on the back of the picture," she said.

Pip looked at the back and grinned. "So it is." He held out his thumb and she offered the tablet with an image of the painting showing at the top of the screen and the particulars across the bottom. He thumbed it and authorized the transaction. "Thank you very much." He smiled and nodded toward the door. "Come, Ishmael. We've an artist to retain."

The maître d' gave him a kindly smile that she probably reserved for the backs of drunken patrons as they left the restaurant—part sympathy and part relief. She offered me one that was all sympathy as I followed him out.

On the sidewalk outside, he peered at the label and then looked around like he was sniffing the air.

"What? You're going to track him down through your keen sense of smell, now?" I asked.

"No, I'm going to use the signpost over there to figure out where I am so I know how to get to this address. Now are you going to continue being a wise guy or are you coming with me? Pick one."

"I never knew you were a mean drunk."

"You still don't. If I were drunk, I'd have missed this and we'd still be looking for a name." He held up the painting.

"That's our name? Firebird?"

"And you call me drunk. Wake up. You're the one with the classical education." He strode off down the street, the painting tucked safely under his arm.

I followed him, having to jog a couple of steps to catch up.

As I fell into step with him, he glanced at me. "Were you paying attention to anything I was saying in there about branding?"

"Yeah. Why?"

"Who are we?" he asked.

"I have no idea where you're going with this."

"You. Yeah, you're stupidly rich, but the love of your life was snatched away."

His words hit me in the chest like a blow. When I could catch my breath, I said, "Well, don't sugarcoat it."

"The business you built? What happened to it?"

"DST bought it for a nice pile of credits. Which is, I'll remind you, how I got stupidly rich."

"Exactly. What do you need now?"

We stomped along for several meters before I shrugged. "I have no idea."

"Exactly. You have no idea what you need. I'll tell you what you need. You need something to do. Something other than hanging around campus scaring students and drinking tea with Margaret Newmar."

"Yeah," I said. "I'm still not tracking."

"And you give me crap about being drunk," he said, turning to port at the next intersection. "You need a new beginning."

I frowned at him. The game was beginning to get a little old. "So?"

He slowed down and looked over at me in short glances as he walked along. "So do I. I'm bored spitless by this fast packet trade. It's too simple. Too small. When I saw the *Chernyakova's* auction fail twice? I went to the old man and made the case that we need to diversify."

"So he agreed to letting you go to Breakall and bid."

"Yeah. And the more I think about it, the more I'm coming to believe he knew I was underfunded."

"So you'd come home and get back to work?" I asked.

"Probably."

"What little I know about your old man, that doesn't sound like him."

He shrugged. "Maybe I'm wrong. I'd be good with that."

"I'm still not seeing what this all has to do with the painting."

"By the all the wrinkly 'nads on Mount Olympus, man. Look!"

He held the painting up in front of me. In the bright light of the late afternoon sun, the ruddy gold flames seemed to dance as the bird rose from the flames. I stared at it for several heartbeats before I twigged.

I looked at Pip. "We need to find Erik James."

Pip seemed to know his way around that part of town so I followed him as he tracked his way through the warren of streets like Theseus in the Minotaur's maze following the delicate strand of Ariadne's thread. In a relatively short period of time, he stopped in front of what looked like a run-down warehouse in a part of town I really didn't want to be wearing nice clothes in as the sun set.

"This is it."

I eyed the building and looked around to see who might be eyeing us.

While I wasn't looking, Pip marched up to a dented metal door and knocked. Loudly.

I followed him up to the building while trying to keep tabs on our surroundings and Pip at the same time.

I heard a couple of bolts clank, and then the door opened a crack. "Yeah?"

"You Erik James?" Pip asked, holding up the painting.

"Maybe."

"Well, sonny-buck, if you're not, tell him to get his rosy red cheeks out here. We need to hire him."

The door opened a little wider, revealing a wraithlike figure wrapped in paint-stained denim. Paint spattered hair hung down to his jawline on either side of his face.

"For what?"

"We need a logo. Based on this firebird."

The young man's face wrinkled in obvious confusion. "A logo? For what?"

"Does it matter?" Pip asked.

"Yeah," he said. "Letterhead? Online? Store sign? They all need a different touch."

"How so?"

"Some things, like letterhead can handle the fine line. Store sign needs to be visible from a distance and detail can get lost."

Pip looked over his shoulder at me, a wild, maniacal grin on his face.

"Yeah. We need this kid," he said.

Chapter Sixteen
Port Newmar: 2374, June 8

The outside of the building looked ramshackle. Inside it looked like a paint explosion. I stepped in from the fading evening light and my eyes couldn't figure out where to look next. Frosted skylights let in light from above. A line of tall windows across the north wall let in even more of the fading daylight, along with a clear view of a brick wall that had been decorated with an eye-searing graffiti mural of arrows and stars that seemed to be moving of their own accord.

The concrete floor, smooth as polished granite under my boots, had paint spatters everywhere. I couldn't make any sense of the shapes left there. Everywhere I looked I saw paintings and posters and even sculptures. They stood in stacks propped against walls. They hung from the walls and even the rafters some five meters overhead.

"I don't get many visitors," the boy said, wiping his hands down the front of his shirt as he backed away from the door.

Pip held out his hand. "We're not visitors, Mr. James. We're clients. I'm Philip Carstairs. That's Ishmael Wang."

James stepped forward to shake his hand briefly and then stepped back again. His gaze flickered toward me and then back to Pip. "What kind of logo do you want?"

"We want to license the design for this firebird." He held up the painting again. "This is much too detailed for what we want, but this is the idea."

"It's for the side of a freighter," I said.

He looked at me. "Like an ocean freighter?"

"Like a solar clipper freighter," I said and pointed upwards.

His eyes and his lips all got very round. "I've never seen one.

In person anyway."

"They're just big boxes out in space. Not very interesting," Pip said.

He blinked several times. "Not to you, maybe."

"We see them all the time," Pip said with a nod. "We're a little jaded in that regard." He put the painting down, leaning it against his leg, and pulled out his tablet. He flipped through a few screens and then turned it to face James. "This is my ship. Our logo? Boring C in a circle. See?"

"Well, it has some identity," James said leaning forward to look at the image. "That's not a just a circle, is it?"

"My father assures me that it's a star."

"Oh, of course. Those are the stellar prominences around the edge. What's the C stand for?"

"Carstairs."

James ran fingers through his hair. "Oh, right. You're Carstairs. And, wait. That's *your* ship?"

"Technically it belongs to the family company, but yeah. That's the one I paid for." Pip lowered his tablet and leaned down to catch the guy's eye. "Focus, lad. We need your help. Logo? Ship?"

He shook himself. "Right." He waved a hand at the table. "I can't tell the scale. How big is that?"

Pip looked at it. "That's probably three meters across, but it's not for that ship." He looked around the warehouse and pointed at the south wall. "We need one at least that big."

James's jaw dropped.

"Probably twice as tall, actually," I said.

Pip looked at me. "Really?"

"Side panel on the forward nacelle is around ten meters tall and twenty wide."

Pip turned back to James. "It doesn't need to fill it. It just needs to be visible from a distance."

The kid's jaw lost its slackness and his gaze swept the wall of his studio as if he'd never seen it before. "That's huge," he said, his voice a bare whisper. He looked at Pip and then at me. "And you want that firebird as the inspiration piece?"

Pip grinned and picked up the painting. "Well, I'd like this painting but it's way too nuanced to program into an industrial painter." He stopped in mid-stream and looked at the kid. "Isn't it?"

James gazed toward the painting, but his focus lay somewhere else. He raked his fingers through his hair again. "Depends."

"On what?" Pip asked.

"How many colors the painter can spray, how fine a resolution it can spray at." He shrugged and looked at Pip. "How long you want to wait for it to process."

Pip turned to me. "Thoughts?"

I shrugged. "We'll need letterhead, maybe stencils. Shoulder flashes." I blew out a breath trying to think of all the things we'd done for Icarus. "Color scheme to tie the branding all together." I shook my head. "I have no idea what those mobile painters can do, but if we're thinking yardwork in Dree, they've got a lot better facilities for that."

Pip's head nodded as I checked off the items, his eyes unfocused. "First things first," he said.

"Feed the crew," I answered.

He shot me a grin. "Well, I was thinking more like base design. The painting gives us a palette. Reds and golds."

"You'll want a ground color," James said.

"Ground color?"

"Yeah. Red and gold go together but you'll need something to put the shape on so it stands up. Black and red are common but difficult to work with because their saturation values tend to be too close. Desaturating red makes it pink, and that's not exactly what you want on the side of your ship."

"Yeah. We're not going to go buy red shipsuits," I said.

Pip looked at me. "No? Crimson suits with gold piping? Sounds nice."

I sighed. "Sounds like a doorman."

"I'd go with a light toned gray," James said. "Neutral color so it won't clash with anything on top of it. Not dense enough to overpower any design and not so clean that a smudge of dirt would stand out."

"You design clothes, too?" Pip asked.

He shook his head. "No. Just practical." He waved his arms around. "White canvas is white. Do you see any white canvases here?"

Pip held up the firebird. "This is white."

James shook his head. "Gray."

"Really?"

James nodded.

Pip looked around and pointed to a large canvas hanging on the wall by the door. It had what looked like a line of ideograms running from top to bottom in a progression of colors from black to yellow and back to black.

"Gray," James said. "Well, more smoke white than gray, but it's the contrast. If you saw it against white, you'd see." He crossed to a workbench that lounged against the south wall and pulled a piece of heavy paper from a stack under it. "This is white," he said. "Or close enough for this." He crossed to the canvas by the door and held the paper up beside it. The canvas wasn't white. I couldn't really tell what it was. It almost looked like it had a bit of blue in it.

Pip walked over and held the firebird up to the paper. It wasn't white.

"The frame interrupts your perception of the color a little, but it's not white," James said.

"What color is it?" Pip asked.

James shrugged and gave an embarrassed smile. "I can't remember exactly. Might be smoke. It's probably ivory." He took the paper back to his workbench and slipped it back onto the pile.

"First things first," I said.

Pip gave me a quick nod. "Yes. First things first. Can you make a logo out of this for us, Mr. James?"

He shrugged. "Sure. Well, probably. You were talking about other uses for it? Besides the side of the ship?"

"Yeah," I said. "We're starting a business and we'll need graphics for digital letterheads, v-cards, that kind of thing."

"So a scalable graphic file. Sure. What else?"

"Shoulder flashes," Pip said.

"What's that?" James asked.

"Embroidered patches that go here." Pip clapped a hand to his left deltoid.

"Oh, like on uniforms and stuff."

"Exactly."

He nodded. "Town constables have them. You want any lettering?"

"Can you do that?"

He gave a shrug. "Don't know why not."

"And the big logo for the ship," Pip said.

"Sure. It's just a bigger one of these with perhaps a bit less shading."

"How soon can you have them done?" I asked.

"When do you need them?"

Pip said, "We're breaking orbit no later than tomorrow night."

"We better get to work then," he said. He waved us over to the work bench and pulled out a sketch pad. "So, the big one," he said and started laying lines on the paper.

Two stans later we stepped out of James's studio. The system primary had set long before and the heat of the day had been broken by the onshore breeze. James had wrapped the small painting in a padded envelope for us and Pip carried it under his arm. Street lights kept the shadows at bay but we didn't linger. It was probably safe, but why tempt fate.

"What do you think?" Pip asked after we'd rounded the first corner on the way back to the shuttle stop.

"Yeah. This is good."

"Think the kid can do it?"

"Yes."

"He didn't want much," Pip said.

"He probably doesn't do much industrial scale business."

Pip chuckled. "Well, the need for freight company logos is pretty limited."

I snorted. "I've needed two in the last two stanyers."

Pip shot me a grin. "You're not going to be making a habit of it, are you?"

"Gods, I hope not."

"I don't know," he said. "You did pretty well with the last one. Once we've settled the model, maybe you can sell your shares and make another fortune."

"You want to buy them?" I asked.

He shrugged. "Not today. Maybe in a stanyer? Who knows?"

We made it back to the main streets of Port Newmar without incident but had to jog to catch the shuttle just before it pulled out of the stop. Except for the driver we were the only people aboard. We didn't speak. I don't know what Pip was thinking about, but I kept imagining the red and gold phoenix rising on the side of the *Chernyakova's* hull.

"We have to come back to meet with Ball and Associates in the morning," Pip said as we stepped off the bus.

"You still haven't heard from your father?"

He shook his head. "That worries me. I should have at least heard a 'no' by now. Or an 'I'll get back to you' or something."

"Well, we have some time."

"We're leaving tomorrow," he said.

"Yes, but we're filing in Diurnia. We only need to get the documentation lined up here. By the time we get to Diurnia? That's still days away."

"True," he said.

"Even if he turns the deal down, we have a Plan B."

"Also, true." He sighed. "I just have a bad feeling. We should have heard something."

"We can only do what we can do. I'm going to do some tai chi in the morning. Meet here at 0900 and get back to Ball and Associates?"

Pip nodded. "Night," he said and trundled off toward his cottage.

My cottage was still strewn with clothes. Most of them had migrated to the "Toss It" bin, but the pile of things I had to keep was very, very small. Part of me felt silly for thinking I needed more. The other part for feeling like I needed what I had. The bulkiest items were my dress uniforms and my civilian clothing, half of which I was already wearing. If not for them, I could probably have packed in a bento box.

I shrugged, clicked off the main lights, and headed for my bed. I felt like I'd run a marathon and worried that it might be only the beginning.

Chapter Seventeen
Port Newmar: 2374, June 9

My morning workout felt rushed. I kept thinking more about what I needed to do than what I was doing. The third time I found myself doing Wave Hands As Clouds when I was supposed to be doing Grasp Sparrow's Tail, I gave it up as a bad job. Working with somebody else had the advantage of making me focus outside of my head, which left my body to do the form unhindered. Tai chi does not lend itself to thinking. It requires concentration to stay on track. I left the studio, making sure to click the light switch on my way out. I felt grumpy and out of sorts, which only underscored how much I needed the tai chi as a relief valve. I filed that away for another day and headed for the cottage.

The disarray smacked me again when I walked through the door and I nearly screamed. Not literally screamed. It came out as more of a low growl of frustration. I had arrived with nothing to do and found myself overwhelmed with a clutter of my own making, inside and out.

"Enough," I said and attacked.

Everything in the "Can Live Without" trunk went into the "Toss It" bin. Mostly onto the "Toss It" bin, to be precise, because I'd tossed almost everything I owned.

I stashed the bundle of whelkies, the printed photo of my father, and my small collection of captain's stars in the lid of the now empty grav-trunk. I rummaged around in the mess until I found the padded package that held my framed master's license and slipped that into the lid as well. I clipped my three dress uniforms to their travel hangers and hooked them into the grav-trunk. I followed them with the three best undress khakis, the two decent pair of ship boots, and my civvies. They weren't great civvies, but they made me presentable without being ostentatious the way a dress uniform would.

"What else?" I asked myself.

I sorted through the pile of ship-tees and boxers that I'd stacked up before and just packed the lot. My patience with the process had worn too thin for me to worry about it. I kept all the socks that had mates and relegated the leftovers to "Toss It."

That left as many as a dozen assorted shipsuits in various stages of decrepitude scattered around the room. I started flinging them. I kept a half dozen of the least damaged—a couple were practically new—and tossed the rest.

I looked around the room, awash in sweat and feeling like I might cry. Or scream. Literally scream. I'd packed everything I planned to keep except for the workout clothes on my back and the hygiene pack in the bathroom. Combined, it amounted to about half of one of the two trunks I'd brought from Diurnia.

The "Toss It" trunk had stuff piled high and drooping down the sides.

I had the sudden panicked thought that I really didn't remember what was in it.

I heard footsteps coming up the walk, then a knock. I opened the door to find Pip standing there with the wrapped painting.

"Oh, good, you're back. I'm getting packed up and this doesn't fit very well in my bag. You got room for it?"

I backed away from the doorway and he followed me into the cottage.

"You really cleaned house," he said, his gaze sweeping around the room.

"We're leaving this evening, right?"

Pip nodded. "That's the plan. Roland is prepping a flight plan for departure around 2100."

"Heard from your father yet?"

He bit his lip and shook his head. "Not yet."

I glanced at the chrono. "So, about thirteen stans."

"We can amend it. If we leave today we'll have five days on station before the auction."

"That includes the stop at Diurnia to register the incorporation?"

"Yeah. One day there should be enough. We'll be there in a week. That leaves a week to get to Breakall."

I laughed and shook my head. "Long legs."

He grinned. "Faster than the *Iris*?"

"By a few days. To be honest, we made better profits running the length of the sector."

"Low mass. High value," he said.

"Better deals in the afternoon."

He laughed. "Of course. What are you going to do with this pile?" He pointed at the "Toss It" bin.

"Leave it for concierge service to dispose of, I suppose. Why? You have a better idea?"

He shook his head. "No." He handed me the painting. "Looks like you've got plenty of room. Do you mind?"

I took it and stashed it in the pocket inside the front of my trunk.

"Thanks. We're meeting Ball at 1000?"

"I thought it was 0900," I said.

He glanced at the chrono. "We better move. You going to wear that?" He nodded at my sweat-soaked workout clothes.

"Too casual?"

He winced. "Maybe just a tad." He laughed and headed for the door. "Half a stan? Out front?"

"I'll be there," I said.

He waved and latched the door behind him as he left. I stripped down and tossed the sweaty clothes into the refresher before climbing into the shower.

I felt the clock ticking so I didn't linger.

The tram into town dropped us within two blocks of Ball and Associates. The receptionist showed us into the same conference room we'd used before.

We didn't have to wait long before Ms. Ball breezed in trailing the ever-present Alexander.

"Gentlemen. I think we have everything in order. Did you decide on a name?"

"Phoenix Freight," Pip said.

"How ... mythical," she said with an odd look. "Isn't that the bird that rises from its own ashes?"

"Yes," I said. "Every thousand years or so, the old bird dies and catches fire. The new bird rises from the ashes."

"If we can't turn a profit in the first thousand years, maybe we'll change the name," Pip said.

"I see." From her tone I wondered if she hadn't gotten the joke. "We can add that, easily. Alexander?"

"We'll have the updated files in one moment," he said.

I caught him tilting his head just a fraction of a degree as if listening. I nodded to Pip and he winked.

"Any word from your father?" Ms. Ball asked.

"Not yet," Pip said.

"We looked at your documentation and we believe that your power of attorney does not actually restrict you from investing in this enterprise in order to facilitate the acquisition of the ship. The terms in the documentation authorize you to obtain the vessel, crew and supply it, and place it into service. It remains silent as to how you accomplish these tasks."

Pip shrugged. "Good to know, but I'm pretty sure my father would be pretty peeved if I changed our understanding without his approval. Legal or not."

She smiled. "Yes, I suspect mine would be too with a hundred million credits in play."

"Did Commandant Giggone contact you with the names of the board members?"

"She did. Shall we review what we have?"

A soft knock preceded the door opening. Alexander accepted a stack of files from somebody on the other side and the door closed again.

We took our seats while he distributed the files. We started at the beginning.

Ball led us through the charters, supporting documents, and contracts. The board of directors named Alys Giggone as chairman, Benjamin Maxwell as treasurer, and Margaret Newmar as member at large. The charter gave the board wide latitude in expanding its membership and issuing stock so long as no single investor controlled more stock than I did. The organizational chart listed Pip as CEO, as we'd agreed.

We got to the end of the file in about a stan and a half. I hadn't seen anything that varied from our notes other than a few additional pieces of boilerplate in some of the mechanical aspects of corporate administration. Our notes hadn't specified how often the board should meet or the frequency of stockholder meetings. Ball's files spelled all those details out.

"And that's what we have, gentlemen," Ball said, closing her copy of the file and folding her hands on top of it. "Any changes? Discrepancies?"

Pip shook his head. "I didn't spot anything."

"Me, either."

"You'll have some time before you file on Diurnia. If you spot anything, message us and we'll amend the files for you," she said.

"Thank you," Pip said. "Do you have an associate on the Diurnia Orbital who can facilitate this for us on that end?"

"We do. With your permission, we'll send your file ahead so that they can make sure that everything is in order before you arrive. I'll forward the particulars to you once we've received confirmation from that end."

"Excellent," Pip said. "We'll be sailing on the *Prodigal Son* this evening."

She gave a curt nod. "We have the contact information from your notes." She spared a moment to look to each of us. "If there's nothing else, gentlemen?"

Recognizing the dismissal when I heard it, I stood. Pip followed suit. Ball rose with us and offered a hand to him and then to me. "It's been a pleasure, gentlemen. I suspect I'll be hearing from you if you need anything else?"

Pip grinned. "You most certainly will."

Alexander opened the door and led us all out to the lobby, Ms. Ball bringing up the rear.

"Thank you again, gentlemen. Safe voyage," she said.

We took our leave and stepped out into the late morning light.

"Margaret Newmar?" Pip asked as we walked toward Erik James's warehouse.

"My tai chi instructor," I said.

"I know who she is, but how does a gardener have ten million credits to invest?"

I looked at him to see if he might be pulling my leg. "Where do you think you are?"

"What do you mean?"

"This town? Do you know the name?"

"Sure. Port Newmar."

"And the planet?"

"Newmar."

"Doesn't that ring any bells?"

He stopped in his tracks. "No."

"Daughter of the founder."

"She's a gardener!" he said.

"She's also the richest person in the sector. She could buy and sell me and you and your family several times over."

"But she's a gardener!"

"She's also a master of tai chi. She's rich enough to do anything she likes. She likes gardening." I shrugged. "Good enough for me."

Pip blinked. "I had no idea. I thought she was just some sweet little old lady who volunteered to work on the academy grounds."

"Well, she is a sweet little old lady who volunteers to work on the academy grounds. It's the 'just' part that you had wrong."

He shook his head and we resumed our walk. I chuckled the whole way.

We found Erik James waiting for us, leaning in the door frame of the warehouse and squinting into the sun. He either hadn't changed or had an extra set of paint-smeared denims. His face lit up in a broad smile when we rounded the corner and started up his path.

"Great! I'm so excited," he said, waving us in.

We stepped into the building and I had to wait a moment for my eyes to adjust.

"Guys, after you left last night, I did some research on solar clipper company logos. I wanted to see what other companies used."

"Good plan, but I thought we'd agreed on what we wanted."

"We did. I did that." He pulled a piece of paper from a basket and laid it down on the workbench. "That's what we agreed on, right?"

Pip and I bumped shoulders looking down at the image.

"That's pretty much what I expected," Pip said. He looked to me.

"Yeah."

"That's what I thought. It's also wrong," James said.

"Wrong?" Pip asked, his eyebrows shooting up.

"Wrong."

"Wrong how?" I asked.

He pointed to the far end of his studio. Two tiny patches of white—which were probably actually gray—lay in a single pool of light. One was a smudge of red and the other was a spiral of red. "Which one of those is your logo?" he asked.

"Neither," Pip said.

"The smudge," I said understanding where the kid was taking us.

"Right," he said. "The smudge."

"What?" Pip asked.

The kid held up the paper from the workbench. "Look, this is nice and all, but it's too fussy. If you look at anybody else's logo, it's not fussy. It's iconic. A crown with wings. A C in a circle. That's yours," he said to Pip. "All of them are simple shapes combined to form an unmistakable pattern."

I looked back down the room and saw his point immediately.

Pip looked again and craned his neck forward, squinting. He had taken only three steps toward the small images when he stopped with an "Oh!" He turned with a grin. "Once you see it, it's obvious."

James pulled out another sheet of paper, this one with the bold spiral iconography in larger scale than the small one on the far wall. Under it he'd lettered "Phoenix Freight." He stood back and waited.

I reached out to touch the paper. I don't know if I wanted to make sure it was real or what. It was exactly what we needed and hadn't known how to ask for.

"It's ..." My brain couldn't form the words.

"Perfect," Pip said, joining me to stare at the image on the paper. Without turning he asked, "Will it work as a shoulder flash?"

James fished in the breast pocket of his shirt and pulled something out, handing it to him. "A buddy down the block does custom embroidery for the tourists. Mostly personalized polo shirts and crap. I asked him to run it up as a shoulder patch. I didn't know what shape so I had him put it on a simple shield and left room at the top for the ship name."

Pip fingered the sample for a moment, then handed it to me. "How'd you think to leave room?"

He shrugged and looked at his feet. "I didn't know what a shoulder flash was, so I looked it up. Then I looked at some samples. Civilian flashes just list, like, the police or fire department name. That usually includes the city or town name. Military flashes list the branch and little else on the official flash, but some of them had ship names and designators as well." He grinned. "Some of them looked pretty elaborate."

"Some of them are," Pip said.

"You can dress that one up with some gold thread or something, but you said something last night. Something like you should be able to look at the shoulder and know who goes with which ship."

"This is good work," I said, fingering the flash for a moment before handing it back to Pip.

"Albert said it was a simple setup, one of the simplest. He just ran it up on a piece of scrap for me." He looked down again. "I know you didn't ask for it, but I wanted to see what it would look like."

Pip grinned. "Do you have the graphics files we need?"

"Oh, sure." He reached into his pocket, pulled out a data cube, and held it out. "Both designs are on there. I gave you the one you asked for and the other one. Albert added the machine layout for the shoulder flash with that design on it. He said it'd work on most commercial embroiderers."

Pip took the cube and wrapped his fingers around it. "If not, I'm sure the graphic is enough to jump-start the process."

The kid beamed. "I still can't believe my design is going to be on the side of a space ship."

"Mr. James, your design is going to be on the side of a space fleet before we're done," Pip said. He winked at me.

"What do we owe you?" I asked.

He rummaged around on the work bench for a moment and pulled up an invoicing tablet. "I—uh—ran up the invoice. We didn't agree on a price before you left last night."

"Sorry about that," Pip said. "We were just so excited." He took the offered tablet and frowned at it for a moment before handing it to me.

I took it and looked at the total. I looked at the designs on the table and then at the two little images across the room and shook my head. "This is not anything close to satisfactory, Mr. James." I handed it back to him with a glance a Pip who had a grin hiding behind his hand.

"Oh. Uh. I can make an adjustment. It's just the normal price, but if it's too much—" He took the tablet back from me.

"You misunderstand, Mr. James. It's not too much. It's not nearly enough. We are purchasing these graphics from you for the sole use of our company in perpetuity. You've charged us for the paper to print it on. We wish to purchase the rights to use it however we deem necessary."

He looked up and the lost expression on his face made me take a couple of stanyers off my estimate of his age. "Well, uh. I've never done that before." He looked from me to Pip and back. "How much were you thinking?"

"Add a couple of zeros to the end of that," I said.

"Then double it," Pip said.

"That's more than I make in a year," James said.

I shrugged. "Not my problem, Mr. James. We'll need a receipt for our records."

"And we're in rather a hurry," Pip said. "If you'd make those adjustments, we've got a ship to catch."

The poor kid fumbled it a couple of times before he got it right, but I thumbed the invoice and sent the receipt to Pip's tablet.

We left him staring at the invoice, his jaw slack and his head shaking back and forth like a loose shutter in a light breeze.

At the door, Pip stopped. "Oh, Mr. James?"

He looked up. "Yes?"

"Thank you."

His breath whooshed out. "Thank you!"

We closed the door and headed for the shuttle stop.

"Was that too extravagant?" Pip asked.

I looked over at the shoulder flash that he still held. "We got the better of that deal," I said.

He looked down at it, flexing it between his fingers. "Yeah. I guess we did."

Chapter Eighteen
Port Newmar: 2374, June 9

Pip and I rode the noon shuttle back to campus. We had a few stans before we had to catch the orbital shuttle from the academy's spaceport.

"How soon do you want to go up?" I asked as we separated at the cottages.

"There's a shuttle at 1700. We can get dinner upstairs and that gives me time to finish wrapping up the loose ends from the convention."

"I've got to see my therapist in a stan, so that'll work."

He waved a hand and disappeared into his cottage while I confronted the mess that remained in mine.

The frantic stan or so I'd spent in the morning had crystallized my thinking on what might be important. I went to my "Keepers" trunk and went through everything there one more time. Rank insignia. Master's license. Uniforms across a range of utility.

I swapped the civvies I'd worn to town for a set of undress khakis and addressed the unruly pile of castoffs. That uneasy feeling I'd thrown away something I shouldn't have still nagged. I had plenty of time before my appointment with Gains, so I spent it pulling everything out of the discard trunk and making sure I'd not left anything in the pockets nor wrapped anything important in a cast-off garment.

Within half a stan, I found myself standing with an empty grav-trunk and a pile of odds and ends of clothing. Rich or not, I had qualms about discarding the trunk. The clothing would go into the recyclers and be extruded as fresh fabric and fittings, but I'd paid good credits for the trunk. I suspected Gains would say my family-of-origin frugality interfered with my new reality.

For a moment I wondered if Pip wanted it.

Then I knew what I'd use it for. I got on the network, placed an order with the academy store, and paid for expedited delivery. It took a bit of math for me to calculate just what I needed, but I was grinning when I latched the door behind me and headed for Mal Gains's office.

He greeted me as always and after satisfying the preliminaries got down to it.

"You've accomplished a lot in a short time," he said.

"I've got more to do, but I'll have to deal with it later."

"You'll manage. Tell me about this deal you've got going?"

"Pip and I are going into business. Again. It's going to be fun, I think."

"I don't usually hear people talking about going into business as fun."

I shrugged. "Yeah, well. I know it's going to be a lot of work. Long hours. Probably some disappointment. We're still waiting to find out if we have the funding we need. And I'm going to have to deal with the *Chernyakova* again."

"What made you decide to do that?"

"Pip made me see that a lot of my emotional response was fear. Rationally, it's just a ship. A ship with an unfortunate past, but just a ship. I know how to fly that ship. How to make it safe."

"You're going to exorcise your demons," Gains said.

"Sounds silly."

"Why?"

"It's such a cliché isn't it? Face your fears and defeat them."

"What are those fears?"

"That I might make the same mistakes they did. That I could kill people out of negligence or stupidity or just bad luck."

"Are those real fears? Or just something you've layered on to help you deal with the horror."

I shrugged. "I don't know how I'd know. The *Chernyakova* was pretty horrible."

"I'm not talking about that horror."

He didn't say it very loudly but it echoed in my head.

The flashes of reality as I'd watched Greta die in front of me while I lay helpless beside her on the deck all came rushing back. I felt the room compress around me, like I was about to pass out from blood loss again. I had to force myself to focus on breathing.

Gains waited me out. I finally said, "I don't know."

His smile—thin as it was—felt genuine. "At least you're paying attention to the right horror, now. We've accomplished that much." He consulted his tablet. "Tell me about this pile of castoffs. Why does it have you so bothered?"

"I just keep looking at it feeling like I'm leaving something important behind." I shook my head. "I've checked and checked. I've got my uniforms and the few things that are important to me all packed and ready to go, but I can't shake the feeling that I've left something important behind."

"What are the important things you packed?"

"Uniforms, license, my captain's stars. A couple sets of civvies and the artwork that was the inspiration for our logo."

"That's all?"

"Oh, I have a photo of my father as a young man. It was my only connection to him growing up. I met him on Diurnia, but that photo is still how I see him in my head."

"Is he very different in person?"

"Not really. Less hair. More wrinkles. The same smile. Same eyes."

"But it's a memento from your life on Neris," he said.

I took a breath and considered that. "I suppose."

"Do you have anything else from then?"

I shook my head. "That's the last physical thing that's survived all this time."

"You have your memories."

"And some digitals that I keep. Pictures of the campus there. Images of my mother. Some of them I took. Some that I recovered from her effects after she died."

"What else is important to you?"

"I have a collection of whelkies from St. Cloud. Those are going with me."

"The spirit carvings?"

"Yes. I purchased some for trade when I was on the *Lois*. I was never able to sell them. I just keep giving them away."

"From what I understand they're very collectable."

"I've had offers to buy them. It doesn't seem right." I reached into my pocket and pulled out the seabird. "This is mine. I had a dolphin for stanyers. It was a gift from a friend. I got that the same time I bought the collection. When I lost Greta, we found this in her effects and I kept it."

"What happened to your dolphin?"

"Christine Maloney has it now."

"You gave it to her?"

"I like to think that it found its new owner."

"Anything else that's important?"

I shook my head. "That's all I've packed."

"And you've left your old clothes to be recycled."

"Yes."

"Like a snake shedding its skin."

I laughed at the image. "Yeah. I suppose."

"Do you think the snake misses its old skin?"

"I'm not sure I'd anthropomorphize a snake to that degree."

"All right then. Do you think you're just missing your old skin? That's why you keep thinking you're leaving something behind?"

Something in his question caught in the corner of my mind and I couldn't quite reach it.

"Don't think about it. Tell me," he said.

"I can't quite get it. It's not the clothes. They're just clothes. Some of them don't fit. Some of them have lost buttons or broken zippers. Boxers with broken elastic. All of them are excess baggage."

"Stay with it. What else are they?"

I closed my eyes and tried to see what lurked in the back of my mind. "They're old. They're stained. They're mine."

"Yes," Gains said.

I opened my eyes and looked at him. "Yes?"

"Yes," he said and nodded.

"They're mine?"

He grinned.

"What does that matter?"

"Our time is almost up so I'll leave you to ponder that in your travels. Consider it a long term research assignment from me."

"How will I know if I get it?"

"I don't think you'll have any doubt." He paused. "You may need to work the question around a little. It'll be a good exercise for you."

"So you think I should take them?"

He shrugged. "I think that's up to you, but you've already determined that they're excess baggage. That you have sufficient resources for your immediate future and the wherewithal to obtain anything you might need but haven't anticipated. Right?"

"Yes."

"No doubts there."

"No."

He shrugged again. "Seems like you have a good handle on it and I want to talk about one other thing. That artist in town?"

"Erik James."

"Yes. While we were getting settled you said you overpaid him for the work he did."

"Did I?" I tried to think back.

"I don't remember the words but something about paid him

more than he asked."

"Yeah. We did."

"Why? He would have been happy to have you pay what he asked."

"It wouldn't have felt right to me."

"Why?"

"I know what that kind of work costs. He provided us a valuable service, even if he didn't know how much that service was worth. Pip and I both did. We probably would have had to pay twice what we actually paid him if we'd bought it from a design and marketing firm in Dree. And it wouldn't have been as good."

"But he undervalued his work and you felt you should—what? Teach him a lesson?"

"No," I said and then had to pause. "Well, maybe. I don't know. He kinda reminded me of me."

"Now we're getting there. What about him?"

"I don't know. When I joined the *Lois* I had one skill that mattered. I could make good coffee. Before then I knew I could make good coffee but I didn't know anybody would value it. The first thing Cookie asked me to do was to taste the coffee and tell him what I thought of it. It was horrible."

"Did you tell him that?"

"Yes. In hindsight, my own arrogance staggers me."

"What happened?"

"He asked me to do better."

"Did you?"

"Yes. It was the bane of my existence for nearly a stanyer. I was always making coffee. I couldn't keep the urns full."

"So, how do you see that applying to Erik James?"

"Cookie taught me something with his little test about the coffee. He could have made better coffee himself, probably. He didn't. The crew wasn't complaining. The coffee was the coffee. When he asked me to make better coffee, he didn't tell me how to do it. He gave me the opportunity to exercise a little initiative. I think he wanted to see what kind of kid I was. If I had the skills to back up my claims."

"And James?"

"James impressed us right out of the box, but instead of giving him his due and letting him guide us, we told him what we wanted."

"You felt guilty for stepping on him so you overpaid him?"

I shook my head. "Maybe, but mostly it was to encourage him to continue to exercise his initiative. To value his work enough to stand up for it. We didn't ask him for a sample of the shoulder flash. Just a design that would work on it. He'd never even seen a company logo on a hull before Pip showed him the image of one. He took what we asked for, added his own expertise, and then did something we probably should have done—might have done if we'd thought of it—and looked at what other companies do. I wanted to reward him for that effort.

"Maybe I was paying it forward for the lessons that I learned from Cookie and Alys Giggone about doing the best job you know how, even if it's more than is being asked for."

He grinned. "That might be the most you've ever said in one go since we've been working together." He stood and held out his hand. "Our time is done for now and you're on your way out. Keep working on this. Keep thinking. I don't think you're a danger to yourself or others, but I think you've still got a bit of inner dissonance about who you think you are and who you think you should be."

I shook the hand and felt myself grinning. "Thanks for all you've done. I have a sneaking suspicion that some of this work will be coming back around to me as we head out."

His grin broadened into a full smile. "That's the plan. So go do your part."

I felt lighter as I left. He was probably right and I still had stuff I needed to work on, but the universe kept unfolding—and in its broad sweeps, I found I needed to work a bit harder to keep up.

Chapter Nineteen
Port Newmar: 2374, June 9

When I met Pip on the path, he eyed my second grav-trunk. "I thought you were going to leave that."

I shrugged. "I discovered I needed it for a few extra things I purchased while here."

We fell into step, heading for the terminal. The system primary was already well on its way to setting, and the shuttle wouldn't wait for us if we weren't there.

He started to say something else but I asked, "Heard from your father yet?"

"No, and I'm really getting worried."

"How long has it been?"

"I sent it on the sixth." He counted on his fingers. "Sixth, seventh, eighth, today's the ninth."

"So. Four standard days and it has to go all the way around the loop to Dunsany Roads and back?" I asked.

He shrugged. "Seems like a lot longer."

"We've been busy."

"True. Did you wrap things up with your therapist?"

"Yeah. I've still got to deal with some internal dissonance and think about whether or not a snake misses its old skin."

He looked at me like I'd grown a third head. "Snakes miss their old skin?"

"There's a class of reptile with no real appendages. They're called snakes. They have various modes of locomotion—"

Pip punched me on the arm.

"Hey! You're assaulting a senior officer."

"I did no such thing. I slugged a wise guy. Qualitative difference."

"I don't think a captain's mast would find it significant." I grinned at him. "You know what a snake is, spaceboy?"

"Don't make me hurt you," he said with a grin. "What about missing its skin?"

"Nothing. We were talking about leaving the old clothes behind, and he asked if a snake missed its old skin."

"Sounds like a therapist. Did he ask how you felt about it?"

I tried to replay the conversation in my head. "I don't think so."

He shrugged. "Go figure."

The trip up to the orbital went without a hitch. The only thing out of the ordinary was when the cadet cargo master came out and shifted my second grav-trunk from the port luggage bay to starboard. He winked at me as he headed back to the cockpit.

"What have you got in there?" Pip asked. "Rocks?"

"Mostly water," I said.

"You're taking water into orbit."

"Don't judge me."

He laughed and settled down in his seat. "Wake me when we get there."

I thought he was kidding, but in a few moments I realized he'd actually fallen asleep.

It was odd. After all the times I've flown into and out of orbitals, I could count the number of times I'd landed as a passenger in a shuttle on the fingers of one hand. I'd never gone planet-side after joining the crew of the *Lois McKendrick* until I went to the academy.

I remembered the trips for orbital orientation courses. I supposed they counted but it only added the digits on my other hand, and perhaps a foot. We'd been flown up by a cadet, worked for a few weeks, and been flown back by a cadet. Somehow it wasn't the same as this; I couldn't really say why.

I had spent my entire adult life since then in space. The feel of the wind on my skin, of the warmth and light on my face? I'd spent two weeks on-planet but still longed for the familiar astringent scent of hydraulics and oil, the machine-scented air that flew with us from place to place. It was a pleasant change, but I felt more at home on the shuttle than I had in the rose-covered cottage.

And, unlike Pip, I couldn't even sleep there.

I leaned down to peer out of the port and saw the orbital appear to fly toward us as we matched orbits. Perhaps it did. One of my problems with shuttle piloting was never being sure if I was supposed to speed up or slow down to approach the dock. I wondered if I would be better at it now that I'd spent nearly two decades speeding up and slowing down, depending on how you looked at it.

We paused just off the traffic horizon while tugs pulled a tanker out of its dock and gave it the first push on its long voyage to somewhere else. We slipped into the shuttle dock and the skids locked down with a thump. I nudged Pip with my elbow.

"Here already?" he asked.

"Finally," I said.

He scrubbed his face with both hands and stretched. "It'll feel good to sleep in my own bunk again." The docking collar snaked out of the shuttle bay's bulkhead and latched on with a soft snap. As the shuttle switched to station power, the lighting failed for a moment and then cut back in. "Looks like we're here," Pip said and waved to me. "Captains first."

The cargo master came back, released the door, and began sliding my grav-trunks out of their slots. "Safe voyage, Captain," he said. He looked barely old enough to shave.

"Thanks. Safe voyage." I took the control handle and tugged my trunks off the ship. Pip shouldered his bag and followed me off.

"When did they start letting kids attend the academy?" I asked as we maneuvered ourselves and our luggage out into the arrival bay.

He shrugged. "Musta been last year." He grinned at me. "That's when you musta turned into an old fart."

I snorted and we soon found our way around to the commercial docks. Pip led the way to the *Prodigal Son*. A long time had passed since I'd followed him from the shuttle bay to the *Lois*, but it felt like maybe it had happened earlier in the week—or perhaps a lifetime past.

Pip must have been thinking about it, too. He stopped in the middle of the docks so suddenly a cargo handler had to swerve his trolley to keep from running him down. The handler flipped Pip a rather rude gesture on the way by. "Do you snore?" Pip asked me with innocent wide eyes.

I laughed with him as we resumed our parade down the dock. He broke trail through a herd of ratings who looked like they'd just been granted liberty, all of them skylarking and catcalling to each other as they trooped by. A couple caught sight of my stars and stared but I followed in Pip's wake without stopping.

We stopped at a lock. P-Son showed on the telltale; the departure time flashed off and on. Pip keyed the lock and we went through into the tidy living space I remembered from our trip from Dunsany to Newmar. An older man lounging on one of the chairs looked up from his tablet when we entered.

"I thought I was going to have to slip the departure time," he said by way of greeting.

"Hello, yourself," Pip said. "Captain Roland Marx, this is Captain Ishmael Wang. Ishmael, Roland."

He stuck out a hand and gave me an oddly judgmental look. "Captain," he said.

"Roland," I replied. "I'm Ishmael. Ish if you like."

Pip interrupted with "Where are we on the maintenance?"

"Done. I told you that before. All systems nominal and we're ready to roll out of here when you are."

"I need to grab a cargo to Diurnia," he said. "Gimme a tick." He pulled out his tablet and started scrolling.

"Crapcakes, Pip. You couldn't have done that before?"

"Keep your suspenders on. I've got five waiting. I just need to pick one." He scrolled a little more. "Or three." He headed back to the lock.

"You're not leaving the ship, I hope?" Marx said.

"Nope." His reply was covered slightly by the sound of the lock opening.

Marx sighed. "I swear this guy is a herd of cats in undress khakis." He raised his voice. "We have to file the departure, you know."

Pip's "I know" came floating down the short passage moments before we heard the lock cycle closed again. He came close behind and plopped a small box onto what I thought of as the coffee table. He looked at Marx. "Well? File it. We're good."

Marx rolled his eyes and flipped through a couple of screens on his tablet.

I nodded at the box. "Cargo?"

Pip nodded. "Low mass. High value."

"What is it?"

He smirked. "If I tell you, you have to tell me what's in your extra trunk."

"Deal," I said.

"Diamonds."

Marx looked up. "What? You scored a diamond drill bit to pay for the run to Diurnia?"

Pip grinned. "No. It's five kilos of gem-grade diamonds. Broker is waiting for them on Diurnia. They'll pay the freight from here to Breakall, including the pit stop in Diurnia."

"You mean five carets?" Marx asked.

"I mean twenty-five thousand carets. Five kilos."

I stared at the box. "Seriously?"

He nodded. "Your turn."

I crossed to the trunk and popped the lid. "Wanna beer?"

Pip's eyes got round and his face lit up. "You filled it with Clipper Ship Lager?"

"It's mostly water."

I reached in and pulled out a pair of bottles. "Want one, Captain?"

He sighed and shook his head. "I'm flying later."

Pip snagged one of the bottles from my hand and flipped the cap off. He stared into the grav-trunk as if it had been filled with diamonds instead of beer. "I can't believe you did this. I didn't think you really liked it."

I popped the cap off mine and took a slug. "I don't really. These are for you."

He clinked his bottle against mine. "Man, I knew I was right about you. We're gonna have some fun."

I thought ahead to the *Chernyakova* and all the work we'd need to do before we flew her. "We've got a long road ahead, yet."

He grinned. "Yeah, but we got a trunk full of Clipper Ship to take with us." He pulled a couple of racks out of the trunk and headed for the galley. "I'll just toss these in the cooler for later."

"You sure two is enough?" I asked.

"It'll get me through dinner," he said. "I'll worry about tomorrow later."

Marx rolled his eyes and sighed before settling back into his tablet.

I plopped into a chair and pulled my own tablet out. "ShipNet?"

"Guest password 'Prodigal' on the default channels," he said.

"Thanks."

He grunted.

On a hunch I typed in "Bad Penny." The tablet linked to ShipNet, and I started reviewing my message traffic. One from Ball and Associates with the information about her colleagues on Diurnia. One from Alys Giggone with a "keep me in the loop" kind of message. I logged out and reset my access to guest.

Marx never twitched.

Part of me sympathized with the guy. I had no idea how long he'd been ferrying Pip around. In small doses, Pip is perfectly charming. I knew from experience that being locked up with him for weeks at a time was anything but a small dose.

Still, I'd been locked up with him on the *Lois* and again at the academy. We'd shared a room for the whole four stanyers. What little I'd seen of him lately didn't make me think he'd changed all that much. His hair was white. He had that little mustache-goatee thing going. It was white, too. He was still completely irrepressible, and yet I'd sometimes found him capable of touching levels of empathy.

"You want dinner?" Pip called from the galley.

"You cooking?" I yelled.

Marx looked up at me like I'd spit on his deck.

"Yes."

"Then yes."

I heard him laugh, and then cupboards started clacking open and closed.

"So? You don't like flying the CEO's kid around?" I asked.

He sighed. "Welcome aboard, Captain Wang. Please let me know if there is anything I can do to make your passage with us more pleasant."

"Yes, he is a pain in the ass."

"This is not a conversation we will be having," he said.

"Do you have a new crew picked out yet? Some cousin from the outer fringes of the Carstairs clan who needs engineering experience?"

"Captain Wang, is there something wrong with your hearing?"

"No. Just curious. I like to know who I'm flying with."

"Do you have any questions about our voyage?" he asked.

"Estimated arrival in Diurnia?"

"Two weeks plus or minus a day."

"How many jumps in the Dark?"

"Two."

"Nice legs. Do you work out?"

Marx stood and walked to the galley door. "I'll be on the bridge if you need anything."

"You want something to eat?" Pip asked.

"I'll grab a snack after we're underway." He offered me a polite glare before climbing the ladder toward the bridge.

I joined Pip in the galley. "He seems a nice enough sort."

Pip paused in his salad construction long enough to look up. "Roland? He's all right. Little prickly at times."

"He's getting a ship out of the deal. You'd think he'd be happy to be skedaddling."

"Skedaddling? Really?" He shot me a pained expression and drained his beer.

"You going to do anything but salad?"

"Feel up to making biscuits?" he asked.

"I thought you were cooking."

"I am." He held out both hands to the bowl of salad. "Look. Greens, tomatoes, a few onions, and a couple radishes. Add a few mushrooms and we're good here."

"What else?"

Pip looked at the salad for a moment before turning to the chiller. He swung the door open and pulled another beer from the rack inside. "There's some chicken. Individually wrapped breasts. Some bacon and eggs."

"Any sliced ham?"

He poked about for a bit and nodded. "Yeah. Doesn't look too slimy either."

"You worry me sometimes."

He straightened up and looked over his shoulder at me. "Only sometimes?"

I shrugged.

"I'll try harder," he said. "What do you fancy with your salad?"

"How about pan-seared chicken breasts and biscuits?"

"Sounds good. You need anything?"

"I'll do the chicken if you'll do the biscuits," I said.

"I already did the salad."

"And I brought the beer."

He held his bottle up and peered at the level. "Fair deal."

I crossed to the galley, pulled open the cupboard under the cooktop, chose one of the frying pans, and slapped it on the burner. "You've not gone alcoholic on me, have you?"

He shrugged. "I just really like this beer. Did I tell you, you can't get it anywhere else?"

"At least twice. Why do you think I brought a trunk full?"

"Because you like me?"

"Because I knew that it would help keep you from whining about it after you drink through the stash you had sent up from the planet."

"I'm wounded."

"What? Are you going to deny that you sent up a shipment from Port Newmar?"

"I don't whine."

I laughed and he tossed me a head of garlic from the bin beside the fridge. "Biscuits?" I said.

He sighed one of the most egregiously put-upon sighs I ever heard, but his grin never faded. Soon he had a good dough in process on the work surface. "Just like old times, sorta," he said.

"How much of a file do you have on me?" I asked as I turned the chicken.

"Enough to know you needed a job. And why."

"Enough to know I had a big pile of credits?"

"Well, I knew you had a lot. The rumors were flying, but I had no idea you had that many."

"So you only want me for my money," I said.

"Well, no. I want you for your license. I'm sure there are plenty of people out there who'd want you for your credits. For me, that's just gravy."

I laughed. I'd been doing that a lot over the last few days.

Chapter Twenty
Diurnia Orbital: 2374, June 23

Walking the passages of Diurnia Orbital with Pip beside me felt almost surreal. I kept looking for Stacey Arellone to step out of a doorway and body slam me into a bulkhead for not telling her I was leaving the ship. That so many people seemed to do double-takes as we passed made me wonder if she might have been right.

I opened my mouth to say something to Pip and realized he wasn't there. Casting about, I saw him stopped at a newsie box, his tablet out as he purchased the latest rag.

He stepped toward me with a huge grin. "You didn't tell me you were big here."

"Big here?" I was scanning the door designators looking for the firm Ball and Associates had recommended.

He held his tablet up so I could see my face peering back at me. It was a grainy shot of me walking along the docks with my grav-trunks in tow. If I had to guess, I'd have said I was on my way to board the *Ellis* for the trip back to Port Newmar.

I laughed. "What's the headline? It's always a question. That way they don't have to have any facts to justify printing it."

"How long have you been off station?"

"I don't know. A few weeks."

"This was published this morning." He scrolled down to display the headline: "Rich Boy Returns?"

"Somebody's paying attention," I said.

"How did they know?" Pip asked.

"Spies? Bribed somebody in traffic control?" I shrugged. "No idea."

"Private vessel. No passenger lists. You're not on our manifest. You should be invisible," he said, his voice more serious than I'd heard for a long time.

"Somebody saw us get off the ship when we went to dinner last night?"

He made a noncommittal kind of grunt but kept staring at the tablet.

"Here we are. Mabon Legal." I pulled the door open and ushered Pip through with a flourish of my free hand. "After you, good sir."

He rolled his eyes and holstered his tablet.

The receptionist smiled as we crossed the carpeted deck. The place was far from ostentatious, but like any good lawyer's office kept up appearances with some wood-grain panels and a quiet hum that seemed so familiar I wondered if there might not be a noise generator someplace that piped the sound on demand.

"How can I help you, gentlemen?"

"I'm Ishmael Wang. This is Phillip Carstairs. We have an appointment?"

She scanned her screen and nodded. "Indeed you do, Captain Wang." She pressed a button and a side door buzzed and popped off the latch. "Mr. Kaplan is waiting for you in Conference Room B."

Pip led the way through the door and before we had time to wonder where we might find Conference Room B, we were in it. The door latched behind us, and a rather dapper man in a three-piece suit that looked like it might have come from Bresheu himself straightened from where he leaned over a pile of documents on the broad table. "Captain Wang?" He held out his hand.

I shook the hand. "Mr. Kaplan, I presume?"

He smiled. "The same." He turned to Pip. "That would make you Mr. Carstairs?"

Pip smiled back and shook the offered hand in turn. "On a good day. Most days it just makes me grumpy."

Kaplan paused for a moment as if his internal programming needed to find the place where the conversation had gone off script.

"Don't let him throw you," I said. "He's like this with everybody."

"Just be glad it's a good day," Pip said and grinned. "You have some papers for us to sign?"

After a couple of back-and-forth glances between us, Kaplan found his place on the page of our conversation and nodded. "I do. I was just reviewing them." He pulled a cover sheet up on his legal tablet and scrolled down. "This says you're to be CEO, Mr. Carstairs?"

"Correct."

"Very good. Ms. Ball's people indicated that you have one

outstanding issue. Which of these two plans will you be executing today?"

Pip said, "Plan A. We'll be forming Phoenix Freight today."

I looked at Pip and started to say something but he shook his head just a tiny bit.

"And do you have the deposits ready?" Kaplan asked.

"We'll be visiting the Confederated Bank Branch here on station as soon as we leave," Pip said.

"And you, Captain Wang. Let me say what a pleasure it is to meet you."

I smiled and nodded. "Thank you. I'm just the driver in this enterprise."

Kaplan's lips puckered in a kind of kiss that I found a bit disturbing. "Surely the majority stockholder is more than the driver?"

I shook my head. "I'm not even that, yet."

He nodded and looked at his legal tablet again. "Very well, then, let's clear up the loose ends so you gentlemen can be on your way."

In a surprisingly short period of time, we stepped out of the firm of Mabon Legal with our lives signed away to Phoenix Freight, Inc.

"So? Did you hear from your father or did you just hang yourself?" I asked.

He shrugged. "I looked over the power of attorney documents and exercised my initiative."

"Meaning, you haven't heard from him?"

He shrugged again. "No. Shall we go to the bank?"

"Yes, but I can't believe you did that."

"It'll be all right. It's not really that much different than what he sent me here for. I'm just taking a slightly different path."

"You just committed Carstairs Ltd. to a partnership with us. With me."

We found the lift and I pressed the call button.

"Yeah. True," Pip said.

The doors whooshed open and three people stepped off before we could get on. One of them turned to stare at me as she walked away and ran into the bulkhead across the passage.

"This could get old, fast," I said out of the corner of my mouth.

Pip chuckled. "We'll be out in the cold again soon enough."

The bankers seemed a bit happier to see us. Of course we were going to leave a few hundred million credits in their care. Not like they didn't have it already, but they appeared to like moving it from one account to another.

It took less time to deal with the finances—setting up the appropriate accounts and arranging for a payroll servicing company—

than it did with Mabon Legal.

As we left the bank, Pip clapped his hands together and then wrung them as if he were washing oil off his palms. "So? What's for lunch?" he asked. "Roland filed for a 1500 departure, which leaves us a chance to get some food we don't have to cook ourselves."

I smiled. "How do you feel about breakfast?"

"I like breakfast," he said. "But it's lunchtime."

"Come on. Let me introduce you to Frank's Finest."

The trip to the oh-two deck took only a few ticks, and we stepped into Over Easy just a bit before 1200. The lunch crowd had already staked out the counter and booth space.

"Looks busy," Pip said.

I looked over the crowd to see Seth behind the counter and pointing to the end away from the door. "Come on," I said and snaked my way through the cheerful hubbub that accompanied the various meal crushes.

Pip and I slipped onto the last two stools at the counter. Seth already had napkin-wrapped silverware and coffee cups in place.

"Usual?" he asked.

"One for each of us," I said with a nod at Pip.

Seth scribbled on a paper pad that might have come out of a restaurant in the previous millennium and clipped it onto the funky metal turn table that hung in the pass-through to the kitchen. "Order up, Frank." He winked at me when he said it.

The wheel spun and the order disappeared.

Pip favored me with a look that was either wonder or indigestion. It might have been both. He leaned over. "What in the name of all the holy water in the Ganges is this place? Did we go through a time warp or something?"

"Best food in the sector," I said.

A voice behind me said, "You're biased."

I turned to see my father standing behind me, a spattered apron hanging around his neck and a sturdy spatula still in his hand. He gave me a big hug. "You on station long?"

"Only until 1500."

"Come see me next time." He grinned and disappeared back through the swinging doors.

Pip arched an eyebrow. "You taken up with older men without telling me?"

I shook my head. "That's my father."

"What?"

"Long story. I'll tell you when we don't have to shout."

He sat back on his stool and shook his head.

Seth refilled our coffee mugs and kept moving down the bar.

Pip took a sip and looked at me. "Bean doesn't fall far from the bush, huh?"

I shrugged. "My mother taught me how to make coffee. Maybe she learned from him."

Seth came back with our plates, slid them into place, and looked to Pip. "Anything else?"

The pile of potatoes and onions laced with bacon and topped with three fried eggs took Pip's entire attention.

"We're good, Seth. Thanks," I said.

He grinned at me and went back to work.

Pip grabbed his fork and dug in. After three bites he looked at me and rolled his eyes up, a look of pure bliss on his face. "How does he do this?"

"No idea."

"You never asked? Never visited the kitchen?"

I shook my head.

"Philistine." He turned back to his meal and dug in again.

He had the right idea so I followed his lead. We soon had our plates scraped down to the paint, and to be honest I wasn't sure he wouldn't try to lick that off.

"Can we go back and visit him in the kitchen?" Pip asked when he pushed his empty plate back from the edge of the counter.

I looked around the dining room and at the line waiting at the door. "Maybe another time when it's not a meal rush," I said, nodding at the crowd.

Seth came back and stashed our empties in a bin under the counter. "Another?" he asked.

I shook my head, but Pip leaned forward. "Can I get one to go?"

"Sure." He scribbled on the pad again and clipped it to the wheel. "Order up, Frank."

"To go?" I asked.

Pip shrugged. "I was too busy eating to pay attention. I want to know what's in that."

"You're going to reverse engineer it?"

He shrugged again. "We have a galley and we'll have a bigger one in a few weeks. Why not?"

I laughed just as Seth brought the box. I made a pinching motion with my thumb to get the tab and he shook his head. "Your money's still no good here, Captain."

"Lemme leave a tip at least."

He shook his head. "He'd kill me. Besides. Finding you was good for him and what's good for him is good for all of us." He nodded around the room to the gang of service staff. "Now if you don't mind, Captain, I got people waiting for that stool." He grinned and we scooted.

We stepped out of the restaurant and crossed the passageway to the lift. The number of eyes on me had grown to a level that gave me a bad feeling. As we waited for the lift, a sultry brunette walked up to us and stood right in front of me. She wore a pair of jeans that might have been painted on and a pink, floofy sweater that should have hidden her assets but only accented them.

"You're Ishmael, right?" she asked. Her voice had that faint whispery rasp that, under the right circumstances could curl my toes, ship boots and all.

She nodded and stepped right up to me, pinning me against the bulkhead with her fuzzy boobs. "Thought so." She gave me a kiss on the lips. Nothing too salacious. She left a hint of cherry-flavored lipstick on my mouth. I think she meant it as a tease because she stepped away and stood there.

Pip stepped up and held out his hand. "Hi, I'm Phillip Carstairs. You are ...?"

She glanced at him, then cast her hooded gaze back to me. "Waiting for Captain Wang," she said.

The lift doors dinged open and a half dozen station personnel rushed off, buffeting us in the wind of their passage.

"Sorry," I said. "We were just leaving." I grabbed Pip and pulled him onto the lift as the doors closed, blocking our view of her pouting red lips.

Pip blew out a deep breath and looked over at me. "Lemme guess. Your ex-wife?"

I shook my head. "My ex works at the pub down around the corner. I think she only works nights."

He blinked. "Seriously? Your ex-wife is still on station?"

"Truthfully, I don't know. She used to be the bar maid at the pub but I don't know what happened to her after we split up."

The lift dinged again and opened onto the docks. I stepped out into the chill and looked around for Pip, who still stood in the lift. The doors started to close so I stuck a booted foot in the way. "You coming?"

He shook his head and followed me out. "You're just full of surprises," he said.

"I thought you had a file on me," I said.

"It didn't mention anything about a father."

"I have one."

He blew out a breath and shrugged. "Well, we can update it when we get back to the ship."

I glanced around at the looks we were attracting. "Sooner is better."

I saw him take in the spectators and strike off across the dock, his breakfast box tucked under one arm.

"Nobody's going to steal it," I said.

He laughed. "Five ticks ago, I'd have sworn nobody was going to play tonsil hockey with you in public. Why take chances?"

"You know that's going to be in a newsie later, right?"

He spared me a glance. "Seriously?"

I shrugged. "Wouldn't bet against it."

We passed a newsie kiosk and he took a detour to look at the teaser display. His steps faltered and he shook his head before catching up with me.

"Already?" I asked.

"How do they do that so quickly?"

"It was an easy setup. Probably had the camera linked to the network in case we noticed and took it. Could have had the image cropped and edited before we got off the lift. Distribution is a button push and my face is on the front of the newsie kiosk."

"Diana's balls," he said.

I raised an eyebrow. "Diana was a woman, wasn't she?"

"Best juggler in town," Pip said. "I got a feeling we might need one."

"What? Juggler?"

"Goddess. If this keeps up, we're going to need divine intervention."

"Or a bodyguard," I said, thinking of Stacy Arellone.

"You know any?"

"Only one that I'd trust, but she's got a job."

"Can we hire her away?"

I thought about it for a few moments as we closed the distance to the lock. "Probably, but I wouldn't want to do that to her."

"What? Make her rich?"

"No. Put her in a position where she'd have to knife somebody else."

Pip paused at the keypad and looked over his shoulder at me. "You are just full of surprises today. Why haven't you mentioned any of this before?"

"We weren't on my turf before."

Pip looked up and down the dock for a few heartbeats before nodding. "Good enough," he said and keyed the lock open.

We ducked in out of the cold. Pip made a beeline for the galley while I went looking for the head and a shower. I had pink fuzz on my chest and a nasty taste in my mouth that had nothing to do with cherry lipstick.

Chapter Twenty-one
Breakall Orbital: 2374, August 1

Pip's predictions proved to be spot on. We arrived on Breakall Orbital on my forty-first birthday. With a week to spare before the auction we registered with the Confederated Planets Joint Committee on Trade office as bidders, placing two hundred million credits in escrow. The functionary gave us a key card, a wand with a number on it, and a copy of the engineering report.

"Would it be possible to see the ship before the auction?" Pip asked.

"No. The engineering report has been certified as accurate and complete. Everything you need to know about the vessel is in that report."

"The report doesn't mention stains on the decking," Pip said. "Nor does it indicate whether the decking has been replaced recently. I was just wondering."

The functionary looked down his nose at Pip. "Stains? What kind of stains?"

Pip shrugged. "Oh, I don't know. Necrotic discharge postmortem from the previous crew?"

"Necrotic discharge." The functionary repeated the words before swallowing a couple of times.

"Bodies rot, even in space," Pip said. "The residue can stain deck coverings, particularly the more porous coverings found on the bridge."

"Not to mention what seeps into the console chairs," I added.

He looked at me with a frown before turning back to the functionary. "We just wanted to know if we could take a quick look to see how much refurbishment will be required."

"I'm sorry, Mr. Carstairs. That's completely out of the question."

He shrugged. "I see. Thanks. Doesn't hurt to ask."

We exited the office and walked a few meters down the passageway before he glanced over at me. "Seeped into the chairs?" he asked.

"We replaced most of them. Nobody wanted to sit on it."

"I can't imagine why," he said.

"Sticks to your shipsuit," I said.

"I really would have preferred not to imagine why."

"You brought me along because I know what's in there, didn't you?"

"I brought you along because I need a captain to fly it."

"Well, sure, but there are a lot of captains you could have gotten."

"Really? Name one."

I opened my tablet and scanned the jobs boards for senior officers. "Well, here's Delman. I know him. He's rated on Barbells."

"He any good?"

"Probably not."

"Why do you say that?"

"Christine Maloney fired him from DST."

He stopped walking to peer at my tablet. "Does it say that?"

"You kidding? They don't put that stuff in public files."

"How do you know then?"

"Because—if you remember my file?"

"Oh, yeah," he said. "Christine Maloney flew with you on the *Iris*."

"Uh, huh. And she cleaned house when she got control of the company. Delman's out. A couple of the senior captains were allowed to retire." I shrugged. "There was something about the cargo handlers that I didn't really follow, and at least one inspection official is now directing traffic on-planet."

Pip frowned at me. "You really haven't changed much. Trouble just falls out of your pockets and lands on everybody around you."

"Stand close," I said.

"So it'll fall on me?" he asked, his eyes bulging and his voice practically squeaking.

"No. So you can stay inside the radius of danger."

He laughed. "All right, fine, but you see what I mean. That's not a long list of available captains."

"Yeah. It's a lot sparser than I'd have expected. I wonder where they're all working."

"Given what you've said? For Christine Maloney. Somebody had to replace all the people she booted out."

"Possible. I hadn't really thought of it."

"Where would you be working if you still worked?" Pip asked.

I shrugged. "I really don't know. That's why I went to Port Newmar."

He chuckled. "And now you're back here."

"Small universe," I said.

"So true."

Pip led the way back to the lift and punched the button for the oh-one deck.

"Where are we going?"

"Traffic office."

"Why?"

"They've got all the ship assignments."

"You thinking you'll sneak aboard?"

He shook his head. "I'm hoping to get a guided tour."

"From whom?"

"The caretaker."

He had a point. A ship like the *Chernyakova* couldn't be left unattended very long. Too much could go wrong that might damage the ship or the orbital.

"Might work."

"I still have a few racks of Clipper Ship left. Just a friendly thank-you from a grateful relative of the dearly departed."

"You'd impersonate a grieving relative?"

"I'd impersonate Alys Giggone if I thought it would help."

"You don't have her legs. What do you expect to find out?" I asked. "I can tell you what shape the ship was in when I left it."

He stopped in the middle of the passageway. "Can you tell me if anything's been taken off while it's been here?"

"No."

He shrugged and continued on his way.

We found the Traffic Control Office hidden behind a sign clearly labeled as Traffic Control Office. Pip pushed through the door and walked up to the counter.

A skinny blonde in an admin jumpsuit stood behind the counter, peering into a computer terminal. "Yeah?" she asked without looking up.

"I'm looking for a ship," Pip said.

"Did you check the docks?" she asked. "Maybe your other pants? Where did you see it last?"

"Last time I saw it it was leaking atmosphere and bleeding fuel all over the deck in the maintenance bay."

She looked up in shock. "What?"

"Well, hello. Now that I have your attention. I'm looking for the *Chernyakova.* Can you tell me where to find it?"

She shot him a sour look. "You and twenty other people. I'll tell you what I told them. It's in a secure parking orbit under guard about twenty-five kilometers away."

"Perfect," Pip said and nodded. "Thank you so much."

Her jaw dropped but she wasn't able to recover before Pip led me out of the office.

"Well, now what?" I asked. "You're not planning on going out there, I hope?"

"Goodness. Why would I do that?"

"I'm still trying to figure out why you want to see the inside."

"Damage control?"

I gave him my best evil eye.

"I want to make sure the computer systems are intact," he said. "I don't really need to get inside for that."

"Really? How are you going to find out?"

"Simple. Ask the people who know."

He led the way to the lift and we dropped down to the oh-two deck. It took him a couple of laps around the station but he finally settled on a disreputable-looking hole in the wall with a shaped neon cocktail glass and a flashing "Breakall Brewery" sign above the door.

He stopped outside and looked at me and then down at himself. "We're a little overdressed, but it'll do." He loosened the collar on his tunic and ruffled the snow-white hair on his head, leaving it stuck out in several directions. "I'll talk. You watch."

"What am I watching for?"

"Somebody watching us."

"Won't that be everybody in there?"

"No. The regulars will keep their heads down and their thumbs in their pockets."

"Then who ...?"

"Just keep your eyes open, all right?" He sighed and staggered into the door, bouncing it off its stops on the inside. He sauntered into the bar as if he were the new owner come to kick butts and forget names.

I followed him before the door could close all the way and watched him weave ever so gracefully through most of the small tables on his way to the bar. He only bumped a couple, the residents grabbing for their drinks and giving him the stink eye.

"Watch it, buddy," one said. That was about it.

I followed him, shrugging in apology to any of the fine folks up to their armpits in the sour-smelling swill that apparently passed for beer. I sidled up to the bar alongside him, leaning over as if to speak to him so I could look down the bar at the dark corners in the far end of the room.

"What ya want?" The gruff voice sounded more bored than hostile.

"Clipper Ship Lager?" Pip asked, hope bright in his voice.

"Pfft," the barkeep said.

"What's on draft then?" Pip asked.

"We got beer. Cheap beer and cheaper beer. Unless you'd like to sample one of our fine vintage wines or perhaps a single-malt scotch."

The guy on the other side of Pip giggled at this. It wasn't actually a very joyful sound, but I counted his amusement as being in our favor. The only person in the bar who seemed to be paying any attention to us, other than the giggler beside Pip, sat near the door with his back against the wall. He must have watched us walk in; he'd certainly watch us walk out.

Assuming we actually walked out and weren't thrown—or carried.

"In that case, I'll have a glass of cheaper beer," Pip said, making a hash of the word glass so it sounded more like "glash."

"You?"

It took me a second to realize he'd spoken to me. "Nothing for me. I'll just pour my friend out when he's done," I said.

The barkeep shrugged and slapped a bottle of beer on the counter. "Five credits," he said.

"I thought you said it was cheaper beer."

"It is. The other is six."

"Classy," Pip said and fumbled something out of his tunic pocket, clattering it on the bar where the barkeep scooped it up, looked at the face of it, and threw it into a bucket under the bar. It clattered when it hit.

Pip upended the bottle, swallowing twice before slapping the bottle down on the counter again. "Yeah. That's cheaper." He left the beer on the counter and headed for the door.

"Hey, don't you want your bottle?" the barkeep said.

"Naw. Let the next guy piss in it," he said and sailed out the way he'd come. He turned to starboard and stepped pretty lively. I had to jog to keep up.

"All right, what was that about?"

"I was looking for the caretakers. Nobody in there in a shipsuit. Did you see anybody watching us?"

"The guy sitting just inside the door."

"Beefy guy? Big gut?"

"Yeah."

Pip sighed. "Just the bouncer. We'll have to look harder."

"Why don't we just take it easy until the auction?"

"I'm bored."

"You're bored?"

He shrugged. "I've got a low threshold, what can I say."

"I've got another couple racks of Clipper Ship," I said.

"No, you don't."

"Sure, I do."

"The ones you had stashed under your bunk?" he asked. "When was the last time you saw them?"

"Couple of days."

"Those are empty."

"You took them?"

"I think of it more as 'trading my empties for full ones.' Why? Were you going to drink them?"

"No, but that's not the point."

He laughed and clapped me on the shoulder. "I'll replace them."

"With what?"

"With more Clipper Ship. What else?" He shrugged.

"I thought you were out."

"Don't be ridiculous. You're the one who's out," he said. "I still have a pallet-load in the hold."

"You have a pallet of it? Why didn't you say something?"

"I did. Back on Port Newmar but you forgot. You made such a nice, considerate gesture by bringing a trunk full of it for me. Who am I to argue with such generosity?"

I didn't know if I should laugh or slug him.

"So? Wanna beer?" He headed back toward the ship. "I need to think about this a little more, and a decent beer would help wash away the foul taste."

"You are crazy, you know," I said to his back.

"Maybe, but get used to it."

I jogged a couple of steps to catch up with him. "Get used to it?"

"Yep. I may be crazy but as long as you're employed by Phoenix Freight, I'm your boss." He grinned.

I laughed and then slugged him in the arm.

Chapter Twenty-two
Breakall Orbital: 2374, August 2

Pip gave Roland a couple of days' liberty so we had the ship to ourselves. I was a little worried that Pip might be considering a boarding raid on the *Chernyakova*, but he settled into the galley with a kilogram of bacon, several large potatoes, a couple of onions, and a dozen eggs.

I sat at the table and watched him peel the potatoes. "What are you doing? Still working on Frank's Finest?"

"Yeah. Cooking helps me think."

I chuckled to myself. "At least it covers the burning smell."

He glanced at me. "That the best you can do?"

"On one cup of coffee? Yes."

"Drink up, the day is young even if you're not anymore."

"And you complain about me?"

He shrugged and grinned. "I'm trying to figure out why they parked the ship off station."

"Keep people from breaking in?" I asked.

His paring knife paused for a moment before he shook his head. "That's possible, but it seems like overkill. With the ship in a parking orbit, they need at least a skeleton crew aboard. Docked, they only need a fire watch caretaker and an occasional visit from an engineer to make sure the scrubbers are working. Everything else is shore power."

"Unless it's not manned."

He glanced at me again. "It's manned."

"You sound sure."

"I am."

"Why?"

"If it wasn't manned, it would have been stolen by now. It's too valuable to be sitting out there by itself."

"What makes it so valuable?"

"I'll tell you when we get it. Hell, I'll show you when we get it."

"If we get it."

"We'll get it."

"How can you be so sure?"

"Because the auction failed twice."

"I don't see the connection."

"You will," he said. He paused in his peeling and looked at me. "I need to play this close for now, Ish. I could be wrong and I'm chasing lightning. If I'm right, that ship is worth way more than a billion credits."

"What if it's not?" I asked.

"Not what? Worth more than a billion credits?"

"No. What if it's not parked in orbit somewhere."

"Wouldn't somebody have noticed?"

"Depends on who was looking," I said. "Wanna make a bet?"

He finished peeling his potatoes and went to work on the onions. "What kinda bet?"

"Let's go up and run some short-range scanner tests."

"Tests?"

"Yeah, we're not supposed to fire up scanners this close to the station, but low-power maintenance testing is allowed with station approval."

"Can we get approval?"

"You're the owner of record, aren't you?"

"Yes."

I opened my tablet and logged into the ShipNet. A few screens brought me to the maintenance menus. I filled out a few fields and held it out for Pip. "Thumb this."

He leaned over to peer at it. "I didn't realize Roland gave you full access."

"He didn't. I know how you think. When he gave me the guest password, I guessed the system one."

Pip nodded. "Interesting." He pressed his thumb to the pad and the maintenance request went to the orbitals maintenance department. "Now what?" he asked.

"Now we wait."

"How long?"

"How long will it take you to peel those onions?"

"Not long."

"Well, get on it." I grinned as my tablet bipped. "Or wait, because here's the permission."

Pip followed me up to the bridge and I sat at the navigation console. It took me a little bit to find the right interface and set the short-range scanners to their low-power test levels. I pinged once and checked the results on the display.

"That's it?" Pip asked.

"Not quite." As might be expected, the area right around the orbital was pretty busy. Every ship, container, and floating barge showed up as a glowing band. I put a twenty-kilometer ring around our position and another at thirty. "If it's out there, it'll be in that ring."

"There," Pip said, pointing at a blob in the right region.

I added the transponder codes and shook my head. "That's a freighter inbound with tugs."

"There are no other signals."

"It's not out there," I said.

"Why would she have lied?"

"Maybe she didn't. Maybe her boss told her that and she thinks it's true."

The sound of the lock opening vibrated through the deck plates moments before the bellow echoed up the ladder. "What the hell is going on here?"

"I thought you were off for a couple of days," Pip yelled back.

"Station communications sent me a confirmation of system testing," he said as he stamped up the ladder, glaring at me and then at Pip. "Testing I didn't authorize."

"I authorized it," Pip said.

"I'm getting more than a bit tired of your little games. I know it pains you, but you are not the captain," Roland said. "I am."

"It's true. I carry the secret shame deep in my heart," Pip said, placing the back of his hand against his forehead and striking a dramatic pose. "I shall never be the captain of my own ship. What ever shall I do?" He shrugged and looked at Roland. "In the meantime, I own this bucket of bolts and my owner card trumps your captain card."

"Your father pays my salary. Not you."

"Then take it up with my father. I still hold the title on this ship and as long as I do, we'll play my little games."

"Or what? You'll fire me?"

"I can't fire you," Pip said.

He folded his arms across his chest and nodded. His smirk made *me* want to slap it off him. "About time you realized that," he said.

"But I can beach you," Pip said.

"What?"

"But I *can* beach you," Pip said again.

"You can't do that, who'll fly the ship?"

"Well, Captain Wang is rated up to five hundred metric kilotons and he has experience on fast packets."

"I don't have the engineering endorsement for this power plant," I said.

Pip nodded. "True, but we need an engineer for the *Chernyakova* anyway so ..." He shrugged. "It's all about the same. We're not going anywhere for a while. I could probably have one here by the time I need him."

"Or her," I said.

"Or her."

Pip shook his head. "Look, Roland. We're family, however distantly related. You've had a stick up your butt about this berth since you took it last stanyer. What's your issue?"

"Would you like the room?" I asked, rising from the console. "I can get some coffee or something."

Roland glared at me. "You accessed a ship's system without authorization. You're a captain. You know better. I could have you arrested and thrown off this ship."

"Actually, the owner authorized me to access that system and supervised me while I did it. The execution of the test protocol fell entirely within the legal parameters as outlined by CPJCT guidelines for maintenance of a ship while docked." I shrugged. "I'll still give you some space if you'd rather not have any witnesses."

"Witnesses?" Roland said, spit flying from his lower lip.

"I never liked being dressed down in front of witnesses," I said. "It can be embarrassing and—frankly—it's bad form."

"If you wouldn't mind, Ishmael? I would like to have some words with the captain here."

I nodded and clattered down off the bridge. I knew where the coffee pot was and Pip could make a decent cup.

I'll give Pip his due. He never raised his voice. I heard only a few low-pitched statements from him, even when Marx yelled back at him. I stood there in the galley, leaning against the counter and sipping coffee, and realized that I sympathized with Marx. It had to be hard sailing with the owner aboard, particularly if the owner was as eccentric as Pip. Still, the captain's word is law only when the ship is underway; we'd been docked for more than a day.

"I don't have to put up with this!" echoed through the ship.

Pip said something I couldn't hear.

"Your father will hear about this. Mark my words."

Pip said something else I couldn't hear.

After that all I heard was boots stamping down the ladder, followed by some thrashing about in the captain's cabin over my head.

Pip strolled into the galley. "That went well."

Something crashed onto the deck above us.

"Captain Marx doesn't sound happy," I said.

Pip poured himself a cup of coffee and shrugged. "You know how it is. Sometimes when your world view becomes too skewed from reality, it's difficult to realign what you think you know with what is real."

"True. Been on the wrong end of that a couple times myself." I took a sip.

Pip winced. "Yeah. Me, too. You hate to see people going through it, but sometimes it's the only way."

Footsteps stamped along the passage above and down the ladder. Marx stuck his head through the galley door. "You haven't heard the last of this," he said. He showed admirable restraint in not screaming, and he hardly foamed at the mouth at all.

Pip said, "Safe voyage, Captain. Please pass my regards to Aunt Emily when you see her." He pulled out his tablet and started flipping through screens as Marx growled and stomped off the ship, presumably with his grav-trunk in tow. Pip stood poised with his finger over a button on his tablet and his head cocked to the side a few degrees.

The lock whined open, stopped, and then whined again as it closed.

Pip pressed the button. "Good-bye, Roland," he said.

"Erased him?" I asked.

"Oh, good heavens, no. Just deactivated his keys and locked his access out."

"You think he'd try to come back aboard?"

"Why take chances?" he asked.

"I can't fly this ship, you know."

"You can if we get an engineer."

"You say that like all you have to do is go out onto the dock and pick one that's passing by."

He laughed and dug back into his tablet. "Don't be silly. Everybody out there already has a berth. Well, except for Roland. He'll be on the next flight to Dunsany Roads, unless I miss my guess." He shrugged. "Besides, I need somebody who's qualified on this power plant, not some random engineer walking by."

"This isn't a Confederated port. It's not a place where engineers just hang about waiting for work."

"Maybe," he said, still rummaging through screens and filling out forms. He pressed a final button with a flourish of his index finger. "There. I should have a new engineer this afternoon, but even if it takes a week? We're not going anywhere until after the auction." He looked at me. "Which reminds me. If it's not out there?"

"It's got to be docked someplace."

"Someplace they don't want people to find it," he said.

"Where can you hide a bulk freighter?"

He grinned. "Feel like taking a walk?"

I tipped up my mug and emptied it. "I could stretch my legs a bit."

He holstered his tablet and took a couple of swigs from his mug before pouring it out and rinsing the cup. "Let's go."

I followed him across the docks and into the lift. He punched a button and we went up one deck. We stepped off into the wide promenade and he headed around to port.

"Where are you going?" I asked.

"Where would you hide a bulk freighter?" he asked back, echoing my earlier question.

"I don't know. They're kinda large and hard to stick in your pocket."

"Don't be a smart ass." We crossed the promenade to the wide glassed-in wall.

I had to admit the view was spectacular. With few exceptions, each docking ring held a large ship. Some were tankers. I spotted a couple of Barbells and a whole raft of mixed freight ships. The smaller vessels, like Pip's fast packet and the tractors, all docked on the other side of the station. As we walked by, a pair of tugs slipped an older Manchester-built hull into the ring practically at our feet. We could see right into the bridge as it nuzzled up to the orbital and the rings clamped on with a clunk.

The view held my attention but Pip didn't slow down. I had to take a couple of quick steps to catch up with him. "Where are you going?"

"To find the *Chernyakova*," he said.

"How do you expect to find it up here?"

He stopped and peered through the armorglass. He had to shade his eyes to see out through his own reflection. "What's that look like to you?" he asked, not looking away from the glass.

I stepped up beside him and looked out. "It's hard to tell. Looks like the docking light's burned out."

"You see any other docking light that's out?"

I looked to port and starboard and saw ships limned in that kind of unreal sharpness that happens in a vacuum. "No."

"And this ship is a Barbell," he said, pulling back from the glass.

I leaned over and shaded my eyes to get a better look. "It's a Barbell but I can't see the name plate from this angle. What makes you think it's the *Chernyakova*? I bet hundreds of people walk by this ship every day." I looked around at all the people passing us. "Who'd try to hide it here? It's right there for anybody to see."

"Where would *you* hide a freighter?" Pip asked. "*I'd* hide it in plain sight."

Chapter Twenty-three
Breakall Orbital: 2374, August 2

We got back to the docks and walked past dock eight-two without stopping.

"There's nothing listed on the telltale," Pip said. "But the port is dark."

"Anybody walking by down here might not even notice there's a ship docked there."

Pip nodded and chewed the inside of his cheek, his eyes on the decking in front of his feet. "Why there? Why not the maintenance dock? Better security. Closed off from the public."

"Cheap?" I asked.

He glanced at me. "What's cheap?"

"Maintenance dock fees are expensive. No station has more than a few, they're always in demand, and they charge through the nose for them."

"What do they care? They're not going to pay it."

"Limited resource. They want to make as much from it as they can. I bet they had her docked there for a while but when they started having trouble with the auctions, they moved her to the cheapest dock on the orbital so they could collect more fees on the expensive ones."

He nodded. "Makes sense."

"Why are they hiding it at all?" I asked. "You'd think they'd want to draw as much attention to it as possible to unload it."

Pip shot me a glance that I couldn't interpret. "Maybe they got too much attention. Or the wrong kind."

"Wrong kind? Like people wanting to see the deck stains?" The thought made me slightly sick to my stomach.

He shrugged. "Maybe. People are weird that way. Tragedy

draws a crowd."

I'd seen plenty of evidence of that myself, so I just shrugged and looked back over my shoulder. "So, we know where it is. What now?"

"Now we need to get aboard and take a look around."

"I'm pretty sure we can't just walk up and key the lock open."

Pip grinned at me. "We can't, no. Gimme a minute."

I followed him to the lock at dock eight-four, where he rang the call bell.

The lock hinged up and a rating came out. "Yes, sars? Can I help you?"

"We'd like to see Mr. Claymath," Pip said.

"Claymath, sar?"

"Yes, Cargo Chief Fredrick Claymath?"

"Our cargo chief's a woman, sar."

"Isn't this the *Hecuba* out of Greenfields?" Pip asked.

"No, sar. *Elwood Dowd* out of Dree."

Pip glanced up at the dock number above the lock and down at his tablet. "Oh, I'm sorry. I've the wrong dock. This is eight-four?"

"Yes, sar."

"I'm sorry, Mr. ...?" He squinted at the rating's chest. "Marvel?"

"No, sar, Martel. Arnold Martel."

"Thank you, Mr. Martel. Sorry to have bothered you."

"No problem, sar." He shook his head and went back aboard, closing the lock behind him.

"What was that about?" I asked.

"You'll see. Let's get out of the traffic." He led us to the station side of the dock and pulled out his tablet. He punched in a few characters, swiped a couple of screens aside, and thumbed the tab. He set off on a stroll back along the curved wall.

"What are we doing?" I asked.

"Waiting and trying not to look too conspicuous." He glanced up at the security camera straight over our heads. "Shouldn't be too long now."

We'd almost made it back to the dock where the *Chernyakova* lay hidden when a kid wearing some kind of red and blue uniform pulled up to the lock on an electric cart. He looked at the empty telltale and then up at the dock number and down at something on his tablet. He shrugged and pressed the call button.

Nothing happened for several ticks. The kid got one foot into the cart just as the lock swung open. A burly guy wearing a generic shipsuit stepped out of the lock, looking left and right before crossing to the kid.

After much gesturing and shrugging, the guy picked up a couple of bags from the back of the cart, the kid picked up a couple more, and they both disappeared into the ship.

"Perfect," Pip said and crossed the walkway toward the cart.

The kid came out and the lock closed behind him.

"Hey, kid," Pip called. "Did Arnie like his surprise?"

The kid looked up and saw Pip walking toward him. "Well, they liked the free lunch fine, but neither of them was named Arnie Martel."

Pip stopped in his tracks and looked up and down the dock. "Really? I coulda sworn Arnie Martel was on the *Elwood Dowd* at dock eighty-two."

The kid grinned. "Looks like the joke's on you, mister. That's dock eight-two, but the ship's the *Crankachova* or something. The *Dowd's* on dock eight-four."

"*Chernyakova*?" Pip asked.

He shrugged. "Something like that."

"You sure?" Pip asked.

"It's painted on the bulkhead just inside the lock. Keep walking that way and you'll find your buddy at dock eight-four."

"Wait! What about the meals?"

The kid shrugged. "I just deliver where I'm told to. Ticket says dock eight-two. I deliver to dock eight-two. They signed for dock eight-two." He shrugged again and laughed. "Ring the bell. Maybe they'll share. Those two guys will be all week eating that order." He laughed, spun the wheel on his cart, and sped back up the dock.

Pip grinned at me and headed down the dock in the kid's wake. "Perfect."

I looked over my shoulder at the lock. "Perfect?"

"We know where the ship is and about how many people are in the caretaker team. We know that at least one of them is muscle, so they're expecting trouble, and we know how to get aboard. That's as much as I could have hoped for."

We walked along and I chewed on the puzzle for a bit before asking, "How do we get aboard?"

"Join the caretakers."

"Oh, they're going to just let us sign up and give us the secret assignment because we ask?"

"Oh, please. Give me more credit than that."

"So how do we do it?"

"Easy. We just get uniforms, show up a couple stans early, claim we screwed up, and offer to leave."

"How's that going to work?"

He gave me that grin. "Would you want to hang around a few

extra stans on a stinking ship when somebody else screwed up and could get stuck with it?"

I thought about it for a few heartbeats. "No, but how do we get uniforms and what do we do when the real crew shows up?"

Pip held up his tablet. He had a picture of the guard carrying the food sacks into the ship. "That's a stock shipsuit and the shoulder flash probably matches one of the caretaker companies on station. We find the logo, take it to the chandlery, get a couple flashes made up and buy a couple of matching suits. They'd probably sew it on for us."

"Why would they do that?"

"Are you kidding? Those guys have stars in their eyes."

I stared at him, trying to figure out what weird mythological reference he was trying to make.

He reached out and flicked a finger on my collar. "Stars. In their eyes. A captain asks them to make shoulder flashes and sew them on a shipsuit. Would *you* say no? To a captain?"

The chandlery clerk proved to be just as helpful as Pip thought he'd be.

"You want just the logo on the shoulder flash, captain?" he asked.

"What else?"

"We have the full mockup already. Minotaur Monitoring gets all their uniforms here. We can even put the names on for you."

Pip stepped forward. "Excellent. Minotaur is sending over two guys named Benjamin and Maxwell. Can you add them?"

"Of course. It'll take just a few moments." He gathered the suits and slipped into the back.

"Benjamin and Maxwell?"

Pip shrugged, a bland expression on his face. "He'd approve."

"How will we know when to show up? You planning on hanging around outside the lock and timing them?"

He tsked and shook his head. "Civilian contractor. I'd bet they change at 1600."

"Why 1600?"

"Because it's exactly eight stans between 0800 and midnight. Civilians don't stand watch. They have shifts." He glanced at the chrono on the wall behind the counter. "We'll know shortly."

The clerk came out with the two shipsuits draped over his arm. "There we are. If you'd just thumb this?" He held out the tab and I pressed a thumb down.

Pip gathered the shipsuits and we strolled out of the chandlery.

"If they get curious, they're going to find it was me who bought the suits," I said as we stepped into the flow of traffic.

"If they get curious enough to investigate, they might." He shrugged. "But you're not actually on station, are you?"

"Where am I?"

"Last I saw, your face was plastered all over Diurnia Orbital. There was this girl in a pink sweater, if I remember."

"Don't tell me you did that."

He shook his head. "Honestly, I didn't think of it. I'm just improvising as we go. We didn't file a passenger manifest. You came off as crew, but you're not listed on my roster. As far as anybody is concerned, you're probably hiding out on Diurnia."

"But I just left a thumb print at the chandlery."

"Exactly. It's probably faked. What captain shops at the chandlery himself?"

"How do you fake a thumbprint?"

He smiled at me. "That's the question, isn't it?"

"How?" I asked.

"That's just it. You can't. You need the thumb." He shook his head. "We'll talk about this later. Right now, we need to take a stroll on the dock."

I followed him up and out onto the dock. I kept flexing my thumbs and hoping nobody wanted to steal them. I'd grown attached to them.

Pip's timing couldn't have been better. We made the turn around the station just as two guys in nondescript shipsuits pressed the call button on the *Chernyakova's* lock. The lock levered open and two guys came out—the big guy we'd seen before and a scrawny one who might have been a technician. After knowing Stacey Arellone's facility with blades, I wasn't going to bet that he wasn't at least as sharp.

The scrawny guy signed off on the tablet he carried and handed it to one of the new guys. We kept walking and didn't look in their direction as we passed them.

"Sloppy," Pip said. "Very sloppy."

Behind us I heard the whine of a lock closing. "What's sloppy?"

"Passing off in public," he said. "Anybody just walking past could see their procedure."

I glanced back and saw the two guards strolling back toward the lift. "Yeah. Sloppy," I said. "So now we wait?"

"Now we wait. Feel like a beer?"

"What now?"

He shrugged. "We've about six stans to kill. What else would we do?"

"Look for an engineer?"

"We could. Feel like a beer?"

I looked at him, trying to figure out what he was up to.

"Do they give you the stick when they give you the stars?" he asked.

"The stick?"

"Yeah, the one up your butt." He grinned. "Come on. Let's go interview an engineer."

He led the way to the lift and we went down to the oh-two deck.

"We're going for a beer?" I asked.

"We could," Pip said. "I thought you wanted to interview engineers."

I shook my head and followed him around to the local pub. Every station had one, at about the same place on the ring—plus or minus a couple of doors. On Breakall it was called "The Corner" which made it stand out in a round station with very few corners. I recognized the barkeep and he smiled at me when we slipped onto bar stools.

"Captain, good to see you again."

"Whistle Wetter for me, Brian," I said. "This is my friend, Phillip. We call him Pip because he is one. Pip, this is Brian. He's the chief cook and bottle washer here."

He stuck a ham-sized hand out for Pip to shake. "Nice to meet you, Pip. What do you like?"

"Big piles of credits and blondes with loose morals and an acrobatic bent," Pip said.

He laughed. "Fresh out and the supplier's not due until next week."

Pip eyed the chalk board behind the bar. "I'll call it a day."

Brian smiled and started shuffling glasses and pulling handles. It wasn't long before he returned with two beers. "Whistle Wetter for you, Captain, and Call It a Day for you, Pip. Enjoy."

We each took a sip while Brian watched.

Pip smacked his lips. "That's a very smooth porter. Thank you."

"I haven't seen you in here in a while, Captain. You still with DST?"

"No, I went out on my own a stanyer ago. Don't get up to this end of the sector much anymore."

"Ah. That would explain it." He looked to Pip. "And you? Just passing through?"

"Yeah. Heading to Dree as soon as I find a new engineer."

"What happened to the old one?"

"We had a difference of opinion and he quit on me."

Brian chuckled. "That'll happen."

"You don't know of anybody looking for work, do you?"

"Engineering officer?" Brian asked.

"Yeah. Fast packet out of Dunsany Roads. Small plant but long legs."

His eyes widened. "I'd say so if you're in from Dunsany. We don't get much traffic from that far out."

"We spend most of our time over that way but had a priority we couldn't pass up." Pip raised his glass and took a pull.

Brian smiled. "Know what that's like. Can't leave credits on the dock."

Pip shrugged. "We'll be here a few days. If you hear of anybody? I'm on the *Prodigal Son.*"

"You'll be here longer than that without an engineer," Brian said.

"Funny, that's what my last engineer thought when he tried to renegotiate his contract."

Brian laughed and I sipped my beer, wondering if Pip really thought he'd find an engineer at a pub.

"Hang on a second," Brian said. He walked down the length of the bar and spoke to a couple of guys with their heads down and hands waving. The two men stopped and looked up at Brian as he approached and then turned to look at us when Brian pointed. They shrugged and picked up their beers, following along as Brian returned.

"Gentlemen, Pip here is looking for an engineer. Know of any?"

I checked their collar pips; both men wore engineering chief tabs. I looked at Pip who shrugged before sticking out a hand. "Nice to meet you," he said. "Let's find a booth where we can chat, shall we?" He led them off to the corner while I stayed with Brian at the bar.

"Known him long?" he asked, nodding at Pip.

"Yeah. Couple of decades. Met him on my first ship."

"He seems nice enough."

"Oh, he has his moments but I'd trust him with my life." I glanced over to where Pip held court with the two engineers. "Either of them looking for a berth?"

Brian shook his head. "Neither of them, but both of them have engineering firsts who might be."

I shook my head. "What're the odds?"

"Here?" Brian asked. "I'm thinking of changing the name to 'The Engine Room.' Don't know what it is about engineers and beer but there's almost always somebody in here arguing about drives or lube or fuel or something. Sometimes I think they just like to argue."

"Maybe Pip shoulda been an engineer," I said.

I looked over to see Pip wave three fingers in the air in a circle over their glasses.

Brian laughed. "He knows how to make friends," he said, and went off to pull more beer.

Chapter Twenty-four
Breakall Orbital: 2374, August 2

Pip and I headed back to the ship to change into our suits around 2000. I felt a little funny impersonating a caretaker.

"Look," Pip said. "It's not illegal. These are not station personnel. We are not pretending to be CPJCT staff. We're not pretending to be anything other than civilian employees of a private company."

"Yeah, but we're doing it to gain access to an impounded vessel. The Trade Investigation Commission will cast a very jaundiced eye in our direction if we're caught."

Pip sighed. "Don't you think it's strange they're not letting bidders see the ship beforehand?"

"Given the difficulties they've had in the past, it's a bit odd."

"Don't you think that other bidders might be trying to get on board, too?"

That thought stopped me.

"Why else would they have told us the ship was in a docking orbit? Why else would it be sitting in a darkened dock?"

"I don't know," I said. "It just feels like cheating."

"All right. I'll grant you we're working to gain extra information. Are we cheating or are we doing due diligence? Don't we owe it to our stockholders to do whatever we can to make sure we know what it is we're spending their credits on?"

I frowned at him. "Seriously?"

"All right," he said with a sheepish shrug. "That was a bit far. But it is due diligence. Who knows who else has snuck on board using this same technique?"

"Maybe nobody," I said. "I still don't know why you're so bent on seeing what's there."

He glanced at the chrono. "I'll tell you when I know," he said. "We need to get over there and get this going."

Pip hiked along quickly once we'd cleared the lock. He walked right by eight-two and stopped in front of eight-four.

"What are we doing here?" I asked. "The *Chernyakova* is one back."

"Diversion," he said, and rang the buzzer.

The lock opened and a different rating came out. "Can I help you?"

"Yeah, we just came off duty and thought you should know that some delivery guy left a bunch of food at dock eight-two for Arnold Martel."

"Arnie?"

"He's one of yours isn't he?"

"Yeah."

"You might wanna let him know. It looked like a lot."

Pip nudged me with a hand. "Come on. I need a beer after that shift." He walked away, leaving me to follow.

The rating scooted back into the ship and Pip dragged me over to the side of the docks. "Wait for it."

Sure enough, Spacer First Class Arnold Martel came out of the ship, marched over to dock eight-two, and rang the bell. The conversation didn't last long before the beefy guard got into Martel's face and started saying things that made Martel shrink away and step briskly back to his ship.

"That's our cue," Pip said and headed for the caretaker standing in the lock and looking away from us.

The guard stood there watching until the lock closed on dock eight-four, by which time we stood almost next to him. He did a double take when he saw the patches on our suits.

"Long shift?" Pip asked.

"Who are you?" he asked.

Pip looked to me and then back at the beef. "Uh? Relief?"

The big guy's eyes narrowed. "What happened to Smitty and Buck?"

"How the hell should we know?" Pip asked matching him scowl for scowl. "We were just told to show up at ten o'clock and here we are. You want relief or not?"

"Ten o'clock?" The other guard came out of the ship.

"Yeah. Twenty-four hundred. That's ten o'clock? Right?" He gave me a shrug and a roll of his eyes.

"New guys?" the other guard asked.

"Yeah. Just came up from planet-side," Pip said. "Got tired of working private security in the dirt."

The two guards shared a look.

"What's the problem?" Pip asked. "You guys want relief or not?"

"Sure," the first guard said and gestured to his buddy. "Sign the log over to them and let's call it a day."

The second guard smirked and thumbed the page before handing it off to Pip.

"Anything we should know about this job?"

The first guard shook his head. "Fire watch detail. Walk the length of the ship once a stan and tag the stations. Same ole, same ole."

The second guard squinted at me. "I seen your face somewhere?"

"Not that I know of," I said. "Unless you hang out down at The Corner?"

He shook his head and looked to Pip. "It's all yours."

He and his buddy walked down the dock toward the lift. "And just for future reference, twenty-four hundred is midnight. Moron," he said.

"What?" Pip shouted.

The two guards laughed and kept going. "Enjoy your shift," the first one said.

Pip led me into the ship and slapped the lock key. "I thought they'd never leave."

I looked around the lock. I remembered the scars on the deck and the peculiar grunge on the bulkheads. The smell brought back memories I really didn't want to recover.

"Now, let's see what they're hiding," Pip said and walked down the passageway into the ship. He stopped at the first turn and looked back at me. "You coming?"

I swallowed hard and followed him.

He made straight for the bridge but stopped at the data closet under the ladder and swung the doors open. He pulled a hand light out of his pocket and shined it around inside. "Well, the grime looks undisturbed," he said. "That's good."

"What are you looking for?" I asked for what felt like the hundredth time.

He closed the closet doors and pushed the light back into his pocket. "Let's see if it's here," he said and jogged up the ladder to the bridge.

With the orbital right outside the armorglass, the bridge was plenty bright even without the docking light. He crossed to the astrogation station and pointed to the seat. "Do me a favor and bring up the chart catalog?"

I sat and fired up the terminal. It took a couple of ticks for it to warm up. "I didn't know you were on a Barbell," I said.

"First time."

"You knew where the bridge was."

He chuckled. "Think of every ship you were ever on. Where was the bridge?"

"Yeah, but how'd you know where to go?"

"Seriously? It's always the first ladder up from the bow. Always."

The screen finally warmed up and I looked up at Pip. "All right. What do you want to look at?"

"Chart catalog?"

"I can show you the list of astrometric data, but there's nothing like a chart catalog. What do you want to see?"

Pip steepled his hands in front of his face and blew between his palms. "All right. I want to plot a path through the Deep Dark from here to Greenfields. How would you do that?"

I pulled up the route planner. "These circles are how far we can jump. I'd just link a line of circles from here to Greenfields."

I could see Pip's frown in the darkness. "Do it."

I shrugged and started laying jump rings down the length of the system.

"What's that?" He pointed at a flashing icon.

"Looks about where Odin's Outpost is. It's halfway between here and Welliver, but it's in the wrong direction."

"Anything look odd on this display?"

I shook my head. "Standard astrogation unit. I've used one like it for stanyers."

"Can you bring up Dunsany Roads?"

"Sure." I did, and looked up at him.

"What's that? And that?" he asked, pointing to two more of the little flashing icons.

"I don't know. Looks like the same icon as Odin's Outpost."

Pip stood silent for so long I looked up at him again. "Perfect," he said. "We're done here. You can shut it down."

I killed power to the console and stood up to find Pip looking around the bridge. He pointed to consoles in turn. "Navigation, Engineering, Astrogation, Systems and Communications. What's that one?"

"Probably spare. Most of the larger ships have at least one spare console in case one fails while under way. The *Lois* had two, if I remember."

He stared at it for a moment and then grunted. "Let's see if they left any of that food."

I followed Pip down the ladder and led him to the galley. All we found were empty wrappers and a rancid pot of coffee.

"I'm not drinking this," I said.

The tablet he'd gotten from the guard bipped in his hand. "Just as well. Time for rounds."

It wasn't too much different from the old VSI watch on the *Lois*. Follow the path. Trigger each test and find the next. Except these were simple manual toggles to prove we'd been there. The entire set took about a quarter of a stan and left us back at the lock.

"It didn't look too bad," Pip said. "A few panels missing. Some of the rubber deck covering is worn and needs replacing."

"No mattresses in the berthing areas. No stores in the lockers."

"I wouldn't trust any stores left here this long anyway," Pip said. "We'd have to completely refit for crew."

"Next to no spares. Tanks probably need purging."

"We need an engineer," Pip said.

"Agreed." I checked the chrono. "Well, we've got a stan before the relief shows up. What do you want to do?"

Pip shrugged. "I've seen what I came to see."

I spun the watch stander's seat around and patted it. "Good. Then have a seat. You've got a lot of explaining to do."

"Explaining?"

"You said you'd tell me what you were looking for when you found it. Clearly you found it. Give."

He started to answer but the call buzzer sounded, cutting off anything he might have been about to say. I checked the port and felt the breath go out of me.

"Who is it?" Pip asked.

"It's been a while, but it looks like Field Agent James Waters and a couple of his friends. Along with some suits and the two guys we relieved of watch."

"That's embarrassing," Pip said.

Waters pressed the call button again, giving it a little extra poke at the end.

I slapped the lock key and watched it lever up. Before it got all the way up, Pip elbowed me aside.

"Good evening, gentlemen. Can we help you?"

"That's them," the first guard said.

One of the suits gave him a nasty look and he stepped back.

Agent Waters leaned in to look at the name stenciled on Pip's chest. "Mr. Maxwell and ..." he looked at me. He looked me straight in the eye and winked. "And Mr. Benjamin." He pointed to the suits. "These two representatives from Minotaur Monitoring tell me you are not, in fact, in their employ. Any comment?"

"Yes," Pip said. "Several."

One of the suits pushed forward and thrust his chin out. "I demand you arrest these two imposters."

"On what grounds?" Pip asked.

"Impersonating an officer, trespass, tampering with evidence. I can probably think of a couple more."

"Unsafe operation of a vessel while in station?" Pip suggested. "Unsanitary working conditions? Are you aware of the conditions these men work in, sir?"

"What? What are you saying?" Bluster got the better of him and his communication degenerated into unintelligible mutterings.

Agent Waters looked to Pip. "How do you explain your presence on this secured vessel?"

Pip showed the tablet to Waters and nodded at the two guards in the back. "They signed us in. Here's his thumbprint. Damn sloppy work. Is this how you keep a valuable asset secured, sir? Just let anybody walk up and take over?" This last was delivered to the blustering suit. "Your security penetration test failed, sir, in a most spectacular fashion. I suggest you tighten up your procedures before the auction next week. Who knows who else might get aboard or what they'll do."

"Anything else?" Agent Waters asked.

"No, I'll file my full report with their CEO in the morning."

Agent Waters growled at the suit. "I'll just pretend this was a friendly walk on the dock," he said. "Filing false charges is a serious business." He nodded to Pip. "Good evening, Mr. Maxwell. Mr. Benjamin." He gathered his agents and the black-suited lot of them strolled away.

Pip crossed to the suit and thrust the tablet into his hands. "You'll want this," he said and stalked off.

I walked up to the suit and lowered my voice. "You'll probably want to ream them out inside the ship. Witnesses ..." I cast my gaze around the small crowd that had gathered to watch the show. I gave him a little shrug and followed Pip.

I fell into step with him as he passed the lift on the way back to the ship. "You're going to have to explain this all to me when we get back to the ship," I said.

He chuckled. "Yeah. About that," he said. "I haven't been exactly truthful with you."

"Really? I'm shocked. Shocked. And by shocked I mean, are you totally out of your mind?"

"Not totally. No." He nodded toward the *Prodigal Son's* dock.

A black-suited figure lounged against the bulkhead and straightened as we came into view.

"Jim. Good to see you again."

"Pip." He said and smiled at me. "Captain Wang. How did you get mixed up with this idiot?"

Pip laughed. "It's a long story. Wanna beer? I've got some Clipper Ship in the hold."

He looked at the chronometer on the bulkhead and nodded. "You brought beer from Port Newmar?"

"You going to arrest me for promoting trade?" Pip asked.

"I'll need to examine the evidence first," he said.

Pip laughed and keyed the lock.

Knowing Pip, Agent Waters would find nothing but empty bottles.

Chapter Twenty-five
Breakall Orbital: 2374, August 3

Watchstanding had gotten me used to being up at all hours, but even watchstanders got to sleep sometime. It was well past 0100 before the lock closed behind Agent Waters and I could corner Pip.

I plopped myself down on the sofa in what I'd come to think of as the living room and glared across the empty bottles on the table. "Give."

"Give what?" he asked.

"What did you find on the *Chernyakova*?"

"What makes you think I found anything?"

"You did. I know you. If you hadn't found it, we'd still be back there looking."

He shrugged and picked up one of the bottles in front of him, shaking it side to side and holding it up to the light before draining what little was in it into his mouth. "You don't want to know about Agent Waters?"

"Jim? No, I think I've got that already. I'm just trying to figure out what I've bought into with this little farce of a partnership."

"Really?" His eyebrows shot up and he looked almost eager. "What do you think?" He said it in a "tell me a story" tone.

I sighed and held up a finger. "You're a TIC agent." I added another finger. "You're on assignment." I added a third finger. "Waters knows what that assignment is." I added the last finger on my hand. "It's something to do with the *Chernyakova*. Those flashing icons are significant because they represent stations beyond CPJCT—and by extension, TIC—jurisdiction."

Pip pursed his lips and nodded. "Pretty good. What makes you think it's a farce?"

"I'm window-dressing. You needed somebody in command of

the ship who has no link to TIC or the CPJCT, for some reason. Logically, it has something to do with those stations and protecting your undercover status."

"True, except for the window-dressing part, but substantially correct."

"Then what am I if not the window-dressing?"

"You're motive," he said, his words so quiet I almost didn't hear them over the blowers.

"Motive?"

He nodded. "The name David Patterson ring any bells?"

"It does, but I can't think of why."

"How about Percival Herring?"

I felt my heart rate spike and I had to bite my tongue.

"He's your reason for going where we're going," Pip said. "I'm just a trader looking to open up some new—highly lucrative—markets."

"And you didn't think you could be upfront with me because why?"

"Orders. Everything is need-to-know." He shrugged. "I never lied to you. Never told you anything that wasn't the exact truth." He offered a smile in apology. "It just wasn't the whole truth."

"So this partnership?"

"That's real. I hope we make a shipload or four of credits. We're investing a quarter billion and I suspect we'll make a few billion in return. Enough to set up a whole fleet."

"Your economic model?"

"Real. I suspect I'll be able to collect a lot of data."

"Your father's involvement?"

Pip picked up another bottle and shook it. "I'm hoping I'll hear from him about the deal soon and he'll be in favor. Failing that, I'll have a lot of explaining to do."

"Is he involved in TIC?"

"No."

"But he knows you are."

"Your words, not mine." He gave me one of his looks. "It's largely irrelevant to the discussion and between my father and me."

I shrugged. "All right. So, he knows."

Pip grinned and leaned forward in his chair, elbows on his knees. "Look. I don't ever want to actually lie to you, but our security depends on having a complete, unassailable story. I need to get to where we're going. You've got a reason to take me there. I really don't want to color your story with mine because if you don't tell a believable story, neither of us gets out alive."

"You're asking me to risk my life for your mission?" I couldn't believe he'd do that. "Without even telling me? I thought you were my friend."

He shook his head. "I'm asking you to risk your life to find the man who killed Greta and bring him to justice." He shrugged. "I'm telling you now. There's still time for you to back out. You might remember we have a clause built into our corporate charter and the partnership agreement. You can walk away any time."

I stared at him for several long moments. I couldn't sort out the hurricane of thoughts and emotions inside my head. "Tell me," I said.

He shook his head in refusal. "I can't tell you everything. Ask me a question. If I can answer it, I will. Honestly. If I can't, I'll tell you I can't."

"Why the *Chernyakova*?"

"She has the charts we need to find the Darkside, and she's a known entity there."

"What is the Darkside?"

"It's where you might have ended up if not for my aunt putting you on the *Lois*. It's where people who fall through the cracks end up."

"What's the TIC interest?"

"I can't tell you."

I paused to gather my thoughts. "What did you mean by known entity?"

"The *Chernyakova* was one of the Darkside's vessels. There might be hundreds of them out there, but this is the first one that we've been able to acquire without tipping our hand."

"The ship has been docked here for months under TIC jurisdiction. Why did we sneak in?"

"They didn't know what to look for."

"How did you know?"

"I can't tell you."

"How did you know the *Chernyakova* was one of their vessels?"

He grinned. "I didn't. Just strongly suspected. That's why I wanted to get aboard."

"Can you tell me why you suspected?"

"They're a ghost. None of their logs match station records. They might have been coming from Greenfields, but not by the route that their logs indicated. They got underway with one cargo and docked with another. That's not supposed to be possible."

"But they did it," I said.

"Apparently."

"So, *Chernyakova* is going to become a ghost again?"

"Not entirely. You're a known entity because of Patterson. You might be persuaded to carry a can or two, but you'll want to keep your reputation unsullied. Most of the cargo will be legit. Once you find Patterson and deal with him, we'll be able to re-evaluate the situation. Probably we'll come in from the cold. At least you'll be able to. By then I'll have established enough cover to stay behind if I need to."

"What about our board of directors?"

"You're forgetting who they are."

"Margaret Newmar?"

He chuckled. "She was the one who asked you how assassins got paid, wasn't she?"

I shook my head, trying to clear the buzzing sound out of my ears. "Do they all know about this?"

"None of them know. They'd all be shocked if they did."

"Because of the mission?"

"No, because it would be a gross violation of operational security to bring them into the loop. They all know that."

"Even Margaret Newmar?"

Pip pursed his lips and sighed. "Even Margaret Newmar." He shook his head. "Don't ask. I can't tell you."

"What are you going to do with the *Prodigal Son*?"

"I'll find us an engineer and we'll fly it to Dree for the refit. Father will have to send a new captain out. Or maybe he'll toss Roland a bone and let him have it back."

"That's why you beached him," I said. "You needed him out of the way."

Pip shrugged. "He didn't like flying the CEO's spoiled brat around. He's old school and half a generation ahead of me and the cousins. I just was a little more bratty than normal. It won't reflect on his career in the long run, and Father will find him a new berth with the family even if he doesn't get the *Son*. It's what he does."

"So you picked a fight with him to force him out."

"More or less."

"Will your father really back this plan of ours?"

Pip chuckled. "Of all the things up in the air right now, that's probably the biggest. He knew I was going to hire you. The only significant difference is being a partner in the deal. He'll back it or I'll apologize." He chewed his lower lip for a moment. "I wish we'd hear from him. I'm beginning to wonder what's going on."

"Did TIC have anything to do with scotching the last two auctions?"

"No. They didn't realize the significance on the first one. When the second one failed, it got their attention."

"Did they get the rules changed?"

"I don't know. Maybe."

"Why are you telling me all this? Isn't it a violation of operational security?"

He nodded. "Probably. I'm telling you because you need to know. I've played pretty loose with the truth for the last couple of weeks, but it's coming down to the crunch. If we win the bid on this ship, we're going to be getting the attention of a lot of people who don't fall into the same level of nice that you were used to on the *Lois*."

"I've run into a few already."

"In the Darkside, most of them will be like that."

"Murthering scum?" I asked.

" 'Murthering?' Is that even a word?"

"Yeah, actually. A very old one."

"Then probably. Yeah. At least some of them."

"I'm still not quite clear on why the *Chernyakova*. Surely with the resources TIC has they can use one of their own ships."

"First, there's the charts. TIC has some of them, but the *Chernyakova* must have all of them if it's traveling about the Western Annex."

"All right, but why not strip the charts out of that deathtrap and outfit a real expedition?"

"We've tried with the fragmented charts we have. Ships never came back out. This isn't a mission to be undertaken in force so they're not going to send in a battle group."

"Why not?"

"I can't tell you."

I sighed in frustration.

"There has to be something about their ships," Pip said. "Some signifier or identifier that tells them the ship is good. Might be a code hidden in the transponder. Might be a tattletale built into the communications array. TIC has never found anything but none of their ships ever came back out."

"And you think we will?"

"I'm betting my life on it."

"And mine," I said.

"And yours. And the whole crew as well, but I suspect some of them will know more than we do about what we're going into. They might well be the missing key, which is why this business of ours has to be just what it seems to be. You're looking for the guy who killed your lover and I'm looking for some fast credits. Neither of us is that concerned about the Confederated Planets Joint Committee on Trade."

"Why would they accept the ship back with a new captain and

crew? That doesn't make a lot of sense to me."

Pip shrugged. "Hunch."

"Hunch?" My voice may have cracked in surprise.

"It's the name," Pip said. "*Chernyakova.*"

"What about it?"

"Anglicized names are always subject to interpretation," Pip said. "On the surface, it's named for the daughter of some guy named Chernyakov."

"What's the significance?"

"One interpretation could be 'Daughter of the Dark.' "

"Or Daughter of the Darkside?" I asked.

He shrugged. "Possible. Somebody scared off those other bidders. I don't think it was the stained decking."

"What's keeping them from scaring us off?"

Pip grinned. "I'm betting they'll want us to win so they can get the ship back."

"I don't follow."

"Neither of the other two bidders had a reason to take the ship back home."

A little finger of ice trickled down my back. "You're not making me feel really comfortable about this."

He shrugged. "Comfort is a luxury neither of us can really afford, is it?"

"Keeping my skin intact—and not vacuum frozen—strikes me as a couple steps higher than simple comfort."

Pip laughed. "If I'm right, they don't actually want the ship."

"What do they want?"

"They want somebody to pick up where the late and largely unlamented crew left off."

"They want smugglers."

"You say smuggler. I say revenue-optimal crewmember. It's a question of perspective."

"And TIC is going to turn a blind eye to this revenue-optimal operation?"

"No, you idiot. They're sending one of their better agents on this mission to keep an eye on things and make sure they know what's happening."

I fell back against the sofa and stared at the overhead. "You," I said to the blank plate above my head.

"I need another beer. You want one?"

Chapter Twenty-six
Breakall Orbital: 2374, August 3

After a late night of skullduggery and soul-baring, I slept in. I'm not sure how I managed to sleep with everything going on. By the time I was ready for breakfast, it was time for lunch. I left my stateroom and found the galley largely as we'd left it.

"Maid's day off," I said to the coffee pot and began the process of infusing water with life.

While the coffee dripped, I took a bucket into the living room and filled it with empty bottles. There seemed to be more of them that I could account for from the previous night's gab fest, but I probably wasn't the most reliable of witnesses by the time we'd broken into the *Chernyakova*, rifled its computer systems, been kicked out by Trade Investigation, and then returned for an extended Hail and Well Met with the ranking TIC officer on Breakall.

Pip shambled into the galley as the coffee gurgled its last gasp and gave up the ghost with a sigh. I handed him a mostly clean cup and grabbed one for myself before pouring for us both. We sat on opposite sides of the galley table. I for one stared into my cup and tried to wake up as the magic molecules worked their way into my brain.

"You know coffee doesn't wake you up?" Pip said.

"Speak for yourself."

"No, it just reverses the effects of caffeine withdrawal. If you didn't drink coffee, you wouldn't need it in the morning."

"If I didn't drink coffee, I wouldn't need morning," I said.

"You're just trying to cheer me up."

I laughed, just a tiny bit. It's not that I was hung over. I'd only had a couple of beers when we got back. I just couldn't wake up.

"So, what do we do today?" I asked.

"Find an engineer?" Pip shrugged. "Gimme a few ticks to wake up and the analgesics to kick in. How much beer did I drink last night?"

I pointed to the bucket of empties with my mug.

He peered at it. "That doesn't seem like enough."

"It's the third bucket."

His eyes were wide—bloodshot, but wide. "Third bucket? Of empty bottles?"

"All right. Maybe only second."

"What did you do with the first one?"

"It's here somewhere. Why? You savin' the empties or something?"

"There's a deposit on them."

"I'm not flying back to Port Newmar for the deposit on empty beer bottles," I said.

He shrugged. "Probably not." He took a slug of coffee. "We're not going anywhere without an engineer."

"Seems like I'm always missing an engineer. Why didn't I go into engineering instead of deck?" I said into my cup.

"You could probably get your engineering endorsement," Pip said.

"I have my steward endorsement already."

"Yes, but you could fly us over to Dree."

"It'd take a week or more to get it. More if the steward endorsement was any indication."

"The auction is in three days. We'd have to arrange for tugs to haul it or at least get it checked out to see if it's spaceworthy."

"And you're still short one engineer. There's no way I can take and pass an engineering chief exam. We need somebody who knows which end the fire comes out."

"Fire comes out?" Pip asked.

"Kickers and thrusters, sure."

He smirked at me and made me laugh at myself. Again.

"Did you post the opening yesterday?" I asked.

He shook his head. "I'm waiting to hear back from Chief Michaels. He said he's got a first who's ready to move up. He's got the license. Just need to see if he's interested in moving."

"How likely is it?"

"Michaels seemed to think it was at least plausible."

I heard a bip and Pip pulled out his tablet. "Well, there's one problem we can cross off."

"Auction canceled?" I asked.

He chuckled. "Father's response. 'Family council approves joint venture. P on board.' "

"P on board?"

"Aunt P wasn't in favor of the original deal."

"She didn't want me as captain?"

"She thought you would have been wasted as simply captain after having owned your own ship." Pip shrugged. "I don't think anybody considered that you might want to buy in. I certainly didn't."

"Why?"

He looked across the table at me and laughed. "I had a hard enough time believing I could convince you to take the helm of that hell ship. That you might want to sink your own funds into it? The farthest thing from my mind."

"Really?"

"That and I didn't realize you had that kind of liquid assets to spend."

"You did know I'd get a share of the salvage claim and that I'd sold Icarus."

"Not ten percent of the salvage, and the rumors about Icarus aren't exactly bankable."

"Well, the salvage will probably be eaten up by fees and administration before it filters through DST's hands."

He shrugged. "We'll know shortly."

"Assuming we win the bid."

"You'll find out regardless as soon as it settles."

"Not that soon. It still has to be sent to DST for disbursement."

"A few days. Maybe a week. You'll probably get a deposit before we can get the ship to Dree."

"I've been thinking about that."

"Getting the ship to Dree?"

"Yeah. If we can fly it there, that's going to save a few million credits."

"True, but is it safe?"

"The hull is sound. That much is spaceworthy. I'm willing to accept the engineering report at face value for the moment. If we get an engineer in there and he finds any serious discrepancy, we can sue for misrepresentation."

"Sue who?"

"The engineering firm that filed the report for one. The auction administrators for another."

"That could take stanyers to clear up."

"But it won't."

"Why?" he asked.

"Because they'd settle quickly and quietly. Nobody wants that kind of blot on their record. I bet that auction house sells repossessed ships, brokers trades, does all kinds of business. I'd also bet that report is precisely correct. We should probably find an engineer to go through it looking for things that aren't mentioned at all. Those would be the ones we'd have a hard time suing over."

"We're back to that," Pip said.

"Yeah."

"Where do we find an engineer?"

"Feel like a beer?" I asked.

Pip lifted his head up and stared at me, his eyes still bloodshot but looking nearly open. "Isn't that my line?"

"Yeah, but I needed it."

"What are you thinking?"

"We only need to borrow an engineer, right?"

"All right. I'll play along."

"Wouldn't it be better if we had two or three arguing over what's in that report?"

Pip sat up straighter. "Why, yes. I believe it would. You can't get two engineers to agree on anything that's not backed up by four years of advanced math. Even then it's touch and go."

"So, let me ask again. Feel like a beer?"

He poured the last of his coffee down his throat and stood up. "Maybe a small one. Shall we go?"

We made it to The Corner just as the lunch rush peaked. Brian had two helpers behind the bar and four wait staff on the floor. "Maybe we need to come back when it quiets down," Pip said.

I saw a couple of khaki-clad arms waving over the heads of the crowd and waved back. "Maybe not. Isn't that your buddy Michaels waving to us?"

"I knew that beer would pay off," Pip said and led the way to the table.

We settled into a comfortable enclave of senior engineers and a couple of affable mates. The names flew around, but I wouldn't have remembered them except for their name tags.

"So, what brings you back to The Corner?" Michaels asked Pip.

"I needed some engineering advice and couldn't think of anywhere else there was good beer."

"Weren't you looking to hire an engineer?" he asked.

"Still am, but this is a different thing. My buddy Ishmael and I are looking to buy a ship, but we've got an engineering inspection report and I don't know if I trust it."

"You want an independent inspection?" one of the other engineers asked. "I know a couple good firms here on station."

"I'm a cargo master. I'm too cheap to hire another one. I wanna know what's wrong with the one I got."

The line got another round of good-natured laughter.

Michaels and three other engineers pulled out tablets. "Beam it and we'll look at it," Michaels said. "You buy the beer."

"Deal." Pip stood up and flagged down the nearest wait staff to bring a couple of pitchers and some more glasses. He then pulled out his tablet, isolated the inspection report from the rest of the documentation, and beamed it to each of the waiting engineers. By the time he'd finished, the beer had arrived and the discussion kicked in almost immediately.

"Unwin Barbell. Is it on station?" one asked.

"We're told it's in a docking orbit somewhere," Pip said.

"Are you looking for anything in particular?" Michaels asked, scrolling through the report on his screen.

"Anything missing," Pip said. "We figure what's there is probably accurate enough to stand up in court, but what's missing could be a problem."

Shortly thereafter the conversation around the table petered out as those with tablets shared with the others, everybody busy reading.

I poured a beer and sat back to gauge the response.

"Nothing on tankage," one of them said.

"No spine X-rays?" somebody said. "If there's a structural lapse, it'll be where the spine joins either the fore or aft nacelle."

"Hours on these fusactors seem awful high for the age of the ship."

"Yeah, and look at that maintenance log. Those generators are due for replacement, not just a realignment."

"Well, you can't just look at hours—" The argument took off from there.

By 1400 the lunch crowd had emptied out and the engineering staff had returned to whatever duty they had been neglecting over beers. Chief Michaels lingered, scrolling up and down in the report for a while. I'd listened to it all but didn't take in many of the details. I just listened to see whether there were any points they agreed on.

Chief Michaels turned to me. "So, Captain. You haven't said much."

"In here I'm just Ishmael, Chief. I'm only the driver on this bus."

"You're going to helm this beast that Pip here is buying?"

"We're actually buying it together," Pip said.

"Well, I figured that much." Michaels looked at my face instead of my collar. "Ishmael. You're that guy that made a mint selling your company to DST, aren't you? Ishmael Wang?"

"Yeah. That's me."

Michaels laughed. "That was a shrewd move." He raised his glass in a toast to me. "But why d'ya want to go back out? I'd have figured that deal would have set you up for life."

"It did. I can do pretty much anything I want. I want to sail." I shrugged. "Pip and I met on my first ship. We've always worked well together, so why not?"

"Good answer," Michaels said. He cast a look around the room, just a casual glance before leaning in over his beer and speaking into the nearly empty glass. "So you two are going to bid on the *Chernyakova*?"

"Was it that obvious?" Pip asked.

Michaels shrugged. "Not so much. There's lots of Barbells around. Couple even for sale if you know where to look. Seemed the logical choice with the auction coming up in a couple of days."

I nodded. "The inspection report is all they'll give us. We're just doing a bit of due diligence to do what we can to protect our shareholders."

"Smart. I wouldn't have thought of it, but I'm just an old engineer." He grinned at us.

"I didn't hear anything that might be seriously wrong other than potential for some weakness in the spine," I said.

"Barbells. That's always the risk. Really? It's not that serious; I probably wouldn't have bothered with X-rays either. The strain is negligible as long as you've got a can on there. Anybody who gets underway without one probably won't dock again in one piece." He shrugged. "I'd be more concerned with flushing the potable water. It's been sitting for a while, it's going to be stale as week-old toast and any contaminants will have had a chance to seep into the system."

"So, it would probably be safe enough to hop it over to Dree for refitting?" Pip asked.

Michaels's gaze focused somewhere in the distance for a moment or two before he nodded. "I'd think so. I'd give her a good cleanout and stock up a bit on spares, but one jump with very little strain? Sure. I'd fly it."

Pip stuck out his hand. "Thanks, Steve. That's what we needed to know."

Michaels shook and nodded. "Thanks for all the beer. Good luck with the auction."

We left him at the table and headed back to the ship. I had a lot to think about before we hit the auction floor.

Chapter Twenty-seven
Breakall Orbital: 2374, August 8

The day of the auction, we got up early and scuffed around the galley. Breakfast mess turned into a desultory affair of eggs, Pip's latest trial with Frank's Finest, and what seemed like enough bacon to feed the crew of the *Lois*.

It wasn't like I'd slept well the night before at any rate. Something about spending nearly two hundred million credits made me a bit anxious, even more anxious than when I started Icarus. Maybe it wasn't just the credits. For two days I'd been mulling over what Pip had told me. Going through with the auction meant starting down a road that might cost me everything. It also meant I might find some closure on Greta's death.

I couldn't quite come to grips with the idea that I might succeed where the entire might and influence of the Trade Investigation Commission had failed. The concept felt oddly foreign and totally logical at the same time. Pip and I would—theoretically, at least—be able to get out into the Darkside in a way that the overt TIC forces couldn't. Assuming we didn't die first. Yet, it still didn't feel quite right, quite real.

In spite of that, the longer I pondered the situation, the more attractive it felt.

That alone should have been enough to warn me.

"How much is our limit?" Pip asked over the shattered remains of breakfast.

"We've got two hundred million in escrow."

Pip nodded. "We can't use all that. We'll be short on the refit."

"There's still sixty million in our reserves."

"Yeah, but we'll need to pay taxes and fees. There'll be registration fees and then there's the cost of stores and spares."

I picked a piece of bacon that I didn't really want off the plate and nibbled it. "True, but we'll get some income from the sale of the cargo. I'll get a back-end payment for my share of the salvage claim. How much are you thinking?"

"We need that ship but anything over a hundred and eighty is going to leave us shorter than I'd like."

"You think it's going to cost that much to get her ready for space?"

"I think it's going to cost more than you imagine to get it ready for the Darkside."

"What do we do if it goes over that?" I asked. "One eighty is barely more than scrap value."

Pip shook his head. "I don't know."

"I say we bid it up to our escrow limit," I said. "Is it too late to add to it?"

Pip blinked at me across the table. "You want to bid more than that?"

"Just a bit. Maybe an extra ten million in case somebody else reaches two hundred million first, so we'll be able to get in one more bid."

"Five million," Pip said. "That's still going to leave us pretty short on the back end."

"Without the ship, we got nothing so it doesn't matter, does it?"

"Won't matter if we get the ship and can't fly it either."

"We can find other backers if it comes to that."

"Like who?"

"I don't know, but I bet Alys Giggone might. She wanted more people on the board anyway, remember?"

"True."

I glanced at the chrono. "We've got three stans before the auction starts."

"Let's do it," Pip said, a grin spreading across his face. "I'd say 'Trust Lois' but I'm not sure that applies here."

"Well the auction starts at 1200 so maybe 'Better deals in the afternoon' applies."

He laughed. "I wonder how many people are actually going to bid on this thing?"

"I'm hoping it's just you and me, but I'll bet I'm wrong."

He snorted at that. "Yeah. That's a bet I'm not taking."

It didn't take us long to get the galley cleaned up and into our khakis. We got to the auction office just after 1000 and eventually got through the line to the harried cashier.

"All funds must be deposited in escrow no later than one hour before the auction," he intoned. "Funds not currently deposited in a Confederated depository can only be added to escrow with a certified check or wire transfer. How much do you want to place in escrow?"

"We want to add to our account," Pip said.

"What's your number?"

Pip held up our bidding paddle and she keyed the four-digit number.

"Current balance is three hundred million. How much do you wish to add?"

Pip leaned forward across the counter. "Three hundred million?"

"Yes, sir. Two hundred million deposit on the first and an additional one hundred added on the fifth."

"Does it say who added those funds?"

She shook her head. "Wire transfer direct from a numbered account in Diurnia in the name of Phoenix Freight. That's you, isn't it?"

"Yes, it is."

"So, how much more you want to add?" Her gaze flickered to the line of people behind us in a silent reminder.

"Ten million," I said and slid our corporate routing numbers across the counter.

She keyed the transaction and pointed to a thumb pad on the counter.

I thumbed the pad and Pip accepted the receipt on his tablet.

"Next?" Business as usual.

We left the office, heading down the passageway to put some distance between us and those who were still negotiating.

"Who do we know with a hundred million to toss around?" I asked. "Waters?"

Pip shook his head. "He's got access to that kind of funding, but the whole point of this is to keep them out of it."

"Your father?"

"He might. If not directly, then through the family." Pip looked at me. "Numbered account from Diurnia to the company escrow account. Who even knows that? Christine Maloney?"

"Unlikely. DST has no interest in us."

"Well, somebody's going to want something from us for that much credit," Pip said. "Nobody spends that kind of dosh without expecting something in return."

"They'll have to tell us at some point, wouldn't you think?" I asked.

"Probably sooner, rather than later and I'd really like to know who's behind it."

I heard a familiar voice behind us say, "There you are. I figured I'd find you somewhere nearby."

I turned to see a bald woman in khakis smiling at us.

"Chief Stevens? I thought you were on your way to Port Newmar," I said.

"I was, but I got a message from Alys Giggone and changed my plans." She held out a hand to Pip. "You must be Phillip Carstairs."

"Oh, yes. Engineering Chief Margaret Stevens, Cargo Master Phillip Carstairs. Pip, Chief Stevens."

Pip shook her hand. "Pleased to meet you, Chief."

She laughed. "Well, I'm pleased to meet you, too, but I'm more interested in this ship we're buying."

I traded glances with Pip before answering. "The auction starts at noon," I said.

"Yes, and I gather you've found the extra funding?" she asked.

"We were just wondering where it came from," Pip said.

"I only arrived on station last night or I'd have paid you a visit," she said. "That's courtesy of your board of directors."

People had started paying us more attention than I was comfortable with. "Perhaps we could walk a bit," I said and set out along the passageway.

"Board of directors?" Pip asked.

"Alys found a few more people who wanted to be part of your venture and took the liberty of bringing them in. Phoenix Freight now has thirty-six shares and a total capitalization of three hundred and sixty million credits."

"She added ten new board members?" I asked, feeling a bit upset that she'd taken that step without even consulting us.

"Oh, no. Only four new board members. I'm one of them, by the way." She grinned.

"That's forty million, where'd the rest come from?"

"From me," she said. "I got the seat on the board and six shares."

I couldn't quite grasp what she'd said. "But why?"

"Why what?" she asked.

"Why get involved at all?"

She leaned back and laughed. "Are you kidding? I was peeved that I didn't have shares in Icarus." As she patted me on the shoulder, she lowered her voice. "That was brilliant. When I signed on with you, I had no idea that would all fall into place."

"It was luck," I said, shaking my head. "Dumb luck."

She laughed again. "Luck, schmuck. You were in the right place with the right ship to do something nobody else had done in that sector for a century." She looked up into my face. "Was it luck that Christine Maloney was on that ship?"

"Well, yeah. Actually, I think it was."

She shook her head. "I'm going with karma. Between the two of you, you did something that neither of you could have done alone. It was a breathtaking accomplishment to anybody who understands the industry."

She looked at Pip. "You've known him a long time, right?"

"Since his first day," Pip said.

"Tell me? Was he always lucky?"

Pip's eyes gleamed and he pursed his lips. "Not always, but he had at least his fair share of breaks."

"That's what I mean," she said. "A lot of what happens in the Deep Dark is skill and planning and foresight, but then there's the luck. No amount of skill will help you if luck runs against you." She pulled me around to look me square in the eye. "I know you lost somebody to that same luck. She'd be the first to agree with me. You're a lucky man, Ishmael Wang, and if half the stories I've heard about this one are true"—she nodded at Pip—"you two are about to kick karma in the ass."

"That's why you invested?" Pip asked.

"Oh, no. I invested because Alys thinks you two will make a lot of credits and I want a share."

"I don't understand," I said. "Why are you here?"

"I invested because I wanted a share, but I'm *here* because I want to go along for the ride."

"But, you can't come with us," Pip said.

She arched a brow at Pip. "Why ever not?"

"You don't know where we're going."

She chuckled and leaned over to him. "You think you're the only one who knows what *Chernyakova* means?"

His eyes looked like goggles on his face and his eyebrows all but disappeared under the fringe of his hair.

"Some of us have been around for a long, long time, my boy. You'd be surprised what I know." She shrugged. "Besides, you're going to need a good engineer to put that ship back into fighting trim. I happen to have written the book on it."

Chapter Twenty-eight
Breakall Orbital: 2374, August 8

The auction company held the event on the promenade above the docks. Pip nudged me and pointed to the docking light, which now illuminated the top surface of the *Chernyakova*. Pip, Chief Stevens, and I stood close together near the station-side bulkhead. I wasn't too keen on having people behind me under the circumstances.

"Quite the turnout," Chief Stevens said.

"It's not every day they auction off a death ship," Pip said with a grin.

As the hour approached, the crowd grew. Some were bidders, others merely spectators. Orbital security formed a perimeter around a small platform near the armorglass, and at 1200 hours a tall, thin woman in a severe black suit stepped up and faced the crowd. She must have been wired because her voice came from the speakers in the overhead.

"Ladies and gentlemen, it is now 1200 hours on August 8, 2374. The auction for lot five-five-three, the *Solar Clipper Chernyakova* and its cargo, will begin in accordance with CPJCT rules and regulations on salvage. Vessel is a one-hundred-forty-meter bulk hauler, Barbell class designed by Unwin Yards. This particular vessel was constructed by Chibba Yards of Martha's Haven in 2369. Vessel is being offered in as-is condition. Interested parties should have received a certified engineering inspection report prior to today's auction. The manifest for this vessel indicates that the cargo container holds approximately two hundred metric kilotons of cold-stabilized phosphate ester fire-resistant hydraulic fluid.

"According to the rules established for this auction, only those bidders who have placed sufficient credits in escrow and received a numbered wand may bid. Bid by raising your wand, and I will acknowledge your bid. If your wand turns red, bidding has exceeded your escrow and you will be out of the auction. Your bid includes all necessary taxes, commissions, and fees, which will be deducted from the settlement. Thank you for your attention.

"Let's begin. Bidding will start at fifty million credits. Who'll give me fifty?"

A well-padded man in a business suit near the front lifted his wand, and the auctioneer pointed a control wand at him.

"We have fifty, who'll make it sixty?"

A woman right in front of the stage raised her paddle.

"Sixty. Do I hear seventy?"

The bidding climbed slowly but Pip held the bidding wand down by his side. "Do you know any of these people?" he asked.

I shook my head. "Nobody looks familiar."

"Those two represent scrap yards. I think the woman is with Manchester and the man works for some knacker over in Martha's Haven," Chief Stevens said. "They'll drop out as soon as the bidding goes above a hundred twenty-five."

Pip gave her a long look, but she smiled back at him and gave a small shrug.

A distinguished man with white hair at his temples and a ruddy complexion, standing near us at the back, raised his paddle and said, "One fifty."

"I have one hundred fifty million in the back. Thank you, sir. Do I hear one sixty?"

No one responded for several heartbeats until somebody on the far side of the crowd raised his wand. "Thank you, sir. I have one sixty. Do I hear one seventy?"

The distinguished man raised his wand.

The auctioneer pointed to him. "I have one seventy. Can I get one eighty?"

I heard Pip inhale and exhale but he didn't raise his wand.

Somebody near the front bid. "Thank you. I have one eighty. Do I hear one ninety?"

The distinguished man raised his wand.

"Thank you. One ninety. Do I hear two hundred million?"

Pip raised the wand.

The distinguished man cast him a dirty look but raised his wand at two ten.

"I have two ten. Do I have two twenty?"

Several bidders jumped into the action then and the auctioneer moved quickly through to two ninety before the bidding tapered off.

"I have two ninety. Do I hear three hundred million?"

Nobody moved. The distinguished man held the bid at two ninety and the promenade was silent. I'd seen several wands turn red. Only a few remained white.

"I have two ninety. Do I hear three hundred million?" she repeated.

"Two ninety-five," Pip said and raised his wand.

She smiled at Pip and acknowledged his bid. "I have two ninety-five. Do I hear three hundred?"

The distinguished man sneered at Pip and held up his wand.

"Three hundred million. Thank you. Do I hear three ten?"

Pip grinned at the guy and raised his wand. "Three ten. Thank you. Do I hear three twenty?"

The man scowled at us and tucked the red wand into the side pocket of his jacket and pushed his way clear of the crowd.

"I have three ten. Do I hear three twenty?"

Several heartbeats went by.

"I have three ten. Do I hear three twenty?"

More silence. I don't know that I'd even seen so many people in one place who made so little noise.

"Three ten. Going once."

More silence.

"Three ten. Going twice."

People started turning to us. Most with smiles. Some with scowls and a few with frowns.

"Sold. Three hundred ten million credits. Bidder seven four four seven."

The crowd cheered and clapped, although I couldn't imagine why. I looked over to see Chief Stevens grinning and waving while Pip stood there with the wand in his hand and the most astonished look on his face. I leaned over to him. "What's the matter?"

"I just spent three hundred and ten million credits," he said.

I laughed.

A pair of orbital security officers appeared out of the crowd and the auctioneer stepped from between them. "Congratulations. If you'd come with us, we'll take you to the ship and arrange for the transfer of title."

We followed them to the lift and down to the dock where the auctioneer keyed the lock open and led us inside and up to the bridge.

She booted up the main console and held out a hand. "Owner's key," she said.

One of the guards pulled a small fob from his pocket and handed it over.

She plugged the key in and typed a few characters to reset the ownership data screen.

"Captain's key."

The other guard pulled out a different fob and handed it to her.

She plugged that one in and erased those contents as well.

"There you are," she said, waving a hand at the console and very carefully not looking at the stained cover on the seat. "Just add your data. You're now the proud owners of the *Chernyakova*. Thank you for doing business with Breakall Ship Auction and Sales." She shook hands all around and then sailed off the bridge. I heard the lock cycle open and closed after a few moments.

I glanced at Pip who seemed frozen in place while Chief Stevens took a turn around the bridge.

"It must have been horrific," she said. "I can't imagine what you must be going through, Captain."

Her words reminded me of the day we came aboard to begin counting the bodies. "It was," I said.

She crossed the bridge to peer into my face at close range. "And yet here you are. Why?"

I jerked a thumb at Pip. "He can be very persuasive."

She didn't look away from me but shook her head. "No. He couldn't have persuaded anybody who didn't have a damn good reason to come back to this. Why?"

I had to look away from her eyes. "I don't really know. Closure, maybe. Seeing the ship made whole again. Undoing what had been done."

"Making it right again," she said.

"Something like that," I said. "Facing my fear."

"Your fear?" she asked.

"That I might make a mistake like this and kill a whole crew like I killed—" I couldn't finish the statement.

She reached out, took my upper arm in a gentle grip, and shook me. "You no more killed that woman than you killed these people," she said, waving her free hand at the stained deck cover. "You're a better captain than that. A better person than that."

"I don't know anymore," I said.

"I do. And I've only known you a short while." She shook my arm again before releasing me.

We looked over at Pip, who hadn't moved as much as a muscle since climbing the ladder to the bridge.

"Pip? You all right?" I asked.

"I just spent three hundred and ten million credits."

Chief Stevens and I laughed.

"Yes, you did. Now you need to load up the owner's key with the company data and hire this guy as captain so he can hire me as engineer and we can shake the dust out of this ole girl." She turned to me. "Will you rename her?"

"I don't know," I said.

"No," Pip said. "She's got to be the *Chernyakova*."

Chief Stevens face took on a knowing smile and she nodded. "I suspected as much."

"One does not simply walk into murder," I said.

Two startled faces swiveled toward me.

"What did you say?" Pip asked.

I shook my head. "It was just something my mother used to say when we'd plan a trip. Never made any sense to me but it was probably from some old book."

"One does not simply walk into Mordor," Chief Stevens said.

"Really?" I asked. "I always thought it was murder. What's Mordor?"

"A heavily fortified city filled with evil creatures and horrible magic," she said. "It's from a very, very old story."

Pip chuckled. "Might be more appropriate than you know."

Chief Stevens shook her head. "No. You'll do yourself a big favor if you get that idea out of your mind and focus on the task in front of you. We have to hire a crew and get this ship back to earning her keep." She pointed to the console with a grin.

Pip shot her a strange look but took the seat and began filling out the forms to register the ship to Phoenix Freight, Inc., of Diurnia. He filed the changes and almost immediately his tablet bipped. When he pulled it out and looked, he sighed. "I should have known."

The chief and I traded glances and crossed to Pip.

He held up his tablet to show a bill for over a thousand days of docking fees. The total came to just over five million credits.

"Well, now we know what happened to the other bidders," he said.

Chapter Twenty-nine
Breakall Orbital: 2374, August 9

Chief Stevens joined us aboard the *Prodigal Son* for breakfast at 0600 while we sorted out our planning for moving the *Chernyakova* to the yard in Dree.

"We can get by with a skeleton crew," she said. "A couple of sections maybe."

"That's what I think, too," I said. "But we'll need a full set of mates."

"Maybe not," Pip said.

"You thinking of applying for a yard permit?" the chief asked.

"If we can sell this load of hydraulic fluid, it would pay off the docking fees with a little extra. Snag an empty can so we're not moving cargo, and we'd qualify for a one-hop permit from here to the yard with basically the three of us."

The thought gave me the creeps. "I'd go watch-and-watch," I said. "Leaving either engineering or the bridge without watch standers is not something I'm willing to do."

"All right. We hire a half dozen able spacers and some engine men. I can probably get by with eight and still keep watches on the main engineering and environmental systems," the chief said.

"Then we can worry about hiring officers and crew when we have an estimate on the refit from the yard," Pip said. "No sense paying crew if we're going to be tied up in the yard for a month."

I ran a hand over my scalp as I thought about it. "That's doable. Can we get people for a short contract like that?"

"We can ask," the chief said. "Maybe somebody just needs a ride to Dree."

"What'll we do with the *Son*?" I asked, looking to Pip.

"If Roland hasn't already left, we could send the ship with him," he said. "Or we could go back to the original plan and have the ship towed to the yards. That's the safest option."

"That'll eat into our reserves," the chief said.

"All right," I said. "Before we make any decisions, let's see what we have." I looked to Pip. "Sell that can. Don't get fancy. Get rid of it. Apply it to the docking fees."

"Aye, aye, skipper," he said with a grin.

I flipped him a rude hand sign. "Are you willing to let Roland have the *Son*?"

"Sure. It was always the plan."

"Then why don't you see if he's still on the orbital and get him back here."

"What do I tell him?"

"Lie. Tell him your father made you give him the ship. It'll make him feel all superior and saves his face, and we'll have one less ship to worry about."

"I like it," he said. "But we keep the beer."

Chief Stevens perked up at that. "We have beer?"

"Half a pallet of Clipper Ship Lager in the hold. We brought it from Port Newmar," Pip said.

"You're holding out on the old chief? I'm wounded."

"We can raid it this evening," I said.

"Sounds good. I started to go through the engineering spaces yesterday. I'll get back to that today and see what I need for basic stores and spares. We've got an account at the chandlery here, don't we?"

"We should," Pip said.

"So, if I update the onboard inventories we can file a replenishment order when we know if we're flying or towing her?"

"Yeah. Order whatever is needed. I'd prefer to fly," I said. "Gives us a chance to see what's there before the yard starts playing with it."

Pip and the chief both looked at me with raised eyebrows.

I looked to Pip. "Operational security?"

He glanced at the chief and shrugged. "She's need to know and probably knows more than we do already."

"About time you realized that," she said.

"We don't know what extra surprises might be on the ship," I said. "Pip thinks there's charts to someplace in the navigation databases. There also might be extra coding in the transponders. We just don't know how they know whether the ship is one of theirs or not."

She rolled her eyes. "You're overthinking it."

Pip looked at her. "You know."

"The Darkside has been there longer than CPJCT has." She shrugged. "You don't fly around out here for the better part of a century without picking up a few bits of less-than-common lore."

"So, I'd like to go through the ship before we get to the yard and we start rebuilding it."

"There's probably a few odds and ends we should add, if they're not already here," the chief said.

"All right, then. If you two can do that, I'll post the berth openings and start going through the bridge to see if there's anything there that might keep us from flying to Dree. How long would it take to get the permit, Pip?"

"Walk in, pay your fee, walk out."

"So, assuming we can get enough hands, we could be almost to the Burleson limit before we could schedule tugs to tow us."

The lock call sounded at almost the same instant as Pip's tablet bipped. He glanced at it. "Well, that's one problem solved."

He stood up from the galley table. "That'll be Roland. Father just told me to put him back on the *Son* and send him to Umber." He went to open the lock.

"We better hope we can fly her, then," the chief said.

"Yeah. That would be a long walk to Dree."

She laughed. "He really has a half a pallet of Clipper Ship in the hold?"

"Unless he's overestimating how much of it he's consumed. We brought a full pallet and my extra grav-trunk full when we left Port Newmar."

"I like the way you boys operate," she said and levered herself up from the table. "We should probably head over and see what we can see while he makes nice with the captain."

She nearly ran into Roland at the galley entrance.

"Who the hell are you?" he asked.

"I'm Chief Margaret Stevens. Who are you?"

"Captain Roland Marx," he said and I saw his gaze flip to her collar tabs. "Engineer?" He looked at me and then over his shoulder. "You hired an engineer?"

Pip stepped up beside him and clapped him on the shoulder. "The bad news is, yes, we did. The good news is, not for this ship. The *Son's* all yours for now. Father says you need to burn for Umber as soon as you can light it up, so we'll just grab our stuff and scoot. You should be able to file for a 1500 departure."

"Nice to meet you, Captain," the chief said. "Safe voyage."

Marx stepped through into the galley, letting the chief exit. "See you on board," she said over her shoulder and disappeared down the passageway toward the lock.

"I told you I'd be back," Marx said, turning on Pip.

"Actually I think you said something more like 'You haven't heard the last of this,' " Pip said. "Yes, that was remarkably prescient on your part. Now, we need to clear out of here so you can fly this ship to Umber for my father."

"That's it? You don't have anything else to say to me?"

Pip stopped for a moment and looked up in confusion. "No, I don't think so. Safe voyage?" He shrugged. To me he said, "I'll have the beer transferred over as soon as I can arrange a cargo handler. How long will it take you to move your stuff out?"

"I never really unpacked. I can be out of here in five ticks."

"Well, there you go, Roland. I need a little more time than that, but we'll be out of your hair within a stan."

Marx stood there for several heartbeats, staring slack-jawed at Pip. "That's it?"

"What else is there? You've got a flight plan to file. Maybe try to snag a cargo to pay for the trip to Umber. I assume the ship's been refueled and replenished because that should have been arranged when we docked." Pip shrugged. "We need to get out of your way so you can do that."

Marx blinked several times, but Pip left the galley with me on his heels.

"Gimme a few ticks to pack up my trunk and arrange for the beer?" Pip asked.

"Half a stan enough?"

"Plenty." He pulled out his tablet and was punching buttons even before he got through the door to his stateroom.

It took a little longer than five ticks for me to toss everything into my grav-trunk, but not by much. It left me with the problem of what to do with the empty grav-trunk. I tried to think if there was anything on Breakall that I wanted to take with me badly enough to fill a trunk with it and came up empty. Lacking any better choices, I slaved the two trunks together and took them both down to the living room to wait for Pip.

Marx's grav-trunk stood in the corner nearest the lock. The captain himself still stood in the galley, apparently surveying the remains of breakfast.

"The coffee's fresh," I said. "You want a hand clearing this away?"

He shook his head. "What's with that kid?" he asked.

"Well, first, that kid is forty."

"He's almost half my age and has no sense of decorum," Marx said. "That makes him a kid in my book. Just because he's the CEO's son he thinks he can get away with anything. With treating people like crap."

"Actually, it has nothing to do with being the CEO's son. Tom wouldn't put up with that kind of behavior." I shrugged. "He treats everybody the same way. As long as I've known him."

"Oh, right. How long have you known him? Couple of stanyers?"

"We met on my first ship, back in '51."

"He didn't go to the academy until '53."

"I know. I flew over with him on the *Bad Penny.* That's how I knew the code for the ship's systems by the way. Might want to change that to something else. We graduated together. Class of '58."

He blinked at me for a few heartbeats. "You're captain already?"

"I caught some breaks."

"Well, tell me how a cargo first gets off talking to a captain the way he does?"

"First, while you're captain of the ship, he's not cargo first. He's owner. As owner, he gets to talk to you pretty much any way he likes. The only time he has to do what you say is when the ship is underway.

"Second, treating a forty-stanyer cargo first like a green third mate is a good way to get your hand bitten off at the elbow under any circumstances.

"Third, he's really not a bad guy. Just a bit eccentric."

"A bit eccentric? He brought a pallet of beer on the ship for personal consumption. We could have used that mass to carry paying cargo."

"Seems to me he paid for that trip a couple of times over with that one shipment of diamonds."

Marx looked down at the galley table. "Yeah. I'll grant you that."

"Has he ever flown a leg without turning a profit?"

Marx ran a hand over his mouth and shook his head. "No. Never."

"Captain's share is pretty decent. You earn more in salary or shares?"

"Shares," he said without looking up.

"So, your biggest complaint is that this 'kid' who picks the cargoes that pay you shares in excess of a princely salary doesn't talk nice to you?"

He glanced over at me. "When you put it like that ..."

I shrugged. "You know what I think?"

"What?"

I grinned. "I think I'm glad he's picking my cargoes now."

Marx laughed and I left him to cogitate in peace. I wondered how long it would take him to realize that the captain's share on the trip to Umber would be zero unless he found a cargo.

Pip clattered down the ladder, his trunk in tow, and we headed out for the *Chernyakova.*

"Where's the beer?" I asked.

"Courier picking it up in half a stan. Where can we put it?"

"Roll it into one of the coolers in the galley."

"What'd you talk about with Roland?"

"What a pain in the butt you are."

"I'm wounded."

I chuckled.

He glanced behind us. "You're bringing both trunks? I thought we drank all the beer out of that one."

"We did. I just can't think of what I would want to fill a trunk with here in Breakall."

"I see. Not coffee?" He gave me a sly smile.

"Chandlery has buckets of the stuff. Besides, the best roaster is on Diurnia."

"Probably for the best, then."

"Did you sell that can yet?" I asked.

"I listed it with a broker here on station. They traded us an empty can for it while they find a buyer. It'll cost us a percentage but they know the market here better than I do. Station services will swap the cans out this afternoon sometime."

"Good enough."

A small crowd waited for us at the *Chernyakova's* lock. As we approached, somebody said, "There he is." All the faces turned toward us and everybody started talking at once.

"What the—?" I asked.

Pip snickered. "Your fan club caught up with you."

Chapter Thirty
Breakall Orbital: 2374, August 9

The crowd slowed us down but allowed us through to the lock, which left me with the conundrum of how to get the lock open without letting them all in or crushing somebody in the mechanism.

I locked my grav-trunks down in front of the lock itself. Pip took the cue and parked his beside mine. Some members of the crowd appeared to be members of the press. A couple had hover-cams above their heads; several held up recorders.

I held up a hand. "Hold on. Hold on. I can't understand any of you."

About half the noise fell away but a couple of people near the back continued shouting questions. "This will go much better if you'd put a clamp on it for a couple of ticks," I said.

As the noise finally abated I heard Pip snickering.

"Thank you," I said. "Raise a hand if you're a member of the press. Yes, you can raise the one with the recorder in it."

About a third of the crowd seemed to have one or more appendages in the air.

"All right. If members of the press would slide off to my left?" I made a shooing motion. "That will let me figure out what these other people want and make more room for you to ask questions and maybe get answers." I glanced at Pip, who took the hint and waved people off to one side.

I turned to a trim, young woman in a shipsuit standing closest to me. "Yes? Can I help you?"

"We heard you're hiring."

"Well, the company is hiring, yes." I looked up and saw more shipsuits in the remaining group. "How many are here about a job? Raise a hand?"

A little more than half, some in civvies, raised hands.

"We posted openings on StationNet this morning. Are you all here from that?"

Most of them nodded.

"All right, then. If you're here for a job, please move to my right, would you? We're a bit short-handed, but if you can hang on for a minute, we'll get some specifics taken care of."

They milled about a bit until I said, "Being able to follow simple directions is one of the qualifications we're looking for."

Some of them laughed but all of them moved aside, leaving maybe a half dozen people in civvies and station coveralls.

"And what can I do for you?" I asked the nearest one, a skinny man with a terrifyingly brilliant smile stretching his face.

"Oh, I just came down to see if we could get a tour."

"A tour?"

Several people nodded and a couple more pressed closer.

"Why would you want a tour? It's a freighter."

The smiling man nodded. "Well, yes, Cap'n, but this boat's been parked here over two stanyers. Most of us have walked by it a couple times a day the whole time. Even when they tried to hide it."

Pip chuckled.

"As much trouble as this ship's seen, I thought I'd like to come and pay my respects to the old girl before she leaves," he said.

"How many of you want a tour?" I asked.

All the remaining people along with half the press and two-thirds of the potential crew raised their hands.

I leaned toward Pip. "Ideas?"

"We can't very well give tours right now," he said. "We're too short-handed."

"Agreed."

"Schedule one? Maybe tomorrow?" He scanned the waiting crewmen. "A couple of them look likely and probably more are qualified. If we can hire a couple who have Barbell experience, that would help manage foot traffic."

I looked at the three groups, all waiting patiently and politely. "All right," I said, raising my voice so everybody could hear me. "Tour people? We weren't exactly expecting company today, and it's the maid's day off." That got some chuckles. "If you'll come back tomorrow at what?" I looked at Pip. "1400?"

He shrugged and nodded. "That should let us take care of the worst liabilities."

"So, tomorrow afternoon, 1400. We'll give you a walk through the ship. There's not much to see, but if you're set on it, I'm game."

The smiling man said, "Really?"

"Sure. If you want, why not?"

That seemed to satisfy them and they wandered off, leaving a gap between the press and the potential crew. I addressed the crew first.

"How many have served on a Barbell before?"

Almost all the hands went up and my breath went out in a whoosh. "I'll admit, that was unexpected," I said. "Deck and engineering? Hands up?"

Many of them stayed up but a few dropped.

"Cargo handlers?"

All the hands went down and several of the people laughed.

"Now I know who the real Barbell people are."

More people laughed.

"That wasn't a joke."

More laughed.

"You're losing ground, skipper," somebody shouted.

"All right. Here's the deal. We're flying this ship to the yards in Dree as soon as we can make her spaceworthy. We'll need a couple of stewards and some watchstanders for deck and engineering to get us there. No share because we're flying on a yard permit but I'll pay scale plus twenty-five. It's a one-voyage contract for now. We'll know more when we get her into the yard and see what she needs. Until we do, that's all I know."

Nobody seemed to object and nobody walked away.

"Very well. Let me answer a few questions for the press here, and Mr. Carstairs will take names and particulars. Then we'll see where we are."

Pip nodded and pulled out his tablet, setting up shop on the top of his grav-trunk and organizing the spacers in a line along the side of the dock where they weren't blocking traffic.

I turned to the press and took a couple of steps away to give Pip some room.

"All right. Recorders on. Cams running?" I asked.

Lots of hands went up and the gabble of questions started.

"Wait. Wait. This is too cold and noisy to work that way. One at a time." I pointed at the man in the front with a handful of recording equipment. "One question. Go."

"Are you the same Ishmael Wang that led the salvage team?"

"That's the best you got?" I asked him.

He blinked.

"Yes, I am." I pointed to the next person behind him. "Yes? One question."

The first guy stepped in and asked, "Why did you want this

ship?"

I looked at him without speaking for a moment. "Standard is not your native language?" I asked.

He seemed a bit surprised by the question and answered, "Well, of course, it is, but—"

"The phrase 'one question' is foreign to you?"

"Well, no. I asked one question," he said. "But—"

"Yes, you did but now you're trying to ask another question and I'm trying to hear this gentleman's one question. You keep interrupting. Would you like me to answer another question?"

"Well, why do you think I'm trying to ask it?"

"All right. I'll answer that question," I said. "Because you're incapable of understanding simple rules or waiting your turn like everybody else. So, that will be the last question I will answer for you. Good day, sir."

He started a bluster storm, but his colleagues soon elbowed him aside.

"So we're clear on the rules," I said. "You get one question. I'll answer it if I can. If you ask me the same question somebody else asks, you'll have to get the answer from them. When we get through, we can go around again. Depending on time, maybe a third round if anybody's still standing. You're all welcome to come back tomorrow for the tour at 1400."

I pointed to the person in front with a hover-cam over her head. "One question."

"With as much of this tragedy as you've seen up close, Captain, why did you agree to come back to the *Chernyakova*?"

I bit my lip for a moment, trying to think of how to phrase an answer that might sound reasonable. I gave up and went with the truth. "I don't really know. Part of it was the tragedy itself. It was stupid. The whole crew paid the ultimate price for somebody's unfortunate decision. I thought I might be able make some piece of that right again by fixing the ship and making it safe again. I'm not sure that makes any sense, but that's what I have."

She opened her mouth but saw the warning look and smiled, stepping aside for the next person.

"What was the other part?" the next reporter asked.

"He made me." I jerked a thumb at Pip.

Pip said, "I heard that."

The reporters laughed.

"Sorry, that was flip, but the truth is bringing that ship in from out there was horrible. It was frightening and I was scared almost every moment for the weeks it took to get her in and safely docked. He made me recognize that and invited me to come along with him to deal with it. Not very heroic, but it's the truth."

The reporter grinned like I'd given him a pocket full of gold but nodded and stepped aside.

"One question," I said to the next one in line.

"After you sold Icarus to DST, why come back at all?"

"After Icarus, I found myself in the position of being able to do anything I wanted to instead of whatever I needed to. I took a few weeks off and visited with some old friends. I tried to think of what I wanted to do. I couldn't think of anything I'd rather do than sail." I nodded to the next one. "One question."

"Have you recovered from losing your engineer?"

"No," I said. "But I'm healing." I pointed to the next reporter. "One question."

So it went for the better part of a stan. I got all the way through the crowd of reporters once and almost through a second time when I realized that the crowd was bigger than when I started. I looked up at the reporter. "Wait a second. You weren't part of the original group."

"No, Captain, I wasn't."

I sighed. "All right. One question and then I'm done. I've got a ship to run."

"And crew to hire," Pip said from his vantage point by the lock.

"Any regrets about outbidding Malachai Vagrant?"

"Not yet," I said. "It hasn't been a whole day yet and I still need to finish checking out the ship. Once I find out how much it'll cost to put her right, I may have a few." I stepped back and said, "Sorry, that's really all I have time for. If you have any other questions or want follow up, contact Phoenix Freight via StationNet and we'll do our best to accommodate you."

"We're still welcome on the tour tomorrow?" one reporter yelled.

"Yes. 1400. We'll figure something out."

Pip shook his head at me. "You're going to regret that."

"Probably," I said. "Who do we have here?"

"Captain, these poor sods think they'd like to sail with us to Dree."

"I'm so sorry," I said.

They all laughed, some with real humor and some more from duty than amusement.

"I wasn't expecting a mass hiring," I said. "I don't know why I wasn't, but there we have it. Mr. Carstairs has all your particulars?"

They all nodded and Pip nodded with them. "I've got everybody's name and contact information, along with a statement on credentials, Captain."

"Very well. If you'd give us until 1500 to find our feet here, we'll start calling people back a few at a time and give you all a chance to get into the ship and see what we're up against. Engineering crew will meet with our chief engineer. I'll meet with deck and stewards. Any questions?"

A hand went up in the back. "I have one, skipper."

"Sound off," I said.

"I know this is a one-off with a yard stay, but will you be willing to hire us on after?"

"If at all possible, yes. I'm a little fussy about who I risk my life with in the long term, but anybody who's willing to risk theirs to help get this old girl into Dree has at least a vote of thanks from me." I shrugged. "And we'll need a full crew on the other end, won't we?"

They seemed to take that in stride and a few even looked a bit more relaxed.

"Anything else?"

"Skipper?" Pip said and nodded me away from the lineup.

We stepped back toward the lock.

"Two stewards. A spec two and a messmate. Both seem competent. They're the only two in the whole lot."

"Only ones competent or the only stewards?"

"Stewards."

"Whew. You had me worried for a second. You're thinking we need somebody to make coffee?"

"It would make the interviews go much smoother if we can get the mess deck cleared away," he said.

"You'd hire them?"

"Yeah."

"Names?"

"Franklin and Sharps."

"Sounds like a law firm."

Pip laughed.

I went back to the line of expectant faces. "Franklin. Sharps. If you two could lounge around with us for a bit, the rest of you we'll see this afternoon."

A man and a woman came forward though the dispersing crewmen.

"Captain, this is Spec Two Melanie Sharps and Messman Alan Franklin."

I shook hands with each. "You two know each other?"

They both said "No, sar" at nearly the same moment.

"I've been operating out of Diurnia for the last bit and I've never met either of you myself. How do you happen to be here looking for a berth, Ms. Sharps."

"You and I were both with DST, Captain. I was with Captain Avery on the *Linda Loren* before he retired."

"Tanker life didn't agree with you?"

"We'll just say I wasn't fond of his replacement and didn't cotton to being a bunk bunny, sar. My contract expired while we were here on Breakall." She shrugged.

"You make biscuits?" I asked.

"Doesn't everybody?" she grinned.

"How's your coffee?"

"I hear you like Djartmo Arabasti."

I looked at Pip who studied his tablet as if it were actually turned on.

"Mr. Franklin?" I asked.

"I got bumped here in June, sar. UFH mixed cargo hauler needed a slot for an able spacer and the cascade bumped me off the ladder."

"A full-share messman got bumped?"

"I was only a food handler at the time, sar. I passed the messman exam while I was waiting."

"Been there, Mr. Franklin. That why you want to get to Dree? Confederated ports have better slots?"

"I just want to get back out, sar. Mess deck isn't glamorous but it pays the same and you eat good."

"Fair enough. Here's the deal. We got a mess in there and we need it made right. You're the only two stewards who came down to call on us today and I like initiative. Even when I'm on the wrong end of it."

They shared a glance.

I nearly laughed at the worry they shared. "How about you come in and look it over. Decide how badly you want the jobs?"

"Sounds fair, sar," Sharps said.

"Yes, sar," Franklin said.

"Come on then." I keyed the lock and pulled my grav-trunks into the ship. They followed me with Pip bringing up the rear. I waited until he'd closed the lock behind us before heading deeper into the ship.

"First impressions, Ms. Sharps?" I asked as we stepped onto the shambles of a mess deck.

She scanned the area, her mouth slightly open and her gaze darting everywhere. "How bad was it when you brought her in, sar?"

"It's been cleaned up a bit," I said.

She looked me in the eye. "Whole ship like this?"

"Some was better. Some worse."

"Mercy Maude," she said.

I crossed the mess deck and stepped into the galley with Franklin and Sharps close behind.

"This isn't so bad," Franklin said.

Sharps gave him a look that was all too familiar.

"What do you think, Ms. Sharps?"

"There may be a galley under all this cruft, sar."

"I think there might be, given a bit of elbow grease and a bucket of disinfectant," I said.

I saw the moment she shifted from shock to planning. The aimless gaze clicked into inventory mode as she looked at sinks and stove tops, skated across the work spaces, and checked off the coolers and cabinets.

"Mr. Franklin?" I asked.

"Looks like a lot of work, sar."

"You up to it?"

"Nothing else on my calendar today, Captain."

"Neither of you has mentioned the smell," I said.

They glanced at each other again. Ms. Sharps asked, "Was that a question, sar?"

"You'll get used to it," I said.

"Oh, I hope not," Franklin said and then looked horrified. "Sar."

Pip and I both laughed.

"I suspect Chief Stevens has the scrubbers on overtime at the moment, trying to clear away the worst of it," I said. "I'm sure you'll believe me when I say it was much worse when I first came aboard."

"You mean yesterday, sar?" Franklin asked.

"I mean back in '71."

He paled. "Oh. Of course, sar."

"What're your priorities on this, Captain?" Ms. Sharps asked. "This will take a couple of days to make right, but you need the mess deck this afternoon, right?"

"Exactly. You should find some cleaning gear in the locker there. Some of it might be good. The brooms won't have rotted, but I'm not sure of the swabs and soaps. Figure out what you need and see Mr. Carstairs to get it from the chandlery. We've an account you can use for replenishment but no inventories set up. You'll be able to order your own once you've signed The Articles."

She nodded to Pip. "Aye, aye, sar. I can't guarantee coffee by 1500 but we should be able to find you a clean place to sit."

"All efforts will be appreciated, Ms. Sharps."

"I'm in, Captain," she said.

Franklin nodded. "Me, too, sar."

I pulled out my tablet and brought up the contracts Pip and I had agreed to, and after some fumbling managed to get both crew signed on. "Thanks, both of you. You've got your work cut out for you, and I need to get on with making captain noises so I'll leave you to it."

I left the galley and picked up my trunks on the way up to the cabin. Pip followed me up the ladder and paused in the passageway for officer country. "Any of these cleaner than the rest?"

I shook my head. "Not really. We're going to need to replace all the mattresses and bedding before we sleep aboard."

"The berthing areas are already stripped," he said.

"Small blessings. Book us a suite at the Rangefinder on deck ten, would you? We'll need someplace to sleep for a few nights."

"Aye, aye," he said and trundled down the passageway, his grav-trunk following in his wake.

"Hey," I said.

He looked at me.

"What happened to the beer?"

"Redirected it to a storage locker on the oh-two."

"Didn't want to share with the new crew?"

"Thought better of trying to store it in that cooler before it's been cleaned."

"Thanks. You did good out there," I said.

"We make a good team. Always have. Anyway, I've got work to do."

I pulled my trunks into the cabin and locked them down out of the way.

On the bulkhead the chrono ticked over to 1054. It felt much, much later.

Chapter Thirty-one
Breakall Orbital: 2374, August 9

My stomach grumbling alerted me to a basic priority. I bipped the chief to meet me on the mess deck and picked up Pip from his stateroom on the way down the ladder.

Sparks and Franklin had done yeomen's work on the mess deck in the scant time they'd had available, clearing away the rubble and bagging it for disposal. They worked with the simple tools of buckets, hot water, soap, and rags to clean off the surfaces of three of the tables. I found them up to their elbows in the muck, sleeves rolled up and smiles on their faces.

Franklin saw me enter and straightened up to attention. "Captain on deck."

Sharps straightened before I could speak.

"Oh, belay that. We're going to work together and we've got too much to do to get all military." I looked around at the progress and nodded. "Nice job here. What do you need most?"

"Mops and wringers, skipper," Sharps said. "A fresh jug of deck cleaner and another for glass would help."

"We'll do that, but I think you're wrong."

She looked at me, her eyes wide. "Captain?"

"I think what you need most is lunch."

Pip nodded. "I know that's what I need most. You two aren't hungry?"

"Well, yes, sar," Franklin said. "No offense, but this isn't someplace I'd want to eat just now."

Chief Stevens stepped onto the mess deck and laughed. "You're not the only one."

"Chief? Spec Two Sharps and Messman Franklin. Our first new crew members. Sharps and Franklin, this is our chief engineer,

Margaret Stevens."

The chief nodded and smiled. "Nice to meet you. You've made some good progress here in—what? A stan?" She eyed me. "I heard you come aboard and wondered if you were going to skip lunch mess."

"First priority," I said.

"Feed the crew," Pip said.

Sharps tossed her cleaning rag into the bucket on the table and rubbed the end of her nose with the back of one wrist. "We calling for takeout, sar?" she asked. "I didn't look in the coolers, but I'd bet we'd like what's in there even less than what's here."

"Who wants a beer?" I asked.

Pip raised his hand instantly, straight up from his shoulder, his face alight with a grin.

I turned to see the chief with her arm up. The ratings stood there with confusion so plain on their faces I nearly laughed. "Let's go find food," I said. I led them off the ship and down to The Corner.

The place jumped with the lunch crowd so we took a round of the washrooms to sluice off the slime from being aboard ship. By then Brian had saved us a table in the corner and I ordered a pitcher of Whistle Wetter while we perused the menus.

"You can have something else, if you don't like the beer," I said glancing at Sharps and Franklin. "Mr. Carstairs will drink it if you just leave it there."

"Sorry, Captain," Sharps said with a glance around the table. "I guess I'm just not used to drinking with officers."

The chief leaned over and asked, "Would it make you feel more comfortable if we took off our collar tabs?"

Sharps laughed. "No, sar. Not really."

"All right," I said. "This is a ship's function. We need food. We need information. And Mr. Carstairs likes beer. We can tiptoe around all day but there's work to do." I grinned. "We may as well enjoy it. Besides the cleaning gear, what does the galley need, Ms. Sharps?"

She shrugged. "Everything, Captain. Cookware to cutlery, flour to roots. I didn't get a good look at the steam tables or other fixtures, but I assume they'll be fine once the crud's cleaned off them. Stainless is pretty durable."

I turned to Pip. "I loaded Ms. Sharps and Mr. Franklin into the crew roster this morning. Can you approve her for chandlery replenishment?"

"Of course, Captain." He took a pull from his beer and slipped his tablet onto the table.

"Chief? How's it going in engineering?"

"I spent the morning in environmental tweaking up the scrubbers and getting set up to flush the potable tanks." She looked to Sharps. "I diverted the orbital supply direct to the ship. You shouldn't see any difference in the galley, and it's fine to drink or cook with."

"Thank you, sar."

One of Brian's servers stopped by the table. "Ready to order?"

Neither Sharps nor Franklin looked ready but I didn't want our meeting to run all afternoon. "Anybody have an objection to burgers? They make good ones here."

Four heads shook so I gave the waiter our order. "Five burgers, deluxe. Fries. I'd like a coffee. Anybody else need anything?"

"I'll take a coffee, too," the chief said, raising a finger.

"How do you want the burgers cooked?" the waiter asked.

We went around the table and in a tick he was off to the kitchen.

"How are you coming on your inventory, Chief?"

"All I've got is eyeball numbers at the moment, skipper. There's a stack and a bit of scrubber filters. The potable tanks are nearly dry so flushing them won't be a problem. I'd like to get a survey of the volatile and fuel tanks. The gauges tell me there's stuff in there, but I don't know what it's like after a couple of stanyers at the dock. That'll take some doing if we have to flush and refill them."

"How soon before you can get a replenishment order?"

"At least a few days. We're going to be that long just getting the decks so our boots don't stick."

"What do you think is a reasonable estimate for getting underway?"

She laughed. "We can get underway now. Getting docked again would be the problem."

She made me grin. "You know what I mean. A week? Two?" I asked.

"If we can get some hands aboard, two weeks is a good target. I'll know better after I've had a chance to dig into the power and gravity systems. Right now, I have no idea what's there. If it's really bad, we're gonna have to tow that baby. We could do that today, but it would cost us dearly."

Franklin raised a hand with a glance at Sharps. "Permission to speak, Captain?"

"You never have to ask permission to speak if you're at the table, Mr. Franklin. It comes with the chair."

"I was just wondering when we might be able to move aboard?"

"Good question. One we should probably answer before we meet with the gang this afternoon." I looked to the chief. "We'll have hot water and power by then?"

"Got it now, but yeah. Once I get the potable tank flushed we'll be just using station services to stay topped up. We'll stay on station services until we can get underway and fire up our fusactors."

"Food services?" I looked to Sharps. "How soon can you feed a dozen or so people?"

She glanced at Franklin before answering. "Just the two of us? A couple of days to make it clean enough. We'd need a replenishment order to get the galley up to snuff, but I'd not want to do that until I had clean spaces to stow it."

"Very well. Let's take a walk around when we get back to the ship."

Our waiter returned with food and we all dug in.

"Berthing," Pip said around a mouthful of potatoes.

"Oh, yes. I don't want to refit the entire ship until we get done with the yards. Deck berthing has what? Twenty bunks?"

"Twenty-four, Captain," Franklin said.

"If we clean up that area and the san, that'll give us a working berthing area. It's already the cleanest because it's where we stayed when we brought the ship in." I looked at Sharps and Franklin. "You don't mind sharing with grease monkeys, do you?"

"Hey, watch it," the chief said with a twinkle in her eye. "I'll have to warn my people they'll need to share with deck apes."

"Twenty-four enough?" Pip asked.

"We'd planned on sixteen. What are you thinking?" I asked.

"There's a lot of work to do and a lot of time to do it between here and the yards. Most of it won't be on the yard work orders," he said.

"You're thinking we hire on more?"

"And buy a pallet of cleaning and painting supplies." He shrugged. "Sooner the ship's shipshape, the sooner we get to hauling cargo."

I looked at the chief.

"He makes a good case," she said.

I looked at Sharps. "Thoughts?"

"Me, sar?"

"You're going to have to feed them," Pip said. "Can the two of you handle twenty-eight of us?"

I saw the doubt in her eyes when she glanced at Franklin.

"Sharps?" I asked.

"We probably could," she said, her words slipping out as if each cost her credits. "I'd feel better about it with one more steward. Even an attendant to help on the line and with cleanup would make a big difference, Captain."

"Noted," I said. "And Ms. Sharps?"

She seemed almost fearful when she looked up to meet my eyes. "Captain?"

"It's been a long time since I worked a mess deck. Your job is to keep the crew fueled. I know only too well how much that takes, and I'm relying on you to make sure I know what you need to make it happen."

"He's not kidding," Chief Stevens said.

"Yes, sar."

"We'll keep an eye open for another likely mess attendant," I said and looked back at Pip. "Twenty-eight?"

"What?" he asked, innocent as new cloth.

"You asked if Ms. Sharps could feed twenty-eight."

"Oh, did I? I must have miscounted."

"You've only had three beers—"

"Two, Captain." He winked at Franklin who seemed a bit nonplussed by our exchange.

"The one in your glass is the third and it's almost gone. The point remains that you haven't miscounted anything since you started sorting your peas on the galley table as a toddler."

"I might have seen a first mate in the list of applicants."

"I didn't realize we'd posted for a first mate."

"We haven't, Captain."

"All right, then," I said, with a glance at the chrono. "It's coming up on 1300 and we have two stans to get enough of the galley cleaned so we can start interviewing crew. Anybody still eating?"

Franklin stuck the last of his burger into his mouth and washed it down with a healthy slug of beer.

I waved for the waiter and added a healthy tip to the tab before thumbing it. We left The Corner and headed for the lift. I pressed the button for oh-one and noted Sharps and Franklin looked confused.

"A little detour," Pip said. "Chandlery."

I led the parade as we descended on the ship maintenance section and pulled out swabs, brooms, dust pans, trash bags, wash rags, sponges, detergents and anything else that seemed likely. I piled Franklin's arms full and then shifted to Pip's before the chief took his place, and I gave her a couple of buckets of deck cleaner. It all happened so fast it left Sharps standing at the end of the aisle in bewilderment.

"Ms. Sharps? Did I miss any cleaning gear you'd need in the next four stans?"

She looked at the loads everybody held and shook her head.

"What else do we need to make the crew interviews go smoothly?" I asked.

"Coffee?" she asked. "I don't know how we'd do that at the moment."

I held out my arms for Pip's load. "Gimme that. Contact Cackleberries on the oh-two and have them cater a coffee service for forty. Paper cups. The works. If they have a pastry service, add that."

He pulled out his tablet and pecked at it.

"Anything else, Ms. Sharps?"

"You want me to carry something?" she asked.

"I want you to go see that nice clerk up there and thumb the tab for this."

"Me, sar?"

"You need to stop asking that, Ms. Sharps. I want to make sure you'll be able to access the ship's account when you start placing replenishment orders and the best way to do that is here, now. Go. This is getting heavy."

"Stars in their eyes," Pip said.

I winked at him.

We were back on the lift in a matter of a few ticks and redistributed the load across the five of us. Chief Stevens grinned at me and shook her head.

"What?"

"I wouldn't have missed this for the world."

"What about the new edition of your book? *Sifu* Newmar said you were supposed to be working on that."

She shrugged and nearly dropped a broom. "I've got the files. I can work on it when we put the ship in the yard."

I laughed.

"What's so funny?"

"You'll be working double watches with the ship in the yard."

She grinned again. "Probably, but the new chapters are on maintenance and supervising yard workers. This will be perfect."

"Book?" Pip asked.

"Chief Stevens wrote the textbook on engineering," I said.

"What?" His eyes got round but before he could say anything else the lift opened onto the docks.

I led the charge across the dock with the ratings right behind me. Pip and the chief brought up the rear. "You're that Chief Stevens? That's what you meant? You literally wrote the book on engineering?"

"Guilty as charged."

"We used your book at the academy. I nearly flunked that

course," he said.

"Don't feel bad. An astonishing number of people do."

I knew what was coming and had the hardest time keeping the grin off my lips.

"What happens to them?" Pip asked.

"They transfer to Deck Division."

I think it was Sharps who squeaked and Franklin who dropped the bundle of toweling. I could have had them reversed.

Chapter Thirty-two
Breakall Orbital: 2374, August 9

We all trooped into the mess deck and dumped our loads on the cleaned tables.

"Now what?" the chief asked.

"We've got about a stan and a half before we open the lock to the ravening horde. You've probably got stuff to do, don't you?"

She checked the chronometer. "I do."

"Carry on," I said.

She grinned and headed aft.

I turned to Pip. "We have coffee coming?"

"I asked for 1445 so we'd be able to get a cup before the crowd arrives."

"Ms. Sharps? Priorities, please?"

She took a breath and blew it out slowly as her gaze swept the mess deck. "Tables, Captain. Then decks. If we have time to clean the pass-through, we can use that as a coffee mess. If we can scrape off the first layer here, Mr. Franklin and I can work on the galley proper while you're busy interviewing. Tomorrow we can deal with the coffee urns themselves. They're going to take a lot of time that we don't have today." She blinked and added a belated "Sar."

"Sounds good. Lemme go get into a shipsuit. You two set up a couple of extra buckets."

I left the mess deck with Pip in tow.

"Gonna be like old times," he said.

"Not exactly, but it's a lesson I want passed to the crew. This is a good way to do it."

"What? That everybody works?"

"The captain's not afraid to get his hands dirty."

Pip nodded. "Good lesson. I take it you want me to be stores officer?"

"If you're not busy buying and selling cans?"

He snickered. "I was planning on it. Only makes sense. You want me to take a deck watch, too?"

I shook my head. "I don't think it'll be necessary, depending on who we hire." I stopped at the top of the ladder outside the cabin. "Which reminds me. A first mate?"

"You'll know her when you see her."

"It's not Bev, is it?"

He shook his head and grinned. "Better."

"Do I need to hit you?"

"You might want to when you see who it is."

"You're not going to tell me?"

He shook his head. "Not in a million years."

"Well, let's get changed and go help Sharps and Franklin."

"You know they're going to flip lids when we walk back in there and pick up swabs?"

I felt myself smile. "Does it make me a bad captain if I said, 'I'm counting on it'?"

He laughed and headed for his stateroom. "Two ticks," he said.

I took one step into the cabin.

"I locked the file," Pip said before I heard his stateroom door close.

I chuckled all the way to my grav-trunk. I needed to find a shipsuit I could burn after we got done cleaning. I flipped open the lid and stared at a trunk full of empty beer bottles. It took me five or six heartbeats to realize I'd opened the trunk I'd thought was empty.

I was still laughing when I stepped from the cabin a few ticks later and found Pip waiting. He grinned when he saw my face and we went down to join the party on the mess deck.

We found Sharps and Franklin standing in the galley filling a couple of buckets with soapy water. They'd stowed the cleaning gear and broken out enough for them to use. I noted that they'd made good use of the trashcan liners and seemed to be working well together. Neither of them heard us over the sound of rushing water. Sharps glanced up when I stepped up to the deep sink and jumped so badly she slopped water onto the deck.

"Mercy Maude," she said. "You scared the...heck out of me, sar."

"Sorry, Ms. Sharps. Where do you want us?"

"Want you, sar?" She turned to see Pip standing behind me.

He waggled his fingers in greeting.

"Cleaning," I said and lifted the bucket out of her hand. "You'll need a couple more buckets."

"Tables," she said sounding a bit dazed.

"Tables," I said and grabbed a scrubby sponge from the stack on my way back out to the mess deck.

Pip commandeered Franklin's bucket and followed. We started on the table tops and seats. The hot water and grease-cutters made short work of most of the grunge. There were still smallish bits that would need a little more effort but I kept an eye on the chronometer on the bulkhead. With the four of us on table duty, we'd just about have time.

At 1445, the lock call bell rang. "I'll get it. That should be our coffee," Pip said and tossed his sponge into the bucket of slimy water.

I finished the last of the tables while Franklin filled a wringer bucket with detergent and hot water. I grabbed a spare swab and the two of us cleared most of the deck by the time the coffee service sat ready on the counter.

"Sar, you'll need to stay off that for a bit so it'll dry," Franklin said, pointing at the deck.

"I also need to get into a clean uniform," I said. "Mr. Carstairs? If you'd get into your khakis and man the lock? I'll get changed and collect Chief Stevens."

"Aye, aye, skipper," Pip said and pounded up the ladder to officer country.

"Anything else you two need before we open the show?" I asked, looking at Sharps.

"No, sar," Sharps said.

"Help yourself to the coffee and some dessert," I said, pointing to the spread on the pass-through. "I'll be back in a bit."

I tiptoed over the wet deck. Franklin brought out a damp swab and backed into the galley, taking all our footprints with him. I grinned all the way up the ladder to the cabin. We could have done a lot worse.

I left the cabin at 1455 and met Pip outside the mess deck. "They're gathering already, skipper. How do you want to do this?"

Chief Stevens joined us, wiping her hands on a bit of toweling. "One at a time for each of us?"

I nodded. "We don't want people wandering around loose too much. Line 'em up in two rows and send them up one at a time. If you'd be so kind as to flash whatever you know about them to our tablets, so we know who's supposed to be coming up the ladder?"

"Sure thing." He backed two rungs down the ladder and paused to look up at us with a grin. "Good luck."

The deck wasn't completely dry but it served well enough. It would need swabbing again before the day was out. The chief and I grabbed cups of coffee and settled at side-by-side tables. At 1500, Ms. Sharps smiled and offered us a little wave as she closed the door to the galley. I could hear them sloshing water and scrubbing over the sound of the blowers.

My tablet bipped; a few moments later, so did the chief's.

"And so it begins," she said.

The first candidate stepped into the mess deck.

"Able Spacer Anthony Burgess, reporting."

"Here, Mr. Burgess," I said and pointed to the table opposite.

The candidate behind him followed his lead stepping onto the mess deck.

"Wiper Walter Bellamy, reporting."

The chief raised a hand. "Here, Mr. Bellamy."

So it began. Some refused coffee, some took extra time. Some were clearly nervous. Some looked relaxed, as if they met with clipper captains every day. For all I knew, they did. If I hadn't kept notes, I would have lost track after the first ten ticks.

One candidate was another messman so I called Ms. Sharps out to sit beside me.

"Messman Rachel Adams, reporting."

"Rache?" Ms. Sharps said, leaning forward, and then cast a horrified glance at me. "Oh, sorry, Captain."

"Here, Ms. Adams." I said with a smile at Ms. Sharps.

When the candidate had refused the coffee and taken her seat, I said, "Apparently you know Ms. Sharps?"

"Yes, sar. We served on the *Loren* under Captain Avery."

I nodded. "Not a bunk bunny?"

She colored but held her head up. "No, sar."

I turned to Ms. Sharps. "Can she make biscuits?"

"No, sar." She smiled. "She's a master of the omelet pan."

"Good to hear." After a few more routine questions I released her and addressed Ms. Sharps. "You'd approve?"

"Of Rache? In a heartbeat. I didn't know she'd left the ship, too."

"Thank you, Ms. Sharps. There's your second hand."

She grinned. "Thank you, Captain." She left as my tablet bipped again.

When Ms. Sharps disappeared into the galley, the chief grinned at me. "You've made a friend."

"Who? Ms. Sharps?"

The chief shook her head. "No. Me. I love a good omelet."

We laughed as the next candidate stepped onto the mess deck. The afternoon disappeared in a sea of faces and names and ratings and specialties.

The chrono clicked over to 1730 before the chief ran out of engineers to interview. I sent my last one off and waited for the next bip.

"Why are all these people out of work?" I asked. "This isn't even a Confederation port."

"That might be why," she said. "They get bumped or shoved off here, and getting back out is a problem. Honestly, I thought there'd be more."

"Really?"

She shrugged. "You've led a charmed life, skipper. With some notable bumps. You had Alys Giggone at your back, and then you went to the academy. Some of these people have been sailing around as long as you have. Some longer. Most give up the life and settle down, but some of the people I've seen today have been sailing for three or four contracts, and this isn't the first time they've been put ashore. They've been around the quadrant a couple of times."

I chuckled and looked at my tablet to see if I'd missed the bip. "I was preparing for the eventuality that I'd be beached before I left the *Lois*. I never was and it doesn't look like that's something I ever need to worry about again."

It bipped just as I reached for it. "Alberta Ross. Why do I know that name?"

A shadow moved in the passageway and a familiar figure stepped onto the mess deck. "First Mate Alberta Ross, reporting," she said. Her naked scalp gleamed in the light of the overhead. Tribal tattoos snaked across her skull, down her neck, and disappeared into her service tunic. I saw at least a quarter kilo of surgical steel stuck through her flesh in various places.

Any normal person would probably have run for the lock.

Chapter Thirty-three
Breakall Orbital: 2374, August 9

I didn't know what to say for several heartbeats. I felt my jaw hinge open and hang just above the tabletop.

Luckily, the chief filled in for me. "Al? My gods, Al." She was up and across the mess deck before I could recover. "What the—? Why are you here?"

"I heard the boy toy here was on station and hiring. Where else would I be?" she asked.

Chief Stevens shot me a quizzical expression. "Boy toy?"

"Long story." I stood and crossed the deck to Al, unsure whether to shake, salute, hug, or some combination of the three.

She solved the problem by holding out a massive paw and gripping my hand in both of hers. "Good to see you." She paused and smiled. "Captain."

"I'm stunned," I said. "I don't even know where to begin."

"Is that good stunned or bad stunned?"

"Delighted stunned." I stepped back and just looked at her. "I can't believe you're here. I haven't seen you in twenty stanyers."

"I've got some new steel. Wanna see?" She reached for the buttons on her tunic.

I laughed. "I'd love to, but maybe another time?" I nodded toward the galley door where Sharps and Franklin peered out. "Give the crew a chance before we scare them off the ship."

She bellowed her great laugh and clapped me on the shoulder. "Good plan, skip."

"So, you want to come crew, Al? Or is that just Carstairs playing games?" the chief asked.

"I'm applying. I know you're not looking for mates. Taking a permit to Dree, are ya?"

"Yeah. Didn't seem really feasible to try to hire mates until the refit's done," I said. "Come in, sit. Have some coffee?"

She grinned. "Love a cup." She strode across the mess deck, sloshed some coffee into a cup, grabbed a pastry, and slung a leg over a chair at the table.

I heard the galley door click closed and chuckled.

Pip came up from below decks with a cheesy grin stretched across the bottom of his face. "Told ya," he said.

"Twenty-eight," I said.

"We finally ran out of applicants," he said. "Should we send Sharps and Franklin off before we settle in for a gab?"

"Probably." I went to the galley door, opened it, and stuck my head through. "Ms. Sharps. Mr. Franklin. Excellent work today. Why don't you hit the docks now? Get some rest. Sort out your business with the orbital. Plan on moving aboard day after tomorrow."

"Thank you, Captain. We'll just take a few ticks to get this gear stowed and we'll be out of here," Sharps said.

I grinned. "I appreciate all you've done. I hope we haven't scared you off."

Sharps glanced at Franklin and smiled. "It's been different, Captain, but no. You haven't scared me off."

"Me, either, sar." Franklin said.

I thought he still sounded a little rank-shy, which seemed odd if he had as much time in grade as the chief seemed to think. I nodded and left them to their stowing.

Al, Pip, and the chief had their heads together over the table by the time I got back. Al's pastry was gone and she only had a bit of coffee left in her cup. "All right, you lot. No plotting against the captain while his back is turned."

They all laughed and I sat.

"So, how do you know our captain, Al?" the chief asked. "This sounds like a story I need to hear."

"Well, a couple of eons ago I was on the old *Hedley.* Second mate. We ran a nice triangle trade out in Dunsany. I knew a lot of the Federated Freight people there. Alys always seemed to snag the talent. I have no idea how she did it."

"How well I know," the chief said.

"So we were somewhere. St. Cloud?" she asked, looking at me.

"I thought it was Dunsany Roads, but it's been so long it could have been Umber."

She squinted her eyes and finished off the coffee. "No, had to have been Dunsany. You'd just been up to that hoity-toity tailor. What was his name? Rutabaga?"

"Roubaille."

"That's it. Anyway we're out for a prowl with the crew from the *Lois* and this buck kid slides in beside me and we have a few beers. Jaw a bit. Not a bad-looking kid. Kinda green around the edges, but he didn't spend all night staring at my tits like some do."

The chief glanced at me and started chuckling.

"I've never heard this story," Pip said, his eyes wide in feigned wonder.

I hoped it was feigned.

"So anyway. About two, three stans into the barn dance, this kid sees Alicia Alvarez across a crowded room. Stars in his eyes and bone in his ... teeth." She winked at me.

"Wait," the chief said. "Captain Allie Alvarez?"

"Well, she was only second mate then, but yeah. That was back when she was running astrogation for ... what was it? The old *Proust*?"

"*Duchamp*," I said.

She slapped the table top with one large palm. "That's it. She was second on the *Duchamp*. Hell of a looker then. Still is. This buck kid snakes in, winkles her out from under half a dozen Lido Deck Lotharios, and he's got her out dancing on the floor." She grinned at me. "Damnedest thing I ever saw, before or since."

"Why, Captain Wang, you have depths I have never suspected," the chief said.

I rolled my eyes and hoped it would be over soon. I suspected I'd never hear the end of it.

Sparks and Franklin stepped out of the galley and tried to scoot past. "Ms. Sharps. Mr. Franklin. This is First Mate Alberta Ross. If all goes well, she'll be joining our little band."

Al nodded to each. "Sharps. Franklin."

"Nice to meet you, sar," Sharps said. She turned to me. "What time in the morning, Captain?"

"Get a good breakfast in you and be back at 0800, if you would?"

"0800, aye, aye, sar," Ms. Sharps said. She led Franklin off the mess deck and down the ladder. I felt the vibrations from the lock more than heard them as they left.

"All right. Nobody here but us chickens," I said. "Al? You're really applying for this post?"

She leaned in and crossed her arms on the table, resting her weight on her elbows. "Yes, Captain. I am."

"You're hired."

My answer seemed to surprise her. "Just like that?"

I shrugged. "Why not?"

"Don't you wanna know why I'm here on Breakall? Why I'm not a captain?"

"I suspect you're not a captain because you either don't want to be, which is fine, or because you've been yo-yo'd up and down the ladder so often nobody wants to take a chance on you, which isn't." I shrugged. "There might be other reasons, but frankly, I don't care why you're not a captain. It doesn't matter any more than why you're a first mate matters. Maybe someday you'll tell me all about it over beers in some dive in the back of the Deep Dark, and maybe you won't. I'm good with it either way. I'm not asking because it doesn't matter."

"If none of that matters, what does?" she asked.

"Alys Giggone once said she'd fly with you to the gates of Hell because she knew you'd get her home."

"Alys said that?"

I nodded.

Al swept her tongue around inside her mouth as if tasting for words that she didn't quite recognize. Her eyes looked a little bright. "How's she doing at the academy?"

"I wasn't back there very long, but she seemed to be doing well. She's on our board of directors."

"She always had the gift," Al said.

I glanced at Pip.

He nodded.

"Before you accept, I should fill you in a bit on where we're going," I said.

A grin seeped from the corners of her mouth and crinkled the corners of her eyes. She might have had a few more wrinkles there since the last time I'd seen her but I was looking more at the humor in her dark brown gaze. "Oh, I know where you're going, skipper. You're going to the Darkside and I'd guess it's to look for that hunk of hull plate that killed Greta Gerheart."

"And you're good with that?" I asked.

"Oh, yeah," she said. "I'm fine with that."

I rose to refill my coffee cup. "Well, then. We should probably get down to making some crew selections and then find some dinner."

"Wait, wait," the chief said. "What happened with Alicia?"

"Half a stan later, she's got him by the tongue and dragging him out of the bar," Al said.

"Allie?" the chief said.

Al grinned and nodded. "Allie."

The chief gave me a long stare.

"I sent Alys my recommendation to the academy the next day,"

Al said. “I figured she’d use it one day, and here he is. All cleaned up with stars on his collar and a ship under his feet.”

“If we’re through?” I asked.

“Not quite,” the chief said. “Boy toy?”

Pip leaned forward. “Oh, that’s what Bev used to call him. Her boy toy. See—”

“Can we save this for another time? We’ve got ship’s business to deal with.” I gave Pip my best captain’s glare, for all the good it did.

He grinned. “I’ll tell you later, Chief.”

“So, how many did we see, Pip?”

“Sixty-seven, not counting Al.”

Even the chief’s eyes widened at that number.

“I didn’t think we had that many here this morning,” I said.

“We didn’t. I had thirty-odd from the morning list. Word apparently spread.”

“For a one-way, one-shot ride to Dree,” I said and looked at the chief.

She shrugged in an “I told you so” way.

We winnowed the lists down relatively quickly. Having that many applicants across a wide variety of ratings meant we had our pick in terms of what we needed. We white-listed the steward, Rachel Adams, and offered her the messman slot. Two messmen and a second would be enough. That left twenty-one berths between engineering and deck. I picked six and we identified twelve for the chief. I wanted round-the-clock watches on engineering main and environmental. I still felt a little gun shy because of the ship’s history, even if a more logical part of my brain chided me about the probabilities. I claimed the last three slots for deck—one spec three bosun, and two able spacers—to be the day-worker cleaning crew. I could move off-duty watch standers to augment them in order to get the inside of the ship cleaned up. I suspected that, having seen and smelled the ship, even the watch standers would be willing to help out.

It took a little over a stan to sort out the rosters. By the time we were done, I was ready for food and the coffee had gone cold.

I turned to Pip. “If you could notify those we’ve hired? Have them report at 0800 day after tomorrow. And send a thanks-but-no notice to the rest.”

He gave me a disgruntled look. “You know I’m not your personal secretary, right?”

“I know, but you locked the file. Remember?”

“Already sent,” he said, with a grin.

“Then why are you complaining?”

"Didn't want you to get used to having me do your scut work."

My eyes rolled so hard I thought they might bounce on the overhead. "Dinner?"

Pip nodded. "And I need to get my beer out of storage."

"You have beer in storage?" Al asked.

"Didn't want to move it aboard until we had a place for it. I asked Sharps to clean one of the ready coolers so we'd have a place to put food."

"We're not going back to The Corner, are we?" the chief asked.

"I'm open. Where do you want to go?" I asked.

"There's a place up on eight that has great seafood."

"I'll eat seafood," I said.

"You'll eat any food you see," Pip said, poking me in the arm.

"That's no way to treat your captain."

"I'm your CEO. I'll treat you any way I like as long as we're docked." He poked me again for emphasis.

"Al? You in?"

She shook her head. " 'Nother time, Skipper. I got some loose ends to wrap up here on station."

"Fair enough. We'll probably meet at Cackleberries on the oh-two for breakfast. 0600 or there abouts."

"Save me a seat. I'll be there."

"What are we going to do about the tour tomorrow?" Pip asked.

The chief turned to him. "Tour?"

"We had a crowd outside the lock when we got here this morning," I said.

"I saw them earlier," the chief said.

"Some of them were stationers who'd been walking past the ship as long as it's been here and wanted to see it."

"So you agreed to a tour?" Her eyebrows crawled halfway up her scalp.

"It was maybe a dozen. Why not?"

Pip chuckled but I didn't see what was so funny.

Chief Stevens massaged her forehead with one hand and groaned. "What time tomorrow?"

"1400."

"What were you planning on doing for this tour?"

"I thought we'd just walk them in, through the galley, down the spine, maybe a quick turn around the bridge."

"Traipse through the engine room?" she asked.

"Well, probably. Yeah."

"And who's going to be the tour guide and answer questions? Keep them from killing themselves—or us—by fiddling with the equipment?"

Pip held up his hands, palm out. "Don't look at me."

I looked at Al. "First Mate Ross, I wonder if I could impose on you a bit tomorrow afternoon and ask if you'd be willing to be just slightly out of uniform when our guests arrive?"

"How out of uniform did you have in mind, Skipper?" Her eyes almost danced.

"Half a kilo of surgical steel?"

"I can go as far as a kilo without breaking a sweat," she said.

"I'm more concerned you should make our guests sweat."

Her rumbling laugh filled the galley.

Chief Stevens looked back and forth between the two of us. "Exactly how well did you know this raw quarter share, Al?"

"I offered to take out some of the sharper bits for him."

"My, my, my," the chief said. "Unknown depths, indeed."

Chapter Thirty-four
Breakall Orbital: 2374, August 9

The day started so well. I should have been prepared for it to turn on me.

Pip and I met Al and the chief at 0600 after a solid night's sleep. The place had a morning rush going, but the four of us got a booth near the kitchen and enough food to keep us until lunch. We even got some ship's business done before leaving the diner and getting swarmed.

It began innocuously. A couple of people asking me to sign a hardcopy of a newsie. A rating stopping us to ask if I was still hiring. Even one rather shapely woman who rubbed against me while asking if I was really single. I found one of her scarlet fingernails stuck in the seam of my shipsuit later.

All before we made it across the passageway and into the lift.

Several people followed us on and I was uncomfortably aware of the way they stared at me.

I'd gotten used to being a clipper captain. People treated me differently. Not exactly deferential but sometimes with a bit of wariness. Sometimes with a jaunty smile and a nod.

These people looked hungry; for the first time in months I found myself wishing I had Stacy Arellone at my back.

When the lock opened on the dock, it didn't get any better. The four of us wasted no time getting around to dock eight-two but before we got there, I asked Al to break trail for us.

"Who are all these people?" I asked.

"You're famous, Captain," the chief said.

"Your face was on every screen on the orbital last night, Skipper," Al said. "They were re-playing your news conference on a loop in the bar."

"You went out to a bar and didn't tell me?" Pip asked.

"You've got beer and didn't share." Al shrugged as if that ended the discussion, but she grinned back at him over one meaty shoulder.

The crowd in front of the lock was even bigger than the one the day before. The noise they made practically rattled the deck plates. So many people clogged the dock that the cargo crawlers had begun lining up along the bulkhead, trying to ease through behind them without running into—or over—anybody. I saw a couple of uniformed orbital security around the periphery, one of them talking on a radio with a hand pressed to his ear.

We pushed through to the lock, and I stopped to look at the sea of faces. Some of them were amused, some clearly drunk. Others had a look of "I wonder what's going to happen now?" and still others had looks I really wasn't happy about. Here and there I saw a hover-cam above the crowd and figured a half dozen recorders had laser mics focused on me.

"You want me to shut 'em up, Skip?" Al asked, her voice pitched so low I almost missed her words in the racket.

I shook my head and pointed to the deck just behind me to the left. She took up station there and I nudged Pip and the chief into a rough line beside her. Facing the crowd again, I raised my left hand and waited.

The people nearest me—a couple within sneezing distance, which made me a little nervous—quieted almost immediately, faces turned to me. Slowly the quiet inched out into the crowd for a bit before somebody said, "What's he doing?"

"I'm waiting for you all to be quiet so I can speak," I said. I didn't raise my voice but those within a few meters shushed those further back.

"Shh. He'll speak if you'd shut up."

"Put a sock in it. I can't hear him."

The pool of quiet spread. Eventually people further back in the crowd raised their hands and it spread even more.

Progress, but I couldn't see very far through the crowd.

I spotted a cargo handler with a pallet of packing crates stuck in the herd a few meters to port and motioned Al to follow. "You two stay here, please," I said to Pip and the chief.

I pushed through the crowd with a little help from Al. The driver wore a station cargo coverall and the scaredest expression I've seen this side of a hull breach. I leaned in to speak to him. "If I could stand up there for a few ticks so I can talk to them, I might be able to get you on your way."

He looked like I'd offered him jewels and dropped the pallet to the deck so I didn't have to climb so high. Al gave me a boost and I found myself chest and shoulders above a sea of humanity.

"Good morning," I said, raising my voice. "I'm not sure why you're all here, but we have a problem and I really need your help."

A wave of nods rippled out across their faces.

"This is a commercial dock. Some of your neighbors are here trying to work and you're blocking the traffic lanes, keeping them from doing their jobs."

I saw them looking around but only the people on the edges of the crowd could see the lineup of cargo handlers and crawlers that would normally have zipped through this passageway.

"If you could open a lane back toward the bulkhead on the station side? A few meters would let them pass and it would save orbital security a lot of paperwork if they didn't have to arrest us all." That got a laugh and people pushed forward from the station side. It made things a bit thicker for us, but traffic started to move again. Security personnel helped form a barricade against the back of the crowd, which moved more of them out of the way.

I glanced down at the driver on my handler with a shrug. "A few more ticks and I'll have you free."

He looked a lot less scared and nodded.

I looked back out at the crowd. "Is the circus in town and nobody told me? What's going on?" I asked.

I got a laugh with that and heard more than one person ask, "What's a circus?"

A squat man with a neck so thick his head seemed to merge with his shoulders raised a hand. "We're here for the tour," he said.

I looked down at Al who just smirked at me in return. Over by the lock, Chief Stevens had her forehead in her hand again and Pip had tears streaming down his face, apparently from laughter.

"The tour? Of the ship?" I asked the man.

"Oh, aye." Everybody around him nodded in agreement. "We saw it on the viddie last night. I never been on a freighter. Ran the hoses, trotted cargo here and there. I never saw one inside. Might never have another chance. 'Specially not one like the *Cherny*."

I stood there looking out at all those faces looking back. "You're all here for the tour?" I asked, raising my voice so it would carry a little better over their heads.

Their response was a rough roar that might have been "Yeah!" and a lot of emphatic nodding.

I think Al said, "Holy Mother of Goats." The noise was so loud, I might have misunderstood her but I shared her sentiment.

When the hubbub subsided a bit, I looked at the people closest to me in the crowd. "It's barely 0700, what are you doing here so early?"

"Well, they said on the viddie it would open at 1400. I just wanted to get a good place in line," the squat man said. His neighbors all nodded in agreement.

"How much are the tickets?" somebody yelled from a few rows back.

I glanced at Pip, who wasn't laughing any more. He was craning his neck to look out over the crowd.

"Hang on. Just a tick." I waved at a reporter with a hover-cam over her head. "You were here yesterday, right?"

"Yes, Captain. Madeline Marsport, Breakall News Forty-Two."

"You have me on cam?" I pointed to the cam above her head.

"Sure do."

"Perfect." I looked straight at the device. "This has grown way beyond anything we expected. Of course, we're thrilled and delighted that the public has taken such an interest in Phoenix Freight and our first ship. Yesterday, a couple dozen people wanted to look at a freighter. Today? You all showed up!" The crowd laughed. "We have some logistics to deal with." I pointed at the line of security waving the cargo crawlers through the narrow passage. Madeline what's-her-name was on the ball because the cam spun to point in that direction. "We'll need to make arrangements with station security to make sure we don't block the flow of goods around the station." The cam pointed back at me. I looked down at the driver near my feet. "This poor guy needs to get this shipment somewhere and he can't while I'm standing on it talking to you." That got a few more laughs. I glanced at Pip who was frantically mouthing a word which I suddenly realized was "lawyers." I looked back into the cam. "We also need to check with station officials to see if we need to have some kind of permit or permission to do this on such a broad scale." That brought some boos. I shrugged. "I know. You should see the reports *I* have to fill out."

I saw a uniformed security guard making his way through the crowd making a rolling gesture with his hand.

"I need to get down now so this cargo can roll and I need all of you to clear a path so we're not blocking traffic. The orbital security people have a better idea of how to do that, so if you'd follow their instructions? We'll get on with our day and see about how we need to proceed. Deal?"

I heard a bit of grumbling but for the most part, the crowd followed security directives to move to one side or the other of the broad dock, opening the center to traffic. I looked at Madeline who beamed. "Got it?"

She nodded. "One question?" she asked.

"One question."

"Are you really going to let all these people tour your ship?"

"I'm going to try," I said. "I'm certainly going to try."

I jumped down then and held out a hand to the cargo driver. "Thanks. Sorry for the inconvenience."

He shook my hand and smiled. "Best show on the orbital and I had a front row seat." He started lifting the load back up, but paused to catch my eye. "How much are the tickets?"

I grinned at him. "You get in free."

He grinned but said, "I was thinking about my boy. He's mad for these ships."

"How old is he?"

"He'll be fourteen in a few days."

"Bring him," I said. "We'll see if we can't make this a birthday he'll remember."

The handler drove off, his warning horn beeping intermittently as he disappeared around the dock.

When I turned around, Al was smiling at me.

"What?"

"If the cargo business doesn't take off, we can always fall back on the birthday party trade."

"I like to have a Plan B," I said.

We crossed back to the lock where Pip and the chief stood waiting. "Any sign of Sharps or Franklin?" I asked.

"It's only 0730," the chief said. "If they're smart, they're still eating breakfast someplace sane."

"What? You find something out of the ordinary here?" I asked.

She shook her head and laughed. "When I met you on the *Iris*, you seemed like such a calm and decent fellow."

I keyed the lock and let them inside, making sure nobody followed us before closing it again.

"We're going to need to set a brow watch, which means we need people on board to do that," I said.

"Which means you need to get the mass allotments set up," Pip said.

"I'm willing to fudge that for the moment, but it would be easy enough to do, I suppose."

"We also need mattresses and bedding for the cabin, our staterooms, and deck berthing, don't we?" he asked.

"Yeah. And all the hygiene products, too." I looked to Pip. "You're the stores expert. How much of that do we need?"

Pip struck a pose. "I'll have you know I'm a cargo master, not a stores expert. I find your question beneath my dignity to answer."

"So you don't know either."

"That's about it," he said with a nod.

The chief snorted. "I understand now. I'll be down in engineering checking on the potable water situation and trying to figure out what's in the volatile tanks without blowing us all up."

"I like the last part of that," Pip said.

"What? The 'without blowing us all up'?"

"Yes. That part. I still have beer in a locker on the oh-two."

"More Clipper Ship?" the chief asked.

"Indeed."

She nodded. "All right then. No blowing up today." She shook her head and chuckled as she headed for the spine.

We followed behind her and had just about made it to the mess deck when the lock call bell rang.

"Don't Sharps and Franklin have keys?" I asked.

Pip nodded. "Yes, and they know how to use them."

"I'll get it," Al said and trotted back down the passageway.

I looked around the mess deck and stuck my head into the galley. The mess deck needed another swab, and the galley needed one more day before I'd be willing to eat from it again. "We need a coffee pot," I said.

"You need a lawyer," Al said.

"What?"

She stepped onto the mess deck with a uniformed security guard in tow. A slender man with a pot belly hanging over his belt followed them in.

"Can I help you?" I asked.

"I'm David S. Powers," he said.

"I'm Captain Ishmael H. Wang," I said.

"I represent the Orbital Management. I am here to serve this injunction to prevent you from holding an exhibition at this location without the proper permits and facilities."

"You couldn't afford a process server?" Pip asked.

"What?" Powers asked.

"Where and/or how can I learn which permits are proper and/or what facilities are required?" I asked, shooting a glance at Pip.

"You must obtain the appropriate application for an exhibition permit from the Orbital Manager's Office no later than one month prior to the exhibition."

"So, if I want to give tours of my ship today, I needed to file the permit last month?"

"No, Captain. You needed to file the application for permit last month. The Orbital Manager's Office will then process your application and grant or deny your permit within fourteen working days."

"So, in theory, if I wanted to hold tours of my ship next month? I would have to file the application for permit today?"

"Correct, Captain." He smiled as if I'd just won the prize.

"And two weeks from today the Orbital Management Office would tell me if I could give tours or not?"

He frowned. "Not at all, Captain. Fourteen working days, not two weeks."

"So closer to three weeks from now, I would be able to give tours of my ship?"

"No, Captain." He sighed. "That is only the period of review after which you will learn if your application has been granted."

"Ah, yes, because I have to file the application a month in advance of the exhibition."

He smiled. "At least a month, but essentially, yes."

Al hid her mouth behind a hand. Pip had his lips folded in and appeared to be biting them.

"So, assuming that I filed the paperwork today and the Orbital Management Office approved the application, I could plan to give tours of my ship in a month and one day from now."

"Precisely."

"Wonderful. You'll tell the hundred or so people outside that they should all go home on your way out?"

His eyes grew round. "Certainly not, Captain. If you have made promises you cannot keep, that is hardly the problem of Powers and Powers or the Orbital Management Office."

"I see." I scratched my jaw and pondered. "I don't plan on being here next month. Is there anything we could do to expedite the process? A month seems a long time."

"The wheels of governance turn slowly," he said. "We must have time to weigh the pros and cons of any such application before refusing it."

"Before refusing it?" I asked.

"Certainly. You can't expect the Orbital Management Office to approve every sideshow huckster that docks."

"Or any of them for that matter, eh?" I asked.

"I'm so pleased you understand, Captain. Good day." He spun on his heel and, after a bit of initial confusion over direction, disappeared down the passageway toward the docks.

"Al, would you see that he doesn't fall and hurt himself on the way off the ship?" I asked.

She grinned. "Aye, aye, Cap'n."

"She was right," Pip said when Al had left the mess deck.

"I need a lawyer?"

He nodded.

“We have one handy?”

“Lemme see what I can do.” He pulled out his tablet and started flipping pages.

Chapter Thirty-five
Breakall Orbital: 2374, August 9

Al came back from showing our visitor to the lock followed by Sharps and Franklin.

"Captain, who are all those people out there?" Sharps asked.

Al started chuckling.

"They're waiting for the tour."

"There's like a thousand people out there, sar. How are you going to get them all through?" she asked.

"Well, we've run into a snag. Orbital Management says we need a permit. It takes a month to get it and they'll refuse it anyway, Ms. Sharps." My brain caught up with my ears. "A thousand people?"

She shrugged. "Maybe not, sar, but a lot more than yesterday."

I looked at Al. "Ms. Ross? Would you check the situation for me, please?"

"Aye, aye, Cap'n."

"Where are we on the galley and mess deck, Ms. Sharps? We've got crew coming in tomorrow, including your friend, Rachel. Assuming she accepts the offer, of course."

"We got the ready cooler clean, sar. We still have a lot of cooler and storage spaces I haven't even looked into yet. The decks will need another swabbing. The steam tables and kettles will come up to boil just fine. The cooktop's a mess but it'll cook. The ovens are the cleanest thing there. They look hardly used."

"How about galley equipment?"

"We've a few pots and pans. No mixing bowls. I think I saw one mixing spoon. No scales. If it could have been taken off, it probably was."

"Yeah. I thought we had more than that before, but given the amount of time the ship's been sitting here, I'm not surprised.

Here's what I want you to do. Strip it down. Clean it up. Place a replenishment order this morning for one of the chandlery's galley packages. Get one for cookware so you can get the pots and pans. They have a kit of spoons, spatulas, whisks, and measuring cups. I forget what they call it. Galley utility pack or something. Grab one of those. Get a good coffee mill. They have a cheap one that's not worth the metal it's made of. There's also a Schmidt. It's big enough to grind a bucket at a time, I think."

"I know the model, sar."

"Good. Get that. Then buy forty settings of flatware, bowls, and stuff. I think they come in incremental packs of ten. Go with something relatively generic so we can add to it after the yard availability and we get a full crew. We need to get some basic foods aboard so we can feed people starting tomorrow with lunch mess. Doesn't have to be fancy. Cold meats, cheeses, breads, and maybe a pot of soup. We'll need coffee and tea, probably should stock some bug juice." I ran down after a couple of ticks and stopped to take a breath. "Got that?"

Sharps nodded. "Cookware, galley tools pack, Schmidt mill, forty settings. Then enough food for lunch and dinner tomorrow."

"Oh, I'll leave the spice and seasoning to your discretion. Get what you need that's fast and easy now. You'll have time later to fill it in before we get underway."

She nodded. "What about the berthing area, sar?"

I winced. "Thank you, Ms. Sharps. I'd forgotten that. We need hands to clean them and then mattresses and bedding, hygiene supplies." I stopped and shook my head. "I'll deal with that, Ms. Sharps. First priority: Feed the crew. We're here now and we'll have twenty-odd more by 0800 tomorrow. Let's see how far we can get between now and then, shall we?"

"Aye, aye, sar," Sharps said and I thought she smiled a little before disappearing into the galley with Franklin on her heels.

"What I wouldn't give for a pot of coffee right now," I said.

"We can get some on the way, Skipper." Pip said, slapping his tablet back into its holster.

"We're lawyered up?"

"Close enough. Meeting in fifteen ticks on oh-one."

Al came back from her reconnoiter and shook her head. "It's not a thousand. Maybe three hundred. More than this morning, and orbital security is looking really thin."

"You've been on a Barbell before, right?"

"Skipper, I've been on just about everything before."

"We're off to the lawyer. Check out your stateroom and see what you need to be able to move in. With crew coming in tomorrow,

I'd really like to get everybody moved in because leaving the ship unattended overnight is getting too risky."

"Agreed. See ya when you get back."

We scooted through the lock and waved to the waiting crowd as we passed. It was rather a lot of people. I began to get a little nervous about what might happen if we had to turn them down.

We got onto the lift without anybody trying to kiss me or hug me or ask me any questions, a blessing I felt most grateful for.

"You all right, Ish?" Pip asked. "You're looking a little stressed."

"What do you think will happen when we tell those people we can't give them a tour?"

"If it's not our fault?"

"How do we convince them of that?"

"Let's see what the lawyer says before we borrow trouble, huh?" he said.

I took a deep breath and blew it out as the lift doors opened. Clipper captains were supposed to be unflappable. I put my best flap forward and stepped out into the swirl of the oh-one deck.

The oh-one deck was mostly ship support businesses, but those included accountants, lawyers, and brokers as well as some of the freight company branch offices and CPJCT and Union offices.

"It's this way, I think," Pip said and headed off to starboard.

Four doors down we stopped at the offices of Singer and Gouge, Corporate and Business.

"We seeing Singer or Gouge?" I asked.

"No idea. Maybe both. Maybe neither." Pip pushed the door open and I followed him in.

"Yes? Can I help you?"

The receptionist wore a tasteful pinstripe suit with a pressed silk shirt and an old-fashioned bow tie. I'd seen pictures but never one in person. Luckily Pip wasn't so distracted by our host's sartorial splendor.

"I'm Carstairs. This is Wang. We've an appointment with somebody."

"Oh, yes, Mr. Carstairs. Mr. Singer will see you immediately." A buzzing door called us inward.

Mr. Singer rose from behind a half acre of polished wood to come around and shake our hands. "Gentlemen. It's wonderful to meet you. I've been watching you on the viddie for the last couple of days and I must say I admire your panache, Captain. It's not every one who can think so well on his feet and handle a crowd so adroitly. Please, sit. Sit."

Pip and I plunged into some overly soft chairs while Singer perched a butt cheek on the edge of his desk.

"Thank you, Mr. Singer—"

"Barry, please."

"Thank you, Barry. I'm just fumbling around trying not to cause a riot. Which is why we're here."

"Yes, Mr. Carstairs said something about difficulty with the Orbital Management Office and a permit?"

Pip sat forward. "Somebody claiming to be from the Orbital Management Office visited us to tell us we couldn't give tours of the ship without a permit. Further, it takes a month to get said permit, and they probably wouldn't grant it anyway."

"Sounds perfectly normal so far. How can I help you?"

I glanced at Pip at the same time he looked at me.

"How do we get around this permit problem?"

He smiled and clapped his hands together. "You don't, of course."

"We don't?" Pip asked.

"Of course not."

"How can we give tours of the ship then?"

Singer pursed his lips and steepled his fingers in front of his mouth, frowning and nodding as if trying to decide which legal remedy we might make best use of. Eventually he lowered his hands. "The only way would be for one of you, probably both of you, to be arrested and charged for holding an exhibition without a permit. You might be able to have as many as a half dozen people on tour before that happened. The unfortunate side effect might be that the Orbital Management Office would be within its legal purview to confiscate the exhibit—in this case, your ship—and dispose of it as they deem appropriate. Generally that would mean selling it at auction."

"I see," Pip said.

"Good! I'm glad we have that out of the way. Now. How can I help you gentlemen?"

"We've got something like three hundred people camped outside our ship. They're expecting a tour. How do we deal with getting them on and off the ship without running afoul of the Orbital Management Office? What if we don't charge admission?" I asked.

Singer went through his deep rumination process again while Pip and I fidgeted in the too-soft chairs. Eventually he emerged from his mental cocoon with a smile. "No, that would still be an exhibition with the same likely result. If you decide to do that, my advice is charge a very high price for the tickets in order to pay your legal fees."

"How do I get three hundred people on my ship without having to pay legal fees?" I asked. The man frustrated me way too much with as little coffee as I had in me.

Singer gave the matter a great deal of thought before responding. "I can only think of two ways," he said.

Pip leaned forward and so did I.

"First, if they book passage for a voyage. Your ship is licensed to carry passengers?"

"No," I said.

He sighed. "Then the only other way is hire them as crew."

Pip clawed his way up out of the chair and took Singer's hand in both of his, pumping it vigorously while I tried to climb back to my feet. It took me two tries but I made it.

"Thank you, Mr. Singer—Barry. You've been most enlightening and I'm sure we'll have no further problems with the Orbital Management Office," he said. "We'll just show ourselves out, won't we, Captain?"

"Thank you, Barry. Most enlightening."

I followed Pip out the door, past the reception desk.

"Oh, Mr. Carstairs?" the receptionist called before we got out the door.

Pip turned. "Yes?"

"A matter of your bill?"

"Of course." Pip returned to the desk and thumbed an invoice before following me back onto the oh-one deck.

"That was enlightening," Pip said. "Not really useful in terms of resolving the problem but enlightening."

"How so?"

"He charges by the minute."

"So the contemplative silences?"

"That would be my guess, but he did shed some important light, if not significant assistance."

"Do I need to beat it out of you or will you freely share this enlightenment?"

"You might consider some anger management therapy, Captain," he said, giving me a baleful gaze from under his bushy white eyebrows. "I don't remember you being so prone to violence in the past."

"I was never so worried that I might be blamed for a riot before."

"There is that," Pip said. "We learned that Powers wasn't spinning something out of whole cloth just for us. Singer knew of previous cases and how they disposed of the offending exhibits. This bears all the earmarks of a class one, blue-ribbon snarl of red tape."

"How do we straighten it out?"

"Generally by oiling the gears of government that turn so slowly, but that was the really enlightening part. We don't. We can't give the exhibition. No tours. If a little oil on the right gear had been an option, Mr. Thinkie would have offered to be the first gear."

"So what do we do? I really don't want to go back and tell those people we can't take them on a tour."

Pip chewed his lip as we got back on the lift. I punched oh-two.

He blinked at me. "Not back to the dock?"

"Not without coffee."

"Good plan," he said. "What was the name of that reporter with the hover-cam this morning?"

"Madeline something. Madeline Marzipan?" I shook my head. "That's not right." I tried to replay it in my head, but without coffee all I could think of was coffee. "Why?"

"If we can't take them on the tour, maybe we take the tour to them," he said.

"It's something."

"Particularly if we get a recording of Powers explaining why we can't do it."

"Might take some of the sting out."

We stepped through the door at Cackleberries and my brain seized up with the smell of coffee. I didn't remember anything else until I got back into the lift with a cup of life cradled in my hands and the warm steam caressing my nose.

"We need to do something about your habit, Ish."

"Getting in over my head?" I asked.

"That, too, but I was thinking about the coffee problem."

"I don't have a problem. I can quit any time I want."

He grinned. "Uh huh."

"Marsport," I said.

"Marsport?"

"Madeline Marsport. Breakall News Forty-Two."

"You sure?"

"No, but it's a start."

Chapter Thirty-six
Breakall Orbital: 2374, August 9

We got back to the ship just a little before 1000, which gave us four stans to solve the problem before the bomb of humanity went off outside the lock. Again we waved at the crowd as we passed. So far, they still smiled and waved back. Most of them sat on the cold metal, propped up against the bulkhead. Some had tablets out. Some were reading. A couple were playing games. One guy was going up and down the line selling coffee and juice, and a woman had a tray of cookies.

"Ah, the entrepreneurial spirit at work," I said.

Pip chuckled. "There's probably a kid selling his service as a place holder while they go to the head."

"I wouldn't have thought of that."

"You've had a lot on your mind, Skipper."

"We need to get Marsport down here," I said as I keyed the lock.

Pip held up a hand. "Wait. I feel something." He pressed an index finger against each temple, eyes pressed closed, his face scrunched in concentration. "Yes. It's becoming clearer now."

"What the—?"

He straightened, eyes wide, and clapped his hands. "Your wish is my command, Captain." He bowed much to the delight of the first people in line.

"Did you put a little something extra in your coffee?" I asked.

He shook his head and extended an arm to point. "Voilà. Ms. Madeline Marsport." He grinned. "You gotta admit, I'm good."

"Timing is everything," I said and waved Ms. Marsport over.

"Good morning, Captain. Mr. Carstairs, is it?" She offered a hand to shake.

"Yes. Yes, it is." He shook the offered hand, then pointed to the hover-cam above her head. "Could you secure that for a few moments while we have a chat?"

She looked to me before looking back at Pip. "Chat about what?"

"We've got a bit of an exclusive story for you, but we'd like to discuss it first before we fire up the presses."

At the word exclusive, the red tattletale on the camera went out and the cam dropped into her outstretched hand. She tucked it into a pouch at her side and smiled. "I'm listening."

"Step into my office, would you?" Pip extended a hand toward the lock in invitation.

She picked her way up the ramp as if it might fold underneath her at any moment. Pip and I followed and I slapped the close key. She gave a little start when the lock began moving.

"So, here's the deal," Pip said. "We've got a problem and we think you can help us. In return for that help, we'll give you a story that nobody else can get."

"Details?" she said, eyes sharp and skeptical.

"OMO says no tours," Pip said.

Her eyes went wide. "They're gonna go nuts."

"You see our problem?"

She nodded. "What do you need?"

"David S. Powers. You know him?"

"Davy Docket? Sure. Everybody knows him."

"Can you record him saying we can't give the tour because we don't have a permit? That if we do, we lose the ship?"

"That's easy. He's a one-button interview."

"One button? On your cam?" Pip asked.

She shot him an impatient glance. "On my blouse." She looked back and forth between us for a heartbeat or two. "What else?"

"News isn't an exhibition, Ms. Marsport. It's the public's right to know. We have the man who led the salvage team that returned the ship and its unfortunate—late—crew to Breakall Orbital. He can walk you through the tragedy. Show you the stains on the deck. We give your holo cam a tour of the ship and you publish it for everybody to see. "

I coughed.

"All right. Maybe not the stains on the deck," Pip said.

Her eyes had gone round and her jaw hinged open. "Mother of dragons," she said, her voice barely audible over the sound of the blowers. "Who?"

I held up a hand. "Uh. Me."

Her expression was one of those comical takes you see on holos that you know can't possibly be real. Hers was.

"You can check the records, Ms. Marsport," I said. "I was only first mate then, but it was me."

"How soon do you want Powers?" she asked.

"You'll do it?" Pip asked.

"Do it? Are you kidding me?" She shook her head. "How many of my clothes do I need to take off? I'd record naked for this story." She reached for her blouse.

"No, no! Please. No," I said.

Pip's face fell and I chuckled.

"That won't be necessary, Ms. Marsport," I said. "We just want to avoid a riot, if we can."

"All right. Let me go get Davy Docket on cam. I'll be right back." She took a couple steps toward the lock but stopped. "You're not going to stiff me on this, are you?"

"Don't put out the Powers piece until you have the tour," Pip said. "The two pieces will have more punch together. A real one-two." He made little punching motions with his fists.

"Good enough." She looked at the lock. "What do I do? Say 'open sesame seed' or something?"

I punched the lock key and the machinery levered open.

"When you're ready, just ring the bell. We'll come get you," Pip said.

She trotted down the ramp like her skirt was on fire and disappeared around the side of the ship in the direction of the lift.

I closed the lock again. "Think she'll do it?" I asked.

"Oh, she'll do it." Pip bit his lip.

"But what?"

"But will it be enough?"

"We need a Plan B," I said.

"We need some crew to do things like run errands and mind the lock," he said. "In the meantime, your coffee's getting cold."

"It's been cold for the last three ticks but it's coffee." We headed back to the mess deck. "A real one-two?"

"It worked."

"She probably doesn't even know what that means."

"Don't bet on it," he said. "You'd be surprised what goes on as sport here."

I paused to look at him.

He shrugged. "What? You want to bet? Against me?"

I laughed. "Not this time." I continued up the ladder to the mess deck. "I prefer to have a little better chance."

"Yeah, I prefer to stack the deck myself."

I gasped. "You cheat? I'm shocked to my core."

"Only when it matters."

I stepped onto the mess deck and tossed the rest of my cold coffee down my throat before throwing the cup away. I could see Sharps had made some significant progress. Little things like liners in the trash cans. Somebody had scraped down the two coffee urns. I wasn't sure how fit they'd be, but at least they were cleaner. I ran my hand down the chromed side of one. "I was probably the last person to clean this urn before today."

"Really?" Pip asked. "Over a thousand days and you think nobody else cleaned it?"

"Caretakers have very little vested interest in that kind of thing."

"True. Bring your own. Do your shift. Leave. As long as the ship doesn't catch fire or drift away on you, it's good."

"You want to get your beer?" I asked.

"What? Now?"

I shrugged. "I figure it'll take maybe a stan for me to walk Ms. Marsport through the ship. That should give you enough time to move it in."

"Past the crowd?"

"Put a tarp on it. We'll be getting replenishments from the chandlery all day, I hope. It shouldn't raise much attention." I shrugged. "If they ask, tell 'em it's beer."

He laughed. "Won't they mug me for it?"

"They won't believe you."

The call bell rang. "That was fast," he said.

I shrugged. "Let's go see."

Sure enough, Madeline Marsport, Breakall News Forty-Two, stood at the lock. I cracked it open to let her in and Pip out.

"Aren't you coming with us?" she asked as he walked by her off the ship.

"I've got an errand. I'll be back before you're done." He gave a jaunty wave and headed for the lift.

"Did you get it?" I asked.

"Oh, yeah. Easy. He loves it when people pay attention. You wanna see it?"

"I believe you."

She laughed. "You shouldn't be so trusting, Captain."

"So I've been told. How do you want to frame this?" I asked.

"How about you just talk to the camera? Pretend it's a friend who's come to see the ship and point out the places of interest as we go. I'll ask a question if I have any or point if there's something I think you should talk about."

"What if you point and it's nothing I can talk about?"

"Pull your earlobe. Like this." She reached up and gave a little tug to her left earlobe.

I followed her example.

"Even less. Just a little touch, like you had a scratch for a moment."

"Very well, Ms. Marsport. How would you like to begin?"

"I'll start out there. You open the lock and welcome me aboard?"

"Like just 'Welcome aboard. I'm Captain Wang, your tour guide this morning?' "

"Sounds perfect. Remember. Just be yourself. You're talking to a friend. You can pretend you're talking to me instead of the camera if that helps. Relax and go with it. I've seen you with the crowd. This should be really easy compared to that." She paused to give me a little nod of encouragement. "Ready?"

"Let's do it."

She walked back off the ramp and stood at the entrance. She pulled the hover-cam out of its pouch and launched it with a toss. It stopped just a few centimeters over her head and I noticed a small control wand in her left hand. She nodded to me and I closed the lock. It had barely closed before she rang the call bell and I kicked the key to open it again. As the ramp extended I stepped down onto it and looked at the camera. "Hello. Welcome to the *Solar Clipper Chernyakova*. I'm Captain Ishmael Wang. Come aboard and I'll show you a little bit of what it's like to live and work between the stars ..."

I walked back into the ship with Marsport a few steps behind. Inside I keyed the lock closed and faced the camera again. "Crewmen coming aboard or leaving the ship use that door. It's an airlock and can be used in an emergency to dock two ships in space as well as keep us snugged up against the side of the orbitals when in port. Come with me and I'll show you where the crew eats."

I didn't get far down the passageway before I ran into Al coming the other way.

"Oh, Captain. I heard the lock call—" She stopped when she saw I wasn't alone.

I turned to give the hover-cam a good look at Al. "I'm giving a bit of a tour to our friends here," I said. "Everybody? This is First Mate Alberta Ross. Ms. Ross? Everybody."

She blinked a couple of times then shrugged. "Hello, everybody. Welcome aboard the *Chernyakova*."

"We're on our way to the mess deck," I said. "Would you care to join us?"

"I need to go see Mr. Carstairs for a moment, Captain. Do you know where he is?"

"Check the lock. He'll be along shortly."

Al grinned. “Aye, aye, Captain.” She mugged for the camera a bit, which almost made me giggle at the thought of what a bald, pierced Amazon would look like grinning and waving on the video. “Enjoy the tour, everybody.”

She flattened against the passage and I led Ms. Marsport past her and on into the mess deck.

The rest of the tour went fairly well, I thought. After surprising Sharps and Franklin on their hands and knees scrubbing out a cooler, we went down the spine to visit with Chief Stevens. After a couple of wide-eyed moments she gathered herself and gave us the three-credit tour of the ship’s engineering spaces, including power and environmental, before waving us away with “Now go look at something more interesting. I’ve got work to do.”

As we made our way back along the spine, my gaze went to the darker patch on the deck. I wondered if I’d ever be able to walk the spine without seeing the messenger’s bloated body sprawled there in my mind. I took about four steps before I realized that Ms. Marsport wasn’t with me. I turned around to see her pointing at the deck.

I touched my earlobe but she pointed again and gave me a firm nod. Her lips formed the word “Please.”

I touched my earlobe again but she pointed again and lifted her right hand to the top button of her blouse.

I took a deep breath and looked down at the stain. “When we first came aboard back in ’71,” I said. “We found the crew where they’d fallen. One of them was there. We think he was the messenger sent down from the bridge to find out what was wrong.” I had to stop to clear my throat. “Needless to say, he didn’t make it.” I turned away from the camera and started walking. “When we get to the end of this long passageway, I’ll show you up to the bridge.”

The bridge wasn’t much to look at in the glare of the orbital’s lights but I gave her a few moments to walk the cam about and get a feel for the space before leading her back down the ladder. I took her through the captain’s cabin and let her peek into a couple of the officers’ staterooms before going down the ladder to crew berthing.

We stepped into the bay and I flipped on the overheads. “Finally, this is where the crew sleeps while we’re underway. We call it a berthing area, and their bunks are berths.” I walked down the length of it, giving her a chance to check out a couple of the sections. “Each quad has room for four crew members, two up and two down. As you can see, a crewman has just about enough room to crawl into a bunk and would have to leave the quad to change his mind. Through there is a sanitation station, what the crew calls the head or the san. What others would call the bathroom. Around the corner and down the passage there's an identical berthing area for the other half of the crew."

"How many people aboard a ship like this?" Ms. Marsport asked.

"Four people per quad. Six quads per berthing area. Two areas. Forty-eight plus a minimum of five officers."

I led her back out and up to the lock where I thought we'd end our tour. "And that's about all I can show you about life aboard the *Chernyakova*," I said. "I hope you've enjoyed your visit."

I expected the light to go out but it stayed lit and I looked at Ms. Marsport.

"I have a couple of questions, if I may?"

I nodded.

"Why are there no mattresses in any of the beds, Captain?"

I ran a hand back over my scalp and took a couple of deep breaths to steady myself. I couldn't look into the camera for this so I stared at the bulkhead. "When tragedy struck the ship, two-thirds of the crew were off duty. Half of those were probably asleep and the other half lounging about in the berthing area."

"In their bunks," she said.

I shrugged. "There's not much room there."

She nodded and motioned me to continue.

"We had to dispose of all the bedding on the ship. We haven't had a chance to replace it."

"Thank you, Captain."

I pressed the key to open the lock and she walked off the ship. I watched the cam fall into her hand as she turned and looked back at me. "We good?" I asked.

"We're better than good. When do you want this released?"

"The sooner the better. We need to let these people know what's going on."

"Will do, Captain."

"Thank you, Ms. Marsport."

"Thank you, Captain. See you in a few stans."

I really didn't know why I felt gut punched. Walking through the ship shouldn't have been that harrowing. Her focusing on the stain in the spine had pegged my meter. I'd had a hard time breathing after that.

I found Al and Pip on the mess deck with three coffees on the table between them.

"One of those mine?" I asked and slipped into the seat.

Pip slid one of the cups over to me.

I took a sip and nodded. "Not bad. Where'd you get it?"

"Guy selling to the line."

"Your beer aboard?"

"It's chilling now."

"Any problems?"

"Nope. Just rolled it in."

Chief Stevens came onto the mess deck and sat with us. "We have coffee?"

"Not yet. You want one? I'll fly," Pip said.

"Naw. We getting some lunch?"

I looked at the chronometer and probably would have been surprised that it was already a couple ticks past noon if I hadn't felt like it was already half past midnight.

"Probably should," I said. "How're Sharps and Franklin doing?"

"I sent them to find themselves some food at 1130," Al said. "Asked them to be back by 1230 and we'd watch the lock for deliveries while they're gone."

"Good." I sipped the coffee and let the sound of the ship wash over me.

"What're we going to do if this viddie thing doesn't work?" Pip asked.

I shrugged. "I don't know. We've done about everything we can."

"Any thoughts on getting the berthing areas cleaned up?" Al asked. "If we get food prep going for tomorrow and the crew can move aboard, that'll take a load off us in terms of security."

"Having a brow watch and messengers would be a big step forward," I said. "How long it would take them to clean out deck berthing? It's a big space."

"We've got what? Twenty new crew coming tomorrow?" Al asked. "Start them on the berthing areas and branch out into the passages."

"I'll need some help in engineering," the chief said. "I'm picking up the loose crap but what I need is about forty people with a gallon of elbow grease and the odd sponge to get that place cleaned up. I don't know what some of that crud on the decks is, and I don't think I want to know."

"You don't," I said. "What do we have left to do to get underway?"

"Besides food and crew?" Al asked.

"Well, and basic supplies. The usual things," I said. "Chief? Any idea yet?"

She shrugged. "I think she's actually spaceworthy now. The volatiles seem to have vented, leaving the tank empty, but the gauge was stuck. I got that cleared this morning. I'll order tankage from the chandlery this afternoon and see if what we get matches what we're missing." She took a deep breath and blew it out her nose. "I'd like to take a day and run diagnostics on the fusactors. Another for the sail and keel generators. They always take a bit of fiddling."

"Burleson drives?" I asked.

"They're running low-level validations now. I'll know this evening whether or not they're what they say they are."

"What do they say they are?"

"A lot better than I expected," she said. "Barbells don't have that kind of leg as a standard fitting."

"What are we talking about?" I asked.

"Class T Origami. If they're up to spec, we're good for six Burleson units. Loaded."

I felt my eyeballs bulging.

Al grinned and nodded as if the news wasn't exactly news to her.

"We had Class O's on the *Tinker*," I said. "We could do three with a tailwind."

"We got a really good deal on a used ship," Pip said, smiling into his cup.

"Don't calibrate your jumps till the diagnostics are done," the chief said. "I'll let ya know when to celebrate."

"Old engineer's saying?" I asked.

She shook her head. "Got it in a fortune cookie somewhere in Ciroda."

Chapter Thirty-seven
Breakall Orbital: 2374, August 9

The call bell interrupted our little kaffeeklatsch. Al volunteered to see who was at the door and returned with some tote-wielding chandlery workers with a delivery for Ms. Sharps. Pip and I ran the manifest and had the workers stack the goods in the galley. I signed the delivery receipt and sent them on their way.

"There's a coffee grinder here, Cap," Al said.

"I saw that. No coffee yet, but we're getting closer."

"Maybe this afternoon," she said.

"I didn't know you were such a coffee aficionado, Al."

"I've heard so much about yours, I'm just lookin' forward to tryin' it. That's all."

The lock cycled open and closed so I gathered my wits. "What'll we do for lunch?"

"Not The Corner," Al said.

"Cackleberries again?" the chief asked.

"I can always eat breakfast," Pip said.

"Works for me," Al said.

"Good enough." I stood and started policing our table for paper cups and used napkins.

When Sharps and Franklin came in, I took a moment to hand off the paperwork and point out the delivery that had arrived in their absence. It only took a tick for us to get out the lock, but what we found made me pause.

"That's a lot of people," the chief said, staring at the crowd that now disappeared around the curve of the orbital.

"I'd think they'd be freezing," Al said.

"I hope this video idea works," I said.

"It better, or there's going to be a mob of really pissed-off people."

"Should we tell them to leave?" Al asked. "At least let them know we're not giving the tour?"

"I'm still hoping there's a way around the OMO," I said.

"Singer said the only way is passengers or crew," Pip said with a shake of his head.

"I know. I got a bit distracted by the video tour," I said. "Let's give Marsport a chance to get the video cut together and we'll make the announcement."

"You want somebody to stay with the ship?" Al asked.

"Sharps and Franklin are aboard," I said.

"They're not officers. What if OMO comes back with some more legal chaff?" she asked.

The thought made my stomach roil. "Yeah. I'll stay. You guys go get some food. I'm not very hungry."

They headed off toward the lift, Pip in the lead. I watched them go but couldn't get over the sight of all those people waiting just to see the inside of a ship. Granted the ship had some history, but the waiting herd seemed way out of proportion. It seemed incredible to me that so many people might be stuck on Breakall Orbital. I suspected the people in line had jobs. Probably shift workers and cargo handlers. The permanent party housing down on oh-seven would certainly hold a small city's worth of people.

I was about to go back into the ship when I saw Pip coming back with something in his hands. When he got closer, he held up a couple of cups of coffee and a bag. "Lunch," he said.

"From Cackleberries?" I asked.

"Vendor set up on the dock just outside the lift."

"Wonder what the OMO permit process for that is," I said.

He laughed. "Orbital security was just calling to find out when I snagged these. I'd guess he'll be closed up and gone by the time they find out."

Something in the waiting crowd shifted. Some movement I couldn't really see but that caught my eye. I stopped halfway up the ramp and looked back at them.

"What is it?" Pip asked, craning his neck to look.

"I don't know. Something's happening."

Pip handed me a coffee and faced them. "It's the video. Must be. They're looking at screens."

Sure enough, the random shifting of the crowd had frozen as they stared at tablets and peedas. Some looked over shoulders, others held up their devices so their neighbors could see.

"Well, that's torn it," I said. I crossed the brow and put the cup and bag on the watchstander's station before stepping back out into the chill and crossing to where the front of the line waited.

"You sure this is wise?" Pip asked.

"No, but I'm the one who made the promise I couldn't keep. I'll be the one who stands here."

The video appeared to go on and on. I stood there in the cold trying to read expressions from the faces in the crowd. A few seemed excited. Most seemed sad. I didn't see anyone who was angry. Eventually, the video must have ended because people started stirring again. The guy at the head of the line saw me standing there.

"This true, Cap'n?" he asked. "OMO won't let you give tours?"

The people behind him began crowding forward.

"It's true. If we give tours, they can take our ship. The only way we can let people aboard is as passengers or crew. We're not licensed to carry passengers and there are way too many of you to be crew."

The man nodded and looked at his peeda again. "The old girl really that much of a mess inside?" He gestured with the device in his hand.

"I haven't seen the viddie yet, but probably."

He ran a wrist under his nose, still looking at what had to be a blank screen. "I'd be willing to help clean her up," he said.

"I'd love to have you help. I could use a few hundred people but I don't have enough people to tell you what to do or how to do it."

Pip stepped forward and put his mouth close to my ear. "You will tomorrow."

"Yes, but I can't expect these people to stay here all night and I'd be willing to bet OMO is going to start having words with all of us if this goes on much longer." I nodded at the orbital security people wandering up and down the line.

"You're probably right," he said and stepped back.

"Wait a tick," I said, and turned back to the guy in line. "Here's the deal. I can't do anything else today. Tomorrow, I've got crew coming who can help organize it but you people are going to start getting heat from the station pretty soon now and I don't mean the warm kind."

They laughed and more people pressed forward.

"If you can come back tomorrow morning, we can do something then."

"And lose my place in line?" the guy asked.

"What if I can deal with that?"

"What? Keeping my place?" he asked.

I nodded.

"Sure, but how?"

I leaned over and spoke in his ear.

He stepped back and stared at me, his eyes the size of walnuts. The grin spread slowly and he nodded. "Darn right!" he said.

"Good. If you'd pass the word? We need to arrange for some supplies."

He set about gathering the people behind him while I turned to Pip.

"How many sponges in a case?" I asked.

"What kind of sponges?"

"The utility ones? About this big?" I held my fingers up to show him.

"A full industrial case? Probably a hundred."

"Would you trot down to the chandlery and get me about three cases? Hire the transport to bring them here as soon as possible?"

"You want three hundred sponges?" he asked.

I looked back at the crowd. "You're right. Better make it four hundred. And a box of chisel tip markers. Black or blue. Whatever they have."

He looked at me like my brain had made the last jump without me. He looked at the smiling people lining up against the bulkhead and shook his head. "Four hundred sponges coming right up."

"Thanks, Pip."

He marched down the dock just as a delegation of orbital security approached.

The ranking officer nodded and waved at the crowd. "Captain? How long is this going to go on?"

"Well, they just learned they can't have the tour they were promised."

"Yeah. We saw it. Nice touch. Why aren't they leaving?"

"I'm trying to make it right with them. I was the one that offered the tour. Seemed only right I should try to do what I could to keep them from getting out of control."

The officer gave me an odd look and then scanned back along the crowd before glancing over his shoulder at the thin line of security shipsuits. "I see," he said. "Can we expect them to leave without causing problems?"

I shrugged. "I think so. I've offered an alternative that most of them seem to be accepting. As soon as my cargo master gets back from the chandlery, we should be able to begin moving them out relatively quickly."

He gave me an informal salute. "Thank you, Captain. I'll pass the word down the line and up the chain."

"Thanks for your consideration today, officer. It's been a long day for all of us."

He shrugged and proceeded to gather and redeploy his flock as he walked through the crowd.

I stepped out on the dock to get a look around the corner and saw that the word appeared to be spreading. Every face I saw had a big smile, or at least a cheesy grin, plastered across it.

"Captain?"

I looked up to find Ms. Marsport walking along the line, her holocam floating above her head.

"Ms. Marsport. Thank you. I haven't seen the video yet, but all these people seem to have."

She laughed. "Everybody on the orbital has seen it at least once at this point, according to our traffic figures. It's the biggest thing Breakall News Forty-Two has ever done. I wanted to come thank you in person."

"Without your help, this might have been really ugly," I said.

"Why are they still here? Don't they know the tour is canceled?"

"Yes, but we've been talking and I think we've got a solution."

"Really? Can you tell me?"

"Not just yet, but if you come back around 0900 tomorrow? I think you'll see—and record—the outcome."

Her eyes lit up. "Another exclusive?"

"Well, let's just say, you're the only one who knows when to show up. Except for them." I pointed at the crowd.

About that time, Pip came around the corner riding on the back of a cargo hauler with four huge cases on the back. The crowd clapped and cheered as he rode by.

"If you'll excuse me, Ms. Marsport. Duty calls."

She shook her head and grinned. "Of course, Captain. Is it all right if I record?"

"It's a public dock, Ms. Marsport."

I walked back to the head of the line just as the cargo hauler pulled up.

"Where do you want these, Skipper?"

I pointed to the bulkhead just ahead of the first man in line. "Line them up there, if you would?"

The driver nodded and in a matter of a tick had the crates off the truck and against the bulkhead. He gave me a quizzical look but rolled his hauler back the way it had come.

Pip strolled up and held out a box of markers. "These what you wanted?"

"Perfect." I snapped the box open and pulled out a marker before walking to the first crate and prying a corner open so I could get a sponge out. I wrote the number 1 on it and handed it to that first guy in line.

He took it like I'd handed him a gold bar before turning for the lift and waving the sponge in the air at the remaining crowd. They cheered and clapped as he passed.

In a matter of heartbeats we had a dozen people all clutching sponges and smiling as they left the line and headed toward the lift.

Pip stood and watched, shaking his head back and forth. The line kept moving forward, and I kept marking sponges and handing them out.

"Don't just stand there. Hand me more sponges," I said.

He stepped in behind me and pulled the sponges out of the cases, handing them to me as fast as I could take them, mark them, and hand them off.

My marker ran out about the same time the first case did, so I pulled another one out of the box and kept going. Pip had to break into the second case and we moved closer to it, pulling the front of the queue along with us.

My wrist cramped after ten ticks, so Pip and I changed places. "Just keep writing the next number," I said. "That's one twenty-two."

I watched him scrawl "123" and then focused on keeping a fresh sponge in his hands as he marked and doled them out.

It took us the better part of a stan to get through the line; we were left with about a dozen sponges. Pip and I had traded places back and forth until the chief and Al returned from lunch and were able to spell us.

I picked up a sponge and took the marker from the chief.

"What was the last number?"

"Three eighty-four," she said.

I scrawled "385" on the sponge and then gathered up the leftovers. The last of the crowd disappeared around the curve of the dock, leaving the four of us and a handful of bemused orbital security.

"Let's drag these empties into the lock. We'll see about disposal later," I said.

"You want to keep them, Cap?" Al asked.

"Might have a use for them tomorrow. If not we can break them down then."

"I still don't know what you think that was all about," the chief said.

"What's the biggest problem we have with the ship?" I asked.

"No crew?" Pip asked.

"Besides that."

"It's filthy," Chief Stevens said. "Stem to stern, keel to bridge."

"That's my thinking as well."

"How long will it take the twenty-eight of us to clean it?"

She shook her head. "Weeks. Probably longer than it'll take to fly her to Dree."

"That's my thinking, too."

Pip and Al were wrestling the big cardboard containers into the lock so I stepped aside to get out of their way.

"That's why I just hired three hundred and eighty-four day workers."

"What?"

Al and Pip had the same beautifully incredulous look. The chief spoiled it by merely looking confused.

"Well, no. Tomorrow morning, I'll hire three hundred and eighty-four day workers."

Pip recovered first. "That's insane. How are you going to pay them?"

"Already did," I said, holding up the numbered sponge.

"I get that the number is their place in line," the chief said. "How is that payment and how are you going to clear this with OMO?"

"Legally, we cannot have an exhibition," I said. "Mr. Singer made it very clear that the only way we can get them aboard is as passengers or crew. Tomorrow, for a very short period of time, they'll be crew."

"You can't bring crew aboard without having them work," Pip said. "Davis S. Whatever will slap you with a summons faster than you can say 'Are you out of your ever-loving mind?'"

"I plan to have them work," I said. "That's why they have the sponges."

"You're going to have them clean," Al said.

"Of course. We'll have to have a day-worker orientation session first. Groups of ten or twenty. For safety considerations we'll need to show them around the ship. Warn them against playing with the engines. That kind of thing. After the orientation each will be given a part of the ship to clean. We'll have crew at 0800 tomorrow to ride herd and keep them pointed. Maybe a half square meter of deck or something, then they leave."

"That many people? You still haven't said how you're going to pay them," Pip said.

"I told you. I already did." I smiled. "They're being paid in sponges."

I heard a voice behind me. "Captain?"

The orbital security detail had lined up behind me at the ramp. "Yes?"

The man licked his lips and wiped his hand on his pants. "We, uh, overheard them talking about what you're planning for tomorrow?"

"Yes? Is there a problem?"

He shook his head. "Oh, no, Captain." He paused and glanced back at the handful of guards behind him. "It's just—we're off duty at 1800 and have tomorrow off?"

I looked to Al who shrugged. "And?"

"Well, Captain. We were wondering. Could we get sponges, too?"

Chapter Thirty-eight
Breakall Orbital: 2374, August 9

After sitting in the open lock for a couple of stans, the bagged sandwiches had grown soggy and the coffee had gone stone cold. Personally, I'd had about enough of tip-toeing around the mess in my own ship. It was probably just low blood sugar but I headed up to the mess deck. Somebody needed to do something and I was riding high from dealing with the crowd.

When I got to the mess deck, I went straight through to the galley. "Ms. Sharps, where are we on coffee?"

"In the urn, Captain." She pointed to a rack of mugs. "Those just came out of the dishwasher. They're probably still hot." She stepped to the oven and pulled out a tray of honest-to-gods cookies.

The smell went right to my head.

She slipped the paper lining out of the baking tray and slid a fresh load of cookie dough onto it before slotting it into the oven and closing the door. "Something wrong, Captain?" she asked, wiping her hands on the sides of her shipsuit.

"Um. No. Thank you, Ms. Sharps. No. Carry on." I breezed back out of the galley, taking a mug with me and filling it from the single polished urn. The coffee smelled not quite divine. The ship still had too much of its own nose, but I was able to overlook it in return for the warm life flowing down my throat and into my body.

Pip, Al, and the chief sat at a table, all with mugs in front of them, all looking at me as if I might not have zipped my shipsuit up all the way. Or perhaps had zipped it tightly enough to cut off blood flow to my head.

"Try a cookie, Skipper," Pip said. "They're delicious and you missed lunch."

I took a seat and snagged one from the tray. "Thanks. Don't

mind if I do."

Al and the chief kept trading glances.

"Something you don't want to tell me?" I asked.

Apparently, the chief had drawn the short straw. "Have you seen the video tour, Captain?"

"No. It made the rounds while I was out on the docks."

Al said, "When you get a few ticks, you might want to grab it."

"That bad?"

"You were quite ..." The chief studied her coffee cup as if the word she needed might be floating on the top. "Eloquent."

"That doesn't sound good," I said.

She smiled. "Eloquent is good."

"It really was good, Cap'n," Al said. "Really."

"Then why are you two warning me about it?" I looked to Pip who simply shrugged.

"It's got a tone that I don't think you intended." The chief shook her head. "You'll have to watch it to see. Later. We still have a ship to prep for tomorrow."

Her words snapped me back from wherever I'd been. Or perhaps it was the coffee. "Diagnostics still running on the Burleson drive?"

"Yeah, but early results confirm we got legs all the way to the ground."

"Another fortune cookie?"

"No. Just something my second husband used to say about his first wife. Seemed appropriate."

"You expecting to divorce the ship?"

"Not any time soon, but I didn't plan on divorcing him either." She shrugged.

"Al? Can we do this thing tomorrow?"

"It'll take some doing, but I think if we limit the number of people who come aboard at once we should be all right. We can put different teams to work in different places. Start with berthing and the san in there with one group, add a couple groups for engineering. The crew coming in seem solid on their records, so if they're not complete drones they should be able to point and sniff."

"Pip? What am I missing?"

"I'm worried about the OMO's reaction. If they see this operation starting up in the morning, will they come down on us like a ton of iron?"

"Should we visit with Singer again?" I asked.

Pip shook his head. "I'd just as soon ask forgiveness for being an idiot than for going against legal advice."

"Well, what are the possibilities? We're hiring civilian day workers to clean the ship. That's done all the time."

The chief and Al both nodded.

"We're fulfilling the health and safety requirements by giving them training in how not to blow up the ship while we're docked."

They nodded again.

"We have a legitimate need. This ship is filthy. We're giving them legitimate tasks to do in cleaning it."

"No arguments there, Captain," the chief said. "It's the 'paying them in sponges' part."

"There's no minimum wage in CPJCT regs."

"No, but there's union scale," Al said.

"For spacers hired on under contract and having signed The Articles. We're hiring civilians on a fixed-term contract for a very, very short duration." I shrugged. "I'm no lawyer but CPJCT regs are pretty clear that the contract binds so long as both parties agree to the terms." I looked to Pip. "Right?"

He shrugged. "As far as I know, it's never been tested like this."

"Pull it back around to the other dock," I said. "Would we be having this discussion if I had hired ten civilians to clean the ship for an hour and offered one credit per person per stan?"

"Nobody would do it for that," Pip said.

Thinking back to the people in line, I wasn't so sure he was right. "Assuming I could find ten people willing to work under those terms?"

"As long as we're not underway, I don't see why that would be a problem. Nobody would blink if we paid fifty credits an hour but you're right. The regs are silent on the terms of the contract. I'm not even sure we'd need to prove we had a need for the labor or that they performed any." He shrugged.

"It's our company. You're CEO. It's our labor. Our ship."

"Yeah, but it's their orbital," Al said.

"No help for it now," the chief said. "How are we going to do this?"

"Crew comes aboard at 0800, those who've accepted," I said. "I think it's what? Twenty-one? Deck and engineering."

"Something like that," Pip said.

"So, seven teams of three. Four aft in engineering and three forward for berthing, bridge, and passages?"

"And how many day workers per?" the chief asked.

"What would make sense? I can't see twenty people trying to clean the berthing area. They wouldn't have room to swing a dead mop," I said. "Ten?"

"So seventy day workers at a time gives us about five or six rounds before we run out of labor," Pip said. "What could go wrong?"

The chief shook her head. "No, we're going at this backwards. We don't want the most number of people in the ship at a time. We want the smoothest flow of people through the ship."

"What are you thinking?" I asked.

She waved a hand. "We got the mess deck cleared away. This should be our staging area. One of our crew teams should be assigned to orientation. So, they go pick up ten day workers, give them a trot through the ship stem to stern and back again. Take them to where they're going to work and leave them with the crew team there. They go pick up another ten and repeat it. We can swap around that duty once a stan or so."

"Yeah, that would get old," Pip said.

"By the time they've gotten the other five groups working, they get the first group and escort them off the ship."

"How long for the orientation tour?" I asked, trying to estimate it.

"We can time it tomorrow and fine tune," Al said.

I looked to the chief. "How long is VSI?" I asked.

"On this ship? No more than half a stan. Generally closer to fifteen ticks."

"And that's a slow walk. Let's start with a ten-tick tour. Bring them here. A little welcome. Take them up to the bridge. Aft to engineering. What there, chief?"

"Main engine room. Take them down to environmental by way of the kickers. Bring them back up through power and grav, then back through the spine to berthing?"

"Makes sense, then off to their assigned duty station. Give them a few ticks to clean?"

"If we follow that pattern, they'll be cleaning for a stan and a half, just waiting for the tour guide group to make a cycle."

"That feels awful fast to me," Pip said. "I don't know that I could walk that path in ten ticks, let alone see anything along the way. We need to move more people through the tour faster or we'll be here the rest of the month. Sixty a stan is over six stans to get them all through."

"All right," I said. "A hundred a stan is still going to be four stans to get them through."

Pip started chuckling. "Even if they only actually work a quarter stan, that's a lot of labor."

"Are we making it too hard?" Al asked.

"Maybe," the chief said.

"At the core of this isn't actually cleaning the ship, is it?" she asked.

"No," I said with a shake of my head.

"Anything we can do will be a plus but I don't really feel like babysitting four hundred day workers who're only going to give us a few ticks of labor each."

"Agreed," I said. "What are you thinking?"

"I'm thinking we put a couple of buckets of soapy water along the way and have them clean while on tour. Drag a sponge along the bulkhead as they walk. Maybe hand out some swabs so they can run the swab along the ceiling." She shrugged. "Walk them in. Show them around. Even if they never touch the bulkhead, we're ahead of the game because we're spending next to nothing and four hundred people slopping soapy water around will go a long way. Especially down in berthing. Then walk them out and swap them for the next group."

"Won't that leave more of a mess?" I asked.

"Than what we have now?" she asked. "Really?"

"I'm just thinking of the liability if somebody slips on the deck."

"Add a waiver to the contract," Pip said. "You ever read yours?"

I shook my head.

"If it's a problem we just send one or two of our boys and girls out to run a fast damp swab around the corners and pick up the drips. Twenty people running field day routines shouldn't take forever. By this time tomorrow, the tour's done. The ship's had a bit of a spiff. We can get back to getting ready to fly her to Dree," Al said.

I looked around the table.

The chief nodded. "I like it. We'll have more cleaning to do after that, but some of it I wouldn't want a day worker doing anyway."

Al nodded. "That's what I was thinking. I don't really like the idea of turning people loose with wet sponges on the bridge."

Pip shrugged. "Seems likely to me. Meets all our goals and gets out from under the riot potential."

"That's what we'll do then. Break our boys and girls into pairs tomorrow. One to lead and one to keep stragglers from straggling. A couple people spare, maybe, to relieve the walkers and keep the soap buckets full," I said.

"Who do you want to stay aboard tonight, Cap'n?" Al asked.

"I will." I glanced at the chrono. "I've got a spare sponge and I'll get a bucket from the galley. If I order a mattress now, I can probably have the rack ready to take it by the time it gets here."

"How many do we need?" the chief asked. "I bet they're all the same size. I'm not above cleaning my own stateroom."

"The cabin, three mates, cargo, engineering, and steward," I said. "There's another one that's named something like supercargo on the plans but we always called it the VIP room on the *Tinker*. Don't remember ever using it."

Al stood and tossed back her coffee before slotting the empty. "Let's go see what we need, then. No reason to rent a bed if we have one here."

I let them go ahead and took a detour through the galley for some cleaning gear.

Sharps and Franklin had their heads together over one of the work counters but stood when I entered.

"What's our status, Ms. Sharps?"

"You found the coffee," she said with a grin. "We were just trying to figure out what we needed to do next. We've got one freezer unit and one dry-goods storage cleaned. They were mostly just empty and dusty. There's a bit of expired food in the other freezer and some canned goods in the other storage. We'll need to dispose of that and we can get it cleaned."

"So you've got room to bring in some fresh stores?"

"Yes, sar. Do you have any preferences in terms of menu?"

"I'm partial to food in adequate quantities. I like it when it's not too much of the same thing all the time, but I confess to being a creature of habit. I like my eggs in the morning, but I'm happy to eat almost anything placed in front of me."

She seemed a little nonplussed by my answer.

"Put together some simple menus, Ms. Sharps. You know better than I do how to rotate them to keep them fresh and still not need to stock an entire grocery store to make them."

"How far out should I plan, Captain?"

"I expect we'll be tied up here for at least another few days. I'd like to be underway within a week. The trip to Dree should be something around eight or nine weeks. Do you have storage for four months?"

"Easily, sar."

"Get us stocked up for four months, then. Use a head count of thirty for your projections. I'll leave the menu planning and replenishment orders to your discretion." I shrugged. "You're more familiar than I with what's needed to keep the crew fed and relatively happy at meal time. Do that and we'll be fine."

"Sounds good, Captain. Would you like to approve the menus before I order?"

"I'd really rather not. Delight me with your choices, Ms. Sharps."

"Thank you, sar. I'll do my best." She paused. "Can I ask how soon we can move aboard?"

"Our skeleton crew will be here in the morning. I'm hoping we'll all be able to stay aboard by tomorrow night. I want to get us on a port-side watch schedule tomorrow, so plan on a simple lunch mess tomorrow and a hot meal for dinner. After that, full rotation. Ms. Adams should be here to help by then."

Sharps and Franklin shared a glance and Franklin shrugged.

"Thank you, sar. We can handle that," she said.

"If I didn't think you could, you wouldn't be here, Ms. Sharps." I smiled. "But I have one request?"

"Certainly, Captain."

"I need some cleaning gear so I can get the cabin put together. A bucket, swab, broom, some cleanser? Mind if I help myself?"

"Of course not, Captain. You're paying for it." She grinned.

I chuckled and set to rummaging around in the stores closet. I stacked what I needed in an empty pail and grabbed a swab and broom. I stopped on my way out of the galley. "Oh, by the way, Ms. Sharps. As division head, you have a stateroom in officer's country. You knew that, right?"

Her eyebrows wagged up and down. "I didn't actually think about it, Captain. I just assumed I'd be in the berthing area with the rest of the crew."

"It's not much of a privilege, Ms. Sharps, but it comes with the rank. The good news is that you've got a bit of privacy and you're sharing a head with an empty stateroom, unless that's the one Mr. Carstairs claimed." I lifted the bucket of cleaning gear. "The bad news is that you'll have to clean it before you can move in. We'll order your mattress and bedding this afternoon with the rest, but everything else is up to you."

"Thank you, Captain."

"Don't thank me yet," I said. "I'm guessing you'll more than earn it before we're done."

I shouldered the door aside and climbed up to the cabin. It wasn't as big as the one on the *Agamemnon*, but that meant I had a lot less to clean. I checked the bunk frame for size and passed the information to Pip before pulling out the broom and getting busy.

Chapter Thirty-nine
Breakall Orbital: 2374, August 10

When we'd flown the *Chernyakova* in from the Dark, I'd slept with the rest of the crew down in the berthing area. Waking in the cabin felt so natural, I barely registered the change. It only took me a few ticks to do the needful and get into a fresh shipsuit. I still had some work to do before I could hang up my license, but my skin didn't crawl when I sat at the console to work on reports.

The chrono had just clicked over to 0545 when I left the cabin and headed for the galley. My thought had been to get an urn of coffee going, but soon I was following the heady aroma of fresh baked bread and coffee as if it had me by the nose.

I found the chief sitting at a table with a cup of coffee. "Good morning, Captain."

"You're up early, Chief." I grabbed a mug and paused to sniff the air coming out of the galley before filling it.

"I'm not the only one." She smiled.

Franklin stuck his head out of the galley door. "We'll have some breakfast ready at 0600, sars, if either of you want it."

"Thank you, Mr. Franklin," I said. "That would be fine."

The chief saluted me with her mug. "You're lucky with crew, I'll give you that."

I slipped into the seat across from her and grinned. "I prefer to think of it as recognizing the best in people and giving them the wherewithal to rise to it."

"Did you read that in a management book?"

"Second year at the academy," I said.

She laughed. "Sounded like it."

"Mostly I've been lucky." I couldn't help thinking of the times I hadn't been.

"So, we've got crew coming in at 0800?"

"I'm hoping some of them come in earlier," I said. "The acceptance was for 0800."

"And you told the day workers 0900?"

"I'm hoping a stan will be enough to get our people up to speed. We shouldn't have to give tours to the crew. Almost all of them have Barbell experience, and other than the Burleson drive, this ship is the spitting image of the *Tinker*."

"True." She sighed. "I'll be glad when we can get her cleared away and off the dock."

"You and me both." I took a sip of coffee. "Remind me of this, the next time I start shooting my mouth off about getting civilians on board."

She laughed. "I will if I can. I wasn't close enough to stop you this time."

Al came down the passage. "Do I smell fresh bread?"

"Breakfast mess at 0600 according to Mr. Franklin."

"We're never going to get those day workers off the ship," she said with a mock frown. She grabbed a mug of coffee and joined us at the table.

"Pip went ashore?" the chief asked.

"Yeah. He'll pack what's left in the room and check out. We'll be staying aboard until we get underway."

"I checked out this morning, too," the chief said. "I'll be here."

"I need to do that today," Al said. "It was so late by the time I got the stateroom together, I just fell into the bunk." She lowered her face to her shoulder and sniffed loudly. "Nobody can smell me over the ship, I hope."

"I think you'll be fine," the chief said after leaning over and giving Al a sniff. "Smells like disinfectant. You'll fit right in before this day is over."

Mr. Franklin stepped up to the pass-through and opened the top door. "Good morning, sars. Breakfast mess is being served."

I stood and took my place in line, delighted to find they'd set up a simple omelet station. A shiny new four-slice toaster was on display behind the counter. "Ham, cheese, onion, and mushroom if you have it, Mr. Franklin."

"Two or three eggs, sar?"

"Three. I have a feeling it'll be a long time until dinner."

He grinned and started my omelet before turning to the chief behind me.

I stepped into the galley door while Mr. Franklin assembled our meals. "My compliments, Ms. Sharps. What time did you get up to get fresh bread going?"

She looked up from her work table. "I set it to proof last night. Came down after setting up my stateroom and set up the loaf pans. Tossed it in the oven at 0430 when I made coffee."

"It's going to be a long day," I said.

She swiped her brow with the back of her wrist. "I'm used to it, Captain. When we get this day-worker business settled and get to some kind of regular schedule, it'll be much easier. Particularly with Adams and Franklin to help."

"Captain, omelet?"

I stepped back to the line and took the plate. "Thank you, Mr. Franklin. Smells great."

I started back to the table and stopped, surveying the room.

"Captain?" the chief asked.

"I wasn't planning on opening the wardroom up until we had a full complement of officers." I nodded to the table across the mess deck from the coffee urns. "If we claim that table, it leaves the rest for crew without having them feel like we took the best seats in the house."

"Designated wardroom?" Al asked.

"Yeah. What do you think?"

"I like it," Al said and collected her mug before plunking down at the other table.

I grinned and joined her.

"No disrespect, skipper," she said. "We got work to do and I'm hungry."

"None taken, Al. Carry on. My frail captain's ego will just have to cope."

She laughed and got busy piling breakfast in as if stoking a furnace.

I realized she was doing just that and followed suit as the chief took a seat opposite and grinned.

Pip showed up at 0700 with a grav-trunk in tow and a bag over his shoulder. "Breakfast?"

"Mr. Franklin makes a nice omelet," Al said. "And the toast is fresh."

Pip sighed deeply and with much dramatic effect. "I've already eaten, but lemme get this stuff stowed and I'll join you for coffee. We've already got spongers waiting out there."

"Crew'll probably start showing up at quarter till," Al said. "That's when I'd show up."

"Me, too," he said and clattered up the ladder to officer's country.

"Can we get some of the early birds moving?" the chief asked.

"One of us would have to do it," Al said. "I'm game if we want to try to keep the backlog down."

"Do we have a contract for them to thumb?" I asked.

Al nodded. "Pip ran one up last night while you were working in the cabin. It's probably in your queue for approval."

A quick look at my tablet verified Al's prediction, and I scrolled through the document carefully. "Clear language. No ambiguities. They work for no more than one stan at duties designated by crewmembers and in return they get a sponge."

"I'm glad the little bugger's on our side," Al said.

"Who said?" Pip asked with a grin.

"This looks good, Pip. Think we should run it past our friends at Singer and Gouge?"

"Honestly, yes. We probably should."

"But?"

"But he's going to take two stans to think about it, offer us a stan's worth of suggested changes which we'll have to reject, and then rubber stamp it."

"Sounds about right," I said.

He grabbed a coffee and joined us at the table. "Nothing magic about contracts. This one expires at 2359 tonight so it's got a sunset clause. It specifies what we expect in terms of *quo* and the *quid* in terms of a stan of labor without getting lost in the weeds of what they can or can't do."

"There's a bit of ambiguity there," the chief said. "What if we order them to do something like beat up their neighbor or screw the captain?"

Pip asked, "Or beat up the captain?"

"How about we change that to 'authorized maintenance duties' instead?" I asked.

"What? You don't fancy getting beaten by sponge-wielding stationers?" Pip asked.

"Not so much."

He shrugged and pulled out his tablet, tapped it for a few ticks, and then our tablets all bipped with incoming traffic.

"Can OMO shut us down?" I asked.

"We'd have to have a lawyer answer that, but they'd have to have some cause. If they invalidate this contract, they're opening themselves up to a system-load of hurt," Pip said. "Contracts have the weight of planets. Would they be willing to risk it for the sake of chopping off an activity that will be over by end of day?"

"They'd have a hard time getting a judge to rule in that amount of time," Al said. "Unless they already had one in their pocket."

"I wouldn't rule that out," the chief said. "But I agree. This should be too small for them to worry about. Voiding a contract would be opening up both doors on an air lock."

"Let's do it," I said. "I'll administer the contracts at the lock as captain, unless you think you should as CEO."

Pip sipped his coffee and squinted his eyes. "Either way. Probably make more sense if I do it, just because they're civilians and I'm the CEO of the company. There'd be no question with Phoenix Freight doing the hiring instead of the ship."

"Change that parties paragraph, then," said the chief.

"Oh, good catch," Pip said. "Thanks."

She shrugged. "Just because I'm an engineer doesn't mean I haven't navigated a contract or two in my time."

Pip gave her a sharp glance, but she only smiled and sipped her coffee. When he looked back at his tablet to make the change, she winked at me.

Tablets bipped around the table again and everybody nodded.

"All right," I said. "We need a table down there."

"I'll take a grav-trunk," Pip said. "Can I use your spare?"

"The one full of bottles?"

"Yeah."

"Sure."

"Bottles?" Al asked. "A grav-trunk full of bottles?"

"Long story," I said.

Pip took a last slurp off his coffee and headed for the ladder. He chuckled the whole way.

"I got time," Al said just as the lock call bell rang.

I lifted my mug and looked at Al. "Somebody's at the door. I bet the crew's here early."

She bussed her empty dishes and shot me a glare followed by a grin before scooting for the lock.

"Bottles?" the chief asked.

"We should probably clear this table, don't you think?"

She snickered and slipped her empty plate onto mine. "Since you're going ..."

I laughed. "This is going to be a long voyage, isn't it?"

"Depends," she said. "Bottles?"

I took the plates to the rack and slotted them in. "I had two grav-trunks full of stuff when I went to Newmar. While I was there I unloaded one of them and recycled the contents. I don't even know why I was dragging it all around." I took my mug to the coffee urn and refilled it. "When it came time to leave, I filled it with beer."

The chief giggled. "Clipper Ship?"

"What else? When we got to the *Prodigal Son*, I shared it with Pip."

"You drank a trunk full on the trip out?"

"Well, and while we were here. We had help. You helped as I remember."

She offered a sheepish grin. "Got me there."

"Anyway, I kept collecting the empties and they kept disappearing. I thought Pip got rid of them."

"He did," the chief said.

"Yeah. I'm still not convinced he didn't take the last few racks out of my trunk to add to his pallet load, but he filled my spare trunk with the empties."

"You had that pallet load *and* a trunk full?"

I shrugged. "Pip really likes that beer."

She was still laughing when Al returned with the first two crewmen to sign The Articles.

Chapter Forty
Breakall Orbital: 2374, August 10

By 0800 the whole crew had arrived. It only took a few moments for them to thumb The Articles and establish their contracts. Ms. Sharps set out a tray of fruit-filled tarts and a stack of napkins while everybody settled in.

"Good morning and welcome aboard," I said. "I'm Captain Wang. I'll be ringmaster of this circus. Some of you know Ms. Ross, first mate. The engineering crew has already met Chief Stevens. The fellow with the white hair and silver earring is our cargo master and CEO of Phoenix Freight, Mr. Carstairs. There'll be plenty of time for you to learn to hate us on the way to Dree, but right now you're probably wondering who those people are outside on the dock."

A spacer in the back raised his hand. "Yes?"

"Who are those people outside on the dock, Captain?" he asked.

The assembly chuckled.

"What's your name, spacer?"

"Bentley, sar. Ordinary Spacer Virgil Bentley."

"I'm glad you asked, Mr. Bentley. Those are day laborers I've hired to help with cleanup. You may have noticed in your earlier visit and this morning that the ship is not exactly shipshape and Bristol fashion. We've a huge task ahead of us in getting her ready for a yard availability in Dree. We want to get there as soon as possible, but the operative phrase there is 'get there' rather than 'as soon as possible.'

"That means we'll be doing a bit of our own clean-and-scrape on the way and only asking the yard to refit damaged systems and equipment. Chief Stevens will make sure the ship is spaceworthy. It's my job to make sure we have the crew necessary to keep us safe on the way.

“Ms. Sharps in the galley there, who made these tarts for us out of thin air as nearly as I can tell, will keep us fed.

“Today’s evolution will be a bit of a change of pace for some of you, especially the junior members. We’re going to hire about four hundred civilians to come in and clean.”

Eyes all around the room got very round at that number.

“If you’ve seen the video, you know that we offered tours of the ship, but the station management shut that down. So we can’t give tours. Everybody repeat that for me? We can’t give tours.”

A bit of rumbling that might have been words left me shaking my head.

“No. You don’t understand. We can’t give tours. Try again.” I raised my hand as a prompt.

“We can’t give tours,” they chanted. I noted a few smiles around the room and a few frowns.

“So if anybody asks you? What do you say?”

“We can’t give tours,” they said.

“Right. These people coming aboard are coming to work. We need to give them a safety orientation which will involve visiting several spaces aboard the vessel including the mess deck, the galley, a trip down the spine to engineering, some of the engineering spaces, the bridge, and one of the crew berthing areas. While that might seem like a tour, it’s a safety orientation. Are we clear?”

A few people mumbled something.

“What is it?”

“Orientation,” said a couple of ratings in the back.

“Try again,” I said. “I know this seems really stupid, but humor me—because failing this could cost us the ship and you’ll be back on the beach. Safety orientation.”

That seemed to have gotten their attention because they all said “Safety orientation.”

“And what about tours?”

“We can’t give tours,” they said.

“When they come in, each person will have a sponge.”

Their laughter stopped me.

“Seriously. They’ll each have a sponge. I need somebody to get swab buckets set up at each end of the spine, one in crew berthing, and maybe in engineering?” I looked at Chief Stevens who nodded.

“You will instruct your day workers to moisten their sponges and wash a piece of bulkhead or deck. Whatever is handy. Just dragging their damp sponges down the length of the spine is sufficient. I know this gets sillier and sillier as we go, but consider what four hundred sponges will do to that hundred meters of spine. If you haven’t seen it yet, you'll know what I mean as soon as you get in there."

The expressions of "are you kidding me?" began to evaporate to be replaced with some thoughtful consideration, particularly among the junior crew who'd be stuck with cleaning that spine if the day workers weren't going to.

"Here's the thing. There are four hundred of them. There are twenty-odd of us. We need to get them into the ship, give them a good safety orientation. Let them wash something and then get them out so the next group can come in. We can't have them stacked up in the passages, so it's going to be a very, very long day to get forty groups of ten through the ship."

I paused to let that sink in. "Get us through today, and tomorrow will be operations normal."

Some of the crew in the back rows snickered. I didn't blame them.

"Any questions?"

An ordinary spacer raised her hand.

"Yes?"

"What's a circus?"

When nobody laughed, I felt very, very old.

"It's an ancient form of entertainment. I'll see if I can find some images or holos of them." I really didn't feel like trying to explain clowns and trapezes with the crowd building outside the lock.

To say nothing of gladiators.

"Anybody else?"

A spec one in the back raised a hand. "So, we're going to pick up ten stationers at the lock, trot them through the ship dripping soapy water, and then show them off the ship again."

"Basically."

"What do we do with the used sponges?" he asked.

The room shared a moment of laughter.

"They keep them," I said. "That's what they're being paid."

One crystal moment of silence hung in the air before the place fell apart with merriment. After they calmed down, I had the chief pick a couple of engineering ratings to go aft and act as sign posts, while I split the rest up into pairs and sent Pip ahead to start getting contracts thumbed.

"Ms. Ross, could I impose on you to take a couple of these strapping lads or ladies and load up a few sponge buckets?"

"Of course, Captain. Any particular places?"

"Ends of the spine. Maybe at the foot of the ladder in officer's country? A couple in the berthing area we've designated. We'll have mattresses coming in later today, and it would be nice to give our people a bit of a head start on that. You probably know the best places as well as I do. I'll leave it to your discretion."

"Sponge buckets, aye, aye, Captain." She turned to the gathered rankings and pulled two pair out. "You four, if you'd come with me?" She left the mess deck without looking back, the ratings close on her heels.

I wasn't sure where she would find the buckets, but I suspected that she'd make do or order some from the chandlery. As I thought about it, I wasn't sure she hadn't already done so. First mates can be terribly efficient as long as the captain stays out from under foot. The thought made me think of Fredi and I fingered the stars on my collar. She'd taught me a lot of lessons I probably never appreciated until I needed them. It occurred to me that I'd need to be much less under foot.

"All right. First pair, down to the lock. The rest of you finish your coffee and pastry. You'll be up soon enough."

An engineman and an able spacer ducked out of the mess deck and the rest settled in. Mr. Franklin lowered the upper door in the pass-through and opened the galley door, locking it back on its latch. I smiled at him and he grinned before ducking back inside. In the moment of quiet I heard Ms. Sharps addressing her small gang, although I couldn't hear what she said. I grabbed another mouthful of coffee and contemplated just how lucky I had been with crew.

I hoped that luck would continue even while girding myself against the disappointment I'd have to deal with when I was wrong.

I heard the tread of many feet coming up the passageway and stuck my head into the galley. Ms. Sharps had Mr. Franklin in the deep sink with a stack of cake sheets and Ms. Adams had her head in the sanitizer. "Ready, Ms. Sharps?"

"I don't have to speak do I, sar?"

"Just a few words about cooking in space, maybe?"

She bit her lip and shrugged. "I'll do my best, Captain."

"I would expect nothing less, Ms. Sharps."

The able spacer led the train of ten stationers into the mess deck and they gathered like a flock of birds, unsure whether to actually enter or turn and fly. I grinned when I saw the man with the number one sponge near the middle of the pack.

"Come in, come in," I said waving them forward. "Whenever possible, don't block passageways. Somebody might need to go through in a hurry."

They shuffled a few steps into the mess deck and stopped again.

I took a breath and began. "You probably know I'm Captain Ishmael Wang. Welcome aboard. We're about to send you on a safety orientation of the ship. The two spacers with you will show you where to go and what to do. Pay attention to their directions because the safety of everybody aboard depends on you."

I paused to let that sink in.

"This is the mess deck. It's our dining room in space. We also use it for crew meetings and generally hanging out when not on duty. Getting everybody fed three or four times a day is important, and this is where it happens. If you'd step this way, I'll show you the kitchen—what we call the galley—where the food is prepared."

I walked into the galley and stepped around the side of the work station to stand with Ms. Sharps. I had to wave them in to get them all in and lined up.

"This is Ms. Sharps. She's our cook. Ms. Sharps?"

"Welcome aboard, everyone. I love to cook but cooking in space has its own challenges. We need to have the right foods in the correct quantities aboard before we get underway. Once we start, we can't swing by the shops on the way home for a loaf of bread or a liter of milk."

They chuckled.

"So, we have to plan menus, order staggering amounts of food and cooking supplies, and store them all in the various freezers, coolers, and store rooms around us here in the galley. It's an important job and one that I'm honored to have." She looked up at me. "Captain?"

"Thank you, Ms. Sharps." I waved them back. "If you'd go back onto the mess deck, your team will take you to the next stop on your safety orientation."

As they shuffled out, Ms. Sharps said, "Was that all right, sar?"

"That was perfect, Ms. Sharps. Can you remember to say it again?"

She laughed. "I better."

"After the first twenty groups I'm sure you'll be able to say it in your sleep," I said and smiled to myself at the horrified look on her face.

After the first group left the mess deck I sent the next team down to the lock to pick up their charges. In due time they returned and we repeated the set piece for them.

When they left, I sent the next.

And the next.

After the last group had disappeared into the ship, I took the opportunity to fill my cup. My head was already spinning from all the talking. I found some relief in the quiet. I settled at the designated wardroom table and waited for the first group to come back around on their way out to the lock. I tried not to think about what could go wrong with fifty stationers with wet sponges and soapy water loose in the ship.

When I got halfway through the cup of coffee without seeing anybody coming back, I began to worry and bipped Al. She hadn't come back either.

I got a response bip but no message. In a moment she appeared in the door to the mess deck shaking her head. "We may need some assistance, skipper."

"What's happened? Somebody slip and fall?"

She bit her lip and shook her head. "They won't stop."

"Who won't stop? Stop what?"

"The day workers. They won't stop cleaning." She bit her lower lip and looked suspiciously like she was trying not to laugh.

"Show me."

She led me down to the berthing area and I found the first group down on hands and knees scrubbing the decks with their sponges.

"Where are the rest?"

"Bentley's got his group in the san with part of that third group. The rest of group three is down at the far end cleaning the quads. I think group four is still back in engineering and group five has claimed the spine."

"I thought this was going too smoothly," I said and stepped forward into the berthing area.

Al barked, "Captain on deck."

Everybody stopped what they were doing. The ratings all came to attention and the day workers looked around and finally stood up where they were.

"Would somebody get Bentley and his team out of the san, please?" I said.

The rating closest to the san stuck his head through the door and spoke. A half dozen people came out, sleeves up and sponges dripping. Bentley followed them and grinned at me.

"If you can't hear me, raise your hand," I said.

From the collected confused looks I figured everybody could hear well enough.

"Thank you for your hard work, folks, but I've got a problem and only you can help me."

The whole room moved forward a half step.

An older woman in civilian clothes stepped forward. "What do ya need, Skipper?"

"We still have a couple hundred people out on the dock who want to come in and play. I need you all to leave them something for when they get here."

Several people chuckled.

"And besides, I only contracted you for a stan and that's almost up."

"Oh, that's okay, Skipper," the woman said. "I got plenty of time."

"I appreciate the offer," I said. "But there are still a lot of people out in the cold and I'm out of sponges."

Chapter Forty-one
Breakall Orbital: 2374, August 10

The civilians accepted my words at face value and began shuffling forward. I nodded at the rating by the hatch and stepped back so he could lead his charges out. I watched them go, smiling and nodding to each. Most of them smiled and nodded back but it looked more like sad smiles than happy ones. When the second rating came by I stopped him.

"Where's the guy with the number one sponge? Wasn't he in your group?"

"Yes, sar. Didn't he come out?"

"Anybody know where the number one sponge is?" I asked, raising my voice to carry down the length of the berthing area.

A kid in a coverall that was soaked to the knees raised his hand. "I think he's up in the long corridor that went to the back of the ship."

"Thank you," I said, and turned to the rating. "I'll get him. Show your guests out and then stand by at the lock."

"Aye, aye, Skipper," he said and trotted down the passageway after his disappearing brood.

It took only a few heartbeats to get up to the spine where I surprised a lounging, grinning rating into a blank-faced attention when he saw me. "Captain on deck," he said.

A couple of ratings further along the spine came to attention and the civilians all stopped to look.

"Carry on." I turned to the rating. "Sponge number one? Know where he is?"

"No, Captain. My group is thirty through thirty-nine."

I slipped behind the day workers and made my way down the spine, looking for the guy in the rumpled coat who held sponge number one. I found him washing the bulkhead above the stained deck. He'd been there for some time, based on the area he'd cleaned. He didn't look up when I approached.

"Excuse me?" I said.

When he didn't turn I touched his shoulder. "Excuse me?"

He turned then, and I saw his face running with tears although his lips curved in a smile. "Sorry, Captain. I ... didn't hear you."

"Are you all right?"

"Yes, thank you."

"I need to ask you to move on so we can let the others have a turn."

"Oh, yes. Of course. I should have realized."

He used the sleeve of his coat to wipe at his face and he collected himself as I watched. He took a deep breath, almost a sigh, and let it out.

"If you'd come with me? I'll show you to the lock."

"Thank you, Captain."

I set out along the spine. After a glance down at the deck, he followed.

When I passed the rating, I said, "We're going to need to move them along. We've still got over three hundred people to go."

"Aye, aye, Skipper," he said and made a spinning motion with his finger in the air. His partner answered and began moving people toward us.

I led number one down the spine and past the galley. "You seem upset," I said. "I hope it wasn't anything we did."

He shook his head and took his lower lip between his teeth for a moment. "No, Captain. I'm quite all right. It's just—my youngest—she's on a freighter over in Ciroda. An Eighty-Eight under Cristo colors."

"You miss her?"

He nodded. "Yes, Captain, but that's not it. I thought I knew what had happened here. It was all over the newsies. Horrible. Sensational. Everybody talked about it for weeks and then we didn't talk about it again." He looked over at me. "Then you did that video and we all saw it. When I came aboard, I thought I understood and then I saw that ... the stain. There are a lot of them around the ship. I saw so many of them." His eyes grew bright again and he blinked. "All I could think of was my Em out there on a ship." He swallowed a couple of times. "Thank you, Captain. For letting us all aboard. For making sure this doesn't happen again. At least on this ship."

He ducked his head and scurried out the lock.

I had to step aside for the group coming out behind us, then followed them off to speak to Pip. "Everything going all right out here?"

He shrugged. "We've got the next couple of groups ready to go, but I was beginning to wonder if something had happened on your end when nobody came out."

"We're having trouble getting them to stop cleaning."

He looked at me for a moment, his face completely blank. "Getting them to stop?"

"Yeah. I found two groups down in the berthing area. I had to ask them to leave some for the rest. I was afraid they'd have it done before anybody else got a chance."

Pip started chuckling and shaking his head.

I didn't really see what was so funny. We needed to give all of them a chance to get some work in or the orbital would seize the ship. "Laugh, but all we need is David S. Powers showing up with a restraining order."

"You had to mention him, didn't you?" Pip asked, nodded at a group of orbital security marching along the dock, the lawyer in question in the lead.

A group of soggy civilians paraded off the lock around me. They walked past Powers, who gave them a strange look. I grabbed the two ratings who'd just released their workers. "You two. Next group. Go."

Pip's eyebrows scaled his forehead but he waved the next group onto the ship right in front of Powers's nose.

I snagged the trailing rating. "Keep them together and keep them moving but make sure they come out with wet sponges."

"Aye, aye, Captain." He followed the team into the ship.

Out of the corner of my eye, I caught the gleam of a hover-cam and turned to find Ms. Marsport standing just around the edge of the lock. She saw me turn and shot me a blazing smile. "Great stuff, Captain."

I nodded at the approaching security guards. "This might be interesting."

She looked and winked. In a matter of moments her hover-cam had taken up station near the lock where it must have had a full view of the proceedings.

"Captain! What is the meaning of this?" Powers said. "I thought I made it clear that you needed a permit for an exhibition."

"You did, Mr. Powers," I said. "I'm not giving an exhibition."

"I've got a warrant for your arrest and an injunction to seize the ship," he said. He stepped aside and waved the lead security man forward. "Serve him."

"Captain, I have a warrant for your arrest," the guard said.

"So he said. I'm not running an exhibition, officer. Do you have probable cause for serving that warrant?"

The guard looked around at the crowd and at Pip standing behind the grav-trunk. "What are all these people doing here, Captain? Looks like you're giving tours to me."

"They're day workers."

"Day workers?" he asked.

"I'm in the process of hiring them to help clean the ship to expedite our departure for the yards in Dree."

"Hiring them?" the guard asked and frowned at Powers. "There's no regulation against hiring day workers, is there, Mr. Powers? If there is, we need to get this warrant changed because it's for operating an unlicensed exhibition."

Powers scowled. "You're not hiring them."

"We most certainly are. Do you want to read the hiring agreement? Everybody entering this ship has thumbed it."

Two ratings appeared at my back and Pip waved the next group in.

"Next group. Step up. Let's get you processed," Pip said. He smiled up at Powers. "I need to ask you to step aside, sir. You're interfering with the operation of a vessel."

"Just wait," Powers said. "I represent the Orbital Management Office and it's within my purview to validate your assertion."

"You want to read the contract?" Pip asked, offering the reader to Powers.

"Hey! No butting in, buddy." The next civilian in line elbowed Powers out of the way. "I got number sixty and I'm the next to get hired."

"One moment, number sixty. If you'd be so kind as to let this official from OMO read the contract you're about to sign?" I asked.

"OMO?" He squinted at Powers. "You're that lawyer guy."

"I am, yes," Powers said and looked very proud of himself when he said it.

I winced and so did the orbital security guard.

"All right, smart guy," Sixty said. "Read it and weep." He thrust the tablet at Powers and stood back, with his arms folded. "But I'm next and ain't nothin' you're gonna do to stop it."

Powers took the tablet and scrolled through the contract once quickly and then flipped it back up, and took a bit longer to read through it. When he got to the bottom he looked at number sixty and then at me. "This is insane. You can't hire them."

"Why not?" Pip asked. "I'm CEO of Phoenix Freight. I've offered these people a valid limited-duration contract for labor. Every single person going through that lock has thumbed it."

"You're paying them in sponges," he said. "That's preposterous." He turned to number sixty. "You realize they're only going to pay you one sponge for an hour of labor?"

Sixty held up his sponge. "They already did."

His neighbors in line waved theirs in support.

As another group of day workers came out of the ship, Powers grabbed one of them by her wet sleeve. "What did you do in there?" he demanded.

She pulled her arm free and scowled at him. "Who the hell are you?"

"I'm David S. Powers from the Orbit—"

"You're that lawyer guy!"

"Yes, I am, and I demand to know what you were doing in that ship."

"Demand in one hand and piss in the other. See which one fills first," she said and started to walk away.

Powers's face, which had been a bit reddened before, took on a whole new hue that bordered more on purple than red. "You can't talk to me that way. Officer, arrest that woman."

"On what charge, Mr. Powers?" he asked.

Number sixty snickered. "Offering advice without a permit."

The woman stopped and whirled on him. "It's none of your business what I was doing on that ship, but I'll tell you anyway if it'll send you on your way. I was cleaning. You want to smell my sponge?" She stalked over and thrust her filthy sponge in Powers's face.

He reached to wrestle it out of her hand but she pulled it away and tucked it behind her back.

"Oh, no. I earned that sponge. Get your own." She stomped away.

"Officer?" I asked. "Do you have any cause to believe that I am running an exhibition?"

The orbital security guy shook his head and looked at Powers. "I can serve this and we can drag him up to the judge's chambers, but unless you got something other than you *think* he's giving tours, I've got a contract that says he's hiring cleaners, a witness that says she's just done some cleaning, and a long line of people who are going to be really peeved if they don't get a chance to earn their sponge." He shrugged. "I wouldn't want to be standing in the prosecutor's boots when the judge hears the case."

Powers ground his teeth together so hard I could hear them squeak. He scowled at me for several long moments. I thought he might say something, but he never found the handle on his tongue.

With a final grunt, he stalked away.

"Thank you, Officer," I said.

He grinned and stuck a thumb in his belt. "Thank you, Captain. You've always treated us right. Nice to be able to return the favor. That guy's a menace to the orbital. Good to see him put in his place."

I looked at the man's face. "Do I know you?"

He shook his head. "Doubt it. We know you, though. You been flying in and out of Breakall for stanyers. We know all the troublemakers," he said with a grin. "You're not one of 'em." He started to walk away but stopped to wave at the line. I thought he was just waving to be friendly until somebody way down the dock waved back. The guard turned. "My brother. He's number three eighty-five. Good day, Captain." He winked and strolled off in Powers's wake, gathering his squad as he went.

By 1500 we had gotten through the line of civilians and the whole crew had flaked out on the mess deck. Ms. Sharps had laid on a lunch mess of bread, cold cuts, and soup, which sustained us through the ordeal. A few members of the crew still had sandwiches in their hands.

"It might have been easier to do it ourselves, Skipper," Al said.

She got a rousing groan of agreement from the assembled crew.

"I couldn't believe people were coming off and going around to get into line again," Pip said. "When we got into the three-fifties, I looked down the dock and the line was almost as long as when we started."

The chief shrugged. "People. This business would be a lot easier without them."

I thought about number one and smiled. "Maybe," I said. While it might have been easier, it certainly wouldn't have been as worthwhile.

I stood. "All right, crew. Excellent job. You each have my thanks for stepping up to the task for the day, even if it was a little unorthodox. Next we need to get people assigned to watches, get the brow covered, get the remaining spaces cleaned enough for us to live in them. Ms. Ross, how are we in berthing?"

"The day workers did a hell of a job, Skipper. All we need is a little polish on the decks and some brass shined and it would pass inspection." She grinned at the crew who dutifully groaned and hid behind each other and their coffee mugs. "Seriously. Bedding is due by 1600 along with the hygiene supplies we need for the head. Anybody who wants to or needs to can stay aboard tonight."

I saw a couple of people perk up at that.

"If you didn't bring your duffel with you or need to tie up your port-side affairs, we'll take a break after we get the bedding in and assigned. You're all sharing the one berthing area for now; there should be one bunk per person."

"A situation I'd like to have remain," I said.

Al chuckled. "What I was getting at is that you'll have to go down and claim a bunk. You'll have to settle disputes among yourselves. Arm wrestling is acceptable but I'd prefer something more equitable like a random number on your tablets. Fisticuffs will be dealt with in the normal manner. We'll let you off at the Burleson limit and you can walk home."

"That brings up something," I said. "How many don't have ship tablets of your own?"

Most of the junior ratings and one of the spec threes from engineering raised their hands.

"Anybody that has one of their own that they don't want to use?"

A couple more people raised their hands.

"Mr. Carstairs, would you order us some tablets from the chandlery? Standard crew models. I think we get ten in a box."

"Aye, aye, Captain."

"Next on the agenda, official Phoenix Freight shipsuits. Tomorrow we'll swing everybody through the chandlery to get your suits with the *Chernyakova* shoulder patch along with any ship-tees or boxers. If you have any personal needs, let somebody know."

I looked around at the exhausted expressions. Even Ms. Sharps and her gang from the galley looked tired.

"Any questions?" I asked.

Bentley raised his hand.

"Mr. Bentley?"

"Any estimate on when we'll leave for Dree?"

"I'm hoping we'll be getting underway within the next few days. I'd like to give Chief Stevens a chance to make sure that we can make it to Dree alive before we undock. That's just my personal preference."

I looked to Ms. Sharps. "Evening mess?"

"Evening mess will be served at 1800, sar. Nothing fancy, but we got a shipment in this morning and we'll have another tomorrow."

"Excellent." I turned to the crew. "All right. I need three watch sections. First watch gets set at 1800, just like a real ship. It'll be the first watch this ship has seen in over two stanyers, and I expect everybody to do their jobs to the best of their abilities. If you have a problem you can't solve, tell somebody. If you see something you don't understand, ask somebody. If you find yourself in a situation that you feel is dangerous, make sure somebody knows. And if you find yourself alone in the night, shut up and stand your watch."

They laughed.

"You've all heard enough pep talks, so you don't need to hear one from me. Remember the best one you ever heard and pretend I'm saying it to you now. I've got work to do and so do you." I turned to Al. "Carry on, Ms. Ross."

I left the mess deck to my crew and climbed the ladder to the cabin. I did have work to do, but mostly it consisted of getting out from under foot so my officers could do their jobs. I ran a finger across the stars that Fredi had given me and wondered where she was, what she was doing.

Chapter Forty-two
Breakall System: 2374-August 18

It took Chief Stevens four more days to get the last of the diagnostics completed and decide the ship was spaceworthy. We'd sold the hydraulic fluid and paid off the docking fees.

That cargo handler brought his son by on his birthday. We weren't able to give him a tour but answered his questions about maybe signing The Articles when he came of age. To do that effectively, we needed to show him areas of the ship like the bridge, the engine room, berthing areas and the galley. He shared lunch mess with the crew and Sharps even made him a little happy birthday cake to celebrate. His father took digitals of him sitting in the captain's chair on the bridge. My hat was too large for him, but it was adorable.

Even after our big cleaning spree, people kept coming to the lock with their sponges. They wanted to know if we needed any more help. I had to leave standing orders for the brow watch to thank them kindly but assure them that they'd cleaned enough.

Murphy, a spec two ship handler who seemed to have some grasp of reality beyond beer and boys, told me about one guy who asked and then started crying when she turned him away. "Not in a blubbery way, sar. He just looked really sad and these tears started running down his face. He thanked me real polite and walked away up the dock."

"Sponge number one?" I asked.

"I don't know, sar. He had a sponge, but I didn't see the number."

I left standing orders that if sponge number one ever came back to page me, but he never did. I looked up his name and address in Pip's records. He worked in cargo handling down on one of the lower decks. I never followed through on looking him up, but something about him stuck with me. Bothered me in a way I couldn't really get a handle on.

When the tugs pulled us out of the dock, I thought of him. A crowd had gathered on the observation deck above our dock. I couldn't see very well through the glare off the station's skin but I thought a few people waved. I wondered if he was up there, waving to us the way he'd never been able to wave to his daughter. I had no way to signal back, but in all my stanyers in space, docking and undocking at orbitals around the Western Annex, that was the first time I ever noticed people waving good-bye.

"Captain, tugs report we're clear of the station and ready to push out for the safety perimeter," Al said.

"Thank you, Ms. Ross. Steady as you go."

"Aye, aye, Captain. Steady as you go."

I rode out in the communications console instead of the captain's chair. I kept track of ship's systems and communications traffic while the chief watched over the engine room in person. Al held down the duty watch station and a spec one ship handler with the improbable name of Horatio Jones sat at helm. Pip joined us and watched from one of the spare seats. I'm sure it was a sight he'd seen as often as I had, but the expression on his face still held a sense of wonder, of awe. I wondered if mine did.

In the week or so we spent on Breakall, we'd gotten our watch sections straightened out. I knew the names of the crew at least well enough to recognize their name tags at a distance even if I didn't actually know their faces. Twenty-seven crew was more than I'd worked with since leaving the *Tinker*. After working with a tractor crew, the ship seemed practically crawling with hands even though we were at half our allocation.

I keyed the travel permit notice into the beacon so ships spotting us would know we were running short-handed on the way to the yard. I set it for automatic broadcast at the required interval. I'd had to look it up because it had been so long since I'd been third mate, I'd forgotten what the interval was.

The tugs slipped us through station traffic and got us lined up in less than half a stan, then signaled they were ready to let us go under our own power. "Tugs report we're clear of station traffic, Ms. Ross."

"Thank you, Captain. Should I notify the chief?"

"If you please, Ms. Ross."

I heard her tapping on her console for a moment. "Chief Stevens reports we're ready to light off the kickers, Captain."

I watched the tugs' links on our systems board until they'd cast us loose. "Tugs have released us. Helm, ahead one quarter on my mark."

"Aye, aye, on your mark, ahead one quarter, Captain."

I stood and walked to the rear of the bridge to watch the tugs fall away astern. I let them get well clear. "Mark," I said.

"Ahead one quarter, sar."

At the stern I saw just a flickering of light as the kickers ignited and started pushing us out to the safety limit where we'd be able to raise sail and begin our passage in earnest. We still had a couple of stans to go before we got there and not a lot to do on the way.

I planted myself in the captain's chair and glanced at Al, who seemed to be absorbed in the minutiae of making sure we stayed on course.

The shadow under the helm's chair caught my eye. My memory overlaid the first time I'd seen it, hung over the after side of the bridge, peering in through the armorglass at the tragedy within. I remembered all the bodies. I remembered the smell. The sense of helplessness that filled me then came back and threatened to overwhelm me.

Never in all the time since had I ever imagined I'd be back on this ship, sitting in the captain's chair.

Pip shifted in his seat to look at me. I could just make out his white hair and goatee and the twinkle of his silver earring in the dim light of the consoles. His teeth flashed in a grin and I found myself smiling back. He'd been right. I had been afraid.

I glanced behind me and looked at the orbital already shrinking away. For a moment I remembered the sapphire daggers that had pierced me so tenderly and felt my chest rise and fall in a sigh. Then I remembered the man in a tatty coat, wet to his elbows, scrubbing the bulkhead in the spine as if washing the face of his child after dinner.

"All I could think of was my Em out there on a ship," he'd said.

I straightened around in my seat and faced forward. I didn't look at the stain, but I felt the pressure of all their deaths. The helmsman, the duty watchstander. The crew in their bunks and the messenger in the spine. All dead. All lost, because somebody took a short cut.

I'd been so quick to judge. To call it stupid. To vent my anger against the forces that put the crew in a position to take desperate chances.

I remembered the sapphire daggers that had stopped me from cutting a corner, from taking a chance that might have left us smeared across two dozen square kilometers of frozen rock all for the sake of a few credits.

"Never again," I said. "Never again."
"Captain?" Al asked.
"How far to the safety perimeter, Ms. Ross?"
"Couple of stans at the current velocity, Captain."
"Thank you, Ms. Ross. Helm, ahead full."
"Aye, aye, Captain. Ahead full."
The ship shook slightly as the massive engines drank fuel and spit fire behind us, pushing us into the Deep Dark. We rode along in near silence, the engine's vibration keeping us company as the ship surged through the cold.
Finally, Al said, "We're coming up on the safety perimeter, Captain."
"Thank you, Ms. Ross. Please notify Chief Stevens to secure the engines, and prepare to hoist the mains."
"Aye, aye, sar. Secure engines and prepare to hoist the mains, sar."
I felt the rumble from the engines die out as we coasted along.
"We are clear of the safety perimeter, Captain."
"Very well, Ms. Ross. Raise the mains, extend the keel."
"Aye, aye, Captain. Raising mains and extending keel."
"Helm, lock course."
"Aye, aye, Captain. Lock course." Jones said. "Helm responding and course locked, sar."
"Very good, Mr. Jones. Secure from navigation stations, Ms. Ross. Set normal watch. I believe first section has the honors."
"Aye, aye, Captain. Securing from navigation stations. First section has the watch."
I gave her a tick or three to make the required announcements and settle back into her seat. We sat there in the quiet for a few moments more. After weeks of frantic activity, I had very little to do. I savored the moment. With a glance at the chronometer I realized I had time for a nap before I had to relieve the watch. I stood and headed down the ladder. "See you in four stans, Ms. Ross."
"Sleep well, Captain."
For the first time in a very long time, I thought perhaps I might. In a few weeks, we'd jump to Dree. A few weeks beyond that, we'd settle the ship in the docks. I had been there at the end of the tragedy and it seemed somehow fitting that I should be there to finally put all the ghosts to rest.
Something about that idea gave me a sense of peace.

Nathan Lowell

The Golden Age of the Solar Clipper

Quarter Share
Half Share
Full Share
Double Share
Captains Share
Owners Share

In Ashes Born
To Fire Called*
By Darkness Forged *

South Coast
Cape Grace*

Tanyth Fairport Adventures

Ravenwood
Zypherias Call
The Hermit Of Lammas Wood

* Forthcoming

Awards

2011 Parsec Award Winner for Best Speculative Fiction (Long Form) for *Owners Share*

2010 Parsec Award Winner for Best Speculative Fiction (Long Form) for *Captains Share*

2009 Podiobooks Founders Choice Award for Captains Share

2009 Parsec Award Finalist for Best Speculative Fiction (Long Form) for *Double Share*

2008 Podiobooks Founders Choice Award for *Double Share*

2008 Parsec Award Finalist for Best Speculative Fiction (Long Form) for *Full Share*

2008 Parsec Award Finalist for Best Speculative Fiction (Long Form) for *South Coast*

Contact

Website: nathanlowell.com
Twitter: twitter.com/nlowell
Email: nathan.lowell@gmail.com

About The Author

Nathan Lowell first entered the literary world by podcasting his novels. The Golden Age of the Solar Clipper grew from his life-long fascination with space opera and his own experiences shipboard in the United States Coast Guard. Unlike most works which focus on a larger-than-life hero, Nathan centers on the people behind the scenes—ordinary men and women trying to make a living in the depths of interstellar space. In his novels, there are no bug-eyed monsters, or galactic space battles, instead he paints a richly vivid and realistic world where the hero uses hard work and his own innate talents to improve his station and the lives of those of his community.

Dr. Nathan Lowell holds a Ph.D. in Educational Technology with specializations in Distance Education and Instructional Design. He also holds an M.A. in Educational Technology and a BS in Business Administration. He grew up on the south coast of Maine and is strongly rooted in the maritime heritage of the sea-farer. He served in the USCG from 1970 to 1975, seeing duty aboard a cutter on hurricane patrol in the North Atlantic and at a communications station in Kodiak, Alaska. He currently lives on the plains east of the Rocky Mountains with his wife and two daughters.

Made in the USA
Coppell, TX
23 July 2023